AN IMMIGRANT'S STORY

THE PROMISE IN THE MORNING SKY

ROBERT STEVEN HABERMANN

outskirts
press

In Memory of my grandfather, Otto Bogner

AUTHOR'S NOTE

As a story-teller, I found it challenging to write a tale about a little-known person who has been deceased for well over one-hundred years. When I began researching this account about the life and times of my great-great-grandfather, Christopher Bogner, I found that there was precious little in the historical record about him before 1846 – the year when he married Margaret Zeilmann.

Also, there are no living eyewitnesses who could have told me relevant things about his personality, his habits, his quirks, his strengths, and his weaknesses. Although I do have a photo of him which was taken in about 1865 (when he would have been age 50), the likeness tells me little about the man. Thus, I almost had to recreate him from scratch.

I asked myself, what makes up a man's life and times? I knew that it is indeed more than the few words engraved on his headstone, and more than those sentences recorded in an epitaph or placed on the pages of an obituary found in the local newspaper. Life is made up of years and months, and hours and minutes. Christopher Bogner lived to be seventy-five years old; that's well over twenty-seven-thousand days – when things happened to him, both good and bad. His life was made up of innumerable times of joy and pain; of fear and bravery; of disappointments and accomplishments; and of dreams which came true and dreams which were elusive. Life takes a lifetime, and it's gone in just a moment.

As a young man, I spent five summers living with my grandfather, Otto Bogner, in Crofton, Nebraska – a small town of about five-hundred people located near the Missouri River. During those summers, my grandfather told me stories about his ancestors as they immigrated to America from Germany in the Ninetieth Century and settled on the Nebraska prairie. I also heard stories from my uncles, aunts, and friends of the family. Whether all of these stories are true, I can only surmise – but they began to fill in some of the gaps of a life well-lived.

As a result of my research, I was able to learn the names and the critical dates of Christopher Bogner's parents, grandparents, and siblings. Furthermore, I believe he departed from the port of Rotterdam, Holland on a sailing ship in September 1840, and that the vessel docked in Philadelphia, Pennsylvania in November. I also learned Christopher remained aboard the boat and that he arrived in New Orleans, Louisiana in early 1841.

But I could never determine with any certainty why he chose to leave his home in Bavaria. Christopher was the oldest son of a family whose ancestors had spent several generations operating a successful cabinetmaking enterprise. Had he not gone to America, he probably would have inherited the business one day.

The historical record also reveals Christopher spent almost two years in New Orleans before traveling up the Mississippi River aboard a paddle-wheel steamboat to St. Louis, Missouri to work for a relative who had a thriving business there. But I still don't know what Christopher did during the time he resided in New Orleans or why he spent almost two years there. I assume, however, he was employed as a cabinetmaker.

Approximately two years after arriving in St. Louis, Christopher met and later married Margaret Zeilmann, and from this time forward, the historical record is much more fruitful. I have located evidence of real estate purchases, the official United States census accounts, marriage and burial records, and several other historical references. However, all of this information would have barely filled up one page of text.

I was also able to gather information and stories found in six brief written family histories which mention my great-great-grandfather. Although these accounts are relatively consistent with each other, there are several glaring discrepancies among these papers. Where the written reports are steadfast, I've set forth a narrative weaving their fact-patterns into this novel. But where the stories are inconsistent, I've chosen the version which seems to be the most plausible.

Even with this body of research and the written and oral family traditions, there are many gaping holes in the historical narrative regarding who Christopher Bogner was and what he believed. In filling in these unknowable details with my assumptions about his past, passions, and values, I've settled upon a curious, intelligent, and optimistic man who was thoroughly engaged in the life and times of the nineteenth century.

At the time when my great-great-grandfather was born in Trockau, Bavaria in 1815, Europe was only beginning to recover from the Napoleonic Wars which had ravaged the continent for nearly twenty years. Many of the surviving monarchies were failing, facing enormous debts, and had severely damaged economies. It was the very beginning of a time of massive changes in Europe which would last until the end of the First World War in 1918.

When Christopher was born, the old political and social ways that had guided Europe since the fall of the Roman Empire were also competing with a new order that had grown up in the late eighteenth century in North America – the rise of the United States of America with its constitutional checks and balances, its republican form of government, and its curious Bill of Rights. This new birth of freedom and feelings of self-worth emanating from the New World would significantly impact on the political and social institutions guiding Europe.

I've also assumed that when Christopher arrived in Philadelphia, he learned that his new adopted country was also struggling with its own demons; such as the matter of African slavery, the displacement of the Indian tribes, and a pervasive prejudice towards the nation's latest group of immigrants.

As the nineteenth century progressed, he would have also faced the problems arising from a violent American Civil War, the opening of the Great Plains and the western lands to white settlement, and the arrival of the modern age. It was a remarkable time in America, too.

Thus, this book is not just about one man and his family. It's about life in the nineteenth century. I strongly suspect that several of the same narratives which I developed in this novel covering the life and times of my great-great-grandfather can be equally applied to many other American families.

In those instances where the story is fanciful, I've tried to keep it well within the broad context of the history of the Nineteenth century. As Bernard Cornwell wrote in *The Historical Note* following the text of his book entitled *The Last Kingdom*:

> I have feathered lavishly, as historical novelists must, yet as much of
> the novel as possible is based on real events.

In my book, I have relied heavily on George Moore's 1844 publication entitled *Journal of a Voyage across the Atlantic* to capture the conditions which were often found on passenger sailing ships during trans-Atlantic journeys during that era. Also, I often used the writings and speeches of William Lloyd Garrison to characterize the words of the abolitionists' movement in America before the Civil War. But in essence, this is a story about a grandfather telling his grandson about his grandfather.

So, turn the pages and read about tall sailing ships and steam locomotives; slaves and emancipators; brave families homesteading on the treeless prairie; and the coming of the railroad. And learn about an American family – begun by two immigrants from Bavaria. As a result of their union, eleven children and sixty-four grandchildren came into this world, one of whom, Martha Bogner Simpson, lived to see the dawn of the twenty-first century.

This tale is, indeed, an American story.

I wish to thank Gary Dwor, Eric Hovland, Marie Panipinto, and Byron Petty for their advice and counsel in bringing this book to completion. You're the best!

If the reader is interested in learning more about the period of history covered by my story, I suggest the following books which I researched in creating my novel: *Centennial* by James A. *Michener* and *Giants in the Earth (A Saga of the Prairie)* by O. E. Rolvaag.

Everyone in a small town has a history. There is a woven chain of ancestors, connecting and interlocking with other families in the community, weaving together sorrows and joys up one street and down the other.

The chain winds and bends and binds up the hearts of all into one.

In Crofton, Nebraska, my hometown, I am Ferd's daughter. Ferd is the son of Otto.

I have been away from Crofton for ten years, but I could go home tomorrow, and I would still be Ferd's daughter, the granddaughter of Otto. I have been woven into the chain. I will never lose my place. And I find comfort in that.

    Home: The Tie That Binds by Diane Bogner Pravecek

THE FOUR FAMILIES

The Johann and Katherina Bogner Family

Father - Johann Martin Bogner (December 14, 1786 - January 17, 1844)

Mother - Katherina Boff (July 17, 1785 - February 10, 1828)

Grandfather - Johann Georg Bogner (1760 - November 23, 1828)

Grandmother - Anna Maria Koehler (1762 – March 17, 1828)

Anna (1813 - 1816)

Christopher (May 4, 1815 – July 15, 1890

Anna Maria (1817 - 1896)

Johann (1822 -1903)

Charles (1824 – 1862)

Georg (1827 - 1851)

The Johannes and Dorothea Zeilmann Family

Father – Johannes (March 21, 1800 - June 15, 1890)

Mother – Dorothea Redel (1799 - May 16, 1864)

Grandfather – Johannes Martin Zeilmann (1765 - 1818)

Grandmother – Elizabeth Hauerstein (1764 - 1840)

Johann (November 2, 1829 - 1919)

Margaretha (October 26, 1830 - June 3, 1864)

Elias (October 9, 1832 - 1899)

Anna (February 6, 1837 - December 24, 1877)

Barbara (April 15, 1840 - 1923)

The Christopher and Margaretha Bogner Family

Father – Christopher (May 4, 1815 - July 15, 1890)

Mother – Margaretha Zeilmann (October 26, 1830 - June 3, 1864)

George (January 19, 1847 - July 16, 1909)

John (March 22, 1848 - June 5, 1922)

Joe (September 27, 1849 - June 24, 1906)

Mike (January 4, 1851 - June 15, 1940)

Frank (April 12, 1853 - August 26, 1911)

Alois (January 30, 1855 - January 29, 1931)

Anna Lena (November 2, 1856 - July 1, 1860)

Barbara (October 30, 1858 - July 20, 1945)

Ignatz (December 2, 1860 - March 20, 1950)

Elias (March 16, 1862 - January 19, 1888)

Dorothy (December 11, 1863 - January 13, 1958)

The Alois and Sibilla Bogner Family

Father – Alois (January 30, 1855 - January 29, 1931)

Mother – Sibilla Pichel (February 1, 1882 - January 9, 1945)

Grandfather – Christopher (May 4, 1815 - July 15, 1890)

Otto (November 20, 1883 - May 11, 1975)

Martin (March 2, 1885 - April 10, 1900)

Alphons (January 9, 1887 - May 11, 1969)

Tony (May 12, 1889 - December 1970)

Bruno (April 17, 1891 - August 20, 1969)

Emil (April 19, 1894 - January 21, 1983)

Martha (February 11, 1896 – May 7, 1998)

Albert (September 26, 1898 - July 24, 1977)

Lawrence (August 12, 1901 - December 27, 1959)

CHAPTER ONE

Crofton, Nebraska, August 1964

"Strike two," the umpire yelled.

Frustrated, I stepped out of the batter's-box and stared down at Jules Sorensen, our third base coach. The umpire has been calling anything close a strike today. Jules flashed me a series of signs and I nodded affirmatively. Pausing for a moment, I lifted my right leg, and with the tip of my bat, I tapped the dirt out of my spikes.

Under a bright blue Nebraska sky, I quickly reviewed the situation. It was the bottom of the ninth inning, there were two outs, and the score was tied at 6-6. My teammate, Tom Hansen (the potential winning run), was standing on third base, and I had a two-ball/two-strike count.

After taking a deep breath, I stepped back into the batter's-box, tapped the head of the bat on home plate, and took my stance. Not wanting to strike out with the bat still on my shoulder, I was determined to swing the bat at anything close to being a strike. Over the summer, I'd faced Plainview's pitcher, Rod Gross, on several occasions without much luck. I hoped this time would be different.

Slowly, Rod began his windup, stopped momentarily to stare at Tom who had taken a small lead off third base and started his delivery to the plate. Instantly, I saw it was a fastball about waist high, and I swung hard and lined it sharply over the shortstop's head into left field. A few seconds later, Tom crossed the plate with the winning run.

As I touched first base, I looked up into the stands and saw Sarah smiling and waving at me. Grinning back at her, I pushed my right arm high into the air in a show of victory and jogged back to home-plate where my teammates were celebrating our twentieth win of the season. They mobbed me.

"Way to go, Bob."

"Nice hit."

"You nailed that sucker."

Our manager, Charlie Depew, shook my hand and asked the team to form a line adjacent to the one made the Plainview's players. Smiling, we walked toward and then passed each of their players, shaking hands and providing messages. We knew we'd see each other again on the ballfield later that summer in the Knox County Playoffs.

After that, my teammates formed a circle around our manager, and Charlie began telling us about our next practice, our next opponent, what we did wrong, and what we did right in the game. Extending our right arms toward the middle of the circle and placing one hand on the top of the next one, we yelled "Go Blue Jays!" in unison and began our journeys home.

It felt so good. The crack of the bat; the sound of a baseball colliding with a well-oiled leather glove – it was the music of my soul. I had always wanted to be tested in such a moment; with the game on the line in the bottom of the ninth inning, a tied score, and me standing in the batter's box.

I'd just lived my dream and became a hometown hero for at least one day. Damn, it felt so good.

After taking off my spikes, putting on my tennis shoes, and picking up my mitt, I left the dugout area and looked for Sarah.

"Bobby, I'm so proud of you."

She leaped into my outstretched arms and gave me a sweet kiss on the mouth. Oh, how I loved that girl.

"You did it! I knew you would."

And then she kissed me again.

I think I fell in love the first time I saw her when she was working as a summer clerk in my grandfather's insurance office. Sarah Hansen was quite a beauty. Standing 5'5" tall, she wore shoulder-length chestnut brown hair and displayed long, tanned, and shapely legs. Then there was that smile – a smile a young boy could not easily forget, especially when laying alone in his bed on a hot Nebraska night. Her smile was what first attracted me to her. She made me feel as if I was the most important thing in her life – and for a while, perhaps I was.

I took her hand in mine, and we began walking out of the ballpark, and up the hill to downtown Crofton. Outside, the day sweltered, and the heated pavement roasted the soles of my tennis shoes. Holding hands, we passed *The Crofton State Bank* on the corner, turned left, and began walking down the street toward my grandfather's office.

Soon Sarah saw her brothers waiting for her in their Ford pickup, and after we kissed goodbye, she climbed into the truck and drove home. We made plans to meet the following night at the Auditorium where *Myron Schaeffer and the Minnesotans* would be headlining a town dance. I couldn't wait to hold her again in my arms as we danced to a waltz or a polka.

As I began making my way to my grandfather's house on Iowa Street, I heard a familiar voice.

"Hey slugger, need a ride?"

It was my cousin, Jerry. He drove one of the coolest sets of wheels in town — a yellow '54 souped-up Mercury coupe with a shimmering chrome grill, big whitewall tires, and flames painted along the sides of its engine so that the fire ran along the length of the car. Smiling, I hopped in, and after popping the clutch, he squealed his tires as we headed on to my grandfather's house where I was spending the summer.

"Well, did you get any?" he asked and grinned.

"Come on, Jerry; Sarah's not like that. She's as sweet as sugar."

"Then you got the wrong girl, Bobby. What you need is a little 'poon-tang' to lift your spirits. You should get a date with Nora; take her down to the cemetery. She'll spread her legs for you. I know she likes you."

"Dammit it, Jerry, just drive. Will ya? Man; just drive."

Cruising down Main Street, Jerry began telling me about something happening in town, but I wasn't listening. In my mind, I was still reliving the winning hit and, of course, Sarah's soft, moist kiss.

A few moments later, we pulled into Grandpa's driveway, and I jumped out of the Mercury. With a cigarette dangling out from the side of his mouth, Jerry said, "Say hello to the Old Duffer for me."

"Yeah — see you."

He backed down the driveway, turned up the radio, and soon he was squealing his tires down Iowa Street.

Slowly, I walked up the back steps of my grandfather's house, opened the door, and after going through the entry cubicle, I went through the second door which led into the kitchen. It was about four o'clock, and not seeing my grandfather in the kitchen, I pushed opened the door to the living room and saw him sitting in a chair reading *The Omaha World-Herald.*

"Bobby, how was your game?"

"We won, Grandpa, and I had the winning hit."

Then I told him all about the game – leaving very little to his imagination.

My grandfather, Otto Bogner, was 80 years old in the summer of 1964. His wife, Bernardina (my grandmother) had died in 1961. Otto had lived all of his life in Nebraska, and he was still active in the insurance business. I was a seventeen-year-old boy from Maryland, and I'd spent the previous four summers living with him in Crofton.

"Do you have plans for the rest of the afternoon, Bobby?"

"Yes, the New York Yankees are sending an airplane to Yankton to pick me up – I need to show Mickey Mantle how to hit a curve-ball. Then I'll be flying to Liverpool later in the evening to help Paul McCartney learn how to play the guitar."

"Paul McCarthy?"

"No, Paul McCartney" – emphasizing the last portion of his last name. "Have you ever heard of the Beatles?"

"Yeah, maybe once or twice. But before you run off to teach Paul McCarthy . . ."

"McCartney!"

"Yeah, McCartney – can you help me do a few things for dinner?"

I smiled, "Sure, the Yankees can wait. What can I do?"

"Well, Othmar brought over some fried chicken, and Norbert gave us a bag of green beans and cucumbers. Perhaps you can snip the beans, and peel and slice the cucumbers. Then, will you go out to the garden and bring in some lettuce for us?"

I loved my grandfather. He and my father were the two most important men in my life at the time.

"Where's the bag, Grandpa?"

After picking up the bag, I found a peeler and a sharp knife in the cupboard and went outside. Walking down the back steps, I sat down on the well-head.

It was a beautiful August afternoon. The sky was Nebraska blue, and the slight breeze from the west brought me the scent of the cornfield, located a half-block away from my grandfather's home. Somehow I knew that this would probably be my last summer in Crofton. I was going into my senior year of high school in Washington, DC, and I'd need to begin concentrating on getting admitted to college.

As I began snipping the green beans, I looked around me. I saw the smoke-house, the steps to the storm cellars, the chicken coop, the vegetable garden, and the two-car garage housing my grandfather's 1962 green Chrysler and the 1924 black Ford coupe (infamous for a night-time run to Yankton so many years ago). I needed Grandpa to tell me the story one more time before I went home to Maryland in September.

Like so many others, my grandfather followed a daily ritual. After getting up, he'd read *The Yankton Press* in the morning before departing for work, and then he looked through *The Omaha World-Herald* when he came home at 4:30. After that, he'd turned on the TV and watched the local news at five o'clock and *The CBS Evening News* (with Walter Cronkite) at 5:30. After turning off the TV, he'd get out of his recliner, walk into the kitchen to prepare supper while listening to Paul Harvey on the radio. My grandfather loved the news, and he taught me to love it, too.

By the time Paul Harvey would say "Good day" we'd be ready to sit down and eat our supper. I had learned early on that in Nebraska, we ate dinner at noon (not lunch) and supper in the evening (not dinner). During these moments, I heard so many of his anecdotes about growing up in Howells and later entering politics. Oh, how I loved his stories. Even when he'd repeat a tale to me, it was always a little bit different yet still mesmerizing.

My grandfather was born and raised before the advent of electricity, the automobile, the airplane, and so many of the comforts we took for granted in 1964. He was reared before the end of the Indian Wars, grew in age during World I, the Great Depression, World War II, and the rise of the Soviet Union. It was a time and a place so distant from my life in 1964 yet so real when he told me his viewpoints. I could listen to him for hours.

"Grandpa, who are those people in the portraits in the front bedroom?"

"Oh, those; they are my grandfather, Christopher Bogner and his wife, Margaretha Zeilmann – your great-great-grandmother. She was known as Margaret."

"Did you know them?"

"Yes, Christopher lived with us in Howells. He died when I was almost eight years old. My grandmother, however, died many years before I was born."

"What was he like?"

"Well, he came to America from Germany in 1840 with his brother, Charles. My grandfather loved children, and he told me so many stories. I loved him, too."

We stopped talking for an instant as I tried to absorb what he had told me.

"You know, Bobby, I need to tell you all about my grandfather someday. Unless you hear these stories, he will eventually disappear from our memories. You know, after we finish the dishes, I'll begin by telling you some things about him. Yes, I've been thinking about his for a long time now. I may die someday soon – gosh, I'll be 81 in November, and . . ."

"Oh Grandpa, you'll live a long, long time. I know it."

"Maybe, but I won't live forever. You need to hear and remember these stories and tell them to your children and grandchildren. Grandpa was a wonderful man, Bobby."

After we put the food away and I wiped the last dish and placed it back in the cupboard, we went to the living room. Although it was after seven o'clock, it was still light outside. Grandpa sat back in his recliner, chose one of his favorite pipes, loaded it up from a can of *Prince Albert* tobacco, and lit it. Reflecting, he took a couple of deep drags from the pie, and the room filled up with a familiar yet pleasing fragrance.

"Well, I guess that's its best to start at the beginning. Do you know anything about my grandfather?"

I shook my head, "No, not much. Until today, I didn't even know his name. I've heard a few things about your father – but not very much about your grandfather."

I sat down in the chair and patiently looked at him. My grandfather, Otto Bogner, stood about six feet high, and in 1964, his hair had turned noticeably grey. He wore glasses and had a hearing aid in his right ear which he often adjusted to pick up or dismiss the sounds around him.

Almost always dressed in a shirt and tie, he was rather thin, and by the time he told these stories to me, he'd developed arthritis in his hands and back. Although still quite mobile, he walked slowly and cautiously, apparently knowing to avoid a fall that had disabled so many of his family members over the years.

Exhaling, he said, "So, let's begin. Christopher was born on May 4, 1815, in Trockau in an area which is now a part of Germany. Then it was called Bavaria, and it was a part of Upper Franconia. Until 1812, his birthplace had been a part of the Holy Roman Empire."

"Yeah, I remember that nation. My history teacher said it was a curious name because it was neither Holy nor Roman nor an empire."

He chuckled. "My father, Alois, told me that Christopher had three sisters and three brothers – but I never met any of them. His parents were called Johann Martin and Katherina Bogner. Christopher's grandparents' names were Johann George and Anna Maria Bogner, and they married in Trockau on August 30, 1784. I still have their wedding certificate – that's how I know the date. But we don't know when or where they were born. Maybe you'll find it out one day."

"Wow; that was a long time ago."

"Yes, it was, but I know his grandparents had parents and grandparents and great-grandparents of their own – all the way back to Adam and Eve I guess. But those names have been forgotten. Bobby, we need to remember our family lineage. You'll remember, won't you?"

"I will; I promise."

He took another deep drag on his pipe but noticed it had gone out. "This seems to happen all the time. Is it the pipe, the tobacco, or me? I don't know."

Picking up his Zippo lighter, he sparked a flame, touched it to the pipe bowl, and inhaled. Soon, the pleasant-smelling smoke was flowing again.

"Like his father, grandfather, and most of the men in his family, Christopher was a carpenter and a cabinetmaker by trade. And I heard he was one of the best young craftsmen in Trockau in his day. Even after he came to America, he continued in this trade. My grandfather made much of the furniture in our home in Howells."

"Do you still have some of his furniture?"

"Yes, I have a table in my office; he made it a long time before I was born."

"Did he tell you about his life in Trockau?"

Grandpa smiled, "Yes, and this is where the story begins to get interesting."

CHAPTER TWO

Trockau, Bavaria, October 1827

Christopher Bogner was the first one to awaken on that cold crisp morning. His brother, Johann, was snuggling close beside him on their straw bed. After wiping the sleep from his eyes, Christopher looked over to his right and noticed his sister, Anna Maria, was also sleeping. It was still dark outside, but he could hear some noise coming from the room downstairs. He rubbed his eyes again and gently took Johann's arm off of his shoulder. After putting on his shoes, Chris tiptoed past his sleeping sister and brother and went down the stairs to the workshop.

It was warm down there; Papa had already started a fire in the hearth and was carefully inspecting the two chairs which he had been working on the previous day. Hearing a noise, he looked at the stairway and said, "Christopher, be quiet. Mother and the babies are sleeping."

The Johann Bogner home was a modest wood-framed building with stone lower floors and a brick chimney. There were three rooms on the first floor: the workshop, a large parlor where the family spent much of their mornings and evenings, and a small kitchen in the back of the house.

Furthermore, there were three bedrooms and one antechamber on the upper floor. Chris, his younger brother, and his sister shared one room. Papa and Mother, along with three-year-old Charles and baby Georg, then eleven months old, shared the larger bedroom, and the grandparents resided in the third bedroom.

"Papa, do you need me today or shall I go to school?"

"Let's wait to see how well Grandpa is feeling today. I have a big order to fill. The Duke wants his tables and chairs delivered before St. Barbara's Day."

Duke Adolph Gottingen and his family lived in the keep of Trockau Castle which had been constructed around the year 700 AD on an outcropping of rock that was formerly the site of a Roman outpost. Initially, the castle was once just a wayside for weary pilgrims and travelers to spend the night out of the rain and cold. But by the year 1100, the fortress had a moat, a draw-bridge, and several fortified buildings – surrounded by a twenty-foot wall. Christopher and his family lived in the long shadow of Trockau Castle in the village that had grown up on the fortress' eastern side.

"Is there anything to eat?"

Johann Martin Bogner, Chris' father, motioned over to the table where a half loaf of bread and some white cheese beckoned. Chris tore off a piece of bread and cut a slice of cheese with the table knife. While tasting the bread and cheese, he walked through the kitchen to a window that looked out to the backyard of the house.

"Chris," Papa said, "when you finish eating, go out to the barn and gather up some eggs, please. See that the horse and cow have enough hay to eat, too."

It was a chilly, early October day, and the sky was roofed with high pale-grey broken clouds. As he stepped out the back door, Chris could see the sun was barely rising over the walls of the ancient castle tower. Although the ground was not yet frozen, he could tell the mush he was stepping on would soon form into permafrost that would probably last until Easter. His boots squeaked noticeably as he carefully traversed the small area of land which was not muddy, and without slipping, he made it safely into the barn.

Opening the door, he immediately detected the reeking smell of manure and rotting fruit. The freeze over the prior week had taken its toll of the apples that had been stored in the bins above the stable area. Although they were last year's crop, Papa had hoped to feed these leftovers to Josephine and Bonaparte before the fruit spoiled. Thankfully, this year's crop of apples, pears, plums, and apricots were safely stowed in the storm-cellar laying beneath the house.

Josephine mooed at the sound of the door opening. She was ready to be milked and anxious for her breakfast. The milking, however, would have to wait a little longer. On the other hand, Bonaparte, the family's twelve-year brown Applegate gelding, seemed undisturbed by Chris's entry.

Stopping by the large bin to the right of the barn door, he grabbed the pitchfork and tossed two or three bunches of hay into the stalls. Without even looking at Chris, Josephine and Bonaparte began munching.

Chris grabbed the egg-basket, and after leaving the barn through the back door, he sprinted to the henhouse. It was still relatively warm in there – compared to the barn – and the rooster and the twelve laying hens cackled as Chris disturbed their nests to find a dozen or more brown eggs. After he carefully placed them in the basket, he slowly walked back to the house.

"Thanks, now go wake up your brother and sister. It's time for school."

"Yes, Papa," and climbing up the stairs, Chris noticed someone was already washing in the anteroom. It was his grandmother, and he instinctively knew she'd be plucking and pruning herself for a long time.

He shook Johann. "Time to get up, brother. We have to get ready for school."

Johann rubbed his eyes and looked at his older brother. "I don't want to go to school. Sister Victoria hates me."

"No she doesn't – now get up."

His brother sat up in bed, and Chris smiled as he observed that all of Johann's garments had previously belonged to Chris. Johann wore a woolen shift which hung down to below his waist and tan leggings with a slight tear in the inseam on one of them. Even Johann's shoes had previously belonged to Chris, but the tailor had sewn them back together and re-oiled them. They would have to do until Charles was ready for them.

Then Chris shook Anna Maria. As usual, she awoke in a bad mood once again.

"Leave me alone," she hissed, clutched her baby-doll, turned over and put her back to him. At ten years old, Anna Maria was still a child – but she'd have to grow up soon. In six more years, she'd probably be married and become the mother of children of her own.

Chris left his bedroom and knocked on the door leading to his mother's room. "Mother, are you awake?"

"Come in, Chris, I'm feeding the baby."

He opened the door and walked into the front bedroom. He could smell the familiar milk aroma. His mother was sitting up in bed and suckling Georg.

Charles, age 3, was still sleeping soundly in the little bed beside her.

The children's mother, Katherina, looked pale in the early morning light. The bedroom was located on the north side of the house, and not much light emerged through the bedroom windows on that cloudy morning. A solitary candle flickered on the small table beside the bed, and it added a strange glow to his parents' bedroom.

"How are you feeling today, Mother?"

"Not as well as yesterday, I'm afraid."

Mother had been sick ever since baby Georg was born in July. She'd experienced a complicated pregnancy and lost a lot of blood during the delivery. By October, her body was still fairly swollen, and she had multiple painful ulcers in her mouth and throat. Furthermore, Mother had a severe rash on her neck and arms, and there was always that fever.

Chris was distraught. He loved his mother so much, and he was afraid she would die like many of the other mothers in Trockau. The town physician, Dr. Meier, had visited her on several occasions, and bled her at least twice to release the bad humors which were flowing in her blood; but she only grew weaker.

"Please awaken Charles and check his diaper. I know he must be wet. Is Anna Maria awake?"

"Yes, Mother."

"Tell her to come in and help me. Then help Johann dress for school, son."

Chris was the oldest living child. His sister, Anna, had died nine years earlier in 1816 at age three. He and his four surviving siblings had been born into a family of carpenters and cabinetmakers. His father, Johann Martin Bogner, and his grandfather, Johann Georg Bogner, had been wood-workers all of their adult lives just as their fathers and grandfathers had been for as far back as anyone could remember. Even at age 12, he had grown to become a gifted craftsman, and Papa believed that one day, Chris would take over the family business.

Chris' grandfather was 67 years old in 1827, and he was bothered by acute respiratory complications (caused most probably by a lifetime's exposure to dust, fumes and the heat from the crafting furnaces in the shop). He had arthritis in his hands and generalized weakness in his back, too. On those days when Grandfather could not help Papa in the wood-working shop, Chris would help out in the family business. On the other days, he attended primary school in Trockau.

Chris' grandmother, Anna Maria Kohler Bogner, was 65 years old and plagued with several disorders arising from consumption and growing dementia. On her good days (which were fewer and fewer), she could help out in the kitchen when Mother was confined to her bedroom. Chris' sister, also named Anna Maria, helped with the domestic work when Mother and Grandmother were bed-ridden. Because the grandparents were feeling well that morning, Chris, Johann, and their sister were able to attend school.

Chris yelled, "Come on Anna Maria and Johann. Let's go, or we'll be late," and with that said, the three of them closed the front door and began walking up Wilhelmstrasse on that crisp October morning on their way to school with the other towns-children.

The primary school consisted of two rooms and was situated next to The Church of St. Boniface, the parish church which served the mostly Catholic community. The younger kids were taught in one room while the older children studied in the other classroom. The curriculum included courses in reading, penmanship, mathematics, literature, history, and of course, religion.

The stone parish church, along with the primary school, stood just inside the castle walls, and by 1827, the town of Trockau had a population of about 600 people. For Anna Maria and Chris, this would be the last year they were allowed to attend school.

He was walking briskly, tightly holding on to Johann and Anna Maria's hands. "Hurry, we'll be late for Mass."

Every morning before the school day began, the children would line up in the vestibule of St. Boniface as Sister Regina would take attendance and then get the children in line for their solemn entry into the main church. When Father Schultz gave his nod, Sister would clap and the children, formed into two lines (one for the boys and one for the girls) and would walk slowly down the central aisle with their hands folded devoutly before them.

After stopping at the designated spot, Sister would clap her hands again. With that signal, all of the children would make 'the sign of the cross' and genuflect before the holy altar. With the third clap of her hands, the children would arise from their genuflect positions and slowly move into their assigned pews.

Once all were standing reverently in the seats, Sister Victoria would begin playing the organ, and the children would start singing the designated song for the day as Father Schultz and four altar boys made their entrance into the main church and walked up to the altar.

As the children were singing that morning, Chris looked over to his right and spied Sonia Therese. She caught his glance and smiled back at him. Sonia was also twelve years old and the daughter of Duke Gottingen. Although she did not attend the parish school – she had her own tutor located in the confines of the castle – she was allowed to play with the other the students during recess. Over the years, Chris and Sonia had developed a special bond.

Secretly, Chris nodded at her and she smiled back at him. He couldn't quite understand the attraction which he had for this young girl but knew two things instinctively: he liked her very much; and that she was well beyond his station in life. Nonetheless, he hoped to see her at recess.

After Mass ended, a similar routine would take place, and as the children exited the church, they – except for Sonia and her younger brother, Joseph – went directly to their classroom in the parish school to begin their day of instruction.

As St. Barbara's Day approached, Chris attended school less and less often. Duke Gottingen had earlier provided Chris' father with the precise specifications for his large carpentry order, and much of the finer detailed work was left to Chris' emerging talents.

By age 12, he was already familiar with the essential tools of a skilled carpenter: such as the auger, chisel, planes of all assortments, square, bevel, gouge, bradawl, sidehook, and saws of all types and descriptions. He could expertly handle a jack, a trying plane, a smoothing plane, a sash fillister, and a plow. He could work efficiently with dividers and calipers and was knowledgeable in traditional dyes, paints, hardeners, varnishes, and glues. As Grandfather became more debilitated, Chris was needed more often to help in the family business.

"Chris, if we can keep up the pace, it looks like we'll finish the job by St. Barbara's Day."

The liturgical feast day of St. Barbara was celebrated on December 4th, and it marked the beginning of the Christmas season in Bavaria. According to legend, St. Barbara lived in Asia Minor during the third century. Her father was a Roman governor who persecuted Christians and kept his daughter a virgin by locking her up in a tower whenever he was away.

Barbara made the mistake of confessing she had become a Christian. Incensed, her father demanded she renounce this heresy. After some time had passed with St. Barbara still stubbornly refused to deny her new religion, her father commanded she be tortured and later beheaded on December 4th. As she was being buried, a cherry blossom emerged from her casket which was taken as a sign that she is now in heaven.

Papa put down his hammer and said, "Did you remember to cut the branch, son?"

"No, but I found a good one. Don't we have to wait to cut it until December 4?"

In Trockau, a tradition arose that a small cherry branch should be cut off and placed in water precisely on St. Barbara's Day. If the branch bloomed on Christmas Day, it was regarded as a good sign for the future.

"Well," Papa replied, "I don't think it would do any harm in cutting it a few days earlier this year— but don't tell Mother. The hard frost last week will probably delay its blooming. Just place it in water and set it somewhere in the barn where it can get light. We'll bring it into the house on December 4th."

A few days later, Papa heard a knock on the front door of his shop, and after opening it, he saw Duke Gottingen and his daughter, Sonia Therese, standing at the doorstep.

Bowing his head, Papa said, "Your Honor, please come in. What brings you to my shop this lovely morning?" It was somewhat unusual for nobility to visit the shop of the ordinary folk.

"I've heard the chairs and tables are finished, and I've come to see them for myself."

The Duke removed his hat, kicked the snow off of his boots, and entered the woodshop.

"Johann, this is my daughter, Sonia."

Johann bowed again to the young girl, respectively accepted her right hand, and softly kissed it.

"I am honored, madam."

Johann took their coats and hats, hung them on the hook next to the front door, and lead them into the woodshop.

"Your Honor, this is my son, Christopher."

Chris extended his hand not knowing he should have waited for the Duke to reach his hand first. Not relying on the subtler aspects of courtship, the Duke accepted and said, "I believe you know my daughter, Sonia."

Still staring at the floor, Chris responded, "Yes, My Lord. I see her in Church on school days."

"Well, Johann, let's have a look at the pieces I ordered."

Papa led the Duke past Chris, and they walked over to the far corner of the shop. A few moments later, he looked up at Sonia and said, "Now you know what I do when I'm not at school."

She smiled and said, "I knew that already. Father says you do outstanding work. I came because I wanted to talk to you alone. Can we go over to the far side? Perhaps, you can pretend you're telling me things about your shop."

After looking at his father and the Duke examining the purchase order, he carefully led Sonia to the far corner.

She looked down at her hands and then she looked deeply into Chris' eyes. "You know next month I'll be thirteen, and soon I'll be a woman. I've never kissed a boy. Have you ever kissed a girl?"

"You mean other than my sisters? No, but I'd like to kiss you sometime – but not here."

When his father briefly looked over at the two children, Chris immediately began showing Sonia some axes and saws.

"When will you kiss me, Chris?"

"On Sunday after Mass. Meet me in the nave near the transept. But we must be quick. The Duke will kill me if he should ever know."

She nodded and smiled at him. Although only 12 years old, Chris knew she had awakened something lurking deep inside of him.

A few moments later, Papa said, "Chris, come over here. The Duke wants to speak to you."

Worried that perhaps the Duke had suspected something untoward, he cautiously walked to the rear of the woodshop.

He bowed to the Duke and said: "Yes, My Lord?"

The Duke said, "Son, your father tells me that you did most of the handiwork yourself. Is it true?"

With his eyes still staring at the floor, Chris replied, "Yes, My Lord."

The Duke rested his hand on Chris' shoulder and said, "You should have a great future in carpentry, my son. I'm already quite impressed with your handicraft."

"Thank you, My Lord."

Carefully, Chris looked at Sonia who smiled back at him. His heart was beating fast, but he was unsure whether it was due to her smile or the Duke's kind words.

Chris never thought the Mass would end that Sunday. He and his family were seated in the back of the church, and soon the familiar trumpets sounded as the Duke, his wife, and their three children made their entrance and sat in their private pew at the front of the Church. As Sonia passed by, she didn't look directly at Chris, but he saw she had a slight smile on her face.

The choir rose to sing, and Papa, the lead tenor, lead the choir in a mournful 'Oh Come, Oh Come, Emmanuel.'

To Chris, the sermon went on forever, and the communion line extended all the way back to the vestibule. His hands were sweating at the thought of the forthcoming kiss, and his heart was pounding so hard he supposed the entire congregation actually might hear it.

As the choir rose to sing the departing hymn, 'Panis Angelicas,' the priest, followed by the Duke and his family, slowly walked down the aisle to the vestibule where the priest and the Duke would shake hands with the congregation as they exited the basilica.

As the remainder of the congregation exited the church, Chris looked in the back and saw Sonia walking down a side aisle to their meeting place. He glanced around the church; no one seemed to be looking his way, and instead of following his family to the vestibule, he genuflected and walked toward the front of the church.

Halfway down the hall, Sister Victoria saw him but did not question his intentions, Chris bowed at her and said, "Good morning, Sister" as they passed and he walked purposely to the front of the church. Genuflecting once again, he turned to his right and noticed Sonia was waiting for him where the nave joined the transepts. There Chris saw a wooden barrier blocking the entrance to the southern end of the church. Slipping under the blockade; he saw her in the darkness.

She ran to his arms, and they kissed. She was about six inches shorter than him, and the aroma of her perfume brought sensations to him that he's never felt before. As their lips parted and she said, "I've dreamed of this day for a long time, Chris."

"Me, too."

"One day, we'll be married."

Suddenly they heard footsteps and looking over his right shoulder, he saw Joseph staring at them.

"What are you two doing in there?"

Sonia said, "Joseph, Chris is showing me the work he's doing on the back altar."

Her brother did not believe a word of it and said, "You'd better come with me now. Father is looking for you, and he won't like what I'm seeing."

She said, "I'm coming – but please don't ever mention this to Father. He won't understand."

Separating from Chris' embrace, Sonia gently touched his sleeve as she passed him and walked over to her brother. At her touch, Chris felt another wave of electricity surge through his body. Frankly, he didn't know what to think.

Joseph eyed Chris suspiciously as she took her brother's hand and they together walked back to the vestibule. She looked over her shoulder and said, "Thank you for showing me your handiwork, Chris. You're quite talented; yes, you are."

Two days following St. Barbara's Day was St. Nicholas' Day when the townspeople began setting up stands for the winter market, called a *Christkindlmarkt*, in the village green to sell baskets, toys, and woodcarvings. They also set up booths for the sale of hot drinks, almonds, nuts, roasted chestnuts, gingerbread, and other baked goods.

The Bogner family traditionally provided a booth in the *Christkindlmarkt*, to sell small gadgets, trinkets, and ornaments the family manufactured over the past year. On the morning of the first day of the festival, the sky opened, and a hard rain fell, flooding the gutters, and the torrents fell off the church and rumbled down the hill to the village green. The Bogners, along with dozens of other merchants who had already set up their stalls, quickly covered their booths with sheets of oiled shacking or felted cloth to keep the water away.

The stallholders responded bravely to the rain and hoped the weather would clear as the day progressed. By afternoon, the wind came up from the north, and as the rain turned into heavy, wet snow, the atmosphere changed from gloom to anticipation. Soon the market was covered in a holiday white, and the spirits of the merchants brighten immensely. Yes, Christmas was coming and so were the shoppers.

Folks from miles away rode to Trockau on their horses and in their buggies or just walked to town to take a good look at the offerings that year. Chris had worked the morning shift and was relieved by his sister, Anna Maria, so that he could buy a sausage or a piece of hot bread.

As he turned the corner, he saw Sonia coming towards him. He smiled at her, and as he got close to him, she motioned him to join her behind a stall that was selling gingerbread. Carefully checking whether somebody was watching them, she threw her arms around him and once again kissed him passionately on the mouth.

Releasing him, Chris asked, "Does the Duke know about us?"

"No, Joseph is sworn to secrecy."

"Good, I can now live for another year."

He looked at her. She was wearing a red cloak which had probably once been her mother's, and her brown leather boots that were laced up to her ankles were already sprinkled with mud. Her long blue skirt flowed down to her feet. Furthermore, she wore green mittens that appeared to be a little too large for her hands. Chris adored her, and she felt his approval.

After looking around again, she kissed him quickly and responded, "I've decided we will marry when I'm sixteen. It's only four more years, but I hope we don't have to wait that long for all that my heart yearns for."

"Sonia, I cannot marry you. You are far above my station in life. Your family will never permit it. It will be scandalous for us."

"Don't worry, my prince. I have a plan, and in a few weeks, I'll share it with you – once I'm thirteen."

The snow had now covered her bonnet, and her face was red from the cold weather. Chris knew her plan would never happen, but in his heart, he believed he would love her for the rest of his life.

In the weeks before Christmas, Mother and Grandmother were busy decorating the house and preparing the Christmas cakes, cookies, and pies that made the season so festive for the Bogner family. Of course, Anna Maria helped out as much as she could but being only ten years old, her contribution was minimal. As the holiday approached, the women hung evergreen boughs over the doors and window – believing evergreens would keep witches, ghosts, evil spirits, and illness far away.

Mistletoe and other greenery were also added in a manner to liven up mantles and tables. Stockings were hung by the fireplace in anticipation of St. Nicholas' filling them with sweets or perhaps an orange, and all sorts of unique food and drinks were prepared for family and guests. And of course, the women shopped in the *Christkindlmarkt* for gifts for the children and relatives.

Four days before Christmas, Papa and Chris hitched Bonaparte to the family carriage and drove it out of town to the countryside where they cut down a large evergreen. After placing it in the wagon and bringing it home, they set the tree up in the downstairs living quarters. The next day, the women decorated the tree with apples, nuts, and festive bows.

In the center of a large table on the outside wall of the residence, Papa placed the cherry branch in a bud vase, and by the week before Christmas, the twig was swollen with buds. The children spent hours looking at the buds and wondered whether the twig would, indeed, bloom on Christmas Day.

In the evenings after supper during the few days immediately before Christmas, the Christmas tree would be illuminated by carefully placed candles, and the family would gather around the tree, drink a cup of warm *glutwien*, and sing carols. Mother and Grandmother were both feeling much better, and all were optimistic for the coming year – 1828.

Soon, it was Christmas Eve, and after supper, Papa and Chris harnessed Bonaparte to the family carriage and brought it out of the barn and up to the front of the house. It was a joyous time, and the entire family had dressed in their most elegant winter clothes. Light snow was falling on the town as they rode in the carriage down Wilhelmstrasse, taking delight in the decorated homes of their neighbors.

After crossing over the moat and passing through the castle's entrance gate, the family saw St. Boniface was surrounded by festive torches and covered with evergreen boughs. A large wreath was attached to the front door and candles were lit in all the windows. Papa helped the family out of the carriage in front of the church as Chris drove the buggy to the field where the coaches were parked.

St. Boniface was already filled with people when the Bogner family arrived. Chris believed he'd never seen so many people in the church at one time. The nave filled up first, and hooded monks, from nearby St. Aloysius' Monastery, held torches to guide the people around the darkened church. Neighbors greeted one another cheerfully, and the mood was joyful for Midnight Mass. Chris looked up into the choir loft and saw Papa had made his way up the steps and donned his choir-robe. Papa would be singing the entrance hymn that night.

The bell tolled eleven times, and at that injunction, the congregation stood up and became silent. Chris looked at the back of the Church and saw Father Schultz and the seven altar boys standing in the vestibule. The deacon entered the rear of the Church and in a profoundly reverent voice, announced the arrival of Duke Gottingen and his family. To a flourish of trumpets, the members of the Royal Family slowly walked down the aisle to their pew in the front of the church.

Then the choir stood up, and the organist began playing as Papa started singing the beautiful hymn 'Stille Nacht.' In 1827, the composition was not yet ten years old. The song was composed just hours before Midnight

Mass on Dec. 24, 1818, by a parish priest, in a small Austrian village called Oberndorf – a town which was located less than fifty miles from Trockau.

After the brief organ interlude, Papa began singing the first two verses:

> *Stille Nacht, heilige Nacht,*
> *Alles schläft; einsam wacht*
> *Nur das traute hochheilige Paar.*
> *Holder Knabe im lockigen Haar,*
> *Schlaf in himmlischer Ruh!*
> *Schlaf in himmlischer Ruh!*

> *Stille Nacht, heilige Nacht,*
> *Hirten erst kundgemacht*
> *Durch der Engel Halleluja,*
> *Tönt es laut von fern und nah:*
> *Christ, der Retter ist da!*
> *Christ, der Retter ist da!*

The organ and trumpets played a musical verse of the song, and finally, the choir joined in with Papa for the final stanza:

> Stille Nacht, heilige Nacht,
> Gottes Sohn, o wie lacht
> Lieb' aus deinem göttlichen Mund
> Da uns schlägt die rettende Stund'.
> Christ, in deiner Geburt!
> Christ, in deiner Geburt!

As the song was concluding, Chris looked around and noticed many parishioners were wiping tears from their eyes, and several others were nodding their heads affirmatively. Chris would hear that Christmas song many more times during his lifetime, but the carol would always bring him back to St. Boniface on December 24, 1827. He claimed to the end of his life nobody had ever sung the hymn any better than Papa did on that Christmas Eve in the basilica.

As the Mass progressed, Mother and Grandmother each began to tire from the standing and kneeling, and Chris sensed this midnight mass would probably be the last time the entire family would be together in church. During the consecration of the bread and wine, Grandmother became noticeably confused and started asking for her mother. During communion, he took Grandmother's hand and led her to the vestibule where they sat quietly until the Mass was over.

While consoling Grandmother, Chris could hear Papa's lovely tenor voice singing 'Ave Maria' as the priest, followed by the Duke's family, genuflected and exited the main sanctuary. Standing up in respect for the Duke and his family walked by, Chris caught the eye of Sonia Therese who smiled sweetly at him. Although he didn't know it then, Chris would not see her again for another twelve years.

When the Bogner family arrived home after Mass, they gathered around the tree, and each drank a cup of warm *glutwien*. Looking over at the table, Anna Maria first noticed the cherry blossoms on St. Barbara's branch had fully opened. Everyone cheered and hugged each other, firmly believing it was a sign from God that 1828 would be a good year for the family.

It wasn't. In fact, by Christmas, 1828, the Good Lord had taken Chris' mother and grandparents to heaven. Thankfully, however, the family members did not know at the time that this would be their last Christmas together.

One week later on January 1, the family returned to St. Boniface to celebrate *The Feast of the Naming and Circumcision of Jesus*. It was New Year's Day. This time, however, Mother and Grandmother were each too ill to attend to service.

New Year's Day had been a moveable feast for many centuries. Under the Julian calendar in pre-Christian Rome, January 1 was dedicated to Janus, the god of gateways and beginnings, for whom January is also named. This early Roman calendar designated the date of March 1 as the start of the New

Year, and March 1 remained New Year's Day until about the year 600 AD.

From that time on and until the adoption of the Gregorian calendar, the first day of the New Year in Europe coincided with *The Feast of the Annunciation*, on March 25, which was called "Lady Day." It wasn't until 1752 when January 1st was designated as the beginning of the New Year.

In 1828, the local people were just beginning to develop their unique traditions for New Year's Day. Because pigs were thought to represent progress and prosperity, Mother began serving a pork roast on the New Year's Day table. She and Grandmother would also bake ring-shaped cakes and pastries. Meanwhile, rice pudding (with an almond hidden inside the dish) was cooked and served to the family; whoever found the almond could expect twelve months of good fortune.

Finally, Mother would serve *Feuerzangenbowle* (flaming fire tongs punch). The hot punch drink's main ingredients are *rotwein, rum, oranges, zitronen, zimt und gewürznelken* (red wine, rum, oranges, lemons, cinnamon, and cloves) as the family gathered around the fire and told ghost stories. Chris would carry many of these traditions with him to America.

Consequentially, 1828 became a time of many changes and challenges for the Bogner family. By the beginning of January, Mother's condition steadily worsened. She became bed-ridden and displayed open, oozing sores scattered all over her body. In early February, she developed severe respiratory distress, and the family called for Father Schultz. Mother received the last rites and died peacefully in her sleep at age 42 on February 10, 1828, the feast day of St. Scholastica. With Mother's death, Anna Maria became the lady of the house at age 11.

In a like manner, Grandmother's confusion magnified considerably as the winter dragged on, and soon she became incontinent and displayed severe bouts of anger and frustration. One morning in mid-March, Grandfather awakened to find that she was not in their bed.

After a search of the house, Papa noticed the back door was wide open. After that, Chris and Papa followed her footprints in the snow and eventually found Grandmother lying dead in a field just outside the town limits. Shoeless and dressed only in her nightshift, she froze to death on March 17, 1828. She was 65 years old.

As for Christopher, he turned 13 on May 4, 1828, and immediately ended his formal education. With Grandfather's physical health declining, and with Johann, Charles, and Georg still much too young to help in the family business, Chris was needed to work in the shop on a regular basis.

Meanwhile, Grandfather, who was devastated by the loss of his wife of almost 44 years, continued his slow physical decline. While working near the fireplace in the woodshop on an afternoon in late October, Grandfather experienced a severe weakness on his left side, and as he lost his balance, he immediately collapsed. Unfortunately, his right hand and arm fell into the hearth causing him extensive burns.

Within a few days, an infection set in, and a surgeon amputated his right arm. The stroke had also produced a devastating loss of cognitive skills and with the use of his left side. He died three weeks later on November 23, 1828. He was 68 years old.

Finally, Sonia Therese moved from Trockau to the city of Bayreuth in early January to become a lady-in-waiting to Princess Mathilde Caroline, the oldest daughter of Prince Ludwig — the pretender to the Bavarian throne. Sonia would reside in Ordensschloss Castle for the next twelve years of her life.

CHAPTER THREE

Bayreuth, Bavaria, July 1839

The land known as Bavaria consists of the region occupying the northern portion of the Alps in Southern Germany. Initially inhabited by the Celts in the 5th Century BC, the area was later conquered by the Romans and made a part of the provinces of Raetia and Noricum. Following the Roman withdrawal from the region in the mid-5th Century AD, the territory was ruled by the House of Agilolfing until the year 800, when Emperor Charlemagne overthrew the dynasty and incorporated the kingdom into the Holy Roman Empire.

When Emperor Napoléon abolished the Holy Roman Empire in 1806, Bavaria became an independent kingdom. The first monarch, Charles, ruled the new nation until his death in 1825 when his oldest son, Ludwig I, assumed the throne. During his reign, King Ludwig and his family lived in five castles, one of which was located in Bayreuth; a small city located about thirty-five miles north of Trockau. Prince Ludwig's marriage to Countess Therese in 1810 was the occasion of the first-ever Oktoberfest, and their union gave rise to seven children, including Princess Mathilde Caroline.

Geographically, Bayreuth is located on the Red Main River in a valley between the Jura and the Fichtelgebirge Mountains. The city's roots date back to 1194 AD. A turning point in the city's history came in 1703 when Count Christian moved his official residence to Bayreuth, and a vast palace was constructed to house the Count and the royal family. In the spring of 1839, the castle was targeted for a significant restoration.

One late July afternoon, Chris was restoring a large table in the grand banquet room on the Upper West Wing of the castle while his brother, Charles, was busy sweeping the dust and wood chips from the floor. A few months earlier, Chris had been hired as a carpenter and a cabinetmaker by the Royal Family, and he brought Charles along with him to Bayreuth to work as his assistant. The brothers were finishing their work in the Upper West Wing on that afternoon, and they'd soon move to the Upper East Wing to begin the restoration there.

Suddenly, the brothers heard voices near the entrance door, and turning, they saw Princess Mathilde Caroline and her entourage entering the banquet room. As the group slowly made its way down toward Chris' work area, the principal architect, Count Frederic Gunther, was describing the progress of the restoration work to the Princess.

The light coming through the hall's massive windows caught the young princess' dress – a French gown, dyed in royal purple – and it showed off the intimacy of the needlework. Her bodice was low-cut and tapered down to a narrow waist. Around the Princess' white-powdered neck hung jewels on gold chains. The Princess was twenty-six years old, and Chris could see she was as lovely as the portraits had depicted her. Several ladies accompanied Princess Mathilde Caroline that afternoon, and all of the ladies were expensively made up and wore brightly-colored silk gowns.

In a show of respect, the brothers put down their tools and immediately stood up straight awaiting the arrival of the royal visitors. As the Princess approached, Chris and his brother bowed deeply, and Count Gunther said, "My Lady, this man here is the lead carpenter whom I've told you about, Herr Bogner. He's done magnificent work, in my opinion."

The Princess' eyes were downcast; seemingly looking at the restored hardwooden floor. As she raised her gaze to look at Chris, he could see her deep blue yet somewhat saddened eyes. Yes, she was lovely.

Smiling, she extended her hand to him, and as he deeply bowed again, he kissed her hand softly. "Yes, Herr Bogner, I've heard a lot of good things about you and your family from Duke Gottingen."

"You are too kind, My Lady."

It was then Chris believed that he recognized one of the ladies in the Princess' entourage, Duchess Sonia Therese. As their eyes met, she brought her right hand to her mouth in surprise. No words were exchanged between them, however, as such a side conversation would be viewed as being highly disrespectful.

As the Princess began asking Chris a series of questions about his handiwork and his plans for the palace's restoration, he replied, "We are about finished here, My Lady. We plan to clean up the dust this afternoon and begin working on the Upper East Wing tomorrow. I hope our work pleases you, My Lady."

"Indeed it has. My husband, Grand Duke Ludwig of Hesse, is already planning for a banquet here later next month when the King makes his royal visit. I will tell him of your progress."

"Yes, My Lady."

"When do you anticipate the work will be finished on the Upper East Wing?"

With that question, Count Gunther interrupted and said, "My Lady, I don't think this man is aware of all of the details of our grand scheme for the remainder of the castle. He's merely the lead carpenter, My Lady."

"Oh, I see."

"Let us leave these workmen to the finishing of this task, and permit me to tell you about our plans to restore the East Wing, My Lady."

Princess Mathilde Caroline briefly looked at Charles, who again bowed deeply, and as the Princess began to leave the banquet hall, Count Gunther pointed out additional improvements to the West Wing and his plans for the autumn season. Chris' eyes, however, were squarely on Sonia, and just as the royal party was leaving the banquet hall, she turned her head and smiled at him.

For a few minutes, the two brothers just stood together in silence. Charles, apparently not recognizing the Duchess, finally remarked, "Brother, I've never seen such fine ladies in my life."

Shaking his head, Chris answered, "Yeah, me, too."

A few days later, the brothers were working in the Upper East Wing when a soldier approached them. "Are one of you men, Christopher Bogner?"

"Yes. I am."

"Duchess Von Furstenberg wishes to have a word with you."

Chris replied, "Who? Me? What's this all about, soldier?"

"Please follow me. The Duchess is waiting in the library."

Chris looked at Charles and said. "I'll be back. I've no idea what this is all about; do you?"

Charles shook his head and shrugged his shoulders as Chris slowly put down his sash fillister, removed his apron, and began following the soldier.

After working in the palace for several months, he had become familiar with its layout. The design of the royal complex was 'stellar.' It had a square central palace building located in the middle of the castle and four wings (each consisting of two floors) on each corner of the palace. An enclosed courtyard lay in the middle portions between each of the four wings, and a twenty-foot stone wall surrounded the entire edifice.

As Chris followed the soldier, they passed a tightly-packed series of remarkable rooms, all different, and all situated in straight rows along the wide middle hallway. After seeing these rooms so many times, even the brightness and the beauty of the interiors of these places were becoming rather commonplace to Chris.

The two men finally reached the library. The soldier knocked on the door, and after hearing, "Come in," he opened the door, stepped into the library, and announced, "Christopher Bogner, as requested, My Lady."

After the soldier stepped aside, Chris walked in. Sonia smiled at him and said, "Chris, is it really you?"

Duchess Sonia Therese Von Furstenberg D'Ousterling was sitting at a writing table and had just put down the book she was reading. She was wearing a riding outfit as if she was prepared to leave for an outing at any moment. Long flowing blond hair was gathered together with a bow and laid softly across her right shoulder.

He looked at her and then gazed across the room at a woman holding a baby. She said, "Yes, Chris, that is my child. Her name is Rebecca Marguerite; she's fourteen months old."

Chris bowed his head, hesitated for an instant, and replied, "My Lady, I don't know what to say."

She dismissed the soldier and then said to Chris, "Please sit here next to me. How long has it been since I last saw you? Has it really been over twelve years?"

He looked up at Sonia and replied, "My Lady, I remember so clearly the last time I saw you. We were at Midnight Mass, and my father was singing in the choir loft. You and your family were announced, and you walked down the aisle to your pew in the front of the church. I smiled at you, but you only looked forward. I remember seeing you later on your way out of church after Mass. Did you know then that you were leaving Trockau?"

"Yes, I did; my father told me the news on that very day. Oh, Chris, we were so young then. What, were we each twelve or thirteen years old then? Do you remember I told you that I'd marry you someday? I know I meant it when I said it; I had such a crush on you, and those memories have gotten me through many tough times."

Then she laughed and said, "Oh, the dreams of a silly little girl."

Smiling, Sonia offered her right hand to him, and he slipped out of his chair, went down on one knee, and gently kissed it. He knew — as he had always known — she was far above his station in life, and a union between them could never happen. But still — but still for all those years — he kept the dream alive deep in his heart.

They talked together for about thirty minutes under the watchful — and entirely proper — eyes of her nursemaid. He learned Sonia had married a Bavarian military officer, Colonel Ernst Von Furstenberg D'Ousterling and that she had two children by him. Soon she'd be departing the palace for Regensburg where he would be stationed at a military garrison on the Danube River.

Soon, their time together was over. As Chris arose from his chair to leave the library, she kissed him gently on his cheek. He bowed, excused himself, and vacated the library. The soldier was waiting for Chris outside the door, and the guard escorted Chris back to the Upper East Wing. Chris was heart-broken.

A few days later, Chris was working in the castle when a soldier handed him a note. It was from Sonia.

Herr Bogner,

Please join me and five others for an evening at the Markgräfliches Opernhaus. The troupe will be presenting Lucia di Lammermoor at 8 PM on Wednesday night. Join us in the Prince's Box (Box 6) a few moments before the opera begins for a glass of champagne. You'll need to wear formal dress, and you can obtain it at the tailor shop on Frederickstrasse near the marketplace.

Please come,

Duchess Sonia Therese Von Furstenberg D'Ousterling.

Chris was spellbound, and reread her message several times. He loved the opera but had never attended a performance in Bayreuth. He decided to accept her invitation.

Later that afternoon, he walked down to the tailor shop and showed the note to the owner, Adolph Richter, who fitted Chris with a handsome ensemble: a dark top coat and matching trousers with a double-breasted vest, a notched lapel which was finished in double points at the lowered waist. The white shirt was made of linen and had low collars (turned down) and a stylish wide cravat. On his head, Herr Richter sold Chris a top hat with a wide brim. Although the outfit cost him about three weeks wages, he gladly purchased it.

Then he went to a bookstore and looked up a summary of the opera. He learned *Lucia di Lammermoor* is a dramma tragico (a tragic opera) written in three acts by the composer, Gaetano Donizetti and that the story was loosely based upon Sir Walter Scott's historical novel entitled *The Bride of Lammermoor.*

On his way to the opera house, he was quite nervous. He had never attended such an elegant affair, and he believed he would be associating with people who were far above his station in life. However, Chris couldn't wait to see Sonia again. Earlier, he had stopped at a barbershop for a haircut and a close shave. The barber also trimmed Chris' mustache and polished his fingernails. He was ready for the opera.

It was a warm summer evening, and when he arrived, carriages were unloading the gentry. He strolled up the stairs to the main floor, showed his invitation to the clerk, and entered into the foyer of the grand opera house.

The Markgräfliches Opernhaus was built in the 'Late Baroque' style between 1744 and 1748 by the French architect Joseph Saint-Pierre. Its exterior façade, crafted of white marble, was designed by Giuseppe Galli Bibiena. To Chris, it was the most impressive lobby he had ever seen – it almost took his breath away.

After admiring the intricate wood-carvings and enormous crystal chandeliers, he climbed the grand stairway to the second floor, and an usher escorted Chris to Box 6. The usher knocked on the door, and a servant opened it, read the invitation, and graciously led him through a dark ante-corridor to the front portion of the Princes' Box.

Sonia was seated when he arrived, and as the servant announced "Herr Christopher Bogner, My Lady," she stood up, turned to Chris, and smiled deeply. "Welcome, Herr Bogner. Permit me to introduce you to my other guests."

He did not hear another word as Sonia began the introductions; he was utterly mesmerized by her appearance. The Duchess wore a floor-length sequined white silk gown with bare shoulders. A matching scarf was wrapped loosely around her neck, hanging over her left shoulder and falling to the front of her dress to a position which equaled the extent of her left arm and hand. Her dress had a low neckline, highlighting her ample bosom, with an elongated V-shaped bodice that stopped at her waistline and met at a point in the front.

She also wore opera-length white linen gloves that curved up to a place just above her elbows, and she walked in light-yellow brocade satin slippers that were tied around her ankles with silk ribbons. An assortment of pearls, lace, and ribbons adorned her hair, and around her neck, she wore a beautiful Safire stone locket attached to a delicate silver necklace.

As Chris continued through the formal introductions, he couldn't keep his eyes off of Sonia. As her gaze met his eyes, Chris could tell she enjoyed his infatuation with her. Following a couple of glasses of champagne and some polite conversation, the servants rang the soft bells indicating the first act of the opera was ready to commence.

The Prince's Box was designed to extend beyond the second-floor balcony an additional twenty feet above the orchestra section of the first floor. The front portion of the box had two rows of three chairs each. The ladies sat in the front row, and the gentlemen sat directly behind them.

As the opening theme began, he gazed in the near darkness at his beloved Sonia sitting in the chair directly in front of him. He could see the gentle sloping of her delicate shoulders, her lily-white skin, and the back of her neck, as she wore her hair in a high bun on the crown which descended to her neck with isolated long 'spaniel curls' dangling down toward the front. The scent of the rich fragrance of her perfume completely intoxicated him.

As Act 1 concluded, the Duchess turned around and asked, "Are you enjoy-ing the opera, Herr Bogner?"

He smiled at her. "Yes, My Lady; I'm having the time of my life. Thank you."

"Good. Do you think Lucia will survive the feud between her own family and the Ravenswoods?"

Chris smiled. "Lucia seems quite fragile to me, My Lady. But we'll see, won't we?"

Sonia smiled and began talking to the lady to her right. All of a sudden, Chris felt entirely out of place, and after a few more moments, he followed one of the other gentlemen out of the box to the atrium for a glass of champagne. He stood alone in a corner just looking at the upper classes mingling and chatting with one another.

Soon Sonia found him and asked, "Why did you leave? I wanted to talk to you."

"We're a long way from Trockau, My Lady, and I'm not so sure I belong here."

She touched his sleeve, and whispered, "You do, Chris. You are as good, if not better, than any man I've ever known. If it were within my power, I'd never leave your side."

Then Sonia looked around to ensure she wasn't being overheard. However, she saw a man carefully watching them. She whispered, "The soldier over there is currently in my husband's employ. I must return to the box, Chris."

He bowed as she left, and he went over for another glass of champagne. The soldier eyed Chris guardedly, and as soon the bell rang, he returned to the Prince's Box for the second act of the opera.

Following the conclusion of the opera, the six of them talked briefly about the performance – set in Scotland – while sipping even more champagne. As the other guests left, Chris and Sonia reminisced about their time growing up together in Trockau. The 'glow' of the champagne was getting to both of them, as she continued talking about her new life in Bayreuth.

"My husband's lover was here tonight – in the box next door to us. She looked at me with such a smirk on her face. I don't know if I hate her or hate him more. It's an open secret, Chris – my friends often look at me strangely – and I wonder, is it pity or dismay, I don't know."

He touched her hand. "I wish I could take you away with me. Sonia, we could go to America and have a life together. I'd be your devoted servant all of my life; you know that."

Tears welled in her eyes, and she touched his hand. "Darling, they'd take away my children. Even now, the guards won't let them leave the castle with me without an armed escort. And I can't deny them their father and their titles; but if it was just me . . . "

He touched her hand again. "You know, sometimes life gets in the way, doesn't it?"

She smiled and nodded.

Soon it was time for them to go, and after agreeing it would be much better for them to leave the Opera House grounds separately, they said their goodbyes. But just before they departed the privacy of the Prince's Box, she wrapped her arms around his neck and kissed him deeply. After gently breaking away from him but looking directly into his eyes, she whispered, "Chris, I love you; I always have and I always will. Never, ever, forget that."

He walked her down the stairs to the first floor, assisted her with her shawl, and helped her into her carriage. She waved at him as she drove away into the August night.

Over the next several weeks, Chris and Sonia took every opportunity to meet somewhere in the castle. Often they'd walk the corridors together; sometimes they'd sneak into a dark room for a few minutes alone, and occasionally they'd meet in the library. Even after taking every precaution, he assumed they were being watched. But his feelings for her were so intense that it made the risks well worth taking.

The 1830s was a time of significant political upheaval in Europe. Initially, King Ludwig had been a liberal monarch, providing his subjects with a limited version of the American-introduced concepts of freedom of speech, press, and assembly. Following the influx of a large number of German Protestants into Catholic Bavaria, Ludwig also fostered the idea of freedom of religion to a limited degree.

Although Protestants were still required to pay the Church tax, they were otherwise free to practice the tenants of their denominations as long as their religious practices did not interfere with the authority and legitimacy of the Roman Catholic Church. Jews, however, were excluded from participating in civil society.

Following the unsuccessful July Revolution of 1830 in France, however, Ludwig's liberal policies suddenly became much more repressive. As in France, the local Bavarian population, pleased with its liberties, began protesting many of the new prerogatives imposed by the monarchy. In May 1832, the social and political upheavals were harshly punished resulting in over one-hundred-fifty political trials and harsh terms of imprisonment. Before the decade was over, Ludwig's government re-imposed strict censorship of the press, speech, and assembly.

In 1837, Bavaria witnessed the rise of the 'Ultramontanes' — a very conservative Roman Catholic movement that aimed to restore Catholicism and the authority of the Pope to everyday life. Then following the election of 1837, the Bavarian Parliament amended the Constitution to remove the civil rights which had been granted to the Protestants.

Among the most controversial enactment of that parliamentary session was *The Edict of August 14, 1838*. In that decree, King Ludwig issued an Order compelling all members of the military to kneel in the presence of the Blessed Sacrament during military ceremonies and festivities. This practice infuriated the Protestants.

Finally, some aspects of Bavarian political and religious thought became greatly influenced by the so-called 'American Experience.' Factions of every stripe of the political and religious persuasions vigorously debated the concept of specific inalienable rights of life, liberty and the pursuit of happiness outlined in the American Constitution.

After that, the various political and religious factions – the monarchists, the libertarians, the anarchists, and the socialists – hotly debated the concepts concerning the wisdom of choosing the country's political and religious leaders, the American freedoms of the press, religion, speech, and assembly, and most importantly, the right of self-determination.

In September 1839, King Ludwig was facing increasing political protests and demonstrations by university students. In response, the monarch ordered the closing of *King Charles College* in Bayreuth just before the beginning of the autumn term. Further enraging the protesters, he sent reinforcing troops to Bayreuth from Munich to guard the castle and state property. However, it did not end the protests.

Situated on Erlanderstrasse on the west side of Bayreuth, Chris and Charles shared a small room above Hapsburg Tavern. It consisted of a single room with two beds, a small chest of drawers, and a window looking out over the busy street below. The tavern, however, was a hotbed of political activity, and it was there the two brothers began to learn more about the outside world. Often, Chris and Charles found themselves deeply immersed in the subtler points of these political and religious dialogues, and the brothers spent many nights in the tavern arguing well into the wee hours of the morning on these principles and strategies.

"We must stand unified with the students," Horst Brinbruger screamed, and almost in unison, seven or eight men at Hapsburg Tavern stood up, raised their glasses of beer in unison and yelled, "Solidarity, fraternity, liberty!"

Almost immediately, a counter-salute was initiated as Clemens Michelson, a leader of the Monarchist faction, who arose from his chair, raised a glass, and yelled, "I give you Ludwig, our gracious King, and Ruler!"

Then four or five others also raised their glasses and responded, "The King! The King!"

It went on like that all evening long.

As Chris sat silently in the corner one evening eating his supper of lamb stew and fresh wheat biscuits, he was listening carefully to the arguments – but not choosing sides. Chris had to be careful; he worked in the castle, and the King's spies were everywhere. Charles, however, was siding with the protesters.

Horst rose again and began another round of dedications. While lifting his glass, Chris could see the branding on Horst's right hand – the letter R for 'resistance.' Chris had learned earlier that Horst had received this branding following his incarceration during a student protest in Munich in 1838.

The process of branding political extremists on their right hand had begun in France during the student uprising of 1830, and it marked the bearer for life as being hostile to King and Country. Many other nations rapidly adopted the tattoo format, and private employers would often refuse the unfortunate bearers work and other privileges for the remainder of their lives. Chris did not wish to be branded.

While finishing his beer, Chris was sitting with a group of men who were discussing the American experiment. One man, Tobias Metzger, a loyalist, was arguing with the others that democracy was not a 'Christian' concept.

He said, "Democracy – I spit upon it – is a pagan form of government emanating from the days of the heathen Roman Republic. The adherents presume they know better than God as to who should rule us. It's not only wrong; it's sinful."

Benoît Bastille, a veteran of the most recent French rebellion, quickly replied, "So, is it better to have one inept aristocrat following another imbecile rule our nation? I say not!"

Tobias replied, "I disagree with your characterization of our gracious King. We Christians believe the power to select our political leadership is God's sole prerogative, not man's. Putting the decision in the hands of men plays directly into the Devil's plan. And, pray tell, what does the common man know about government? We'll get mob rule – not reason."

Benoît retorted in a heavy French accent, "The process has worked well in America for over fifty years now. I've been there. I've seen it firsthand. The office-seekers need not be from an aristocratic family – ordinary men can select their government officials including their president. Then these elected men serve for specific terms and are accountable to the people for their actions. Kings are not accountable until they are forcibly thrown out."

As the participants became drunker, the debates became more heated and were considerably much louder. Chris finished his meal and remained silent, but he wondered about America – what is this new world like? He had heard Benoît talking about the gleaming cities, the majestic mountain ranges, the millions of acres of land for the taking, and the fact there is no requirement for any citizen to bow down before a member of the upper classes. Chris wanted to learn more about America. Perhaps one day, he'd go there and see it for himself.

A few nights later, Chris sat down for his dinner next to Benoît to learn more about this exciting new world. "Have you been to America?"

"Yes," Benoît began, "I went there first in 1831 – right after the student riots in Paris. Oh, so many good men were killed and butchered by the police in the French uprising; I was lucky to escape that last night. I'd been one of the organizers, and I knew my name was on a subversives list."

"Really?"

"Yes, after our barricades were broken, I was lucky to avoid the police dragnet. With the help of friends and strangers, I escaped to England one night from Calais on a freighter. The police were everywhere, and I had to pay a lot of money for my concealment aboard ship. Chris, I can never go back to France again unless the people overthrow the government."

"Please tell me more about America. I may want to go there someday."

"Well, my father is a businessman in Marseille, and although he deeply disapproved of my attempt to topple the French government, he made arrangements for me to sail from London to New York and join the family's export business in Connecticut."

"Is it near New York?"

"Maybe one hundred miles north of New York City – but not far."

Benoît had a sip of beer – a lager beer from Swabia – took a deep breath, and continued. "You know, there is so much to tell you about America, I don't know where to start. While the nation was originally founded by the British, it's full of people from all over Europe now – including many Germans. There are no aristocratic titles or inherited levels of society in America. While there are certainly the rich, the poor, and the middle classes, these designations are often determined by one's wits, talents, and willingness to work. That fact alone makes it so different from Europe."

"That's what I've heard – but is it true?"

"Yes, quite true – but you need to have a dream, and you need to learn English if you go there. You know, the English language is not much different than German – but it's significantly different from French. It took me a long time to learn the language, but you cannot succeed in America without speaking English."

"I've also heard there is no official religion in American. Correct?"

"While it's true, the majority of the people in leadership are Protestants. Being a Catholic, while permitted, can be a disadvantage, my friend. But there is no Church tax; the American Constitution forbids such levies."

Benoît and Chris talked for another hour or so that evening, and then again on several subsequent occasions. Unfortunately, Benoît was in Bavaria on family business for only a short period, and soon he'd have to leave for Hamburg and begin return voyage back to America.

Like many of his countrymen, Chris became enchanted by the prospect of going to America someday. From a young age, he began reading everything he could get his hands on about the subject: such as the translated novels by Washington Irving, Nathanial Hawthorne and Ralph Waldo Emerson, copies of *The Farmers' Almanac*, and even political documents such as the American Constitution. He simply could not find enough information.

On a Tuesday afternoon in early December, Chris had finished his restoration of a broad chest in the Upper West Wing. As the varnish was drying, he began removing the coverings which protected the floor and the wall in the area around the chest. The light through the windows was dimming as the hour was getting later. By January, Chris supposed, there'd be hardly any light at all.

As he was about ready to begin his restoration work on the next piece of furniture, Duchess Sonia and an escort walked into the room. Chris immediately stood up and bowed deeply. "Good afternoon, My Lady."

She smiled and turned to her escort and said, "Would you mind waiting in the other room? I need to have a private conversation with this gentleman."

The soldier, a young man of perhaps twenty years of age, looked suspiciously at Chris, but nodded and left the room. Sonia and Chris both knew the escort would be listening attentively on the other side of the wall.

"I've come to say goodbye. My husband and I leave soon for Regensburg."

"Have a safe journey, My Lady. I will miss you."

She took a deep breath and said softly, "For the first two or three years here, I could think of little else but you. I dreamed of our life together, and only when I realized it was impossible, I married my husband. Ours is a marriage of convenience to strengthen our family alliances. Thankfully, it has produced two fine children whom I adore; but I rarely see my husband these days."

Chris was now looking directly into her eyes; knowing perhaps it was a violation of societal norms between people of different social classes. "I'm so sorry to hear that, Sonia. I've dreamed of you and me, too."

"My husband has taken a mistress, and he has left me with so little hope regarding our future together. I guess that while his action is not uncommon, I don't know how much longer I can go on this way. If I didn't have my children . . ."

And she started to cry. Chris went up to her and took her in his arms. Looking into her eyes, he kissed her on her lips, and then she placed her head on his chest and wept much harder. He held onto her, and they swayed gently in a rhythm which only their hearts could feel.

At that instant, a man charged into the room and yelled: "Get away from that woman, you dog."

She pulled away from Chris and said, "Alfred, Chris is an old friend of mine, and I was only saying goodbye to him. He. . . "

Alfred grabbed the Duchess and pushed her forcefully to the side. Looking at Chris, he yelled "You bastard workman. How dare you touch this woman?" And with the back of his hand, he struck Chris across his face. The blow was so hard it knocked him down to his knees. Alfred then kicked Chris as hard as he could under his chin, and he went somersaulting into the wall.

"Get down on your knees, you conniving bastard, and beg for her forgiveness. You know damn well you must never touch your betters. Now, pick up your tools and leave this palace, and never come back. If I ever see you in the confines of the castle again, I'll have you castrated. Now, get out."

Chris looked long and hard at this man, Viceroy Alfred Dressler. Sonia was crying and just looked at Chris as the Viceroy was leading her away. Slowly, Chris got off of the floor, gathered up his tools, and looked around the room once more. After nodding at her, he vacated the work-area of the castle for the final time.

However, he would see the Viceroy again.

Initially, Chris tried to make as best he could of this unfortunate situation, and he eventually found small carpentry jobs elsewhere in the city. However, without steady work, he knew that he could not afford the costs associated with living in Bayreuth for too much longer. If they could not obtain employment by Christmas, the two brothers would have to return home to Trockau.

But Charles – who had also been fired – became immersed in the political arguments raised by the various student groups and worker associations. Charles would spend most of his time drinking beer in the taverns and attending assemblies of protestors. Chris, aware of his obligation to protect his younger brother, tried to separate Charles from these associations but his efforts were mostly unsuccessful.

For several months, student groups and representatives of the working class met at various venues to discuss ways to petition the King and Parliament for relief from the government's increasingly restrictive practices. The main demands of the student's group concerned issues of liberty, civil and political rights, and national unity. On the other hand, the workers called for improved working conditions, fairer wages, and a reduction in the working day to ten hours.

Initially, no consensus was reached among these groups regarding the specific demands for action. Feeling frustrated by this inaction, a few uncoordinated violent acts were carried out by a few members of the student groups.

Eventually, the combined assembly of protesters agreed to stage a peaceful march on the Bayreuth Palace on December 16, 1839. The groups did not see this movement as a revolutionary or rebellious act, and all of the participants hoped a peaceful gathering and presentation of a petition of grievances to the governmental representatives would encourage the King and Parliament to address their many concerns.

To foster unity, the representatives of each of the groups spent weeks drafting a proposal which would incorporate a list of all of their demands. The final approved petition was written in subservient terms, and the document ended with a reminder to the King and the members of parliament of their obligations to serve the wishes of the Bavarian people.

On the morning of December 16, approximately two hundred men and women gathered in the town square, and after they listened to speeches by several of their leaders, the groups began a nonviolent march down Maximillianstrasse toward Bayreuth Palace. Although Chris had decided to watch the events from the sidelines, Charles had been radicalized and marched near the front row of the protesters.

Because the King was not in residence at Bayreuth Palace at the time of the protest, Viceroy Dressler was officially in command, and on the evening before the Sunday march, the Viceroy had developed strategic measures to contain the marchers. He deployed a substantial military force in and around the environs of the Palace, the principal government buildings, and the churches. These brigades were components of the Imperial Guard, troops from the Bavarian Army, and elements from the local police. Many of the soldiers were seated on horseback and carried swords and batons.

Riding in plain view at the head of the joint military group, Viceroy Dressler set up a perimeter located just in front of Sternplatz. Using a megaphone, he ordered the marchers to halt and disperse. For several minutes, there was silence as the opposing sides just looked at each other in anticipation of the next move. When the organizers of the march ordered the crowd of students and workers to press forward, Viceroy Dressler gave a preemptive order, and the cavalry charged ahead, using their clubs and horses as a means to trample the protestors.

Chris was carefully watching the activities from a short distance. While not wanting to be a part of this protest rally, he observed Charles who was standing in the front row waving a banner. As the horsemen charged into the crowd, Chris watched as a soldier viciously struck Charles on his head with his baton, and as Charles fell to the ground the soldier's horse trampled Charles' unresponsive body.

Seeing this affront, Chris rapidly entered into the melee in an attempt to rescue his brother but the surging military component promptly crushed Chris. As he attempted to lift himself off the ground, another mounted soldier struck Chris on the back of his head with his pistol, and Chris collapsed unconscious on the pavement near his brother.

The battering was over in well under five minutes, and the remaining protestors quickly dispersed and retreated down Maximillianstrasse. Viceroy Dressler ordered the horsemen to halt, and lying there between the halted cavalry and the Viceroy was a scene of several dozen bleeding and injured protestors.

Once the horsemen regrouped and returned to the formation in the front of Sternplatz, the police entered the street and began arresting and gathering up the dead and injured protesters, including Chris and Charles. The protestors were loaded into wagons and slowly removed from the site.

Although the total number killed in the day's clashes remained uncertain, the King's officials recorded two dead and fifty-six injured protestors. An additional thirty-eight demonstrators were later rounded up, arrested, and placed in police custody in the Bayreuth jail. Very few of the King's forces were injured that day.

About an hour later, Chris awoke in a dark cell which he shared with twenty other men, many of whom were bloodied and had broken bones. A few men were still unconscious. His head hurt terribly, and looking around the cell, he was unable to find Charles.

However, Chris saw Horst and asked, "What's going on?"

Horst looked frightened, and before he could answer, they heard a scream from somewhere deep inside the prison complex. Then Horst replied, "Many of our colleagues are being interrogated and branded. I can't believe the brutality."

"Have you seen Charles?"

"No, I haven't seen him, but there are at least two or three other holding cells somewhere inside this prison – each cell is full of protestors. He's probably in one of those cells."

"How long have we been here?"

Horst looked around, "I don't know. Perhaps an hour; perhaps a bit more. I've been watching the cell over to the right. The soldiers seem to be taking two or three of us at a time – and they're bringing them back after each man was branded. Chris, I'm worried."

Chris sat down on the cold floor and rubbed the back of his head. He had a pounding headache, and his shoulder hurt terribly. He wondered to himself, what has happened to Charles?

About fifteen minutes later, three soldiers approached Chris' cell. Oh no, he thought, they're coming for us now. One guard held a lit torch, and another had a drawn pistol. The third man appeared to be an officer.

The officer banged on the cell with his set of keys and yelled, "Christopher Bogner; is there a Christopher Bogner in this cell? If so, show yourself."

Initially, Chris remained quiet, but soon several of the prisoners looked at him, revealing his presence. He said, "I'm Christopher Bogner."

"You will come with us."

Chris stood up and looked at Horst. Sighing, Chris made his way up to the cell door. After telling the other prisoners to step back, the officer opened the door, grabbed Chris' shirt and hurriedly pulled him out of the cell. Upon locking the door behind them, Chris was shackled and led down the path to another door. The officer closed and locked the cell door behind them, and the group began walking down the hall to another part of the prison.

Once again the guard ordered, "Open the door," and passing through the door, the group walked up a flight of stairs which led to another room. After knocking on the third door, it was opened, and the four of them entered into a well-lighted area. Abruptly, Chris was shackled to a ring attached to the back wall and told to sit down at the table. The officer and the other soldiers left the room leaving Chris there by himself.

He sat in the room for another hour when he heard approaching footsteps. The door was unlocked and opened, and five people entered the door including Viceroy Dressler and Duchess Sonia. Chris tried to stand but could not do so because of his restraints.

She said, "Oh, Chris, what have you done?"

He began to respond, but Viceroy Dressler smacked him on the mouth, "Be quiet, swine. Be quiet. You will speak only to me."

Dressler laughed, looked at Chris, and said, "Didn't I tell you never to enter the palace again?"

"My Lord, I was brought here involuntarily. I was not a part of the protest."

"Well, I remember distinctly seeing you attack one of my soldiers. Am I wrong, swine?"

Chris looked at Sonia. She looked angry. He replied, "My Lord, I was trying to assist my injured brother after one of your soldiers struck him; I simply came to his aid. I've no quarrel with the King or with you, Sir."

"You expect me to believe that? Do you think I'm stupid?"

"No, My Lord, but it's true. I only want to find my brother and go home to Trockau."

Dressler laughed and then struck Chris again hard across his face. Sonia screamed and yelled, "That's quite enough; I order you to stop, Viceroy. Stop right now!"

Dressler looked at the Duchess. "You are ordering me to stop; you, a promiscuous woman?"

"My father, Duke Gottingen, orders you to stop." She was clenching her fists, and Chris saw the anger on her face. "And you will release this man immediately; that's an order!"

Dressler stared at her and knew she had gotten the better of him. "You want me to release this criminal who attacked the authority of our King and country?"

"Yes, and do it quickly. That's my order, Viceroy."

Dressler thought for a second, looked at Chris, and replied. "Once we brand you and give you three lashes, perhaps I will."

Sonia was unperturbed. "Now, Viceroy; now!"

Dressler looked hard at the Duchess but realized she outranked him. Slowly, he bowed and said, "Then, Madam, I'll leave this man to your care." He walked to the door and said, "Guard, open the door," and after the door was opened, the Viceroy hastily vacated the interrogation cell leaving Sonia and two guards alone with Chris.

She sat down at the table; she looked perplexed. She lifted her eyes to Chris and said, "You must leave Bayreuth immediately. I can't protect you after tomorrow when I leave for Regensburg. You must leave tonight or tomorrow morning at the latest."

"I won't leave here without my brother, My Lady."

The Duchess looked at the guards and said, "Immediately, go and find Charles Bogner and bring him here. Now."

The senior guard answered, "My Lady, should we leave you alone with this man?"

"Yes, he's a friend of mine – and Christ, he's chained to the damn wall. I'll be okay. Now go and find his brother."

After the guards left the room, she shook her head and just looked at Chris. "The Viceroy has made many passes at me, and I detest him. I hate so many things about Bayreuth that I'm glad to be joining my husband. Perhaps, we can start over if he stops his philandering."

"My Lady . . ."

"Please call me Sonia when we're alone."

He took a deep breath. "Sonia, I'm sorry I've caused you so much trouble. You know, it'll probably be much better if you never see me again."

They held hands and talked for about thirty minutes. Then there was a knock on the door. "My Lady, we have the other prisoner. Shall we bring him in?"

"Yes, please bring him in."

The door opened, and the two guards dragged Charles into the cell. He was dazed, his right hand was bandaged, and there were several oozing welts on his back. His feet were still shackled. The guards sat him down at the table. Chris again tried to stand up, but his restraints would not budge.

"Charles, what have they done to you?"

Charles looked up at his brother. "They whipped me several times and branded by hand. Then they beat me with a club. Those bastards; I didn't deserve this torture."

Sonia was horrified by the appalling sight, and she held her hand close to her mouth.

Chris said, "Brother, we're getting out of here and leaving Bayreuth immediately. Do you think you can walk?"

"Perhaps a little, if you help me."

They sat for another for ten minutes or so as Charles tried to regain his strength. He was crying hard. "I want to go home."

Finally, the Duchess said to the sergeant of the guards, "Unchain these men and take them to Sternplatz. Release the men outside the gates, and return directly to me, so I know they are out of custody. Any questions, Sergeant?"

"No, My Lady, I fully understand."

Sonia looked once more at Charles and just shook her head. "What is happening to my country?"

Chris and Charles remained silent.

A few moments later, she said, "You must leave Bayreuth now before the Viceroy changes his mind. I'll never forget you and our time together in Trockau – please believe that, Chris. May God be with you."

She leaned over and kissed him softly on his cheek, lingering perhaps a little too long.

He said, "My Lady, thank you for helping my brother and me. I'll trouble you no more."

She looked at him; tears were welling in her eyes. She stood up, asked the outside guard to open the door, looked back one more time at Chris, and left the cell. Both of them knew they'd never see each other again.

Then the guards led the brothers down the hall into a stink of damp floors, past ancient stone walls, and by other dark cells which were filled with huddled men. Finally, there was a clank of keys, and a massive door opened. Finally, the brothers were outside the castle walls, and eventually, they were unshackled and released in the plaza. The clock tower noted it was nearly four o'clock in the afternoon, and it was already getting dark.

After treating Charles' wounds and putting him to bed, Chris went downstairs to the tavern for supper. He saw Benoît sitting alone in a corner and decided to talk to him. Initially, they spoke about the day's events including his incarceration and Charles' wounds. Benoît was supportive, having gone through a similar incident in Paris nine years earlier. Some of what Benoît told him that afternoon, Chris had heard before.

Then Chris asked, "How is the quickest way for me to sail to America?"

Benoît put down his fork, and said, "You want to leave Bavaria and go to America? You know you'll never see your family again."

"I need to go. I have lost faith in the politics here. I'm tired of the nobility and the class distinctions – you know, the bowing, the kneeling, the disrespect; I'm sick of being careful regarding what I say and who I love. I want to go to America while I'm still young and can begin anew."

Benoît looked at Chris for a while and then affirmatively shaking his head, he said, "I suggest you go to Rotterdam and sail to Philadelphia."

"Rotterdam – it's in Holland, right? How do I get there?"

"Well, go south to Regensburg and take the Danube River west to the city of Ulm, and then go overland to the Rhine and sail north to Rotterdam. It's a long way, but I'd leave from Rotterdam."

"I don't have much money. Will there be work along the way?"

"You're a carpenter, and there's always work for a carpenter. Furthermore, my father's company has an export office in Rotterdam. Allow me to give you their address. When you arrive there, give them my name and a note from me. They can help you. Who knows, perhaps I'll see you there? I plan to be back in Rotterdam in April or May, God willing."

Once again, it was Christmastime in Trockau, and the family home was decorated in the holiday fashion. In 1839, Anna Maria was twenty-two years old and recently married. She and her husband, Domonic Buttrick, lived in an upstairs bedroom (which was once occupied by her grandparents) with their infant son, Heinrich.

Johann, age 17, was turning into a master carpenter himself, and one day, along with his brother Georg, would inherit the family business. One of Johann's masterpieces, an elegantly carved table, would be later purchased by Richard Wagner, a well-known and respected German composer.

Almost immediately, Chris began to finalize his plans to immigrate to

America. He learned that a first cousin, Christopher Bauer, and his family, were living in St. Louis, and Chris believed he could get a start there in Missouri. Papa, however, was solidly against the idea and presumed that his sons were safe in Trockau.

On Christmas Eve, the family rode in the carriage to St. Boniface for Midnight Mass. As usual, Papa would be singing a solo during the offertory. As trumpets sounded, the congregation stood as Duke Gottingen and his family were announced, and they took their places in the front pew.

After the sermon concluded, Papa rose and began singing Schubert's version of 'Ave Maria' in Latin:

Ave Maria
Gratia plena
Maria, gratia plena
Maria, gratia plena

Ave, ave dominus
Dominus tecum
Benedicta tu in mulieribus
Et benedictus

Et benedictus fructus ventris
Ventris tuae, Jesus
Ave Maria.

Whenever Papa sang, Chris could almost believe he was already in heaven. It wasn't just Papa's beautiful tenor voice but his masterful delivery – it had a way of piercing Chris' heart. Papa sang slowly and richly and delivered the hymn in such a way Chris wished that Papa would never end singing that hymn.

As Chris shut his eyes, Papa's voice began to wipe away those horrible memories of Bayreuth, and the hymn delivered the full solemnity of the Christmas season to the weary brothers. Tears formed in Chris' eyes and looking around the church; he noticed many of the parishioners probably felt the same way. One day, he would be his father's equal in carpentry, but Chris could never match Papa's lovely voice.

After Mass ended, the Duke and his family walked back up the aisle and then paused momentarily near the Bogner family pew. Spotting Chris, the Duke asked one of his servants pass a note to Chris as the Duke continued his slow walk to the vestibule.

Chris opened the note, and read it. It said, "See me immediately after Mass. I have news."

As Chris entered the vestibule, he saw the Duke chatting with several of his subjects. Hesitantly, Chris walked up to the Duke, and catching his attention, the Duke motioned Chris to join him in a tiny room located just off the vestibule.

The Duke shut the door and looked up at Chris. He said, "My daughter has filled me in on the unfortunate demonstrations in Bayreuth. I now have it on good authority that Viceroy Dressler has persuaded our gracious King to sign arrest warrants for many of the protestors. Unfortunately, your name and your brother's name appear on the warrant. You must leave Trockau immediately or plan to be arrested and charged with treason. Like my daughter, I'm convinced of your innocence, but I cannot help you now that the King is involved. Use this information wisely."

"I will. Thank you, My Lord."

The pending arrest warrant greatly distressed the Bogner family, and Papa knew that his sons would have to act quickly. After Christmas supper, Chris and Charles loaded all of their earthly possession into a brown, leather-bound, trunk, said their prayers, and went to bed for the last time in their family home. Nobody slept well that night.

On the morning of December 26, 1839, the two brothers hugged Papa and the other family members for the last time. With the indictment pressing, the brothers understood they would need to leave Bavaria as soon as possible. Everyone knew that once the brothers sailed to America, they would never return home.

Before leaving the house, Papa handed Chris a potato with a branch sticking out of it.

"What's this, Papa?"

"I've inserted a shoot from our grapevine into this potato. My great-grand-parents did the same over a hundred years ago when they moved here from Rothenberg. The potato will nourish the grape cutting for six months or more. When you get to America, plant it, and then whenever you leave, take another cutting of the vine, place it into a potato, and carry it with you to your new home – wherever that may be. This way, you'll always have a piece of your heritage with you."

Chris looked at Papa; they both had tears in their eyes, and they embraced for a long time.

Before their departure from Trockau, the brothers arranged for suitable transport south to the city of Regensburg. Upon arriving there the follow-ing night, they booked passage west on the Danube River to the Kingdom of Baden-Württemberg where they would be safe from King Ludwig's indict-ment. The ride to Regensburg lasted almost two days; but once they arrived, they were out of immediate danger of arrest and imprisonment.

In 1840, Regensburg had a population of approximately 20,000 inhabitants. Situated at the confluence of the Danube, Naab, and Regen Rivers, the first settlements in what would later become the city of Regensburg date from the Stone Age. Around 90 AD, the Romans built an outpost on the site, and in 179, Emperor Marcus Aurelius constructed a new Roman fort named Castra Regina. In the late Roman times, the city was the seat of a bishop, and St. Boniface re-established the Bishopric of Regensburg in the year 739.

Before boarding the riverboat that evening for the city of Ulm, Chris com-posed a short note to Sonia and delivered it to the guard at the barracks where she and her husband were stationed.

It read:

To Duchess Sonia Therese Von Furstenberg D'Ousterling:

My Lady, I wish to thank you for all of the graciousness you have shown to Charles and me over these many years. We leave Regensburg tonight to begin our long journey to America. I will never forget your kindness. You and your family will always remain in my prayers.

Affectionately, Christopher

He never learned whether the Duchess ever read his note.

CHAPTER FOUR

Rotterdam, September 1840

The Danube River is Europe's second-longest river. It originates deep within the Black Forrest of Southern Germany and flows mostly eastward for almost eighteen-hundred miles until it enters into the Black Sea. During the Roman period, the Danube formed the northern border of the Empire.

Following a two-day journey on the Danube, the brothers arrived safely in Ulm on December 31, 1839. Finally, they were safe from King Ludwig's indictment. While Charles was doing somewhat better physically and emotionally, he was still not his prior self. Also, their money was running low.

The brothers found accommodations in a gasthaus located in the central part of Ulm, and within a few days, Chris secured a job in a local carpentry shop. After they were settled, he wrote a letter to his father:

11 January 1840

Charles and I made it safely to Ulm, and we are now living in a gasthaus above a tavern on Koenigstrasse. Winter is upon us, and the Danube is now frozen solid to the west of the city. The Alps are snow-covered and magnificent; towering much higher than anything I've seen in Trockau.

The tavern owner, Herr Hesse, assures me that we are now safe from the indictment and you can write to us here. Charles is doing much better, and I have found work in a carpentry shop not far from the tavern. We plan to stay in Ulm until the rivers thaw so we can continue our journey to Rotterdam.

Yesterday, I climbed to the top of Ulm Minster. It's the tallest church in the world measuring 568 feet high, and the spire has 768 stairs to the very top. The final platform has barely enough room for one person to stand. Looking out over the city, I could see Bavaria on the other side of the Danube.

Papa, I'm still worried about Charles. The beating and the branding have changed him. I hope that once we get to America, he'll forget that awful incident in Bayreuth.

We deeply miss you and the others but believe our decision to leave Trockau was the right one. You always remain in our thoughts and our prayers.

Affectionately, Christopher and Charles

About two weeks later, a letter arrived for the brothers in Ulm:

25 January 1840

About three days after you left Trockau, a military officer appeared at our shop with a copy of the indictment. He searched the house, and when you were not found, the officer took me to the castle for interrogation. Thankfully, Johann sent word to the Duke, and I was rapidly released. I suspect, however, we are still being watched.

The authorities are not aware of your letter. Please don't send any more messages to me until you safely arrive in Rotterdam. I am not so sure the police cannot cross the river and arrest you. So be careful, my sons.

The weather is cold here, too, but we have plenty of work to keep us busy for a long time. Johann and George have been a great help to me, and Anna Maria keeps a good house. I know she would be happy to tell you that she and Domonic are expecting another child come summer.

The Duke does not seem to be well. I've heard he suffers from consumption. His son, Count Joseph, has been taking over the official duties in the Duke's absence. Do you remember his daughter, Duchess Sonia? I hear she's now married with two children and living in Regensburg with her husband.

Let me know when you arrive in Rotterdam. I'll send you a letter there at the address of your friend, Benoît Bastille.

The family sends you their love. Papa

The brothers remained in Ulm for about three months, and as Charles recovered, he tried to find skilled-work, but he was unsuccessful because of the branding on the back of his right hand. Prospective employers were hesitant to hire someone presumed to be a troublemaker. Consequently, Charles found himself often in the tavern and usually drunk when Chris returned from work.

Toward the end of March, the weather warmed somewhat, and soon the ice on the Danube began to break up. Chris and Charles secured passage westward on a log barge, and on March 30, they left Ulm. The next day, the brothers exited the barge at Zwiefalten and began the two-day walk to the city of Tübingen.

Occasionally, the boys hitched a ride on a hay cart or a milk wagon, but they usually walked side-by-side, holding the handles of the brown leather trunk, for most of the thirty-mile journey. The first signs of spring were present all around them, and the brothers were filled with optimism.

They remained in Tübingen for two weeks where Chris secured carpentry work at the local castle, Hohentübingen, to cover the cost of their lodging, food, and transportation fees. During the evening, the brothers would often stroll on Neckar Island where the Neckar River briefly divides its flow into two streams. From the point where the currents merge once again north of the island, the river becomes navigable all the way to the Rhine.

One night, the boys found a tavern in an area of town called Neckarfront. They ordered two glasses of beer and hot meals. It was a beautiful spring evening, and as they waited for their order, Chris gazed around the crowded tavern. It looked so much like the Hapsburg Tavern in Bayreuth and overhearing some of the conversations, the customers were discussing similar topics – women, pay, and politics. So little had changed, he thought, from his days in Bavaria.

Charles asked, "When do you think we'll sail for America?"

"By late summer, I hope. The almanac suggested crossing the Atlantic when the water is the warmest, and the seas are the calmest. However, the book warned of a powerful windstorm called a hurricane."

"A hurricane?"

"Yes, they often occur in the South Atlantic, but these massive winds and rain can do considerable damage along the shipping lanes all the way from South America to Greenland. Many ships have sunk in these storms."

"Does it say anything about sea monsters?"

Chris laughed. "No, there are whales but no sea monsters."

He laughed again and put down his fork. "Charles, we need to make some money. Although I know you don't like to do menial work, you have to help me raise additional funds for our trip to Rotterdam. It will be much more expensive for us to travel once we get on the Rhine."

"No one will hire me because of this goddamn branding. I'm a carpenter; not a sewer rat or chimney sweeper."

"I agree, and once we reach America, no one will care about your scar. But for now, I need your help even if it only involves only menial labor. Do you understand?"

Charles nodded his head, but Chris could tell that Charles was not happy about it.

Traveling up the Neckar River on horse-drawn riverboats, the boys left Tübingen a few days later, and they eventually passed through the cities of Stuttgart, Ludwigsburg, Heilbronn, and Heidelberg before reaching Mannheim in mid-May. As the days were growing much longer, the temperatures were rising, too.

The city of Mannheim is located at the confluence of the Rhine and the Neckar Rivers in the northwestern corner of Baden-Württemberg. Situated along Europe's great waterway, the city had recently experienced massive industrial growth, and it became a logical terminus for the Baden Railway.

The railway revolution in the Kingdom of Baden-Württemberg began in earnest on December 7, 1835, when the first train ran between the cities of Nürnberg and Fürth. The Alder locomotive pulling the first railcars was built by Robert Stephenson and Company in Newcastle, England, and was one of the first steam-powered trains to operate on the European continent. By 1840, rail lines were being constructed all over Western Europe.

Upon arriving in Mannheim, Chris quickly found work as a carpenter in the construction of the new railway depot in the downtown portion of the city whereas Charles could only find suitable employment in building the bed for the rail line. But the work was steady, and thus, the brothers postponed their travel to Rotterdam for nearly four months until the rail line was completed.

One afternoon in late May when the boys were returning to their gasthaus after work, a person handed Chris a handbill. It read:

THE TWENTY-SECOND ANNUAL LOWER RHINE MUSIC FESTIVAL

On Whitsuntide, May 24 at Noon

On the lawn and between the hedges of Mannheim Palace

PROGRAM

Wie nahte mir der Schlummer	Carl Maria von Weber
Jenny Lind, soprano	Piano Concerto in A minor: Op. 54
Robert Schmann	Clara Schumann, piano

Intermission

Requiem	Wolfgang Amadeus Mozart
Symphony No. 9 in D minor, Opus 125 "Choral"	Ludwig Von Beethoven

The Lower Rhine Musical Orchestra

Combined chorus from Dusseldorf, Cologne, and Bayreuth

Felix Mendelssohn, Conductor

Johann Schornstein, Choirmaster

After going through all of the challenges which they'd faced since leaving Bayreuth the previous December, Chris and Charles decided to attend the festival and celebrate their arrival in Mannheim.

Whitsuntide (also known as Pentecost Sunday) turned out to be a lovely spring day, and the crowd attending the concert was massive. Not being able to afford the cost to rent chairs on the upper lawn, the brothers bought general admission tickets. Arriving in late morning, they also brought a picnic basket and a bottle of red wine, and after finding a spot among the hedges and walks along the great lawn, the brothers spread a blanket in the middle of several thousand other concert enthusiasts.

The setting, on the grounds of Mannheim Palace, was an impressive venue. To the southwest, the lavish gardens faced the Rhine River, and to the northeast, the palace presented a four hundred foot long frontage to the City Centre. Surrounded by an area of over twenty acres, the castle was one of Europe's biggest palaces, and it was the second largest one built in Baroque style, second only to Versailles. Construction of the manor was commenced solemnly on June 2, 1720, and the edifice was not completed until 1760. After undergoing major reconstruction in 1827, Mannheim Palace was in a splendid condition in the spring of 1840.

The orchestra was rather large, containing nearly one hundred pieces including keyboards, brass, woodwinds, strings, and percussion, all led by the world-renown conductor, Maestro Felix Mendelssohn. Moreover, the combined chorus from the cities of Dusseldorf, Cologne, and Bayreuth was over two hundred voices strong. Chris wondered whether any of the choir members from Bayreuth had participated – either as a soldier or a civilian – in the demonstrations in Bayreuth during the prior December. Perhaps, he even knew a couple of them.

It was an exquisite day, and Chris and Charles sat on the blanket and soaked in the beautiful music that was enveloping them. Occasionally looking from side to side from his perch on the lawn, Chris watched as other members in the audience seated all around him swayed their hands in rhythm, moved their heads left-to-right and up and down to the percussion sounds, and gently joined in the vocal portions of the chorus. To him, the trials and tribulations the brothers had experienced over the prior six months had somehow been made worth it on that lovely springtime afternoon.

During the long intermission, the brothers walked around the grounds and gazed at the fountains and statues which were placed almost everywhere in the gardens. During these festivals, the breaks often lasted for about two hours; plenty of time for drinking, smoking and friendly greetings on the garden-walks. Occasionally, the brothers would eaves-drop over conversations about the performances.

One gentleman lamented, "Felix Mendelssohn's direction was an embarrassment; he was both aloof and bewildered. He seems to be incapable of making his intentions known to the other performers; he's an embarrassment, I say."

Chris, on the other hand, thought Maestro Mendelssohn's direction was brilliant.

Another gentleman commented upon Clara Schumann, calling her "the most distinguished pianists of the era," and another person referred to the soprano, Jenny Lind, as the "new Swedish Nightingale." Chris wondered at these comments.

As the afternoon faded into early evening, Maestro Mendelssohn and the combined chorus ended the performance with a rousing rendition of Ludwig Von Beethoven's Symphony No. 9 which left no doubt among the audience as to the brilliance of both Beethoven and Mendelssohn.

As the final notes sounded that night, Chris and Charles were almost breathless, and they sat on their blanket for nearly an hour after the performance concluded talking about the marvels they had witnessed during that warm May afternoon and evening.

Mannheim was the most prominent city the brothers had ever visited; in fact, Mannheim was significantly grander in both population and industrialization than either Bayreuth or Ulm. In 1840, the industrial revolution was beginning to hit the Kingdom of Baden-Württemberg, and it was a fantastic time for the brothers. They had never seen a railroad locomotive or a steampowered riverboat. Many houses had installed gaslights, and much of the manufacturing in the city of Mannheim was being converted from wood-burning to coal-fired to make steam to power the new machinery. The jobs were plentiful for skilled workers.

The first rail section between Mannheim and Heidelberg was opened on September 10th. The brothers, along with much of the townspeople, waited outside the Mannheim Depot and listened as they heard the Alder engine chug around a corner and dash through the forest on its way to the terminus.

The crowd cheered as they smelled the smoke, saw the light illuminated on the front of the massive iron engine, and heard the distinct whistle blow. The Alder, along with a coal car and three passenger cars full of people, came to a screeching stop alongside the platform leading to the depot to the cheers of the townspeople. Although it was the first, it would not be the last time Christopher would see a train.

With the work on the railway completed, the brothers bought tickets on a steam-powered riverboat for their journey from Mannheim to Rotterdam. After coming back to their room in the gasthaus for the last time, Chris composed another letter to his father.

September 11, 1840

Tomorrow, Charles and I leave for Rotterdam, and perhaps by the time you receive this letter, we'll be on our way to America. Since I last wrote to you from Olm, we have traveled up the Neckar River to Mannheim. We have found work all along the way, and I think we may have sufficient funds now to purchase our passage to America.

Charles is doing better both physically and emotionally although the branding on the back of his right hand has been an obstacle for him to obtain carpentry positions. I hope his scar will not hamper him once we arrive in America.

Papa, I am filled with competing emotions: from the sweetness of the great adventure to America to the bitterness at the thought of never seeing you again. While I long for the Trockau of my youth, I know Charles and I are taking the best course to resume our lives safely away from the King's men. Our future lies in America.

I will write to you once more from Rotterdam before we begin our journey across the Atlantic Ocean. Give our love to the family and tell them that they will be forever in our prayers.

Affectionately, Christopher and Charles

The next morning, the brothers gathered up all of their worldly possessions and boarded *The Steam Ship (S.S.) Edelweiss* for the three-day journey to Rotterdam. *The S.S. Edelweiss*, a paddle wheel steamer, was 56 feet long, 18 feet wide and 40 feet tall. The steamship traveled at an 8 feet depth and had a 90-horsepower low-pressure engine. It was state of the art for river travel in 1840.

The ship's wrought-iron paddlewheels were 16 feet in diameter with eight buckets per wheel. To power the steam-engine, the vessel carried 75 short tons of coal and 25 cords of wood. Like the rail locomotive, the steamship was built in England. When fully loaded, the boat could carry up to 1000 passengers.

The Rhine is the second-longest river in Central and Western Europe (after the Danube), at about 760 miles in length. After departing from Mannheim, *The S.S. Edelweiss* would make intermittent stops in Koblenz, Cologne, and Düsseldorf – discharging and picking up passengers – before arriving in Rotterdam.

Upon boarding the steamship, Chris and Charles found a spot near a window on the first level to store their belongings and swiftly climbed the stairs to the massive second deck to locate an area by the railing to watch the steamer slowly leave Mannheim. They also learned the ship would travel at an average speed of 8 to 10 miles-per-hour – roughly twice as fast as the conventional ships. The fact the boat was moving downstream was helpful, too.

Also, the brothers were amazed at the width and depth of the Rhine River; it was much larger than any river the boys had ever seen, and *The S.S. Edelweiss* passed many slower vessels on its way north, blowing its whistle as a salute to her slower and older sisters.

Chris was surprised to learn that many of his fellow passengers were traveling to Rotterdam to board ships sailing for the New World. Many passengers had already acquired their tickets for their voyages to America, and Chris spent much of his time talking to them about their plans, fears, and aspirations. He learned a lot from them.

Between the cities of Bingen and Koblenz, the river flowed through the narrow Rhine Gorge, and the brothers marveled at the passing scenery. The gorge was over one-hundred feet deep from the water-line to the top of the cliffs, and the surrounding area was well-known for its castles, churches, and vineyards.

Several hours into the cruise, *The S.S. Edelweiss* made its first stop in Koblenz, and passengers were permitted to get off the boat for two hours before the steamship continued its journey to the North Sea. The brothers used this opportunity to stretch their legs and buy additional provisions after hearing that there was little to buy on ship aside from bread and beer.

After re-boarding, the steamship resumed its journey past the mouth of the Moselle River. Exiting the Rhine Gorge, riverboat stopped at Cologne which was by far the largest city the brothers had ever seen. After leaving Cologne and later Düsseldorf, the Rhine River turns west and enters Holland, where, together with the Meuse and Scheldt Rivers, the waterway forms the vast Rhine-Meuse-Scheldt delta. A few hours later, *The S.S. Edelweiss* ended its three-day journey in Rotterdam – one of the most significant ports in all of Europe.

As *The S.S. Edelweiss* steamed into Rotterdam in the late afternoon of September 15, 1840, Chris marveled at the enormous stone warehouses and mighty wharves of this bustling anchorage. The shipwrights, chandlers, caulkers, sailmakers, and carpenters were busy at work. Merchants and traders from all over Europe were selling their cargoes of grain, cotton, linens, furniture, and lumber.

Moreover, stevedores, sailors, and ships' officers, speaking in dozens of languages, were likely giving orders, taking orders, or exchanging information on prices, weather conditions, pirates, politics, and the latest gossip. Hundreds of workers were busy unloading shipments from the arriving boats, and local tax collectors and customs agents were boarding the vessels to calculate tariffs and to guarantee the validity of the manifests. Many other ships were being readied to leave the harbor on the next high tide.

After gathering up their meager belongings and disembarking the ship, Chris and Charles found directions to the mercantile, *Henri Bastille & Co.*, which was located only two blocks from the pier.

"Can I help you, Sir?"

"Yes, I'm Christopher Bogner. Is Benoît Bastille here?"

"No, he left Rotterdam about a month ago. Can I help you?"

Chris explained the circumstances of his appearance at the shop, and the man replied, "Yes, Benoît mentioned you. In fact, we have a letter from your father, I believe."

He reached under the counter, searched for an instant, and handed Chris a letter addressed to him. It was from Papa.

The man looked at Chris and said, "Benoît asked me to help you should you come to the shop. By the way, my name is Pierre – I'm Benoît's brother. I'll be happy to assist you."

"Great, my brother Charles and I want to find a passage to America. Are there boats any sailing there soon?"

"Yes, I assumed so. You know, ships leave Rotterdam almost every day for New York and Philadelphia. Give me some time to look into the matter. Why don't you come back at six o'clock? We can have supper at the tavern down the street, and I can tell you what I find out."

"Thanks. We could use your help."

Pierre smiled, "Benoît told me that you are both carpenters. Shall I look for vessels which need carpenters? Perhaps, you can get a reduced rate if you're willing to work aboard ship."

Somewhat puzzled, Chris looked at Pierre; Chris hadn't considered that possibility.

Pierre continued, "When I go to sea, I'd rather be a sailor than a passenger. At least they're paying me for my troubles. You know, sailing can be a wholesome experience – lots of physical exercise and plenty of pure air. It's much better than sitting in a hell-hole for six to ten weeks waiting for the ship to reach America. Should I inquire for you? We might be able to make it happen, you know."

"Yes, that would be wonderful."

The brothers left the shop and walked down the street to a small park close to an old church. They sat down on a bench in the afternoon sun as Chris opened the letter and began reading it aloud.

June 21, 1840

I pray that you have found your way safely to Rotterdam and soon you'll be beginning your voyage to America. Let me start by telling you some sad news. Duke Gottingen, may he rest in peace, died last month. The family held a Requiem Mass at St. Boniface, and Count Joseph and Duchess Sonia attended the funeral.

After Mass, I offered our family's condolences to them, and Duchess Sonia inquired about you, Christopher. I told her you were safe in Ulm, and that you and Charles were going to America. She asked me to give you her best wishes.

Perhaps you haven't heard, but following a show-trial in Bayreuth, three men were sentenced to death. I think one of them, your friend Horst Brinbruger, has already been hanged. I was also told Charles was tried in absentia and sentenced to three years of hard labor. Charles can never come home again.

Christopher, you were acquitted along with perhaps ten or more other students and workers. Several of the convicted men have appealed to the King. I have not heard the result, but most people here are pessimistic. The King wants to set a stern example. Did you know that one soldier died in the protest march? Apparently, he was shot in the head by Horst.

The workshop is doing well. Count Joseph - who will soon

become Duke Gottingen – has asked us to help him modern-
ize the castle. So, there will be plenty of work for your broth-
ers and me.

I have sent a letter of introduction to my cousin, Christopher
Bauer, who lives in America in a city called St. Louis. Like
us, he is a carpenter, and I have asked him to help find work
for you. I have written his address below.

Godspeed, my beloved sons. Please write to us when you ar-
rive in America. I know it will be a difficult crossing, but I
believe you're in store for a great adventure. May the Good
Lord watch over and keep you safe.

Your brothers, sister, and her family send their love. I pray
that I will see you again. Papa

Later on in the evening, Pierre met brothers at a tavern near the mercantile. He had information for them.

"I found an old schooner named *The Ballantine* which may fit your needs. She will be arriving in Rotterdam either tomorrow or the next day. After discharging a load of rice, cotton, and sugarcane, the vessel will be to be reconfigured so it can transport passengers to Philadelphia. It is not a steamship but rather an old-fashioned sailing ship."

"I guess I was hoping for a steamship. I've been told it cuts the time in less than half."

"Yes, I steamships are much faster; but they are much more expensive and probably wouldn't need the services of any carpenters. An American company owns the shipping line, and I was told the ship, *The Ballantine,* will make only one more Atlantic crossing this year. It's scheduled to leave Rotterdam around September 28th."

"That's less than two weeks for now – but yes, we can be ready."

"My source told me that if you are willing to help reconfigure the boat, the owners will reduce the cost of passage. Because it's fairly inexpensive compared to the cost of a steamship, it has a pretty full passenger list but needs a couple more ship-hands. The representative's name is Wilhelm Schmidt, and he speaks German. He thinks *The Ballantine* will unload its cargo at Pier 7, and they have an office at the head of the pier. It's called 'Central Yankee Lines.' I suggest you go and talk to him."

The following day, the brothers met Wilhelm Schmidt, and after some discussions, Herr Schmidt offered them a reduction in the cost of their passage in exchange for their agreement to help unload and reconfigure *The Ballantine* for its return voyage to Philadelphia. The brothers would work on the ship as needed during the Atlantic crossing, and their degree of participation would even further reduce the cost.

Once in Philadelphia, the brothers also agreed to refit the vessel for the transportation of coal and freight, and remain with the ship for its journey to the Port of New Orleans.

On the morning of September 29, 1840, Chris posted a farewell letter to his father, gathered up their belongings, and boarded *The Ballantine*. At about 2:30 that afternoon — shortly after the crest of the high tide — the crew of *The Ballantine* loosened its lines, and the ship slowly exited Rotterdam harbor.

CHAPTER FIVE

Crofton, Nebraska, August 1964

Grandpa stopped talking for an instant. He checked his watch and said, "Well, look at the time. The news will be on in a moment. Do you like my story so far?"

I smiled, "Yes, I do. I didn't know a lot about him, Grandpa."

"I can tell you some more about him tomorrow. But wait; there is one thing I do want to show you before we stop tonight."

He got out of his chair and slowly walked into his bedroom. He opened the closet door and began searching for something. "Oh, here it is. Yes, here it is."

He walked back to me with a well-worn brown satchel in his hand. Sitting down, he opened the bag and pulled out a folder. "This is my grandfather's journal. He told me that Pierre had met the brothers at the dock just before *The Ballantine* loosened its ropes and gave him this dossier."

I looked at it; now weathered and torn. "Christopher's journal?"

"Yes, Pierre suggested that my grandfather keep a chronicle about his voyage across the sea. Pierre told him it would be a unique opportunity to capture a vanishing means of crossing the oceans. He predicted that in a couple of years, all boats would be steamships and the age of sailing ships would be over."

"Can I look at it?"

"Well, be careful. It is well over one-hundred years old, and it's written in German. Your mother didn't teach you much German, did she?"

"I only know a few words."

"You know, my father taught us German when we were young children. I didn't learn any English until I was four or five years old. Mama and I did the same thing for our children – at least for the three oldest. It's too bad your mother didn't speak German to you. She's fluent, you know."

After looking at the journal for a few moments, I handed it back to him.

He smiled at me and said, "Let's see what's on the news tonight."

The local anchorman first talked about the national news; noting that the International Olympic Committee banned South Africa from the Tokyo Olympics because its teams are racially segregated. Then he reported Fannie Lou Hamer, a civil rights activist and the Vice Chair of the Mississippi Freedom Democratic Party, addressed the Credentials Committee of the Democratic National Convention, challenging the all-white Mississippi delegation's legitimacy.

Grandpa listened intensively and said, "You know, the Democratic National Convention begins in Atlantic City in about two weeks. I wonder whether President Johnson will pick Hubert Humphrey as his running mate."

Once the national news ended, the anchorman turned his attention to local events (mentioning a county fair in Cedar County), the weather (it would be hot and humid tomorrow with the high about 92* and a good chance of thundershowers) and finally, the sports (the Cubs beat the Cincinnati Reds as Ernie Banks hit a three-run home run in the bottom of the 8th inning).

When the news concluded, we said 'good night,' and I went upstairs to the bedroom I shared with my brother, Dick. The room wasn't much. It had two beds, two chests of drawers, a nightstand and a lamp. In between the beds – which were situated along the outside walls of the room – Grandpa had placed a little blue rug. The windows were almost floor level; they went for nearly the length of the upstairs and opened to provide ventilation and light. There was also a small closet off the bedroom but no bathroom. To wash our faces, we had to go downstairs and share the only bathroom in my grandfather's home.

Dick was still working at the steakhouse and would probably not be home until midnight or later. I took off my clothes, crawled into my bed, and pulled the sheet over me. The room was still quite hot, but I could barely feel a slight breeze coming through the west windows. Outside I could hear the crickets buzzing up fury, and lightning bugs illumined a dark Nebraska night.

Not being able to sleep, I got out of bed and looked up at the August sky. I wondered, where these the same stars Christopher saw as he crossed the Atlantic so many years ago? Was he afraid or was he eager for this grand adventure? Then I thought about the journal; what did it say? How much detail did Christopher provide? I hoped Grandpa would read the entries to me. I wanted to know much more.

Later on in the evening, I woke to the sound of thunder. Dick had slipped into our bedroom while I was sleeping and was not aware of the electrical storm which was rolling into town from the southwest. Going to the window, I could see the streaking bolts of lightning as the rain began pouring on the roof.

I put on my jeans and quietly walked down the stairs, tiptoed through the living room, opened the door to the front porch, and sat down on the rocking chair. I began thinking again about Christopher and his long voyage to America. The wind was chilly – forecasting the autumn that was waiting for us just around the bend – and I watched the storm as it passed through our little town like a ferocious monster.

The rain fell in enormous drops, and I could smell the wetness of the squall. After just a few minutes, the rainwater gathered and began flowing in a torrent down my grandfather's gravel driveway and puddled in low places until even more water forced it further down Iowa Street.

Alone on the porch, I thought again about Christopher's sailing ship as it crossed the cold North Atlantic, and I wondered about his dreams, his hopes, and his fears in his quest to begin a new life in America.

Although I was uncertain about where the story would eventually lead, I was ready to continue the adventure with my grandfather – as I watched the fury of storm weaken as it blew its way through our town and north toward the Missouri River.

CHAPTER SIX

Liverpool, England, October 1840

"**I**s that Liverpool over there?" Chris stood at the railing of *The Ballantine* looking east over the bow.

"Well, there's the entrance to the River Mersey. But Liverpool is still way upstream," responded Dieter Kohler, the lead carpenter. He was a short, stout, ruddy man of about age 50 who had served on the crew for the previous seven years. Like many ship carpenters, Dieter was experienced in multiple trades and callings collateral to the vocation of a carpenter.

As the lead carpenter, Dieter was expected to maintain the tender boats, fix broken oars and lifts, insert bull's eyes in the deck, repair yardarms and planks, and sustain all things wooden. Also, he would oversee and supervise the work of the subordinate carpenters on the ship. And of course, when necessary, he was expected to accomplish all other tasks as assigned to him by a ship's officer.

The two men watched as the river pilot boat slowly approached their vessel, and after tossing a rope to the men, the crew tied the vessel up to *The Ballantine's* stern. Soon another pilot ship was tied up to the bow.

Chris asked, "Is the pilot aboard?"

"Yes, I watched him climb off from the first boat. I see him with the captain now."

"I guess we need one, huh?"

Dieter scratched his beard and replied, "Yeah, it's shallow here, and we need some help getting safely to our berth."

A slight breeze was blowing off the land, and the smell of rain was in the air. About a half hour later, the coal-powered pilot ships began guiding *The Ballantine* into the Mersey estuary. The size and mass of *The Ballantine* made it difficult to maneuver in tight channels; the stopping distance of a large sailing ship – even with the sails down – is typically measured in terms of miles. Just a slight error in judgment can cause extensive damage to the boat and the harbor.

Chris and Dieter carefully secured the stern-lines and helped the crew members assigned to the pilot ships tie the vessels together. Maneuvering a ship through the shallow water requires teamwork, and the pilot must have acquired a considerable level of skill as he moves the vessel through the channel toward its assigned dockage.

The Ballantine had sailed out of Rotterdam almost two weeks earlier and was still only floating in the middle of the Irish Sea. Dieter estimated that once the ship leaves Liverpool, the crossing would take another six weeks at a minimum.

"There we go; we're off. Soon we'll be in Liverpool," yelled Dieter.

After spending the morning at anchor in the Irish Sea just off of the entrance to the River Mersey, *The Ballantine* was moving again. They'd spend the next seven days in Liverpool.

The Ballantine was an old creaky sailing ship. Built in Baltimore about 1810, it measured 738 tons and was 143 feet long, and thirty feet wide. It had three masts, could carry approximately 290 passengers and freight on its three main decks, and it had a crew of 45 men. Dieter referred to her as ". . . very old, very ill-mannered, and very ill-found."

Long-seasoned and weather-stained from hurricanes and severe storms from multiple crossings of the Atlantic Ocean, her hull had been darkened like a fine port wine. Her masts were hewed in the thick forests of Vermont, and her main deck was worn and wrinkled. At her helm on the navigation deck stood a turnstile wheel and a tiller which was both long and thick.

The pilot boats methodically guided *The Ballantine* through several the twists and turns of the Mersey channel, and soon the city of Liverpool came into view. In 1840, the booming town had a population of about 250,000 people, and the municipality was a major port of departure for Irish and Scottish emigrants to the United States.

Along with handling general cargo, freight, and raw materials such as coal, sugarcane, and cotton, Liverpool was also the home-port to both the Cunard and White Star Lines. By the start of the 19th century, a large volume of trade was passing daily through the port, and the construction of the significant buildings in the growing city reflected this wealth. All around the harbor, Chris could see brick buildings – long and tall – with almost endless rows of wharves, piers, warehouses, and offices.

The White Star Line's vessel, *The Royal William,* had been the first 'steamship' to cross the Atlantic in 1833, and the first Cunard liner, *The Britannia,* created a flurry of excitement when she arrived in Boston in 1840. By 1870, almost all of the cross-Atlantic ships were steamships, and the era of transatlantic sailing ships had disappeared into history. But in 1840, virtually all of the transoceanic vessels were still the old-time sailing ships.

It was a bright morning, and the ship shuddered as it struck against the pilings at its assigned berth in the large harbor. As it was in Rotterdam, the port was alive with men and machines, loading and unloading ships, checking inventories, settling accounts, and busy going about the days' work in this active port.

Over on the right, Chris saw masses of people – probably emigrants – waiting for the opportunity to board their vessel for the long sail to America or Canada. Also, there were ships of all sizes and descriptions – some vessels appeared to be much older than *The Ballantine.* Several carriers, however, such as *The Britannia,* were sleek modern steamships which were loading cargo and waiting for their guests (primarily from the upper classes) to come abroad for the two-week ocean-crossing.

Six days later, Dieter, Charles, and Chris met at a small pub called *The King's Arms,* in the heart of Liverpool, to celebrate their last night in England. Over the previous week, the crew spent their days and nights loading, unloading, and refitting *The Ballantine* – getting the ship ready for the anticipated six-week transatlantic sail for Philadelphia.

The pub was busy that evening. Sailors from all over the world gathered for a hot meal and a glass of ale, porter, or stout. Skimpily dressed women circulated within the bar seeking to entice customers with their particular types of services. Bartenders and barmaids took orders, delivered food and drink, and satisfied the debts incurred.

The tavern was a dark and noisy establishment; made of brick walls and well-worn wood floors, covered with decades of the remains from spilled beer, discarded food, and the ashes from hundreds of pipes and cigars. One wall held a painting representing a frigate caught in a massive hurricane – half floundering with its three masts still visible but its sails torn to fragments. Harpoons, clubs, spears, oars, and other nautical items were hung on another wall.

The main room had a low ceiling with crudely hewed massive wooden beams, and on the shelf behind the bar were all sorts of bottles, decanters, flasks, pitchers, tumblers, cups, and glasses. And the room was full of men – mostly sailors – sitting at tables in their shaggy watch-coats, torn and soiled woolen trousers, heavy boots, and heads covered in hats and comforters of all descriptions – mostly unkempt and raggedy.

There were sailors of all types and job duties: chief mates, second and third mates, sea carpenters, coopers, blacksmiths, ship-keepers, loomers, hatch-workers, and deckhands, many with bosky beards, and long and filthy shaggy hair. Most had hard skin – sun-toasted in hue and blistered from too many years exposure to the elements.

As the clientele grew louder and more boisterous, a sole musical performer, sitting on a stool and strumming a guitar sang traditional laments and bawdy songs. An occasional fight broke out in one corner or another, and the bouncers took turns grabbing the unfortunate troublemakers by their shirts and tossing them out of the bar and onto the muddy street – all to the laughter and applause of the remaining customers.

As the men settled down for their last night in Europe, Dieter, a native of Stuttgart, was proficient in English, and he ordered rounds of a creamy Irish ale and plates of steaming Shepherd's pie for Chris and Charles.

"Do you like the music, boys?" Dieter asked them after the guitarist played several traditional English and Irish folk tunes.

Chris responded, "Yes, I do; but I can't understand a word of it. Will you teach me English on our way to Philadelphia, Dieter?"

"I will – but I want to listen to one song. Let me see if the man knows it. The tune has such a beautiful melody."

Dieter stood up and walked over the guitarist, handed him a coin, and requested a particular song. When Dieter returned to the table, he said, "I asked him to play a song called, 'The Leaving of Liverpool,' and I'll translate it as he sings it. Whenever you hear this song in America, you'll remember our night together."

The singer nodded to Dieter and began playing the song in a slow, mournful way.

> Farewell to you my own true love
> I am going far away.
> I am bound for North America
> But I'll return to you someday.
>
> So fare thee well my darlin' dear
> And when I return united, we shall be.
> It's not the leaving of Liverpool
> that grieves me
>
> But my darling when I think of thee.
> Oh, the sun is on the harbor low
> And I wish I could remain.
> But I know it will be a long, long time
>
> Before I see you again.
> So fare thee well my darlin' dear
> And when I return united, we shall be.
> It's not the leaving of Liverpool
> that grieves me
> But my darling when I think of thee.

As the song concluded, Chris said, "That's lovely; thanks."

Dieter responded, "I thought you'd like it."

Whenever Chris heard or sang this song, he'd remember his last night in Liverpool.

He took another taste of the ale and asked, "How many times have you crossed the Atlantic?"

"In this ship – about six trips; but I guess I've crossed over and back a total of twenty times or so."

Almost unnoticed, Charles had gotten up from the table and walked over to a group of five or six Germans who were drinking and telling tales. Every once in a while, Chris could hear a cheer, and looking over at Charles, Chris could see Charles lifting his stein and singing,

"trink was klar ist; lieb was rar ist; trinkin; trinkin, trinkin!"

Chris turned back to Dieter and said, "That twelve-day sail from Rotterdam was quite a jolt to my system. I've never seen so many sick people. Is it normal or was the English Channel just rough on those days?"

"It was rather calm; you haven't seen anything yet, my friend. It can be, and I must say, will be, a lot worse once we leave the Irish Sea."

Dieter took a long drink of beer, wiped his sleeve over his mouth, and slowly looked around the pub. He was fifty-two years old, and his face and hands looked like cracked leather caused by too many days in the sun. Most of his teeth were missing, and flecks of gray were showing in his light brown hair. His short beard, however, was mostly white.

"Yes, I've sailed for over thirty years now – and I've gone all over the world – from several ports in England and Scotland – to Germany – to France – to the Isthmus of Panama – to all points on the western coasts of North and South America – to the West Indies, Africa, and Brazil. And I've had, of course, ten or more crossings to Philadelphia."

He stopped and took a mouthful of ale, "Have you heard of the 'three-cornered trade' route? You know, that's what we're doing now."

Chris replied, "No. What's that?"

"We leave New Orleans with a hold full of sugar, rice, and cotton and sail to Liverpool and pick up emigrants, and take them to Philadelphia where we pick up coal and timber, and then we sail back to New Orleans. For want of a better cargo, we need to load passengers on the western portion of the triangle. While these people are often an annoyance, it's better than sailing only with ballast. It's most profitable."

"So, why did the ship sail to Rotterdam?"

"Well, half of the cotton he hauled there was sold to European traders, and the emigrants we loaded from Holland are wealthier – thus, it makes better business sense. Now, most of the folks we pick up in Liverpool are Irish and Scots; and mostly pretty poor at that."

"Do many people die on the voyages west?"

"Oh, yes. The death rate is commonly about one person in forty, and sometimes it exceeds ten percent. If typhus or some other calamity breaks out, it can get pretty bad."

"That's pretty high."

"Indeed but only a few years ago – before the laws changed – boat owners sold their excess ship space to agents whose only interest was to fill the boat with as many passengers as possible. They just shoveled them in. Conditions are bad now – but it was much worse only a few years ago."

"Wow," Chris replied, "it sounds horrible."

"Yeah, it is – but it was even worse than that in some situations. Sometimes ships would leave port after a satisfactory inspection by the government agent and proceed to a remote spot on the Irish coast and pick up even more passengers. It makes a hideous journey much worse."

Chris just shook his head. "So, an outbreak of disease must be a big problem onboard ship?"

"Yes indeed. That's why people are scrutinized so carefully before we allowed them to board. Once we're on the high seas, there is no turning back to a port. Epidemics can wipe out entire communities of passengers. Typhus, cholera, and dysentery are some of the biggest threats. I heard that last year, over 10% of the Irish emigrants died at sea due mostly to cholera.

It can be horrible."

"What happens to the dead?"

Dieter frowned and said, "Well, we try to do a brief Christian service for them, but after the blessing, they are stripped naked, wrapped in a sheet, and tossed overboard. The emigrants often don't know it but children under seven years old rarely survive the journey in steerage class. It's much better, of course, for those staying in the private cabins."

Chris said, "Really?"

"Yes, it's true. The parents are often so heartbroken by their loss because their children find no resting place in the earth but are devoured by the sharks and other fishes. Also, children often get smallpox on board ship, and most of them die. It can be quite bad for young children."

Another round of ale arrived. This time it was a dark porter – so unlike the pilsners and lagers that Chris used to drink in Bavaria.

Dieter continued, "Often the captains and first officers have been accused of using rations to entice sexual favors from the female passengers. Sometimes these women and young girls are starving, and to get meals for their husbands or families, they are enticed to visit the captain's quarters."

"Wow that's hard to believe."

"But it's true. I have heard frequent complaints of ill-treatment and abuse from certain captains and officers but there is no sheriff on board ship, and once the poor beggars arrive in New York or Philadelphia, the charges are difficult to prove. Our captain, however, is not one of those men, God bless him."

Chris and Dieter talked for another hour. He asked Chris about Charles' branding, and Chris provided him with a small summary of the facts and circumstances.

Dieter said, "He need not worry about his scar in America – in fact, it may be a badge of honor."

Soon, it was approaching midnight, and it was time for the men to return to their ships. Charles, however, could be not found immediately. Apparently, one of the ladies of the night enticed him for a brief interlude on the second floor of the pub. Smiling from ear-to-ear, Charles finally descended the stairs, finished his tankard of ale, and clumsily made it back to the ship on the arm of his brother. Charles slept well in his rack that night.

The following morning – their last day in England – Chris wrote a final letter to his father before the afternoon sailing to America.

October 17, 1840

After thirteen days under sail, we made it safely to Liverpool. Tomorrow, Charles and I leave for America.

As I may have mentioned in my last letter, we are sailing on a ship called The Ballantine. It's an old American wooden ship commanded by Captain Ambrose Worthington. The boat has three passenger decks. The upper deck consists of twelve separate cabins: one for the captain, one for the three officers (the first officer, the quartermaster, and the navigator), and the other ten cabins are reserved for first-class passengers. Also, there is a mess galley.

The middle deck is earmarked for second-class passengers and the other members of the crew. Most of this deck consists of sleeping quarters where there are rows and rows of double bunk beds lined almost wall-to-wall with little space between them. There is also a great room in the center of the middle deck and four toilets. There are two-foot windows at the top of the outside walls to let in ventilation and sunshine. Charles and I sleep near the center of the middle deck near a bulkhead.

The lower deck is set aside for third-class passengers (called the steerage class). The rooms located on this deck are configured in much the same way as those found on the second deck with the exception that there is no ventilation other than the air flowing in from the stairways which lead up to the middle and upper decks.

The Ballantine is a 738-ton three-masted sailing ship which can accompany about 290 passengers. It is 143' long, with the decks measuring 6'5" high and the breath of the main hatchway is 25' 3". Aside from the captain and the three officers, the ship has a crew of 45 men consisting mostly of seamen, engineers, firemen, cooks, stewards, and carpenters.

We left Rotterdam with 189 passengers, and the sail was quite rough. About twenty of the original passengers decided to get off the ship in Liverpool – their plans for a voyage to America are now over. The boat will board about another 75 emigrants in Liverpool today – mostly Irish and Scots.

Charles is doing much better. His wound has completely healed, and he was gotten his spirit back. He was, however, terribly seasick for the first three or four days of our sailing but he has recovered nicely. Luckily, I was nauseated for only one day.

Also, Charles and I have been working on board as carpenters or sailors for the majority of our time since Rotterdam. I am hoping our labor will eventually pay for the cost of our trip.

My boss, Dieter Kohler, is a 52-year-old carpenter from Stuttgart. He has taken a liking to us, and he is teaching me English. I hope to have some proficiency in the language once we arrive in New Orleans next year.

I acquired a journal in Rotterdam, and I plan to begin a log of my travels starting tomorrow. I wish I would have started it earlier.

I will write to you again from Philadelphia. Dieter estimated that, with luck, we should be there in about seven weeks – perhaps in early December. This voyage will be The Ballantine's last transatlantic crossing of the year, and God willing, we will have a safe and uneventful journey.

Please give our love to the family and tell them that they will be forever in our thoughts. I miss you and the others so very much. Please keep us in your prayers.

Affectionately, Christopher and Charles

Dieter, Charles, and Chris stood together at the railing watching the last of the Irish passengers being screened by the ship's medical unit. As Dieter had mentioned earlier, Captain Worthington was well aware of the problems of rampant disease aboard ship. Outbreaks of illness could rapidly overwhelm the passengers and cause enormous problems for the officers and crew.

Dieter explained that doctors employed by the steamship lines made most of the seaport medical examinations, but all too often, the exams were performed much too hurriedly to disclose anything other than the most apparent maladies and defects. One overlooked medical issue could be devastating when out to sea. Captain Worthington, however, was much more cautious than most captains.

Staring to the shore from the forecastle deck, Dieter noted, "The shipping company has a financial obligation to its shareholders to ensure the passengers who board the ship are in reasonably good health. Diseased ships impact on stock prices and cost the company money. Furthermore, those passengers rejected by U.S. Customs after the ship docks in America will be sent back at the shipping company's expense. This practice can be expensive, too."

Chris looked out at the city of Liverpool. Within a few hours, the ship would be on her way once again. In his heart, Chris knew that he'd never see England again.

A few moments later, the First Officer walked up to them and said, "Okay boys, let's begin getting the ship ready for departure. Once those people are safely onboard, we'll drop the lines. The pilot boats are approaching. Let's see to it now."

Chris and Charles were not only working as carpenters on the vessel; they were doing whatever needed to be done at the time – often hard labor. Soon they were busy securing lines, stabilizing cargoes, and readying the canvas.

Around noon, the pilot boats attached themselves to the bow and stern on the starboard side of the ship. Once the lines were dropped, the pilots began maneuvering *The Ballantine* out of Liverpool harbor and into the River Mersey channel.

After supper, Chris began writing his journal. Then before laying his head on the pillow on the lower bunk, he thought of Trockau – his father, his siblings, and all of the friends he left behind. Then he thought about Sonia, and with his heart breaking all over again, he whispered a silent prayer before falling off to sleep.

CHAPTER SEVEN

At Sea, Autumn 1840

SAILING LOG OF CHRISTOPHER BOGNER

Day 1 – Saturday, 17th October 1840, One o'clock, P.M. — left Liverpool on *The Ballantine,* Captain Worthington commanding, for Philadelphia, with 243 passengers. Wind N.W., blowing a strong gale. In less than two hours, only a few passengers were remaining on the upper deck; the ship is rolling heavily. At 4 P.M., the captain discharged the pilot boats – well out in the Irish Sea. At half-past five, we passed Holyhead. Went to bed at midnight slightly squeamish.

Day 2 – Sunday, October 18th — rose at six; was awakened due to ponding of loose cargo on the upper deck. Seas are rough. The smell of vomit was overwhelming. Passed Tuskar Light at 6 P.M. Had public worship at noon: Father O'Neill, an Irish Catholic priest, celebrated Mass; about ninety people attended. So many are seasick – the toilets & chamber-pots smell horribly. Hopefully, it will be calmer tomorrow. Worked all day long; I'm exhausted. Charles is sick again & he remained in bed all day.

Day 3 – Monday, October 19th – the routine of each day at sea appears to be as follows: the bell sounds at seven for the passengers to rise; breakfast at nine; at twelve, lunch; & supper at six; lights are turned out at nine punctually. I worked all day fastening loose bunk beds. Charles is feeling somewhat better.

Day 4 – Tuesday, October 20th – there was very little light or air on the middle deck. A dangerous storm; water poured in through cracks & joints, drenching the emigrants & their belongings. There are no washrooms on the middle & lower decks – only one bathing facility on the upper deck & it's reserved for the first class passengers & the ship's officers. If an immigrant or crew member wants to wash, he has to do it in salty water. Most of those in steerage class will likely wear the same clothes for the entire voyage. Some are beginning to smell already.

Day 5 – Wednesday, October 21st – the food so far has been generally ill-selected & poorly cooked, because of the insufficiency & lousy construction of the cooking areas. The supply of water, hardly enough for cooking & drinking, does not allow for washing dishes or pots. The meat is of poor quality.

No work for me today; spent my time sleeping & talking to the German emigrants. Still practicing my English – learning lots of new words. Charles is doing better.

Day 6 – Thursday, October 22nd – found out that many emigrants have relatives in America; most on board were given pre-paid passage tickets. This enabled those who had migrated earlier to America to bring over their friends & family.

Charles has taken a fancy to an Irish girl named Colleen McConnell. He speaks little English & she speaks no German – it is fun watching them try to communicate with each other. She's very attractive.

Today, we are making miserable progress from want of wind, but the seas were favorable.

Day 7 – Friday, October 23rd – worked for two hours cleaning toilets & scrubbing decks. Unless I have carpentry work, this will be my usual routine. With so many sick passengers, the common areas are always nasty after only a few hours. Many spilled chamber pots & lots of vomit is on the floors. Bedclothes & linens are often soiled, & the emigrants are usually too ill to care. If they wish to wash soiled items, it's with seawater.

For many of the emigrants, it's a family affair. Advice was sought & help was freely given by mothers, fathers, sisters, brothers, aunts, uncles, friends & even entire villages. It is not unusual for a whole family to work to earn money for a single family member who wanted to make the trip. If the person (often the eldest son) prospers in America, he sends tickets & money back for others to follow him. Sometimes, the father travels alone first & sends back prepaid vouchers to the next family member.

At seven P.M., we passed Cork, Ireland; Latitude, 51° 58# N.: Longitude, 6° 34#.

Day 8 – Saturday, October 24th – cleaned toilets & chamber pots again today. After gathering up the contents, Charles & I carry the overflowing buckets to the side of the ship to toss the contents into the sea. We need to be careful. Often the wind drives some of it back onto me or others. After toilet duty is over, we spend hours scrubbing the decks & floors. After stormy nights, Charles & I spend many hours fixing torn canvass. Usually, the torn sail is taken down & a new sail goes up in its place; but at times, we need to climb up & repair the sail while it's still on the mast. Saw one crew member fall & break his arm yesterday. Not a lot of carpentry work to do lately, so we've been assigned other duties.

Day 9 – Sunday, October 25th – at three o'clock, passed Cape Clear; I saw only a distant view of the most rugged part of Ireland. Perhaps it's the last land we'll see until America. The ship is running smoothly.

On those days when I'm not working, I've established the following rules, which I hope to be able to keep: rise at half-past seven; walk on deck till breakfast; read my books & work on my log; practice English until lunch; talk to passengers about America – a few have been there before & most have relatives there; have dinner; take stock of the passengers, being some of all sorts here; then read the Bible & turned in. I prefer the working days because the time passes much quicker & it helps pay off our crossing fare.

The weather continues to be calm with a fair breeze, & the sea smooth. Lat. 51° 32# N.; Long. 11° 59#. We're making good progress.

Day 10 – Sunday, October 26th – often on Sundays, if the weather is favorable, the captain sets up fireplaces on the upper deck so the emigrants can cook a warm meal. People usually have to wait for hours to get access to one of these grates. The fire is contained in a large wooden case, lined with bricks, the coals are confined by 2 or 3 iron bars in the front. The fireplaces are extinguished at 7 p.m.

Light westerly winds, with the beautifully clear weather. All sails set.

Day 11 – Monday, October 27th – the amount of water to be supplied to each passenger varies slightly from time to time, but under American law, it is required to be three quarts per day for each adult. As the voyage goes on, the water becomes of less suitable quality. Often efforts are made to collect fresh water from the sails during a storm. Sometimes the quartermaster adds vinegar to the water so it can be usable. It was not uncommon that on rainy but calm afternoons, emigrants will bring cups up from steerage to gather as much rainwater as they could, using smart, imaginable ways of capturing the rain.

Day 12 – Tuesday, October 28 – for many, just getting to either Liverpool or Rotterdam has been the first significant journey of their lives. The emigrants would travel by train, wagon & donkey or even by foot. Often the emigrants had to wait for weeks for their paperwork to be completed or for their ship to arrive due to the unpredictability of transatlantic travel.

At 7 PM, we're off the Irish coast near the town of Kinsale. Latitude, 51° 61# N.: Longitude, 6° 34#. Couldn't see land.

Day 13 – Wednesday, October 29 – a most beautiful morning. Spent the day working on toilets & scrubbing the decks, as usual. During dinner, the wind changed to E.N.E. Re-set all sail front & aft. Spent time talking to Captain Worthington about the ship's operations. Later, Charles & I sat & listened to some German, Irish, English, & Yankee songs on the middle deck. The passengers were generally in a festive mood & several were dancing, especially Charles & Colleen. I turned in at half-past ten.

Lat. 51° 26# N.; Long. 17° 3#. Light winds, westerly, with smooth water. All sails set.

Day 14 – Thursday, October 30 – the space reserved on the upper deck for steerage passengers is insufficient & situated in the worst part of the ship. Also, it's subject to the most violent motions of the sea & the odors from the hold & galleys.

Dieter told me the three officers take turns steering the ship from the navigation deck. Each officer is officially on duty piloting the boat for eight hours & then off the steering duties for the next sixteen hours – their shifts from 10 PM to 6 AM, from 6 AM to 2 PM, & from 2 PM until 10 PM. After their turn ends at the wheel, each officer goes to bed for eight hours & then begins another 8-hour shift performing their other specific duties (such as acting as the quartermaster) before retaking the helm. In this way, each officer is relatively fresh & up to date regarding the ship's overall performance & location.

Captain Worthington always remains in the overall authority of the ship & he only navigates the boat in an emergency. Should the captain become impaired, the first officer takes his place. Dieter also told me that even in the dead of night, several crew members are always on deck to secure the ship & assist the officer steering the vessel.

Winds from S.W. to N.W., light, with hazy weather & light rain.

Day 15 — Friday, October 31 — here are some more observations. The ventilation is almost always inadequate on middle & lower decks; the air is usually rather foul with unattended vomit, overflowing toilets & piss-pots & the odors of filthy clothes & bodies. Many emigrants will choose to sit or lie in their berths for most of the voyage, often in a stupor caused by the foul air except for the few hours each day when they can walk on the upper deck. But then, only if the seas are calm & no rain. The food often repels the passengers & it's almost impossible to keep oneself personally clean.

Wind N.E., light, with clear weather & smooth water.

Day 16 — Saturday, November 1 — All Saints' Day — had a Mass on the upper deck by Father O'Neill — many folks received communion. Today, we are more than two weeks into our journey — hopefully, we're over one-third of the way to America — only four weeks to go.

Moderate breeze & clear weather; wind easterly with a heavy sea.

Day 17 — Sunday, November 2 — those who have money on board need to be very careful because there's no secure location aboard ship in which it might be deposited. Dieter said that on some voyages, there were robberies almost every night & that several members of the crew were suspected to be the culprits.

Light breeze & favorable weather; wind southeasterly with a head sea.

Day 18 — Monday, November 3 — still foggy & dark, cold & comfortless. Saw lots of porpoises & whales who came along the ship. The First Officer told me that often the distance of four or five miles is all there was to show for a whole day of sailing. He also said there are even times when the ship is further away from its destination at the end of twenty-four hours than at the beginning. The length of the voyage to Philadelphia can vary from 40 to 138 days & sometimes ships that leave Liverpool at the same time might arrive in America as much as eight or nine weeks apart. He said, as of now, we're ahead of schedule. Hooray!

Spent the day as usual. Strong easterly gales with dark cloudy weather & a heavy sea running. Lat. 45° 43# N.; Long. 55° 10#.

Day 19 – Tuesday, November 4 – rose at my usual time. Fine weather. For the first time, I saw a sailing ship off the port side; a brig, standing to the south, but too distant to exchange signals.

Still working on my English. Dieter mentioned that many English words have different meanings. He told me about the word 'spring' – which could mean a season, a place to find groundwater, a mechanical device located near a wheel, & as a way to lurch at somebody. It's fairly confusing.

Spent the day as usual. Lat. 51° 24# N.; Long. 23° 6#. The wind fair, but light.

Day 20 – Wednesday, November 5 – worked all day on mending torn canvass along with regular duties. I haven't had a day off in a long while. Earlier this morning, the wind changed to the south; a lot of the passengers were on the upper deck, the sea smooth; & the sails bellowing nicely. The ship made good progress today. Some heavy card-playing on board with imprudent losses, which I much regretted to see.

Lat. 51° 5# N.; Long. 28° 54#.

Day 21 – Thursday, November 6 – the halfway point – only three weeks to go, God willing. Once again, the captain set up grates, called 'cabooses,' on the upper deck & the passengers lined up with their supplies to cook their food. The cabooses are few, & each passenger required about 15 minutes at least preparing his food. As before, some often waited from early morning to late afternoon for their turn. Many, unable to stave off the pangs of hunger, ate their rice or oatmeal raw.

Moderate breezes once again & clear weather; wind easterly with a favorable sea.

Day 22 – Friday, November 7 – a dense fog. Sea smooth. Spent the day as usual. Charles & Colleen are still seen together. Today, we had a death aboard – the first one so far but Dieter says that probably more will follow.

A young boy from Ireland; he had been unwell for a week or more. So sad.

Lat. 47° 5# N.; Long. 50° 44#. After the fog lifted, the weather abruptly changed with strong S.E. gales; dark & gloomy weather & heavy N.E. swell.

Day 23 – Saturday, November 8 – the navigation officer told me the Gulf Stream brings a current of warm water fifty miles wide & a thousand feet deep from the Caribbean Sea & north along the eastern American coastline. He explained that flows like an ordinary land river & it terminates some-where beyond the Banks of Newfoundland which is still far off to our west. The warm water often causes icebergs that melt & eventually produces cold water.

Day 24 – Sunday, November 9 – in spite of the miserable conditions aboard ship, most of the emigrants seem to have faith in their future. To pass the time, they play cards, sing, dance, read & talk. I often hear wild rumors about life in America & many emigrants like me, are trying to learn English.

Winds strong with N.E. breezes & drizzly rains: dark cloudy weather & heavy northerly swell running off the starboard side.

Day 25 – Monday, November 10 – the ship was rolling from a nice southern swell with a small muster at breakfast. The wind came from the S.E. & the ship was covered with canvas to make up for some days of little progress. Later in the afternoon, the breeze came from the West; it was quite rough with lots of water on deck. During dinner, all the sails were taken in, but the heavy pitching of the ship made eating almost impossible.

Lat. 50° 33# N.; Long. 34° 59#.

Day 26 – Tuesday, November 11 – smooth sailing today; good wind & favor-able direction. Spent some time with the Navigation Officer who told me about the navigator's tools: such as the compass to determine the course of the ship; a barometer by which he perceives the conditions of the atmo-sphere with respect to changes in density & pressure (to ascertain upcoming storms, clear weather & wind direction); the sextant where he observes the angle of the sun every day at noon so as to identify the ship's exact position on the map.

Also, he told me about the chronometer, which notes both Philadelphian & Liverpool time & shows, by comparison, the actual time on the ship at our particular point on the map; a graduated quadrant with a pendulum attached to it that indicates the position of the boat upon her keel. Finally, he talked about the thermometer, used to calculate the likelihood of ice flows through the increasing coldness of the water & he mentioned many others devices aboard ship. It was a fascinating day for me. He identifies our precise position on a chalkboard every day so the passengers & crew members can see exactly where the ship is positioned on a particular day.

Day 27 – Wednesday, November 12 – it's very rough once again. Lots of passengers are ill with dysentery, boils, fever & seasickness. Many emigrants in steerage have lice. When a gale rages for two or three nights, the smell of vomiting & diarrhea is atrocious. I often hear lots of folks crying & perhaps some even praying. Another Irish woman died yesterday & we committed her to the sea this morning. So sad; she came a long way just to perish in the middle of the ocean. I remembered her in my prayers before bed.

The day ended with a beautiful sunset. Hopefully, tomorrow will be calmer.

Day 28 – Thursday, November 13 – seas are calmer & no work for me today. Read; talked; walked; lunched; walked & read again. Dreamt last night about home. I sure miss my family. Charles & Colleen are still friendly. I wonder what will happen once we arrive in Philadelphia. I believe he's in love with her!

Another beautiful sunset – we'll have smooth sailing tomorrow. At nine, went to bed.

Lat. 49° 27# N.; Long. 40° 55#.

Day 29 – Friday, November 14 – a beautiful morning early, but cold & foggy later, as we begin to approach the Banks of Newfoundland. Saw the first seabirds since departing Ireland; we must be getting closer to land. Worked in the morning on the sails. A stiff breeze came up & ran the canvass causing me to get a nasty burn on my left hand. A lot of the sailors have lost fingers; Dieter said I'm lucky not to have lost my hand. Worked the rest of the day on the decks & toilets.

Dieter & I practiced my English – I'm getting better he says.

The sea calm, but it's quite damp on board. I'm so tired of sailing.

Day 30 – Saturday, November 15 – another death this time in First Class which is unusual according to Dieter. Mrs. Larson had been seasick since Liverpool. She was only 27 & left behind her husband & three children. They are mourning her tonight.

Light baffling winds & clear weather with a heavy northerly swell. Lots of folks are seasick again.

The first effect of seasickness is a sense of giddiness in the head, which gradually becomes a pain. The First Officer told me the digestive organs, especially the liver, begin soon to be affected. But as nausea & other such affections are only symptomatic of disturbance in specific functions of the brain, any remedies applied to the digestive organs must necessarily fail, as they always do, producing nothing more than a palliative effect. We are advised to drink as much water as possible, but unless we can catch the water off a sail during a storm, the water is pretty putrid.

Day 31 – Sunday, November 16 – life is not all drudgery here for the emigrants; there are always reasons for celebrations such as marriages, birthdays & anniversaries. On calmer days, they often find time for fun, sometimes dancing on the upper deck, music, writing letters & playing games. Despite the difficulties, many are genuinely excited by their adventure & the approach of their new lives in America.

Tonight, an Irish man played his guitar & I asked him to play *The Leaving of Liverpool*. I can understand the words better now.

We are taking bets on when we'll first see land; it's any day now, I'm told.

Day 32 – Monday, November 17 – Dieter said that the best season for transatlantic sailing is in the late autumn; no icebergs, warmest water, lots of wind but no hurricanes. In the winter, it's too cold; springtime can be pleasant but often lots of icebergs & it can be hot & still early in the summer but then hot with hurricanes later. Captain Worthington reported we are now on the outskirts of the North American continent – we've left Greenland & Europe behind us. Soon we'll be located south of Prince Edward Island – perhaps three hundred miles east of British Canada.

Strong breezes & thick hazy weather with rain. I can't wait to see land – I hope the worst part is now over.

Day 33 – Tuesday, November 18 – another severe storm. There was lots of confusion above deck & the tramping around frightened those in steerage – some seem almost out of their wits with fear. We had our first snowfall & an icy rain. The temperatures are rather cold & the air is foul on the middle & lower decks; the hatches had been battened down for almost a week because of the cold.

With each roll of the ship, the emigrants in the crowded berths are bumped & bruised as they are hurled from side to side against the rough partitions. Water has leaked through the decks in such quantity that most of the beds are soaked & the floor is ankle-deep in salt water. For the last two days, candle lanterns could not be lighted nor has there been any cooking. It's quite miserable; many passengers are ill.

My left hand is still somewhat painful & the saltwater hurts when it gets into the sores. I need to be careful of infection.

Day 34 – Tuesday, November 19 – lately our meals usually consisted of salt pork or fish & hardtack. Sometimes, we can eat handfuls of dried peas & beans, cheese & butter. If the weather permits, beef or chicken can be cooked over charcoal fires in the cabooses, but it's often too dangerous to have a fire & so the food must be eaten cold. Some of the grains are now infested with bugs, the hardtack biscuits are too hard to swallow, the cheese is moldy & the butter has spoiled. But there still seems to be some quantities of whiskey, Madeira & tawny port remaining aboard.

Strong southerly winds, with dark hazy weather & heavy seas running. Saw a vessel pass us steaming eastward; Dieter said it's not unusual now for ships to travel east in winter if it's a coal burning steamer.

Lat. 44° 44# N.; Long. 60° 25#.

Day 35 – Wednesday, November 20 – the quartermaster told me the ship stocks the following foodstuffs for its voyage per passenger: fifteen pounds of oatmeal; ten pounds of hardtack biscuits; four pounds of flour; two pounds of sugar; two pounds of molasses; & six ounces of tea. He also stocks coffee, eggs, candies & other delicacies for the first class passengers & the officers.

I'm so anxious to see land. Several passengers still seem to be ill & we're worried about having more deaths. The weather is now quite cold & we often have snow or sleet instead of rain. Dieter said it's good that the ship sailed when she did – winter storms can be pretty devastating. I hope we don't see what he calls a nor'easter.

Had a beautiful sunrise today; there's always promise in the morning sky.

Lat. 43° 4# N.; Long. 64° 14#.

Day 36 – Thursday, November 21 — the sky was beautifully clear at day-break; but the usual fog came in at about ten o'clock. We've not had a full day of fair weather in about ten days or so; patching canvass, toilet patrol & repairing bunks & tables today.

Strong breezes from the west later on with dark cloudy weather & rain & a heavy sea running.

Day 37 – Friday, November 22 — the wind was dead ahead with a heavy sea. Many emigrants remained in bed. At four o'clock, the wind changed round, the sea smoothed down & we had the most brilliant sunset I ever saw: it was past all description! It gave me a good impression of an American nightfall. The emigrants broke out into applause. We are getting closer now.

Charles & Colleen spend too much time together. She'll break his heart when she leaves the ship. Dieter hit his head & remained in bed today. I assumed his place on the sailing line. I did okay, but he'll have a lousy bump for several days. Still not much carpentry work for us.

Day 38 – Friday, November 23 — saw land today for the first time since we left Cape Clear; I'm heartily sick of the Atlantic. Dieter said it's the island of Nantucket. The atmosphere is mild & warm for late November. We've made it to America. Hooray!

Lat. 41° 18# N.; Long. 68° 18#.

Day 40 – Saturday, November 24 — another beautiful morning. The wind changed to the northwest. Most of the emigrants were on the upper & fore-castle decks as we passed Long Island. Dieter said New York City is only fifty miles to the west. Most of the ill-passengers are feeling much better now. The Irish man is playing his guitar again & many of the emigrants are danc-ing. One Irish man got down on his knee & proposed to a woman. I hope the Charles is not going to try the same stunt.

Day 41 – Sunday, November 25 – on the upper deck, Father O'Neill held a thanksgiving Mass for our safe passage. Even many of the Protestants attended. We sang hymns & everyone shook hands. Captain Worthington said that we are passing down the coast of New Jersey & should enter the Delaware Bay by dawn.

Lat. 40° 22# N.; Long. 69° 20#.

Day 42 – Monday, November 26 – for the first time since we left Liverpool, we have dry land on both sides of the ship. It's snowing again & blustery winds from the southwest. We hope to make it as far north as Wilmington by noon where we'll drop our sails & wait for the pilot ship to arrive. Perhaps, we will lower a boat & pick up some fresh food on the Delaware shore if the pilots are delayed.

Day 43 – Tuesday, November 27 – we waited all day for the pilot ships, but none came to assist us. I was allowed to be on one of the tender boats to Wilmington. Stood on dry land for the first time in over six weeks. Had a cold beer & a sausage before going back to the ship. Hopefully, only one more day until we arrive in Philadelphia. It's still freezing but not too windy.

Day 44 – Wednesday, November 28 – the pilot boats (who had to come down 70 miles to get us) attached to our starboard side & guided us the rest of the way to Philadelphia. We arrived too late to be secured at the dock, so we dropped anchor in the middle of the Delaware River. All were on the upper deck & marveled at the city of Philadelphia on the west bank & the small town of Camden on the east side. For the emigrants, this will be their last night aboard ship.

The captain & the officers sponsored a 'Farewell Party' in the afternoon. There was drinking, singing & dancing. Only one emigrant remains ill – Mr. O'Farrell – but it looks like he'll be okay. He was carried up to the upper deck by his sons & he smiled at those around him. It's still cold but the afternoon sun was welcoming for all.

Day 45 (and last) – Thursday, November 29 – the pilot ships reattached themselves & The Ballantine lifted anchor. It took about three hours to get us tied up on The Central Yankee Lines home dock; but within a couple of hours, our first class passengers were discharged followed by the emigrants on the middle deck & finally those on the lower deck. Saw Mr. O'Farrell walk off the ship with only minimal help. Most of us assumed he'd die below, but God is merciful. He was sick for most of the crossing.

Charles & I will remain aboard ship for the next month, refitting it & then loading coal & other goods for the trip south to New Orleans. Dieter said that the boat must leave Philadelphia by early January – before the Delaware River freezes – or we'll be stuck here until March. We have lots to do.

CHAPTER EIGHT

Philadelphia, December 1840

Chris asked, "Shall we have another beer, Dieter?"

Chris, Charles, Dieter, and dock-worker named Manfred Schlender were sitting in *The Rising Sun Tavern* on Market Street following a long day of loading coal onto *The Ballantine*. The ore was being deposited in the tryworks portion of the ship which is located between the foremast and the mainmast. The try-works – often called the hold – is the roomiest part of the lower deck.

The timbers beneath the lower deck were engineered to be of a particular strength to hold a mass of several hundred tons of coal. The floor was secured by cumbersome knees of iron bracing on all sides of the lower hull, and it was screwed down tightly to the main foundation timbers. Also, the flanks were encased in dense wood, and the opening to the upper deck was covered entirely with a battened hatchway.

It was December 14th and the men had spent the last two and a half weeks refitting the vessel for its upcoming sail to New Orleans.

Dieter replied, "Yeah, but let's try the porter this time."

During their time in port, Dieter, Chris, and Charles resided together in one of the First Class passenger cabins on the upper deck of the ship while the middle and lower decks were being refitted. Once the vessel was transformed, the ship's owners were piling the coal into the hold and on-loading other merchandise and materials onto the confines of middle deck. The new man, Manfred, was a longtime resident of Philadelphia who had been hired by *The Central Yankee Lines* to help prepare the ship for its upcoming sailing to New Orleans.

"So, are we about full in the hold?"

Dieter took a sip of his remaining beer, and replied, "Yeah, after tomorrow, we'll seal the hold and begin loading the middle deck. It'll be a lot easier then. You guys have done a good job."

The weather had turned dreadfully cold as Philadelphia had just experienced its first significant snowfall of the winter. Seven inches of new powder had fallen on the city over the preceding two days, and the wind from the west had dropped the temperature down to 21*.

"Will we be gone by Christmas Day?" Charles asked.

"Well, if not by Christmas, then certainly by New Year's Day. You know, Captain Worthington and the ship's officers have families residing in the area, and I suspect they'll want to spend Christmas with their loved ones before beginning another loop. So, yeah, I think we'll leave right after Christmas."

The porter arrived in two large pitchers, and the thirsty men began pouring the beer into their tankards. Even though the city had been experiencing a cold front, the chilled beer was still refreshing.

A few moments later, a man from the next table over stood up, lifted his mug of ale, and sang:

> We'll drink tonight with hearts as light.
>
> To lovers gay and fleeting.
>
> As bubbles that swim on the beaker's brim
>
> And break the lips while meeting.

A cheer rang out from the men in the tavern, and the 'poet' sat down to the applause of his mates.

Then another man rose, lifted his glass and shouted:

> Here's to ruby red wine
>
> So fine, so cool, so clear.
>
> It's not as sweet as a woman's lips
>
> But a downside more sincere.

In sequence, several other men rose and provided similar toasts to the amusement of the customers, and the tavern seemed to be a festive place to be on that cold December evening.

Chris asked, "Manfred, how long have you lived in Philadelphia?"

Manfred appeared to be about 40 years old and still spoke good German. He set down his beer mug and replied, "My folks came across in 1811 – so I've been here over thirty years now, I guess."

"Tell us a bit about Philadelphia. I still hope to take a day off and look around before we sail south."

"Well, you know it was the capital of the United States for ten years before the seat of government was moved to Washington City in 1800. Geez, Philadelphia is growing like crazy – I believe we're well over 250,000 people now – and over half of the newcomers here were Germans at one time. Now with all of the Irish settling in, the city is changing – and not for the better, if I may say. These filthy people are bringing in all kind of diseases – malaria, smallpox, tuberculosis, and cholera – it's a damn shame, you know."

Dieter said, "We're lucky something bad didn't break out aboard ship – it's happened to lots of other boats. Some vessels were even turned away from the port; not allowed to dock. Captain Worthington made damn sure that the folks getting on in Liverpool and Rotterdam were healthy. God forbid an epidemic breaks out in mid-ocean."

The table was quiet for a while and then Manfred remarked, "Yeah, a lot of the new people are Catholics, too. The original Germans coming here were Lutherans, but now we're seeing a lot of Papists. The locals don't like it much, but I mean no offense to you guys. It's just I'm saying the locals don't like it."

Chris asked, "Why; what matter could it be to them?"

"Well, there's talk that the Catholics want us to take the King James' Bible out of the public schools. Folks don't like their meddling in our business. People also wonder about their allegiance; is it to the President or the Pope? Yes, we wonder. I know two or three Catholic churches were burnt to the ground this year. And there was a riot in July; the Mayor called out the soldiers to guard the other churches."

"Is it that bad?"

Manfred replied, "Yes, and we're also being flooded with free and runaway Negroes from the South. I hear there are nearly 20,000 of them in the city now – poor, dirty, and uneducated – and those damn beggars multiply like nesting rabbits."

Dieter responded, "There are that many of them here in Philadelphia?"

Manfred took a sip of beer and replied, "Yes, indeed, or more of those black beggars. You know the Governor abolished slavery in 1781, and it's what drew them all here in the first place. But they've caused a lot of trouble, and because of that, the Legislature changed the state Constitution last year and smartly canceled their right to vote. Can you imagine a colored mayor here someday? It was bound to happen had the law not been changed, you know."

"Yeah, I've seen a lot of them around town," said Charles. "And I'd seen a few of them bastards in Liverpool, but there's none in Bavaria that I know of."

"It's terrible you know; so bad that all of the rich white folks have moved west of 7th Street to get away from the Irish and the colored," Manfred replied, "and those fine old houses have recently been converted into grimy tenements and boarding houses. Other landlords have built row houses on vacant lots and down alleyways, and Jesus, those areas are now so damn dirty; filled with garbage, pigs and chickens, and the smell of manure from horses, cows, and goats. It's a goddam awful place to be."

Chris asked, "Are the Germans still settling in the Philadelphia area?"

"No, not so much anymore. The new ones are boarding trains and going west to towns such as Scranton, Wilkes-Barre, and Harrisburg. The land is too damn expensive around here now."

"Trains – you said they're boarding trains?"

"Yeah, *The Philadelphia, Wilmington and Baltimore Railroad* opened in 1838 as far north as Grays Ferry and the following year all the way into downtown via a connection with the *Southwark Railway*. Now, you can take a train now from downtown Philadelphia south to Washington City, or north to Boston, or west to Scranton. It's been an amazing couple of years, you know."

Dieter said, "And that's not the end of it, I believe. Soon coal from the

Central Pennsylvania coalfields will be placed on railcars and sent south to Mobile and New Orleans. In ten years, we'll be out of the coal-hauling business – once the rail lines are completed."

"Well, Liverpool will always need cotton."

Dieter responded, "And in ten years, we might all be dead."

And they all laughed.

The four men sat quietly for a few minutes sipping their porter and enjoying a night of gaiety in the crowded tavern. They were hungry after a long day's work, and each one was relishing a heaping plate of beef stew with buttermilk biscuits.

Then Chris noticed a small commotion near the outside door. A man in a three-cornered had entered the tavern and started yelling.

"Come to rally – *The American Abolitionist Society* is meeting in Pennsylvania Hall on 6th Street near Franklin Square on Sunday afternoon at 2 PM. William Lloyd Garrison and Maria Chapman will speak on the horrors of slavery. Come and hear them!"

Many of the customers began booing the gentleman, and a few told the man to shut up. Finally, a bouncer grabbed the man by the collar and tossed him out into the street. The crowd cheered, but Chris was intrigued. He walked over and picked up one of the fliers which had fallen to the floor. He read the announcement and details of the meeting and shook his head.

"I believe I might go and see what it's all about," Chris mumbled.

A man to his right replied, "You won't be alone, but be careful. There are not a lot of abolitionist sympathizers in this part of town. Those coloreds are taking a lot of jobs away from the Irish and the Germans, and they don't like it."

Somehow, Chris didn't think that particular man would be attending the meeting.

On the following Sunday afternoon, Chris put on his suit, tie, and overcoat and found his way from the vessel tied up on the waterfront docks to

Pennsylvania Hall. Charles had decided to spend the afternoon with Dieter and a couple of others in a tavern located not far from the ship.

The meeting place for the Sunday afternoon lecture was already packed with people, but Chris located a seat near the back of the Hall on the left side. Despite his location near the rear of the building, he had a good view of the stage. He promptly noticed seven empty chairs set up in the middle.

At precisely 2 PM, seven people walked onto the stage and took their assigned seats. Shortly after that, Rev. Charles Dunkin arose out of his chair and stepped to the podium to the thunderous applause of the audience. Following some brief introductory remarks, he invited William Lloyd Garrison to speak.

Mr. Garrison, age 35, had been a leader in the abolitionist movement for over ten years. He hailed from Massachusetts and was the editor of the *Liberator* – the leading anti-slavery periodical in the United States. The editor was a small man but had a bellowing voice.

He stepped up to the podium, briefly looked at his notes, smiled at the audience, and began speaking.

> I am aware that many people object to the severity of my language, but is there not cause for severity? I will be as harsh as truth, and as uncompromising as justice. On this subject, I do not wish to think, or speak, or write, with moderation. No! No! Tell a man whose house is on fire to give a moderate alarm; tell him to moderately rescue his wife from the hands of the ravisher; tell the mother to gradually extricate her babe from the fire into which it has fallen, but urge me not to use moderation in a cause like the present one. I am in earnest – I will not equivocate – I will not excuse – I will not retreat a single inch, and I will be heard. The apathy of the people is enough to make every statue leap from its pedestal and to hasten the resurrection of the dead.

The crowd roared its approval, and he resumed talking about the evils of slavery and the abomination it was causing to the good Christian people of America. He provided example after horrible example of the institution of slavery, and he talked about the history of the 'freedom' struggle in

Pennsylvania and the work which was still needed to be done.

Chris began to feel the enthusiasm of the folks sitting around him, and he started standing and cheering with them as the words of the speaker drove the crowd into a frenzy. Although Chris was still not proficient in the English language, he knew enough to understand the flavor of the subject at hand.

Garrison continued:

> I am a believer in that portion of the Declaration of American Independence in which it is set forth, as among self-evident truths, 'that all men are created equal; that they are endowed by their Creator with certain inalienable rights; that among these are life, liberty, and the pursuit of happiness.' Hence, I am an abolitionist. Thus, I cannot but regard oppression in every form and most of all that turns a man into a thing with indignation and abhorrence.

He said he would not be silent, and he referred on several occasions to Biblical verses and the evils of slavery. He said:

> Convince me that one man may rightfully make another man his slave, and I will no longer subscribe to the Declaration of Independence. Convince me that liberty is not the inalienable birthright of every human being, of whatever complexion or clime, and I will give that instrument to the consuming fire. I do not know how to espouse freedom and slavery together.

The audience was in a frenzy, and baskets were being passed around the hall so people could contribute to the movement. Chris put in a dollar – much more than he could easily afford.

Garrison resumed:

> The abolitionism which I advocate is as absolute as the law of God and as unyielding as His throne. It admits of no compromise. Every slave is a stolen man; every slaveholder is a man stealer. By no precedent, no example, no law, no compact, no purchase, no bequest, no inheritance, no combination of circumstances, is slaveholding right or justifiable. While a slave remains in his fetters, the land must have no rest.

He was reaching a crescendo; his voice was smooth, powerful, and demanding. Chris was mesmerized by Garrison.

> If the slaves are not men; if they do not possess human instincts, passions, faculties, and powers; if they are below accountability, and devoid of reason; if for them there is no hope of immortality, then there is no God, no heaven, no hell; if, in short, they are what the slave code declares them to be, rightly deemed, sold, taken, reputed and adjudged in law to be chattels personal in the hands of their owners and possessors, and their executors, administrators and assigns, to all intents, constructions, and purposes whatsoever; then, undeniably, I am mad, and I can no longer discriminate between a man and a beast.

Garrison stopped speaking for a moment, waiting for the crowd to settle down until he concluded:

> But, if they are men; if they are to run the same career of immortality with ourselves; if the same law of God is over them as over all others; if they have souls to be saved or lost; if Jesus included them among those for whom he laid down his life; if Christ is within many of them 'the hope of glory'; then, when I claim for them all that we claim for ourselves, because we are created in the image of God, I am guilty of no extravagance, but am bound, by every principle of honor, by all the claims of human nature, by obedience to Almighty God, to remember them that are in bonds as bound with them, and to demand their immediate and unconditional emancipation.

The crowd leaped again to their feet, and soon Garrison began nodding and bowing to the audience. He looked to his right and waived five or six Negroes on to the stage. He hugged them and said:

"These are my brothers in Christ!"

After that, several other speakers came to the podium, and each one provided more commentary on the matters facing the Nation of the issues of slavery, tolerance towards Indians, and the question regarding the suffragettes.

Chris walked out of the hall a different man on that Sunday afternoon.

After the conclusion of the lecture and a brief reception in the rear of the hall, Chris slowly walked around snowy Philadelphia, deep in his thoughts. He welcomed the crisp, fresh air and the opportunity to stroll around the city alone. The matter of slavery in America bothered him. It wasn't part of the nation he had read about while he was still in Trockau; it wasn't part of the American ideal he'd created in his mind while living in Bayreuth.

He kept on going over the infamous words of Thomas Jefferson: that all men are created equal, and all men are endowed by their Creator with certain inalienable rights such as life, liberty and the pursuit of happiness. Chris asked himself, how does slavery square with these principles?

He knew that the goal of the Constitution was to create a 'more perfect Union' and the drafters of the document could only go so far in reaching a compromise in 1787 between the competing camps on the matters of freedom and individual liberty. He also recognized the new government had departed dramatically from the imposition of a British imposed limited-monarchy.

Furthermore, he remembered that after a few years of governance under a confederacy of independent States, the founding fathers established a republic; the first one since the days of ancient Rome. That in itself was a significant step in an enlightened government. But did it go far enough?

Chris understood that the original signers of the Constitution had entrusted to future generations the obligation to redefine and to expand these individual rights. One of the speakers at the anti-slavery meeting mentioned that the process of obtaining true freedom was like a relay race: the current generation would take the baton from the preceding group, carry the truncheon as far as it could, and pass it on to the succeeding generation. But when would these rights be expanded to cover other oppressed groups, such as the slave population and the native people?

He wandered slowly down Market Street pondering these difficult concepts. The shops were closed on his cold but sunny Sunday afternoon and the world around him was encased in winter white. Shivering from the cold temperature, the snow crunched under his feet as he walked across the long wooden bridge over the Schuylkill River, and he meandered for an hour or so along the narrow streets, the closed shops, and the modest houses on the western shore.

While walking, he noted many of the family homes had hung evergreen wreaths on their front doors, and curiously, hung drawings of pineapples in their main front window. Breathing deeply, Chris could smell the fragrance of supper cooking on a stove, and he smiled as he watched a family of four walking their dog along a snowy street.

As he passed by a vacant lot, he also noticed where two competing groups of young boys had built snow-forts and were busy engaging each other in a snowball fight. All of this made Chris feel a little homesick for his family and the life he had left behind in Trockau.

Then he strolled through a neighborhood full of trees. In the summertime, Chris surmised the streets would be lined with maples, chestnuts, and oaks in long avenues of green and silver and which in autumn would become a bright canopy of gold, orange, red and brown hues. Suddenly feeling a stiff northern breeze, he turned his collar to the wind and put his hands deep into his coat pockets. It was time to begin his long walk back to the ship.

Crossing back over the bridge, he walked down to Christ Church – built during the reign of King George III – and went around to the back of the church to the burial-ground to visit the tomb of Benjamin Franklin, a man whom Chris read about extensively while he was still residing in Ulm and Bayreuth. After pausing for a short time, he placed a small stone of the mausoleum and said a silent prayer. He wondered what Franklin would think of the current political arguments involving matters of slavery and freedom.

Upon leaving the church grounds and turning left, he sauntered passed the building formerly housing *The United States Bank*, and he entered *Independence Hall,* built in 1733, where the merits of the Declaration of Independence and the Constitution had been discussed and debated during the last twenty-five years of the previous century.

He stopped for a few moments by the statue of George Washington and then looked at a portrait of William Penn, the man whose name was eventually given to this State. While he was still perplexed at the arguments and issues which framed his mind on that cold afternoon, the sun was setting rapidly, and he decided it was time to return to the ship.

A full moon was looming just above the horizon as he walked down Front Street and turned right onto Elfreth's Alley, a cobblestone path which meandered a distance of two short blocks past the warehouses and ended at the waterfront docks. It was twilight time, and he walked down a street of blackness. Once in a while, he noticed a candle glowing in a window, but at that hour of the evening, this portion of the town seemed to be all but deserted.

Still deep in his thoughts, he believed he heard a noise behind him. Turning around, he saw a man walking purposefully toward him with a knife in his right hand. Then turning forward again, Chris saw there were two men in front of him blocking his way to the ship. Instantly, Chris stopped and reached into his pocket for his knife. He was outnumbered three to one.

"Well, what do we have here?" the first man asked. "Are you lost, mate?"

"No," Chris said, "I'm on my way to my ship. I have no money, and I don't want any trouble." He felt a chill go up his spine.

The man started laughing, "So, you're afraid of me?"

"I told you I don't have any money. I'm a sailor going back to my ship."

"A simple sailor, are you now; dressed in a fancy suit and tie? I'll bet you have a gold pocket watch and a bulky billfold, don't ya?"

"No, I have no money. Now, let me be."

The three men started circling him, and anticipating an assault, Chris crouched a bit and stretched his hands out in front of him to fend off any attack. The first man lurched toward Chris, and although he swiftly stepped aside, the man's knife caught Chris' upper left arm and sleeve – cutting both.

As the first attacker skidded past Chris, the man tripped on a cobblestone, and in that instant, Chris turned and struck the attacker in his face with his right elbow, throwing the first attacker hard into the wall. He let out a brief cry and slumped to the ground, twisting in pain.

Then the other two attackers began encircling Chris. One man said, "You shouldn't have done that, boy. Now, we'll have to hurt you."

As the two remaining attackers circled Chris, the third attacker's face became illuminated by the bright moonlight. Looking up at the third man, he thought he recognized him.

"Manfred Schlender, it that you? I'm Chris Bogner. I had beers with you last week. Tell them who I am."

The second attacker turned to the third one and asked, "Do you know this boy?"

Manfred replied, "Aye, I know him. Chris, what in blazes are you doing here?"

"I'm off to *The Ballantine*, Manfred. Captain Worthington would be fairly upset to learn that one of his sailors was roughed up by robbers."

Manfred responded, "Believe me, I didn't know it was you, Chris." Turning to his mates, Manfred said, "Let him pass. There'll be others coming home tonight down this way."

Manfred stepped aside and motioned Chris to pass. "I hope you won't be reporting me to the Captain now, will you?"

Chris looked at Manfred and finally said, "We sail in a few days, and I wouldn't like to see you in jail over Christmas. I won't mention it to anyone if you decide you've caught a nasty cold and won't be able to work anymore on *The Ballantine*. Do we have a deal, Manfred?"

He nodded, and Chris walked hurriedly down the alley to the ship, holding his bleeding left arm. He never saw Manfred Schlender again.

The church bells began ringing precisely and joyfully at noon. It was Christmas Day, and Chris and Charles were attending Mass at St. Mary's Cathedral in downtown Philadelphia. The crew had almost fully loaded *The Ballantine* for its journey to New Orleans, and unless a winter storm blew in, the ship would depart on the morning of December 27. After a short walk from the boat in a cold, icy rain, the brothers shook of the sleet from their ice-glazed hats and found seats on the left near a side door.

The massive cathedral, St. Mary's, was built in 1763 and subsequently enlarged in 1810. Its cemetery included the earthy remains of several prominent Philadelphians, such as Commodore John Barry, known as the 'Father of the American Navy'; General Moylan, an aide to General George Washington; and Thomas Fitzsimmons, a member of the Continental Congress who helped draft the United States Constitution.

The interior of the church was decked out in a Christmas splendor on that morning. Poinsettias were placed on the floor all around the altar, and festive holiday plants – including mistletoe, red amaryllis, and holly – were positioned appropriately in the front portion of the church.

When the bells stopped chiming, the choir rose and began singing:

> Hark! The herald angels sing,
> "Glory to the newborn King."
> Peace on earth and mercy mild
> God and sinners reconcile.
> Joyful, all ye nations rise.
> Join the triumph of the skies.
> With angelic host proclaim
> "Christ is born in Bethlehem."
> Hark! The herald angels sing,
> "Glory to the newborn King."

It had been a full year since the brothers left Trockau, and Chris vividly recalled their last Christmas together. Papa sang 'Ave Maria' at The Church of St. Boniface and the family enjoyed a festive dinner in the family home on Wilhelmstrasse. So much had happened since that time exactly one year ago.

As the choir began singing the second and third verses, the priest, the choir boys, and the lector walked slowly down the central aisle to the steps of the altar. After the song ended, the group genuflected and slowly proceeded up the four steps to the altar-mount with each person taking his position in the tabernacle.

Then the priest turned and faced the congregation. While making the Sign of the Cross, he said:

"*In Nomine Patris, et Filii, et Spiritus Sancti.*"

The congregation responded, "Amen."

Then the priest said, "*Dominus vobiscum.*"

And the people responded "*Et cum Spiritu tuo.*"

Although the Mass was celebrated in Latin, the readings and the sermon were spoken in English. Over the previous four months, Chris became quite comfortable in the English language and understood most of what the priest was saying. For Charles, English was still a significant challenge.

During the Mass, Chris' mind wandered to the tasks remaining ahead of them – sailing to New Orleans and completing their journey up the Mississippi River to St. Louis which had taken over three months' time thus far. Silently, he wondered what had become of the passengers who sailed the Atlantic Ocean with them. Were they safely in their new locations? Were things working out well for them? He hoped so.

Then he wondered what would happen when the brothers reached Louisiana. They were running out of money; would they find work in Louisiana? He remembered Dieter was encouraging them to 'make another loop' with the Captain and crew aboard *The Ballantine*, but Chris was ready to begin his new life in America. The brothers had a second cousin, Christopher Bauer, living in St. Louis, and hopefully, his cousin would help the brothers find work and settle comfortably in Missouri.

But all in all, it had been an extraordinary year for them, and on December 27th, their journey would continue.

Later on Christmas afternoon, Dieter, the two brothers, and a few of their shipmates left the ship and walked along the streets of snow-covered Philadelphia to The Rising Sun Tavern on Market Street for a Christmas supper. Like St. Mary's, the tavern was decorated in a Christmas fashion. Creeping cedar ran along the rafters, mistletoe was hung from the doorways, and a Christmas tree was decorated in a corner, covered with candles and ornaments.

The custom of placing a Christmas tree inside a room had been introduced to Britain in the mid-1830s, first by way of Queen Charlotte, wife of George III, and more successfully by Prince Albert during the reign of Queen Victoria. By 1840, the Christmas tree had become widespread in homes throughout America.

That Christmas afternoon, the tavern was a joyful abode for the lonely men – who were far away from their families and loved ones – to gather. Other traditional decorations which were decorating The Rising Sun on that afternoon included bells, candy canes, stockings, wreaths, and angels. Illuminated candles were placed in each window to demonstrate the fact Christians believe that Jesus Christ is the ultimate light of the world. It was quite a pleasant sight.

In one corner, a guitarist played and sang traditional Christmas carols such as 'Deck the Halls,' 'God Rest You Merry Gentlemen,' and 'The Holly and the Ivy.' Many of the customers sang along with him.

The men from the ship each ordered a dinner of suckling pig with all the trimmings and round after round of American brown ale, and they talked about their homes. Chris asked, "How many days sailing to New Orleans, Dieter? What are we facing?"

"Well, I'd guess about thirty days or so. Of course, it depends on the conditions; but we'll be closely following the Atlantic coast, so if bad storms are coming at us, we can quickly find a safe harbor to drop anchor and wait them out."

"Any other stops along the way?"

Dieter took a drink of ale and said, "Maybe one stop – if we need provisions; perhaps in either Savannah or St. Augustine. Both are pretty good ports."

The men ate, drank, and told stories. Dieter talked of his home and family in Stuttgart, and as Charles consumed more and more ale, he once again proclaimed his love for Colleen – lamenting the fact he did not follow her to Scranton.

"Have you ever been in love, Chris?" Dieter asked.

"Yes, I was in love with a duchess — way far above my station in life. We were childhood friends, and she promised me that we'd marry one day."

"So what happened?"

"She moved away, married a Duke, and they now have several children. But I ran into her while working a job in a castle in Bavaria. She said she still loved me."

Dieter smiled and patted Chris' hand, "So, do you think you'll ever see her again?"

"Well, no. For me, Sonia may as well be a million miles beyond the moon. No, I know I'll never see her again."

He took the last swallow of ale and sadly thought about her.

On the afternoon of December 26, *The Ballantine* was fully loaded and ready to sail for Louisiana. It would leave the following morning. After supper, Chris composed another letter to his father.

December 26, 1840

I hope you have received my last letter where I described our crossing of the Atlantic Ocean. With much reluctance, Charles and I will be departing for New Orleans tomorrow. We are not looking forward to another month or more aboard The Ballantine.

It was exactly one year ago today when Charles and I kissed you goodbye and began our adventure to America. With so much happening to us over the last year, it seems like we left home much longer ago. However, it also feels like yesterday.

America is much better than I'd anticipated. If the city of Philadelphia is representative of our new nation, we're in for a good life here. I'm still somewhat worried about Charles, though. He's exceedingly homesick and has not taken the time to learn English. Also, he fell in love for the first time – with an Irish lass named Colleen – and now that she's moved on to Scranton, he is quite moody and down-hearted. I hope he'll be better once we arrive in St. Louis.

In that regard, I've written to Christopher Bauer, telling him that we are on our way to New Orleans. I'll contact him again when we arrive there. I don't know how long we'll remain in Louisiana. We need to find work so we can pay for our trip up the Mississippi River to Missouri.

Philadelphia is a bustling city of around 250,000 people, and it is estimated that well over fifty percent of the people here are from German stock. There are also a lot of English, Scots, Irish, and Negroes, too.

The United States held a national election in November, and it is remarkable insofar as the current President, Martin Van Buren, lost his race for re-election but will peaceful-ly relinquish his power to his opponent, General William Henry Harrison. Furthermore, there is no talk of impris-oning President Van Buren or requiring him to leave the county. This would never happen in Europe.

There are two political parties in America: the Democrats and the Whigs. I was told that over 80% of the eligible elec-torate voted, and the winning ticket used the slogan of "Tippecanoe and Tyler, too." Harrison earned the name "Tippecanoe" from a battle he won against the Indians in Ohio. He will be the first Whig president.

One of the most significant issues facing the Nation now is the matter of slavery. Most of the Northern States have elected to abolish slavery while the Southern States have decided to keep it. The United States Constitution permits each state to determine whether to have slaves. Papa, I think that slavery is an abomination, and it will eventually lead to a confrontation between the North and the South. How can Christians keep slaves?

Dieter sends his best wishes, and he mentioned that when he goes home to Stuttgart next year, he'll try to visit you in Trockau. I only wish we could be there with him.

Happy Christmas to you and all in our family. I'll write to

you again when we arrive in Louisiana. Please remember you are always in our thoughts and prayers, and that we love each one of you so very much. Please keep us in your prayers.

Affectionately, Christopher and Charles

The following morning, the pilot boats reattached themselves to the bow and stern of *The Ballantine* and slowly towed the ship off the pier and out into the main channel. It was a chilly, cloudy, blustery day, and Chris noticed a slight sheet of ice had encased the upper reaches of the harbor. As the ship pulled slowly away, he could hear a crunch and a snap as the boat made its way down the Delaware River. Dieter had been correct; a couple more days at the dock in Philadelphia would have frozen the river until March or even later.

It was a busy morning as the sailors made the canvass ready for the long sail south to the Florida Keys and then northwest to New Orleans. This time, three passengers joined the ship for the trip: Charles Periwinkle and Jonathan Klein (the partners who owned the shipment of lumber stowed on the middle deck) and Josiah Merriweather (who represented the coal company whose product filled the hold). Each one had his own cabin on the upper deck.

As the ship passed the city of Philadelphia, the three businessmen stood watching at the rail on the starboard side of the vessel – wrapped up tightly in their business suits, top coats, and bowler hats. Suddenly, a swift breeze blew up, and two of the men's hats flew off their heads and settled softly in the Delaware River. There would be no retrieving of their hats today.

As the day advanced, the ship made good progress in tackling the seventy-mile tow down the Delaware River to the Port of Wilmington. By the time the boat reached the position where the pilot boats had unhooked themselves from *The Ballantine*, it was too late to begin the unescorted portion of the journey down the Delaware Bay to the Atlantic. Thus, the captain dropped anchor in mid-harbor and waited for the dawn to break to resume the voyage south.

"This will probably be as cold as you'll be for a long time, Chris," Dieter said, noticing Chris shivering in the cold wind off the Bay. "Once we pass Cape Hatteras near North Carolina, we'll get into the Gulf Stream. The air and the water will be much warmer and calmer there. You'll see. But from here to Cape Fear, we'll have pretty rough sailing. I'll bet you a Yankee dollar that those businessmen will not see the light of day on deck until we approach the Port of Charleston."

Early the next morning, the crew raised the sails of *The Ballantine* for the first time since November 26, and the canvas was cold, tight, and heavy from the snow and rain. Once the last sails were firmly in place, the captain lifted anchor and set the sails into jaws of a fierce northeastern wind.

As if anticipating the next move, the ship jumped – almost hesitatingly – as the sails bellowed and tightened, and as she began moving into the main channel, a screaming seagull flew overhead – howling in an apparent protest. The crew, feeling the ship's movements south gave up three heavy-hearted cheers of hooray, and *The Ballantine* was on its sail south into the blustery Atlantic.

By nightfall, the ship had reached the mouth of the Delaware Bay, and Captain Worthington and his officers prepared the crews and their guests for a hard right turn near Cape Henlopen. As predicted, a strong gust filled the sails, and Chris could hear and feel a definite crunch in the ship's main mast. It suffered a minor crack near the deck line, but after an inspection by the First Officer, the captain presumed the vessel and crew could continue at least as far as Port of Norfolk – and maybe much further.

The sea was angry, and occasionally, waves burst over the left side of *The Ballantine* and flooded the upper deck. But with all hatches battened down tightly very little water seeped into the two lower tiers. However, it was too rough to feed the crew, and Chris and Charles – among several others – were seasick once again. It was not until morning that the seas had subsided to the point where the mess galley was open.

"We've survived the worst part," yelled Dieter. "It should get better from now on." And it was.

Soon the days became weeks as *The Ballantine* slowly made its way down the coasts of Maryland and Virginia, and passed the mouth of the Chesapeake Bay at Hampton Roads. The seas were rough at times and the air temperatures, while warming somewhat, remained rather cold.

Late one night while standing on the forecastle deck during the middle-watch, Chris observed a full yellow moon rise out of the dark Atlantic, and he marveled at the silhouettes of the moonbeams which danced across the water. Astonished by such beauty, he wondered at the stillness of his dark-colored world – only broken by the occasional flap of a mainsail and the steady drone of the unceasingly advancing keel.

On other occasions, he noticed how schools of porpoises, dolphins, and whales would follow the boat, and how seagulls often found their rest on the yardarms and masts in the upper reaches of the ship.

Usually, night-watch was a time of reflection for Chris – even as he was faithfully performing his duties abroad ship. He thought about where he had traveled over the past thirteen months and where the journey might eventually take him. He also worried about Charles who seemed to have fallen into a deep depression, and of course, Chris dreamed of Sonia – who was never too far away from his thoughts.

By late January, the ship was sailing alongside the coast of North Carolina. The seas were much calmer and the winds favorable.

Dieter put down his pipe one late January afternoon and said, "You know Chris, we are sailing through what many sailors called 'the graveyard of the Atlantic.' This portion of the sea was once considered quite a treacherous route from here to the city of Charleston."

"I think I heard one of the officers mention that phrase to me earlier. What does it mean exactly?"

"Well, this stretch of sea contains numerous shoals and frequent rough seas."

The precise area where Dieter was probably referring to – known as

Diamond Shoals – has caused the loss of thousands of ships and an unknown number of sailors. The so-called 'graveyard' extends along the whole of the North Carolina coast, past Chicamacomico, Bodie Island, and southward in gently curving arcs to the points at Cape Lookout and Cape Fear.

Chris looked at the horizon. He believed he could see land off to the west. "Are we in any danger now?"

"No, not now. But at one time – before modern-day instruments and accurate nautical charts – it was a devil's deal. The route through this channel is shorter – being much closer to land – but the area is full of shoals, reefs, and oftentimes, pirates."

"Pirates?"

"Yes. Perhaps you've heard that in the last century, Edward Teach — better known as Blackbeard, the Pirate — ran his flagship, *The Queen Anne's Revenge*, out of Beaufort Inlet – just off to our west. He captured lots of merchant ships and often executed the sailors and officers. He was a holy terror."

"I read a little bit about him. Wasn't he a privateer who primarily raided Spanish galleons but later accused of piracy and subsequently hung by the British?"

Dieter smiled, "Actually he was killed in a battle with an English warship. It is said that Teach's corpse was later thrown into the inlet while his head was suspended from the bowsprit of an English sloop so the reward could be collected – or so the story goes."

By the time *The Ballantine* made its way south in the waters off the coast of Georgia, the temperature had risen considerably, and seas were, for the most part, rather calm. One evening after his work was over, Chris went into the mess galley for supper. Most of the tables were full, but he noticed one of the passengers, Jonathan Klein, was sitting alone at a table for four.

"May I join you, Sir?"

Looking up, he replied, "By all means; please join me, Chris."

Jonathan Klein was undoubtedly a modern man of means, and his well-dressed presentation that evening – even while aboard *The Ballantine* – established his place in the hierarchy of American gentlemen. He looked to be about 40 years old and sported curly brown hair and long full sideburns. His whiskers filled the space on his throat between his jaw line and his shirt-collar. Unlike many gentlemen of his day, he did not have a mustache, and the remainder of his face was cleanly shaved.

Dressed in a white cotton shirt featuring a lower standing collar, he wore a broad cravat, tied firmly around his neck and knotted into a bow tie. He also wore a dark brown frock coat, calf-length and double-breasted (with its shoulders narrow and slightly-sloped) and he wore full-length tan trousers with a fly-front.

Chris put his tray down and took a seat to the gentleman's left. A heavy pewter whale oil lamp, suspended above his head, rocked rhythmically with the slight roll of the ship. They had met before on several occasions.

Chris smiled and said, "Sir, I've been admiring your cargo – beautiful walnut, cherry, oak, and mahogany. Is it to be used for making furniture?"

"You have a good eye. Are you a carpenter by chance?"

Chris told him a little about his life in Bavaria and how he and his brother were on their way to Louisiana and then up the Mississippi to St. Louis. He said, "But we hope to find work in New Orleans. Charles and I are getting near the bottom of our currency."

"Perhaps I can help you. I know most of the carpentry and cabinetmaking shops in Louisiana."

"Thank you sir; yes, that would be most helpful."

The two men continued eating their dinner in silence for a while, and then Klein asked, "What are your initial impressions of America?"

"Well, I like it so far, for the most part."

"What particularly?"

"Well, a man isn't chained as much to consequences of his birth. There are no nobles, no aristocrats, and no orders of rank here. Ordinary men have opportunities in America which are not available in Bavaria. There, we are tied to our social class with little hope of raising ourselves above it."

Klein smiled, "But don't be fooled; we have social classes here, too, Chris. The rich white Protestants control just about everything and everyone on the East coast, but I believe there is still hope for those of at least some means and education in the South and on the frontier. From what I've observed of you, I think you'll do just fine."

The two men slowly ate their dinners and talked for another thirty minutes until it became apparent the mess-steward was ready to close the doors to the galley. Klein asked, "Looks like we have to leave; would you like to continue our chat in my cabin over a glass of tawny port and a Cuban cigar?"

"I don't wish to bother you, Mr. Klein."

"No, it's no bother. But I need to tell you something first; I'm Jewish. Sometimes that makes a difference to some folks."

"Why?"

"I'm not sure – and it shouldn't. Well, I certainly don't have horns nor cloven feet – and Chris, I'm certainly not interested in men. I have a lovely wife and family in New Orleans. What do you say? I could use a little more conversation."

"Great. I assume the captain won't mind."

The two men exited the galley and stopped at the rail to look at the sunset for a moment. The coast of Georgia was no more than five miles away to the west, and the sun was beginning to set behind the rising hills just passed the shoreline.

After they arrived at Klein's cabin, Chris asked, "Is it hard being Jewish in America, Sir?"

Klein smiled and said, "It's hard being Jewish just about anywhere these days. My family has been in America for four generations. My father fought in the Continental Army under General Nathaniel Greene, and my brother served with General Andy Jackson in New Orleans. In many quarters, we're still not accepted as Americans."

"I'm sorry to hear that, Sir."

"Thanks. Yes, it's been tough at times. You know, I've been called a 'Jew boy,' a 'Christ-killer,' a 'kike,' and many other despicable names. My business partner won't share a room with me, and he rarely sits with me for a meal. I'm sure you've seen how I sit alone on most evenings. My partner, however, likes my business savvy, my negotiations skills, and the money I bring into the business. But he's only once met my family – almost by accident, you see – and we've never been invited to his home or his social clubs."

Chris shook his head. "I assumed America would be different."

Klein smiled again. "Let me pour us a nice glass of tawny port, and permit me to tell you some things about your new country."

He reached into a cabinet and removed a bottle. Then he grabbed a couple of sniffers and poured two glasses of port. "It's from Portugal, and I can only find it in Boston. Try it; tell me whether you like it."

Chris took a sip. It had a golden-brown color, a nutty flavor, and a medium dry texture. After tasting it, he smiled and nodded his head affirmatively. "It's the best one I've ever had. Thank you, Sir."

"Yeah, I thought you'd like it."

Klein sat down at the small table and offered Chris a chair. He lit the oil lamps but left the cabin door open to provide ventilation and to avoid any perception of indecent activity. After experiencing the bitterly cold winter weather of Pennsylvania, the Georgia evening air was warm and sweet.

Klein continued, "Contrary to its reputation of welcoming immigrants, America has always despised its latest bunch of newcomers. First, it was the Scots. After Bonnie Prince Charlie lost the Battle of Culloden against England in 1746, thousands of Scots came to America. They were despised at first."

He took another drag off of his cigar and then continued, "They were isolated, chastised, and forced to move to the west – the land just beyond the Blue Ridge Mountains of Virginia and North Carolina. But God bless the Scots. They hate the English so much that they were willing to join the rebels in ousting the Redcoats during the War of Independence. Without them, we would not be an independent country today, I fear."

He had another sip and said, "Then came the Germans – beginning about fifty years ago. I remember seeing the posters and cartoons in the local newspapers. They were characterized as being fat, smelly, and ignorant; and often referred to as pork-eaters, drunks, and nasty people with nasty habits."

"Wow."

"Now, it's the Irish whom the locals despise – they're not to be trusted because of their allegiance to the Pope and their legendary bouts of drunkenness and outright laziness. They're also branded as thieves, womanizers, and buffoons. Once they are absorbed into polite society, however, it will be another group of newcomers who'll be despised. It's quite shameful, I think."

"But doesn't our country want more immigrants?"

"Yes, but it's primarily for political reasons. Congress wants them to come and fill up the land procured by Jefferson in 1803."

"Fill up the land, Sir?"

"Yes. You know that the easterners don't want these new arrivals to stay in the northern cities but rather, to settle in Ohio and beyond – and then encourage them to go up the Missouri River and populate the nation all the way to Oregon. Productive, stable and healthy farming families are considered to be the key to growing our new nation. Both Franklin and Jefferson saw population growth as a sign of national strength and the key to holding the land against military moves by the British and Spanish."

"Hmn? That seems to explain a lot."

"Yeah, it should. How about a cigar? Have you ever smoked a Cuban?"

Chris smiled, "No, I've never smoked anything before."

"Well, you're in for a treat, my friend."

Klein arose and picked up a box of cigars off the counter. The ship was gently rolling in the calmer Southern Atlantic, and the sun was setting just below the western horizon. "Let me show you how to smoke one."

He removed two cigars out of the humidor and laid them flat down on the table side-by-side. He licked his right palm, and after setting it flat on the cigars, he began rolling the cigars several times from left to right and then back to the left again, sealing their outer leaves.

Then he picked up one of the cigars and handed it to Chris saying, "Before you light up, you need to clip the end of the cigar. Watch me; the best way to do it is with a cigar-clipper. Cutting it with a knife is acceptable – but only if you don't have a clipper handy."

Then he laughed. "Biting the end off should be avoided at all costs. For best results, snip the end off with a quick, sharp motion like this; it will also help you avoid tearing the end."

Chris followed the instructions.

Klein resumed, "Then, take hold the cigar in your hand, and place the tip just on the flame of the matchstick."

Klein took a long thin stick out of a bowl, held it to the flame of a whale-oil lamp, and brought the fire over to Chris.

Then Klein said, "Just do what you need to do to light the tip – but don't puff on it yet. Before you place the cigar in your mouth, you want to burn the end of the tobacco to seal it."

Then demonstrating the process, Klein said, "Then spin the cigar around several times as you light the cigar. Once you can see a bit of an orange glow over here at the end, you're ready to puff it."

Chris followed the instructions. He had a deep draw on the cigar and soon began coughing heartily. Klein said, "Gently puff; don't inhale the smoke. Once the cigar is fully lit, it will burn on its own for a long while; thus, constant puffing is unnecessary. To keep it going, take a drag or two about once every minute or so."

Klein watched Chris, and then said, "Great; you're doing it right. Now relax, and enjoy the flavor of the smoke. Ah, yes."

The two men spent the remainder of the evening enjoying each other's company. The tawny port, the gentle swaying of the ship in the calm Georgia waters, the tantalizing aroma of the cigars, and the dimness of the cabin from the whale-oil lanterns caused each of them to attain a sensation of well-being and satisfaction.

Chris talked about Trockau and his long voyage to Rotterdam. He mentioned a few pertinent facts about his family, Charles' run-in with the nobility in Bayreuth, and of course, Sonia.

Klein talked about his life growing up in Vermont, his travels throughout the United States and Canada, and his home in Louisiana. He said he'd lived in a house on St. Charles Avenue in New Orleans for the past ten years with his wife, Racheal, and their three children. Louisiana was now home for them.

Chris asked, "How often do you travel to Philadelphia?"

"Well, I guess about once a year. My partner and I obtain timber in Pennsylvania and sometimes in New Hampshire, and then we catch a ride with it back south to New Orleans on a ship. This time, though, we rode a ship north as far as Wilmington, North Carolina, and we rode a train the rest of the way to Philadelphia. You know, the rail line was completed to Wilmington earlier this year. It certainly saved us a lot of time and aggravation. Have you ever ridden on a train, Chris?"

"No, but someday soon I hope."

"You know, it's so much faster and more comfortable than riding on a sailing ship; so is travel on a steamship, by the way."

"Yeah, I know. Charles and I rode a steamship up the Rhine River to Rotterdam. It took us half of the time of a sailing ship – or less – but it was much more expensive."

"You know, I tried to get Captain Worthington to make a stop in North Carolina and pick me up – but to no avail. But one day soon, we'll be able to take a train from New Orleans all the way to Philadelphia and then ship our timber back with us by rail. That time can't come quick enough for me, I say. I suspect this may well be my last adventure on *The Ballantine*. Its time has come and gone, I believe."

Chris nodded his head in agreement.

A few moments later, Charles popped his head in the door asking about Chris. The cigars were almost burnt down to their fingers, and after another swallow or two of the port, Chris excused himself, and the two brothers returned to their cabin. It would not be the last Cuban cigar for Chris; or his final sip of tawny port, for that matter.

Over the next two years, Jonathan Klein became an excellent mentor for Chris, and he would be a frequent visitor at the Klein mansion

It was a warm January day, and Chris, Charles, and Dieter stared from railing at the sleepy city of St. Augustine. Chris asked, "Have you ever been here before, Dieter?"

"Yeah, perhaps three or four times. It's a lovely area this time of year, but it can be a hell-hole in the summer; maybe even worse than Louisiana. The captain usually stops here before we begin our Atlantic crossing to Liverpool."

The Ballantine was anchored near the western shore of Matanzas Bay just outside the city. Earlier, Dieter mentioned that St. Augustine was the half-way point on their trip to New Orleans and it was the last significant seaport before entering the mouth of the Mississippi River. Captain Worthington had decided to stop for supplies and repairs to the foremast before completing the journey.

From the sterncastle deck, Chris could see the American flag flying high above the ramparts of *Fort Marion*. Constructed in 1672, the old Spanish fort (named in honor of an American Revolutionary War hero, Francis Marion and formerly called *The Castillo de San Marcos*) is the oldest masonry fort in America.

Although previously attacked by the British, the French, the Dutch, and many bands of marauding pirates, the old bastion had never been taken, and it remained a prime example of Spanish colonial fortifications. In 1819, Spain signed The Adams-Onís Treaty which ceded the territory of Florida to the United States.

The sky was turquoise blue with only a few puffy-white cumulus clouds hanging low on the horizon. "You see the larger building on the left?" Dieter asked while pointing toward the city.

"The one next to the church?"

"Yes; it used to be the State House before the government moved the capital to Tallahassee. Now it's the Customs House. I assume the captain is there right now."

"Do we need to pay a tariff?"

"No, not this time; only when it is the first stop after coming from Europe.

But I'll bet he's getting updated charts and learning about local conditions. Things change quickly in this part of the ocean as the result of the bad storms and hurricanes. Once we leave here, there's nowhere else to stop – aside from maybe a quick stop at Fort Monroe on Dry Tortuga – before we reach Louisiana. We need to be ready for the next two weeks of open water; hence, the stop here."

The three men stood and looked at the old city for a long time. It had a population of approximately 2500 people in 1841, and the town was used mostly as a trading post between the locals and the Creeks and Seminoles. But it also was a harbor where ships could drop anchor for a few days either before or after their crossing of the Atlantic.

After their month-long bout with winter only fifteen days earlier in Philadelphia, the brothers were amazed at the warm temperatures and tropical breezes. The sun felt warm on their chapped faces, and the breezes pushed gently at the yardarm as the boat stood at anchor.

A few minutes later, Dieter asked, "Have you boys ever swam in the Atlantic?"

"No, never before."

"I guess you know how to swim, right?" The brothers nodded affirmatively. "Well, let's take a reach and go over to Anastasia Island. What do you say? It will do Charles well. He's been a bit melancholy lately."

Anastasia Island sits near a small peninsula on the east side of Matanzas Bay. With the help of a few of the sailors, they lowered a long boat – often called a 'reach' – into the water. The three men climbed into the reach from an entrance on the upper deck and rowed the short distance to the barrier Island. Securing the rope to the trunk of a dead tree, they scampered over the berm and through a maritime hammock of pines, palms, and oaks to the ocean side of the island.

"Take off your shoes, and let's walk in the water." The brothers did as Dieter suggested, and timid at first, they walked a few steps into the shallow water. The waves were breaking about fifteen feet off the shoreline, and the tide flow was gentle, warm, and rushing.

Dieter exclaimed, "Ah, it's just as I remember it. Let's take off our clothes and go for a quick swim."

The boys looked doubtful – what swim naked?

"Ah, don't worry. There's no one around to see your sorry white asses but the birds and the fishes. Come on. Let's go in; give it a try."

Dieter rapidly removed his shoes, shirt, and trousers, and letting out a yell, he charged directly into the breaking waves. As he came close to a larger swell, he dove into it, and after coming up, he stood and yelled, "Come on boys, the water is wonderful."

Chris and Charles first just looked at Dieter, and then for a few moments, at each other. Finally, Charles began taking off his clothes, smiled at his brother, and began running toward the cresting waves.

"Ouweeee!" he screamed as he followed Dieter into the surf. For a second or two, Chris stood there alone on the shore – but hearing the sound of his brother's screaming and yelping with joy finally caused Chris to strip off his clothes and join the other two.

For the next hour or so, they splashed in the waves – over, then under, and then up for air – screaming and laughing at the joy of it all. It would be the only time in their lives in which the brothers would swim in the ocean. And from that time forward, Charles was freed from the prison of his pain. Somehow, he had turned a corner and began to enjoy life once more. It was indeed a magical time.

After they came back for their clothes and let the warm sun and ocean breezes dry them, the three men strolled along the shore; looking at the seabirds, picking up shells, and lost in their thoughts. As the sun was getting low in the January sky, they made their way back to the ship.

It was a day Chris would never forget. Along his walk on the golden-sandy beach, he bent over and picked up two large sand-dollars and a pinkish conch shell. He would treasure these gifts from the sea for the rest of his life.

CHAPTER NINE

Crofton, Nebraska, August 1964

It was almost time for the ten o'clock news, and I could tell that my grandfather was getting tired.

He said, "I remember my grandfather taking the conch shell out of his bedroom one day, and handing it to me, he said, 'Hold it close to your ear; you can still hear the ocean.' And for the longest time, I believed I could hear the waves crashing. You know, I still have the shell in my bedroom, and every once-in-awhile, I pick it up, listen to it, and think of my grandfather."

I smiled; how I loved my grandfather – and probably as much as he had liked his.

"Bobby, what do you have going on tomorrow?"

"Well, I'll be working in the vegetable garden in the morning, and then tomorrow afternoon, we have a ballgame in Verdigre. The team bus leaves here at 1 PM, but I'm sure we'll be back for supper."

"Good. Let's turn on the news and see what's going on in this crazy world of ours."

After he went to bed, I sat on the front porch and looked up at the clear night-sky between the branches of the maple and sycamore trees. The crickets and tree-frogs had already started to chirp, breaking the evening's silence. Above me, I could see a canopy of stars in the moonless Nebraska sky.

The home across the street from my grandfather's house was almost formless in the darkness with only one window illuminated. Max Sprakel was probably awake and watching TV. For a while, I listened to the wind as it made its way through the leaves and branches, and I thought about my great-great-grandfather as he walked on that empty Florida beach so long ago; and so happy to be alive.

A few days later, Sarah and I climbed into my grandfather's Chrysler and drove north to the Missouri River. We crossed the bridge-span at Gavin's Point Dam and parked the car at the swimming beach which, at one time, had been the original channel of the river before the dam was completed in 1955. It was a beautiful summer day, and after we found a spot not far from the water's edge, and we laid our towels on the warm sand.

My transistor radio was playing all of the top songs of the summer of 1964: The Beatles sang 'A Hard Day's Night,' The Drifters crooned 'Under The Boardwalk,' and The Beach Boys played 'I Get Around.'

For no apparent reason, Sarah kissed me, and then she removed her sandals, tee shirt, and khaki tan shorts, and asked, "Well, what do you think?"

For a few moments, she stood looking there at me in her modest two-piece pale yellow bathing suit; I couldn't keep my eyes off of her.

"Wow!" I said, and she kissed me again.

Then she removed a tube of suntan lotion from her beach-bag and began rubbing the lotion on her legs, arms, abdomen, and chest. With a smile and yet another sweet kiss, she invited me to spread the cream on her back and neck.

As she held her ponytail off of her shoulders, I spent time – probably way much too time – gently, but thoroughly, covering the back and shoulders of the girl I loved with creamy white lotion. The thoughts going through my mind were indescribable.

After she returned the favor, we lay down on our blankets – holding hands and feeling the warm Nebraska sunshine kiss our bodies. Peter and Gordon began singing "A World Without Love" – a reality which I couldn't imagine at that instant.

A soft breeze enveloped us, and as we listened to the radio, we could also hear the sounds of children splashing and giggling in the water. Sitting up, we watched lovers holding hands and walking along the shoreline. After laying back down, Jan and Dean sang "The Little Old Lady From Pasadena" and somewhere in the middle of The Righteous Brothers' singing of their song

"See That Girl," I rolled over and kissed Sarah deeply on her lips.

She smiled, gently touched my face, and whispered, "I love you, Bobby." She closed her eyes, and we soaked up a few more minutes of the warm July afternoon sun.

I knew I loved her, too, and I wondered about my great-great grandfather as he stood at the railing of *The Ballantine* looking out from St. Augustine harbor. Was he dreaming of Sonia? Did he feel for her what I felt for Sarah?

I must have dozed off for a while when Sarah shook me, and I opened my eyes to the smiling face of my first true love.

"Come on Bobby; let's go for a swim."

I sat up and watched the beautiful form of my girlfriend slowly walk to the edge of the water. Turning around, she implored, "Well, are you coming in?"

Blowing me a kiss, she took perhaps five more steps and dove into the warm water of the Missouri River. I got up from the blanket, smiled, and shook my head, and then I headed off after her just as Johnny Rivers began crooning "Memphis."

CHAPTER TEN

New Orleans, Louisiana, March 1841

On March 6, 1841, Chris and Charles walked into the Sala Capitular ('Meeting Room') of the Cabildo on the Vieux Carré ('Old Square') in the French Quarter of the city of New Orleans. They were filing their paperwork to be admitted legally as immigrants and to begin the process of applying for American citizenship.

La Ville de la Nouvelle-Orléans was founded May 7, 1718, by Jean-Baptiste Le Moyne de Bienville, the founder of The French Mississippi Company, on land which had previously been inhabited by the Chitimacha Indians. The city was named for Philippe II, Duke of Orleans, who was Regent of the Kingdom of France at that time. With a population of approximately 110,000 people in 1841, the city was the wealthiest and third-most populous city in the nation.

In 1803, the city and the French province of Louisiana were sold by the French Emperor Napoléon Bonaparte to the United States, and by 1841, New Orleans was a major American port. The Mississippi River, which flows through the city, was regularly filled with steamboats, flatboats, and sailing ships of all descriptions which were carrying goods from the interior of the new nation to the industrialized ports located in of the Northeast and Europe.

The city was also home to the most substantial slave trade in the nation, gathering Africans from all over America and selling them primarily to buyers residing in the Deep South. Although the city had been populated initially with citizens of French and Spanish descent, large numbers of Americans began migrating to the city starting in 1803, and numerous German and Irish immigrants began arriving in the 'Crescent City' beginning in the early

1830s. Also, there may have been as many as 45,000 free persons of color in 1841 – most of whom originated from Haiti.

After registering with the American officials, the two boys gathered up their paperwork and returned to their tenement on Rue Chartres – a boarding house situated close to the docks. Provided with a reference from Jonathan Klein, Chris soon began working in a cabinetmaking facility just two blocks from their new residence. Charles, however, continued to work on refitting *The Ballantine* until the ship departed in April for Liverpool – with its holds filled to the brim with bales of cotton and huge bags of sugar.

One night after work, Chris wrote another letter to his father:

> *March 20, 1841*
>
> *We arrived safely in New Orleans about three weeks ago. I waited until now to write to you so that I'd have a mailing address. I've placed it at the bottom of this letter. I have also contacted Christopher Bauer to advise him of our plans and our new address.*
>
> *The Ballantine left Philadelphia last December in the dead of winter facing a cold north wind and streams of ice pellets. By the time we reached St. Augustine in the Florida Territory two weeks later, the weather had turned relatively balmy.*
>
> *One day, Dieter took us for a swim in the Atlantic Ocean. It was marvelous! The water was warm, and the sand was the color of snow. The beach was full of seashells, and the breeze was soft and soothing. We must've walked for miles on the sand after our swim.*
>
> *The remainder of our trip was mostly uneventful except that the water was the deepest color of blue I've ever seen, and the sunsets over the Gulf of Mexico were often quite spectacular. With the wind in our sails, we ran with the porpoises, whales, and dolphins.*
>
> *On several evenings while aboard ship, I had the pleasure*

of dinner with a businessman from New Orleans named Jonathan Klein, and he helped me find work once we arrived in Louisiana. He's an excellent man! I hope we remain friends.

Two pilot boats met us near the town of La Balize and guided us slowly up the Mississippi River to the city of New Orleans. After we lowered the sails, we had little to do except to stand by the railings and watch the bayous and swamps pass slowly before us.

On one sunny afternoon, Mr. Klein handed me his spyglass, and he pointed out eagles, owls, hawks, herons, and egrets sitting in the tops of the trees or soaring over the bayous.

He also showed us alligators, snakes, and lizards laying on the banks of the tributaries or floating along in the swampy backwaters. We'd never seen such sights! Curiously, many of the cypress and pine trees were covered with a strange looking moss which he referred to as 'Spanish moss' - because it looks like a Spaniard's beard.

In the days following our arrival in the city, Dieter helped Charles and I find a room in a boarding house in the French part of the town. A few days ago we registered with the United States government and applied for citizenship. The process should be resolved for us in two to three weeks. Soon we'll be Americans!

One evening, Charles and I were invited for dinner at the Klein's home in the American part of town. He and his family live in a magnificent house - akin to a Greek temple - on St. Charles Avenue, and his wife made us a terrific meal.

Later Mr. Klein gave me a letter of introduction to Monsieur Deveraux who owns a cabinetmaking shop not far from our boarding house on Rue Chartres. I began working there last week at a reasonable salary, but I had to promise Monsieur Deveraux that I would remain in his employ for at least one year. While this will delay our trip to St. Louis, I believe it's an ideal opportunity for me to make some money.

Charles is doing much better. The scar on his hand - while still quite visible - is well-healed, and his mental state of *mind is now okay. I think he's over Colleen and his home-sickness. He's helping Dieter and the others off-load the coal and timber from The Ballantine, and then on-load cotton and sugar for the ship's return trip to Liverpool in late April or early May. Perhaps after that, Charles can also work for Monsieur Deveraux.*

Papa, there is so much more to tell you – but I'll leave that for my next letter. I'm so anxious to hear from all of you and to learn about what's going on at home. I miss you all so very much. But don't worry about us; we're doing fine in our new home.

Please remember you are always in our thoughts and prayers, and that we love each one of you so much. Please keep us in your prayers, too.

Affectionately, Christopher and Charles

In late April, Chris was working on a table leg in the shop. He was kneeling and manipulating a trowel to complete the design on its heel. In just six weeks, the weather had turned from being delightful to hot and humid, and the working conditions inside the shop were almost stifling.

Unexpectedly, the ring-bell on the top of the door leading into the shop from the street sounded, and as the door opened, a young lady, followed by an older man, entered the store.

Immediately, Monsieur Deveraux stood up and recognizing the people said, *"Bonjour, Monsieur Bastogne et Mademoiselle Marie. Entrez, s'il vous plaît."*

The gentleman responded, *"Bonjour, Monsieur Deveraux, merci."* Then the two men began talking business.

A few moments later, Marie casually looked around the shop and eventually settled her eyes on Chris. As she smiled at him, a sensation, like a bolt of lightning, entered through his eyes, crashed down the pinnacle of his spine, and exited through his feet. Chris was utterly in a state of shock at her sensuality, and his feeling was so unexpected.

Although he still felt an abiding love for Sonia, Chris felt a rush of sensations which he had never quite felt before. From the precise instance Chris first saw her, he was smitten as surely as if Cupid himself had shot Chris in the heart with a magic arrow. He couldn't keep his eyes off of her for very long.

As the two men were conducting business, Marie slowly walked over to Chris and asked, "*Bonjour, parlez-vous français?*"

Chris stood up and extended his hand to her, saying, "No, Mademoiselle. I am German, but I speak pretty good English." He bowed and said, "Christopher Bogner, at your service."

She smiled and melted his heart all over again.

Accepting his hand, she replied: "My name is Marie Bastogne. The gentleman accompanying me is my father. I'm pleased to meet you, Christopher. Do you work here?"

"Yes, Mademoiselle. I am a cabinetmaker. I've been working for Monsieur Deveraux for almost a month now."

For the next ten minutes or so, they talked about their lives. Chris told her of his journey from Trockau to America, and she stated that she was born in Marseilles but came over to Louisiana with her parents about in 1826. She also mentioned that her father was setting up a restaurant on Rue Bourbon called *François'* and Monsieur Deveraux would be making furniture for their new enterprise. They seemed to like each other.

Suddenly, her father called to her. "*Chéri, c'est le moment de partir. Viens maintenant, s'il te plaît.*"

Chris looked perplexed and asked, "Chéri?"

She blushed, "Yes, that's what my friends and family call me. It all began with my father. As a baby, he called me '*Marie, ma chérie*'; I hope you'll do the same, Christopher."

He smiled, "Chris. My friends and family call me, Chris."

She nodded and called back to her father. "*Je viens, mon père.*"

She touched Chris' arm and said, "Well, I hope we see each other sometime soon, Christopher. Au revoir."

"*Au Revoir, Chéri.*"

Chris stood silently as we watched her walk over to her father. The businessmen shook hands, and as the gentleman and his daughter exited the shop, Chéri looked back over at Chris and smiled as they went on their way. Slowly, he exhaled; he was still in a state of shock.

On April 21, *The Ballantine* was ready to sail to Liverpool. It was fully loaded with sugar and cotton, and two pilot boats were called to guide the vessel back down the Mississippi River to La Balize. On the evening before sailing, Dieter and a few of his shipmates met with Chris and Charles at Prise de la Bastille – a local tavern near the waterfront. It was a lively crowd, and after nearly six weeks in port, many of the sailors were anxious to return to the sea.

Dieter put down his ale and asked, "So, Charles, have you made a decision yet? You know we're sailing tomorrow, and if you're coming with us, you have to be on the dock at sunrise."

Chris looked perplexed and turned to Charles. "No. You're not thinking of staying on board are you?"

Sheepishly Charles replied, "I'm still thinking about it."

"Why on earth would you want to sail back to Liverpool?"

"Well, I'd have a job, and I like the crew. I'm almost seventeen; I can make my own decisions."

Chris just shook his head. "It's a bad idea. We came all this way to see America and begin our lives over here. With such a mark on your hand, you'll not be welcomed back on the continent. You know that, right?"

But Charles was insistent, and he gave many other reasons for staying aboard the ship. What's more, Dieter agreed with Charles. "Chris, let the boy go. It's a good life, and we'll be back here someday soon – probably next winter. I'll look after the boy; he'll be okay."

Although the conversation continued for another hour or so, in the end, Chris eventually convinced Charles to remain in New Orleans on the condition that when the ship came back to Louisiana, and should Charles decide to rejoin the crew, Chris would agree to let Charles go.

After one last beer and many hugs and wishes for 'fair winds and following seas,' the crew was off to the ship, and the brothers were off to their beds. In the end, Charles made the correct decision.

As the months passed, Chris and Chéri began seeing each other more often. When he was not working in the shop, he was constructing walls, installing floors, and hanging ceilings at the site on Rue Bourbon. A competitor, *Antoine's*, had opened by Antoine Alciatore the prior year around the corner.

By the end of June, the restaurant was ready to open and serve the public. The facility, named *François'*, consisted of two large rooms downstairs. The main entrance off of Rue Bourbon lead into a ten table dining room, and a small kitchen was constructed at the back of the structure. Moreover, the second floor housed the living quarters of the owner, Monsieur François Bastogne, his son René, and of course, his daughter, Chéri.

The family planned a grand opening lasting for two-weeks. After the last coating of paint dried on the front of the restaurant, Chris and René suspended an enormous banner across the façade with a message which combined the opening of the restaurant with the Nation's 4th of July celebration and the French national celebration called 'The Festival of the Federation' on July 14th.

The banner read:

> *Célébration de l'inauguration - 1er au 14 Juillet.*
> *Venez célébrer le jour de l'indépendance Américaine et le Fête de la Fédération*
> *Tout le monde est bienvenu!*

On opening night, Chéri acted as the hostess and waitress while Monsieur Bastogne and René were the cooks. After work, Chris assisted them by doing the dishes, busing the tables, and helping out wherever he could. Often Charles would help, too. Furthermore, Monsieur Bastogne's lone slave, Marcel, also worked in the kitchen when not standing outside the restaurant and holding a sign advertising the facility.

The menu consisted mostly of Creole cooking with strong French traditions, and it offered wines imported from France. After a slow start, the restaurant soon became a robust business enterprise.

One evening in September, Chris sat at a table in the restaurant sipping a cup of coffee while reading a copy of *The Picayune*. After a busy day in the shop constructing tables for a business office in Metairie and then working at *François'* washing dishes and clearing tables, he needed to rest before walking home to his boarding house on Rue Chartres.

The headline on the front page of the newspaper read:

PRESIDENT TYLER VETOES SECOND BANK OF U.S. LEGISLATION

He swiftly scanned through the story and then read another one about Frederick Douglass who had been speaking before the Anti-Slavery Convention in Boston. Turning the pages, Chris saw an item about the coronation ceremony for the new emperor in Rio de Janeiro, Brazil. Suddenly, an article near the bottom of the page caught his eye.

THE BALLANTINE LIKELY SINKS IN NORTH ATLANTIC ALL ON-BOARD FEARED LOST

The frigate, *Ballantine*, carrying a crew of 42 officers and a cargo of sugar and cotton left New Orleans on April 21 and was last spotted in St. Augustine in mid-May. The ship was due to arrive in Liverpool in mid-July but has not been seen since departing the Territory of Florida. The vessel had made many trips to our city and was expected to be back later this year. The De Felice Company and the Reutters Brothers have each filed insurance claims.

Chris exclaimed: "Oh my God!"

Chéri put down the broom and rapidly rushed over to him "*Amant, qu'est-ce qui ne va pas?*"

He looked up at her in a state of disbelief. "*The Ballantine* has probably sunk, darling. Oh, no, poor Dieter and all of the others perished. This is terrible!"

She kissed him on the forehead as she sat down next to him and glanced at the article in the newspaper.

"Is it true?"

"I don't know, but that's what the newspaper is reporting. Good Lord, I'm so glad Charles wasn't on the ship. It must have been horrible for them. I can't believe it."

Chris and Chéri talked about the disaster for the next hour. He told her all about his memories of the ship, and during a couple of the storms, how he had feared that *The Ballantine* would flounder. Chéri said she didn't remember much about her crossing from Marseilles except for the fact that her mother had died during the journey to New World.

He said, "I don't know how to tell Charles. He was much closer to many of the sailors that I was. He'll take it very hard."

Chéri held his hand as he talked. They were devoted to each other, and Chris wondered whether he would marry her someday. He loved everything about her: her smile; her gentle touch; even her French accent. Chris thought she sounded more feminine.

In turn, she liked his German accent, too; she thought he seemed more masculine. Her father – while initially having severe misgivings about Chris due to his ancestry – had come to respect and admire Chris, as did René. Chris felt welcome in her family's home.

Because Chris and Chéri were both Roman Catholics, each of them knew some things must wait for marriage. Nevertheless, they kissed frequently, held each other's hands, and were often quite affectionate – especially when out of her father's sight.

They attended St. Louis Cathedral together on Sunday mornings. Chris had learned that three churches had stood on the site on the town square since 1718 when the city was founded. The first church had been a crude wooden structure. Construction of more substantial brick and timber church was begun in 1725 and was finished in 1727.

Along with numerous other buildings in the general vicinity, the church was destroyed by fire on Good Friday, March 21, 1788. The cornerstone of a new building was laid in 1789, and the present church was completed in 1794. In 1819, a central tower with the clock and bell was added. It was a magnificent building – inside and out.

The following Sunday morning after Mass, Charles, Chris, and Chéri lit candles for Captain Worthington and the gallant crew. Although she never met any of the members of the sailors on *The Ballantine*, she had tears in her eyes as she whispered "*Reposez en paix, mes amis.*"

Chris responded "Yes, rest in peace, my friends. Rest in peace."

During the candle lighting, Charles couldn't contain himself and ran out of St. Louis Cathedral crying heavily.

After a long, hot, and humid summer, the weather abruptly changed for the better in mid-October. Luckily, there had not been any hurricanes striking New Orleans that summer, but everyone knew fierce storms were still possible along the Louisiana coast until the end of November.

On one Sunday afternoon, Mr. and Mrs. Klein invited Chéri, René, Charles, and Chris out to dinner at their home with the sole condition that René would agree to prepare a lovely French meal.

About five o'clock that afternoon, Mr. Klein sent his servant, Enoch, and a carriage to pick up the guests and carry them from their homes in downtown New Orleans to the Klein residence on St. Charles Avenue. Enoch first picked up the brothers on Rue Chartres and then rode a few blocks to pick up Chéri and René on Rue Bourbon.

Stepping out the door to the 'closed on Sunday' restaurant, she looked magnificent wearing a lovely azure blue gown and bonnet to match. She wore her dress off the shoulder, and it featured wide lace flounces which reached to her elbows.

She also wore a sheer shawl and white gloves and carried a white satin and embroidered bag. Her shoes were made out of the same material as the handbag, and they were tied around the ankles with a silk ribbon. Also, she had a small brimless bonnet with a ribbon left untied at the nape of her neck. After assisting her into the waiting carriage, Chris couldn't keep his eyes or his hands off of her for long.

Driving slowly down St. Charles Avenue under a canopy of Live Oak trees and palms, the road curved to the right as it followed the crescent of the Mississippi River. The Klein house was most impressive. Built of red brick with white wood trim just a few years earlier, the three-story monolith had twelve thirty-foot tall Corinthian columns and a large open portico with an encased wrought-iron Spanish balcony which stood just below the curved lintel. It was truly magnificent.

Mr. and Mrs. Klein were standing on the top step as the carriage drove up the circular driveway and stop at the base of the steps. "Welcome to our home. We've picked a beautiful day, haven't we?"

Mr. Klein walked down the stairs and stood waiting as Enoch opened the door and helped the passengers out of the carriage.

Chris said, "Thanks for inviting us, Mr. Klein. The carriage is a much nicer way to travel."

Mr. Klein had met Chéri and Charles before, and after he was introduced to René, Mr. Klein introduced their guests to his wife, Rachel. He opened the front door, and the guests entered the house.

The entrance hall was made of polished slate, and a large chandelier hung down from the ceiling of the second floor. Just inside the entrance hall, several tall floor-to-ceiling windows faced the street side of the home, and a spectacular circular staircase, ascending seemingly without any support, went up to the second floor. To the left of the entrance hall stood a paneled study, and a large dining room with another chandelier was located on the right side.

The guests were quickly ushered to back portion of the home and into a large oak paneled living room. A large sitting porch went off the end of the living room. The floors, aside from the kitchen and entrance hall, were made from solid oak.

In the dining room, an oval table, matching the shape of the room, was made of polished mahogany, and it had four animal-paw feet and six leaves. The other furniture in the dining room included, among others, fourteen arm-chairs in the French Restoration style. It was an impressive room.

The guests were offered mint juleps followed by a meal prepared, in large part by, René. He called the main course '*canard orange à la sauce aux prunes*' followed by 'pêche *Melba et sauce à la crème.*'

As coffee was being served at the conclusion of the meal, Mr. Klein commented, "That's what I call a lovely dinner. René, you'll have to teach Mathilda to prepare some of those dishes. They were delicious. So, where did you learn to cook?"

"I have been cooking all of my life; it's a passion for me. I'm glad you enjoyed it, Sir, and I'll be most pleased to have her come to my restaurant at any time to learn more about French cooking. It would be my pleasure."

"Well, it was marvelous. As the ladies retire to the parlor for a glass of sherry, how about the men joining me in my study for cigars and a glass of port – unless you'd rather play another game of billiards, Charles?"

Charles and René decided to play billiards in the game room as Chris and Mr. Klein retreated to the study.

Mr. Klein's study was lined with shelves crammed with books, and a large mahogany folding-top desk stood against the far wall. Two overly-stuffed leather easy-chairs filled up much of the remaining usable space. Looking through a front window curtain, Chris could see the end of a lovely sunset.

A few moments later, Mr. Klein offered Chris a glass of port and a Cuban cigar. "Well, Chris, Chéri is lovelier every time I see her. When are you going to marry that girl before somebody else woos her away from you?"

"She is lovely, isn't she? And I do like her family very much, but I believe it's too soon to think about marriage. We've known each other barely six months."

"Sometimes, all you need is a few days – or perhaps, mere hours – to make that decision. You know, I fell in love with Miriam the first instance I saw her in Biloxi some twelve short years ago. It didn't take me more than a couple of minutes to decide to marry her."

Chris nodded and smiled.

A short time later, Enoch came in as asked if there is anything more which the men required.

"Thank you, Enoch; we're fine."

With that, Enoch bowed and softly closed the doors to the study.

Mr. Klein took a long draught off his cigar and said, "Enoch is a fine man. He and Mathilda have worked for me a long time. I purchased them about ten years ago, and they have served me quite well. Last year, I manumitted them, and they now work for me and live together in the small cottage behind the house."

"That's nice, Sir."

"Thanks, I care for them very much. Although Louisiana does not recognize – or even permits – Negroes to marry, they were joined together many years ago by a Negro preacher. They have three children who are slaves and work on plantations somewhere in either Mississippi or Alabama. I've tried to find them but so far to no avail. You know, I've grown to detest the institution of slavery."

The two men sat quietly for a few moments, and then Chris asked, "I can't understand how Southerners can justify slavery. What exactly is the Southern argument to permit such an atrocity?"

Mr. Klein tasted the sherry and responded, "You know, they give lots of reasons, including economic, historical, religious, legal, social well-being, and even humanitarianism explanations. In my judgment, they seem to spend a lot of time attempting to justify an unjustifiable tenement of Southern culture."

Chris just shook his head. "Tell me more, please. What are these arguments precisely, Sir?"

"Well, first of all, the defenders of slavery argue that servitude is the foundation of the Southern economy, and they argue a sudden end to slavery would have had a profound and killing economic impact in the South. They maintain that the cotton economy would collapse; the tobacco crops would dry in the fields; and sugar would cease being profitable."

"Yeah, I understand the economic argument – slave labor makes plantations more profitable, but it doesn't make it right."

Mr. Klein smiled and nodded, "And then there's the religious argument. The proponents emphasize that in the Bible, Abraham had slaves and God was fine with this practice. They also point to the Ten Commandments, noting the mandate, 'Thou shalt not covet thy neighbor's house, nor his manservant, nor his maidservant.' They argue that this commandant condones servitude."

"That's almost unbelievable, Sir."

"I know – but they seem to believe it. Finally, the slavers point to the New Testament where the Apostle Paul returned a runaway slave – named Philemon, I recall – to his master. To their way of thinking, Paul has thus endorsed the institution of slavery. Of course, they mention Jesus never spoke out against it."

Mr. Klein got out of his chair and walked a couple of steps to a bookshelf. Looking for a moment, he picked out a book and sat down again.

"This book contains their religious justifications." He handed it to Chris. It was entitled *Southern Slavery and the Bible – A Scriptural Refutation of the Principal Argument upon which the Abolitionists Rely,* by Nellie Norton.

"Take it home and read it carefully, Chris. This book is precisely what the good, holy Christian ministers preach on Sunday morning from almost every pulpit in every church in the south."

"Thanks, I will."

Klein took another puff on his cigar. "Then, of course, there are the historical reasons; they argue slavery has existed throughout history and it's the natural state of humanity. They point out that the ancient Greeks had slaves, the Romans had slaves, and even the English had slavery until recently. To them, slavery is merely a part of the normal flow of commerce."

"Unfortunately, that's true, I guess."

Mr. Klein stood up and poured himself and Chris another glass of port. "They also have the 'Oh my God' argument."

"The 'oh my God' argument, Sir?"

"Yes, they maintain that if all the slaves were freed, then, 'oh my God,' there would be widespread unemployment and chaos. Wholesale freedom would also lead to, 'oh my God,' uprisings, bloodshed, and anarchy. They point to the mob's 'rule of terror' during the French Revolution, and they argue for the continuation of the status quo, which provides for affluence and stability for the slaveholding class and for all free people of this country who enjoyed the bounty of the slave society."

"Wow."

"Finally, there's 'the Divine Plan' argument."

"Huh, 'the Devine Plan' argument?"

"Yes, the proponents contend the tradition of slavery has brought Christianity to 'the heathens from across the ocean.' Slavery is, according to their argument, a good thing for the enslaved. Let me read to you what former Vice President John C. Calhoun has said recently."

Picking up the book, Mr. Klein read, "Calhoun said, 'Never before has the black race of Central Africa, from the dawn of history to the present day, attained a condition so civilized and so improved, not only physically, but morally and intellectually.' Yes, there's yet another justification."

"Well, I guess anything can be justified, I guess."

"Yes, and legally, slaves have no legal standing 'as persons' in our courts. They are considered property, and our Constitution protects the slave-holders' rights to do with their property as their masters see fit. Finally — and perhaps the most egregious reason — most slaveholders believe Negroes are biologically inferior to their masters. You know, everyone's a king when they have somebody to look down on."

Soon, winter was approaching. Monsieur Deveraux had plenty of business in the carpentry shop, and Charles began working alongside Chris on a full-time basis beginning in late September. With everything going so well, he started to think about whether he should stay in New Orleans beyond May 1 when his commitment was over; François' was a commercial success, and Chris was spending much of his off-hours at the restaurant with Chéri.

On Christmas Day, Chéri, René, Monsieur Bastogne, Charles, and Chris went to Mass at St. Louis Cathedral, and during the offertory, the choir and people sang 'Silent Night' in French:

Douce nuit, sainte nuit !
Dans les cieux ! L'astre luit.
Le mystère annoncé s'accomplit
Cet enfant sur la paille endormi,
C'est l'amour infini !
C'est l'amour infini !

Saint enfant, doux agneau !
Qu'il est grand! Qu'il est beau!
Entendez résonner les pipeaux
Des bergers conduisant leurs troupeaux
Vers son humble berceau !
Vers son humble berceau !

Halfway through the first verse, Chris began singing the hymn in German.

Chéri looked up at him, nudged him with her elbow, and whispered, "Christopher, we are not in Bavaria."

He smiled and replied, "This isn't France either, my love."

She winked, kissed him gently on the cheek, and said, "It's not?"

Then she laughed and won his heart all over again.

That evening, René cooked a traditional French Christmas dinner for the five of them at the restaurant, consisting offerings of oysters (*les huîtres*), snails (les escargots), and caviar as starters, followed by a roasted goose (*oie rôtie*) and all the trimmings for the main course.

Almost unexpectedly, *Père Noël* – also known as Father Christmas – arrived just in time for dessert.

A few days later, Chris received a letter from his father.

December 4, 1841

Today is St. Barbara's Day, and it has been almost two years since you left Trockau. Soon it will be Christmas Day. I hope you are well. We have enjoyed reading your letters, telling us all about America. It must be an exciting time for you, my sons.

Also, I have read where Charles was smitten by an Irish girl, and now Christopher by a French girl. We have learned from the newspapers that so many German people are immigrating to America.

Aren't there any suitable German girls in New Orleans? My sons, I believe it is best if each of you finds a wife who is both German and Catholic. It will make things so much easier for you.

We also read in the newspapers that your city has been experiencing massive outbreaks of Yellow Fever, and last year there were over 500 deaths. I hope that once your year is completed with Monsieur Deveraux, you decide to move north to St. Louis where the climate seems to be much better. I know my cousin, Christopher Bauer, will help you get settled there.

Anna Maria and Domonic's daughter, Margaretha, is almost six months old now. It is such a delight to have two young children back in our home. All of us still dearly miss your mother and grandparents, but I am sure Anna Maria will make this Christmas very festive for all of us once again. She reminds me so much of your mother.

Johann is becoming a skilled cabinetmaker, and Georg is speedily learning the craft. Business continues to be good as Duke Joseph always has plenty of orders for us to fill.

The previous political matter in Bayreuth has quieted down, and it appears King Ludwig is keeping his word to restore Catholicism to our divided country. We all pray for peace, especially during this time of the year.

All of us wish you, my beloved sons, a Happy Christmas. I still plan to sing at Midnight Mass - perhaps for the last time, though.

May the Good Lord continue to watch over you and keep you safe.

The family sends you their love,

Papa

As the weeks and months passed, Chris continued to consider his options. His second cousin, Christopher Bauer, wrote to tell the brothers that they were welcome to come to St. Louis in the springtime when Chris' year was over. He knew, however, that any future which he would plan must include Chéri, and if she wouldn't leave her father, he'd probably remain in New Orleans – at least for a while longer.

Charles, however, was anxious to move on.

On February 13th, Chris escorted her to *Antoine's* to celebrate her twenty-first birthday, and soon Easter was upon them. They attended Mass at St. Louis Cathedral and enjoyed another excellent holiday dinner at *François'* with the family. This time, the Kleins attended along with their children at a large table and they were seated in the center of the restaurant. Monsieur Bastogne also set up a smaller table in the back of the restaurant for Enoch, Mathilda, and Marcel.

The winter of 1841-1842 had been an unusually warm and wet one in New Orleans, and the outbreak began at the end of April, which was remarkably early for a yellow fever epidemic. In fact, the return of yellow fever caused general disbelief in the community regarding the prevalence of the disease, an event well documented in *The Picayune*. The newspaper wrote that most merchants essentially ignored the presence of the fever for fear of a loss of business and many ordinary citizens failed to take the necessary precautions.

The Picayune also reported there are three stages of the disease process. During the first part, several different symptoms begin and grow in severity over the space of a couple of days. These symptoms include: a severe headache, chills alternating with hot flashes, bruised pain in the loins and lower limbs, discomfort in the epigastric region along with nausea, vomiting, delirium, a fast pulse, a white tongue (which is furred at center and appeared to bright red along the edges), a dry mouth, dry breathing, and of course, fatigue.

In the second phase, the newspaper stated these symptoms become more severe along with some new signs arising, such as vomiting, black stools, nosebleeds, intense stomach pains, terrible headaches, a periodic loss of consciousness, and the condition were the skin and the eyes turn a betraying 'yellow.'

The third phase includes a total suppression of urine and, after that occurs, death is relatively sure to follow.

In 1842, the most common treatments for yellow fever were bloodletting, and after that, inserting a tonic into the lower bowel to encourage the patients to purge themselves. Other therapies which were utilized during such an epidemic included asking the patients to soak their feet in mustard, to inject themselves with a sugar-based vaccine, and to drink 'heroic' doses of quinine.

On successive days, Charles and later Chéri began to show the telltale signs of the disorder. Finding himself in a state of constant panic, Chris was continually running back between his rooming house on Rue Chartres to care for Charles and Chéri's home situated above the restaurant.

Physicians were called to both residences, and all of the available treatments were tried – but without much success. Each doctor noted that there was very little medicine could do to help their patients, and any recovery would be primarily in God's hands.

While Charles appeared to be getting somewhat better as the days passed, Chéri's condition was growing more worrisome. On May 8, Chris walked over to the restaurant to see her. Her father looked ashen as he answered the door to their upstairs home.

"How's she doing, Sir?"

"The doctor is with her now, and he's not encouraged. We may lose her, Chris."

A short time later, Dr. Duvalier walked out of her bedroom shaking his head. "You can see her now – but only for a few moments. She needs her rest, Chris."

He nodded and went into Chéri's bedroom. She was laying on her back and seemed to be asleep. Her complexion was both yellow and pale at the same time. He knelt by her bedside, and as he took her hand, she opened her eyes.

"Christopher, is it you?"

"Yes, darling, it's me."

"How is Charles, my love?"

"Better; yes, he's better."

She closed her eyes and began breathing deeply – as if she was having difficulty getting air into her lungs.

She opened her eyes again and said, "Christopher, I am so afraid. Please don't let me die."

His heart was breaking. "I won't let anything happen to you. I promise."

"My love, I'm so afraid of dying. I only want to be with you."

He squeezed her hand. "Chéri, will you marry me?"

She smiled. "Yes, my darling. I've waited so long for you to ask me. Yes, I will marry you, Christopher."

He kissed her, and they talked for a little while, but soon Dr. Duvalier came back into the room. "Chris, she needs her rest."

He nodded and said, "Darling, I need to check on Charles. I'll be back very soon, my love."

He got up and kissed her softly on her cheek again, and said, "*Au revoir.*"

She smiled. "*Au revoir mon amour. Reviens bientôt.*"

Chris had tears in his eyes as he left her bedside. Her father patted him on the back as Chris left the apartment and strolled back to check in on Charles. Chris had a heavy heart.

Charles was sitting up in bed when Chris arrived. His fever had broken, and he was hungry.

"How's Chéri?"

"Not well; the doctor is with her now. Father Gaston gave her the last rites this morning."

Chris was sobbing as he helped his brother change his bed-clothes – they were wet with sweat – and he gave his brother some bread, cheese, and water. After making sure Charles had all that he needed for the next couple of hours, Chris walked back to Rue Bourbon and up the stairs to the apartment. Then he saw it; a black veil was hung across the front door.

He slowly opened the door and entered the apartment; René and his father were crying. "*Chéri est morte; elle avec les anges maintenant.*"

Chris put his hand over his mouth and gave out a sound which came from somewhere deep inside himself; a sound he had never heard before. "Oh, no; no; not my Chéri; no."

He stared at her father and brother; how did this happen in the short time he was away with Charles? A few moments later, he asked if he could go in and see her one more time, and René nodded affirmatively and opened the door.

When Chris entered the room, she was laying on her bed with the sheet pulled over her face. He knelt by her bedside and began praying for the repose of her soul. Then Chris stood up and leaned over the bed, and removed the sheet from her face. Chéri looked so peaceful – as if she was sound asleep – and he leaned over and kissed her softly on her cheek.

Upon sitting down on the side of her bed, he began telling her about all of his plans which he had for their future: their children; their names; their lives together; their home; and all of the places they would see. Tears were running down his face as he explained these plans over again in great detail.

Soon her father knocked on the door and came back into the room. "Chris, it's time for you to help Charles. Say goodbye to Chéri now. She's no longer here; she's with her mother in heaven. She'll never feel any pain again."

Chris stood up, leaned over her, kissed her once more, and gently pulled the sheet back over her face.

"*Au revoir, mon amour*; until we meet again in heaven."

Three days later, Chéri's funeral was held in St. Louis Cathedral – along with the funerals of seventeen other victims of yellow fever. What once had been a sanctuary of joy and celebration for Chris – attending Mass on Christmas Day, Easter Sunday, feast days, and regular Sundays – had become a place of grief and sorrow.

The Requiem Mass was recited in Latin, but the benediction was said in French – much of which he did not understand. Toward the end of the service, Father Gaston read a passage from *Isiah 56, 8-12*. Chris quickly found the translation in his Bible. It read:

For my thoughts are not your thoughts,

Neither are your ways, my ways, declares the LORD.

For as the heavens are higher than the earth,

So are my ways higher than your ways

And my thoughts higher than your thoughts.

For just as the rain and the snow come down from heaven

And does not return there but waters the earth,

Making it bring forth and sprout,

Giving seed to the sower and bread to the eater,

So shall my word be which comes out of my mouth;

It shall not return to me empty,

But it shall accomplish that which I purpose,

And it shall succeed in the thing for which I had sent it.

Reflecting on this passage, he took some comfort.

After Mass, Chéri's internment occurred in the St. Louis Cemetery on Basin Street. Several years earlier, Monsieur Bastogne had constructed a memorial crypt on a lot in the cemetery for his wife who had died at sea during their crossing to America. He also expected to be buried there one day. Chéri was entombed into one of the four vaults – next to the one memorializing her mother who had been interred at sea.

As the ceremony ended, Chris picked up one of the roses which had draped her coffin and stuck it to his lapel. He would later place pedals from the rose in his Bible where they'd remain for the rest of his life.

Charles – who was feeling much stronger – walked with René from the cemetery to the restaurant for a brief reception. Chris and François followed behind them at a short distance.

"I had hoped you would marry my daughter one day and give me many grandchildren. Now that will never happen."

Chris patted Monsieur Bastogne softly on his shoulder and replied, "Well, you'll get grandchildren from René, I'm certain."

Monsieur Bastogne stopped walking and looked at Chris. "I'm afraid not; I question . . . how do you say it in English . . . his *virilité,* his *masculinité* . . . his manliness, I guess. No, I don't think I'll ever have any grandchildren now." He had a sorrowful look in his eyes.

As Chris and Charles walked back to their rooming house on Rue Chartres after the reception, they made the joint decision to leave New Orleans as soon as possible.

After giving their fond farewells to the Kleins, Monsieur Deveraux, Monsieur Bastogne, and René, the two brothers picked up their brown leather chest and carried it down to the waterfront. Along with many others who were attempting to escape the yellow fever epidemic, the brothers boarded *The Mississippi Queen,* bound for St. Louis.

At approximately 10:30 AM, the whistle blew announcing the immediate departure of the paddlewheel steamer. Chris and Charles stood silently at the railing on the second deck and watched as the slaves began untying the ropes securing *The Mississippi Queen* to the pier.

While looking at the city that the brothers had called home for the last fourteen months, Chris started swatting at the pesky mosquitoes who were buzzing his head. As he watched St. Louis Cathedral pass before him, he suddenly could not control himself any longer, and he began cursing and swatting at the mosquitoes with the morning edition of *The Picayune*.

He screamed, "You bastards; you fucking bastards!" and in a fit of rage, he started attacking the mosquitoes with a ferocity which shocked Charles and began frightening the other passengers.

Soon his brother grabbed Chris and put his arms around him saying, "Stop, please stop; we need to sit down. You need to control yourself; killing mosquitoes won't bring Chéri back."

As Chris regained control of himself, Charles helped his brother into the covered passengers' section and sat him down in a corner on a bench.

A few moments later, he said, "You know she's in the newspaper today."

Charles replied, "Who? What?"

"Chéri; she is listed as one of the recent dead."

Chris opened *The Picayune* and read, "Mademoiselle Marie Eugenia Bastogne, age 21."

Chris stopped for an instant and then resumed, saying, "You know, brother, I never even knew her middle name."

By July 1, there were over five-hundred deaths from yellow fever in the City of New Orleans. So many people died during this scourge that it became difficult to bury the dead appropriately; the infected citizens died quicker than graves could be provided. During the epidemic that year, City officials would often fire cannons or burn tar 'to purify the air.' Very little succeeded, however, to stem the progress of the disease.

The Picayune later reported the City Council adjourned during this crisis from July to October, leaving the city virtually without a government. A staff reporter also wrote:

> In this chaotic environment, one person described the entire city as functioning as a hospital, with every able-bodied person assisting the sick.

Charles and Chris would never return to New Orleans again.

CHAPTER ELEVEN

Saint Louis, Missouri, February 1844

Chris yawned as the front door opened and a customer walked into 'Bauer Mercantile.' The brothers had been living in St. Louis for over two years while working in their first cousin's general merchandise store. Aside from working behind the counter, the brothers had started a small business making furniture and performing carpentry work around town. By February 1844, New Orleans was just a dim memory for them.

The customer looked around the store and soon walked up to Chris.

"I'm looking for some lumber. Can you help me, please?"

As the customer continued talking in German, Chris believed he recognized his accent.

"Are you originally from Bavaria, Sir?"

The customer responded, "Why, yes; I'm from Hintergereuth. It's a little village which is located about twenty miles southwest of Bayreuth. Why do you ask?"

Chris smiled. "Well, my family is from Trockau. We're neighbors! Before coming to America, I spent several months working in Bayreuth."

The two men stared at each for a moment and then shook hands. The customer said, "My name is Johannes Zeilmann. It's a pleasure to meet a fellow countryman."

"I'm Christopher Bogner. Where do you live now, Herr Zeilmann?"

"My family and I live in a little village called Rich Fountain. It's situated about one hundred miles west of here. We came into town this morning on the railroad to buy supplies and see family. How about you?"

Chris smiled and replied, "My brother Charles and I have been here in St. Louis for almost three years now." Chris told Herr Zeilmann a little about their adventures when coming to America.

Finally, Chris asked, "How about you? How long have you been in this country?"

"Well, my family and I left Bremen on a ship called *The Apollo,* and we arrived in Baltimore after sixty-five brutal days at sea on November 2, 1838 – I remember the day quite well."

Chris replied, "How can anyone ever forget our journeys across the ocean?"

"Yes, I never will. Then we rode *The Baltimore & Ohio Railway* as far as Harpers Ferry, Virginia, which was as far as the line went at that time. After that, we rode on a clumsy freight wagon west to Pittsburgh, and finally, on a riverboat for the rest of the way to St. Louis. We have family here in town whom we're visiting right now. How about you?"

"My brother, Charles, and I are living with my uncle, Christopher Bauer, in a house just around the corner. He owns this business; he's also from Trockau. We've been here about four years now."

Herr Zeilmann smiled. "You know, Herr Bogner, I'd been to Trockau a couple of times several years ago. I distinctly remember the castle and the church; it's called St. Boniface, as I recall."

Chris nodded, and he told him a little about his family in Trockau, including his father's cabinetmaking shop.

Herr Zeilmann replied, "I've been there, and I may have met your father. It's a small world, isn't it?"

The two men talked for another fifteen minutes or so when Herr Zeilmann said, "One of the other reasons we're in town today now is because my oldest daughter will be singing after Mass in the Old Cathedral. She and serval others will be staging a recital in the parish hall at 2 PM on Sunday afternoon. I believe she'll be singing three songs."

"I see."

"Why don't you come, listen to the performance, and meet my family? They'll be delighted to meet a former neighbor. After that, we'll be having supper at my uncle's home. You can join us there, too. What do say?"

Chris smiled and accepted the invitation.

The city of St. Louis was founded in 1764 by two French fur traders, Pierre Laclède and Auguste Chouteau. They named the new settlement after King Louis IX of France. In 1764, following France's defeat in the Seven Years' War, the area was ceded to Spain and later retroceded back to France in 1800. In 1803, the United States acquired the territory as part of the Louisiana Purchase.

In 1804, St. Louis became the capital of the Louisiana Territory, and the city had a population of fewer than 3,000 people. By 1844, St. Louis' population had grown to approximately 36,000 inhabitants making it the second largest city west of Pittsburgh. With this massive surge in population, Bauer Mercantile (which had been founded in 1819) was a doing a booming business.

On Sunday afternoon, Chris walked the short distance from the Bauer home to the 'Basilica of St. Louis, King of France,' commonly known at the time as the 'Old Cathedral.' The church was the first Roman Catholic Church to be founded in St. Louis. From 1826 to 1843, the St. Louis Diocese, headquartered in the Old Cathedral, covered nearly half of America – from Louisiana north to Michigan and from Kentucky west to Oregon. It was also the sanctuary where the two brothers and the Bauer family worshipped on every Sunday.

Chris found a chair near the rear of the Parish Hall and politely listened to the first three young performers sing in front of the mostly empty building. He had earlier observed Herr Zeilmann and his family sitting in the front row.

After the host called her name, Margaretha Zeilmann got up from the chair next to her father and slowly walked on to the stage. She was a pretty girl, with long flowing brown hair tied loosely in a ponytail behind her back, and she was dressed in a red and white floor-length dress.

After nodding to the nun playing the piano off to her right, Margaretha began singing a traditional Catholic hymn entitled "O God of Loveliness" followed by "Out of the Depths" – a song written by Martin Luther. Chris was astonished at the young girl's presentation and the tonal quality of her voice. She was one of the better sopranos whom he'd ever heard, and her stage presence resembled the composure of one who was much older than a girl of thirteen years.

After she finished her second song, she looked up at the audience and said, "Now I wish to sing a song which probably originated with Canadian and American fur traders traveling down the Missouri River in canoes. It's called "Across the Wide Missouri."

She nodded again to the pianist who played a short introduction, and then Margaretha began singing:

The Missouri is
A mighty water.
Away, you rolling river.
The Redskins' camp
Lies on its borders.
Away, I'm bound away,
'Cross the wide Missouri.

Oh, Shenandoah,
I love your daughter,
Away, you rolling river.
For her, I'd cross
Your roaring waters.
Away, I'm bound away
'Cross the wide Missouri.

Oh, Shenandoah,
I long to hear you.
Away, you rolling river.
Oh, Shenandoah,
I long to see you.
Away, I'm bound away
'Cross the wide Missouri.

As she finished the last verse, Chris and the other members of the audience gave the young girl a standing ovation. Chris, like several others in attendance, had tears in his eyes.

After the last performers had finished their recitals, Herr Zeilmann stood up and motioned for Chris to walk down and join them at the front of the hall.

After shaking hands with him, Herr Zeilmann turned to his wife and said, "My Darling, this is the man I've told you about from Trockau, Christopher Bogner. Herr Bogner, may I introduce you to my wife, Dorothea."

Chris accepted her outstretched hand and bowed, "Frau Zeilmann, it is, indeed, an honor to meet you."

"Likewise, Herr Bogner. I'm from Oberfranken, a little village not far from Hintergereuth. Do you know it?"

"Yes, I believe I've been there, madam."

Then Herr Zeilmann said, "Herr Bogner, permit me to introduce you to the rest of my brood. The young man over here is our oldest son, Johann, who is fourteen. Johann, please shake hands with Herr Bogner."

The young man extended his right hand and said, "Please call me John, Sir."

Herr Zeilmann retorted, "Ah, yes, my children wish to be known by their American names. So, Herr Bogner, this is John, and please meet our oldest daughter, Margaretha. She is thirteen and wishes to be called Margaret."

She curtsied, and Chris said, "Fräulein Zeilmann you have a lovely voice. Your last song brought me to tears. It was beautiful."

Then Herr Zeilmann introduced the rest of the family to Chris: Elias, who was age 11 and wished to be called Eli; Anna, who was age 6 and wanted to be referred to as Ann; and finally, Barbara, the youngest at age 4. She was known as Barbie.

"You have a lovely family, Herr Zeilmann, and Sir, please call me Chris."

"Okay, Chris it is, and please call me Johannes, and join us for supper at my uncle's home. He's expecting you."

The Heinrich Zeilmann home was a two-story wood frame house situated on Walnut Street — about four blocks from the Old Cathedral. The worst of winter was probably over for that season in St. Louis although a late February snowstorm was still a distinct possibility.

As Chris walked over to the Zeilmann home from the parish hall, he felt the sun warm his face, and all around him, he saw groupings of crocus — the first signs of spring in Eastern Missouri. Heinrich Zeilmann, Johannes' first cousin and their initial benefactor in America, welcomed Chris into his family's home, and after a short visit, they all sat down for a fried chicken supper.

Heinrich asked, "Chris, tell us about your journey to America."

He put down his fork and wondered to himself, "Where shall I begin?" He started by mentioning his family's business in Trockau and the events which took him and Charles to Bayreuth. He told them about working in the castle and their encounters with Viceroy Alfred Dressler — when Johannes stopped him.

"Did you say Viceroy Alfred Dressler?"

"Yes, do you know him?"

Johannes frowned. "Unfortunately, we do. He's the reason we left Bavaria. In essence, he confiscated our land."

Chris replied, "Tell me more. I despise that bastard. What he did to Charles was despicable."

"Well, for over a hundred years, my family lived on a small farm just outside of Hintergereuth. It wasn't much to the rich landlords in the area, but we were eking out a living nevertheless. Viceroy Dressler owned an adjacent property, and he wanted to purchase our farm and add it to his ever-growing estate."

"Wow. So what happened next?"

"When we declined his initial offer, Dressler sent over several soldiers who set fire to our barn and killed several heads of cattle. A few days later,

Dressler's representative made us a second offer – much lower than the first one – and he hinted that should we decline his generosity, there'd be further consequences."

"Couldn't you go to the constable?"

"No, apparently Dressler had the constable firmly in his back pocket. Even our parish priest wouldn't interfere; in fact, the priest told us to accept the offer and go to America."

Chris could tell Johannes was bitter about the events of the summer of 1838.

Then Johannes looked down at his food, shook his head. "A few days later, Dressler himself rode out to our farm with another contingent of soldiers. I met with him near my smoldering barn, and I rapidly accepted his 'generous offer.' There was little else for me to do; to oppose him would only cause more trouble. Then, he gave us two-weeks to vacate."

Johannes stopped for a moment, looked around the room, and then resumed, "Gratefully, my father had passed away nearly twenty years earlier – in 1818; he would have died beside his burning barn rather than accept the 'offer' to vacate."

Chris shook his head; he had heard a similar tale previously. A surge of disdain arose in him concerning the capriciousness of the powerful Bavarian nobility.

Then Johannes continued, "I still feel some shame in capitulating but, Chris, I had a wife and young family to protect. My mother – God bless her soul – was too frail to join us on our voyage to America. Instead, she went to live with Dorothea's sister in Oberfranken. Mama died there four years ago – a broken woman. But Chris, please finish your story; I believe I've already told you the rest of my sad tale."

Then Chris mentioned the riot in Bayreuth, Charles' branding, their escape to Ulm, and their long journey to Rotterdam. After that, he told them about the forty-six day sail to Philadelphia on The Ballantine, the period when the brothers worked for Monsieur Deveraux in New Orleans, and finally their ride up the river on The Mississippi Queen to St. Louis. By then, it was time for dessert. Chris, however, didn't mention Chéri; her memory was still too painful.

After dessert, the three men went into Heinrich's parlor for cigars and brandy. A few minutes later, Chris asked, "Tell me, Johannes, about Rich Fountain; how did you end up there?"

Johannes drew a deep draught off his cigar, twisted his head upward, and slowly exhaled the smoke. "Well, we arrived in St. Louis around Christmas, 1838, and Heinrich – although he's my uncle, he's only four years older than me, so I call him by his first name – graciously allowed us to stay here until we found a permanent place to live."

Johannes bowed at Heinrich who returned the gesture."After that, Heinrich also introduced me to a land agent who drove me westward in his buggy to look for land in the vicinity around Rich Fountain. Eventually, we purchased a forty-acre tract where we now reside. In some ways, it's much better here in Missouri; in other ways, I deeply miss Bavaria."

"What's it's like in Rich Fountain?"

"Oh, it's barely a community at all; maybe one-hundred people live there. It's an unincorporated community in Osage County, and it lies about fifteen miles southeast of Jefferson City. Our little town had its start in about 1838 when our friend and neighbor, John Strumpf, built a gristmill there. He told me he named the village for a spring that flows near his mill."

"Are there any Indians still in your area?"

"Not many now" Johannes chuckled. "In 1828, Andy Jackson expelled them – primarily the Osage and Missouria people. I guess a few of them still hide in the hills, and I've seen a couple of them near the mill. But they seem pretty harmless to me."

"So, how big is the actual town?"

"Well, we have a general store, a livery stable, a post office, and a church – it's called 'Sacred Heart.' That's about it. As I said, it's pretty small. The church was started about five years ago by our priest, Father Ferdinand Helias d'Huddeghem; he's from Belgium. I guess most of us who live in Rich Fountain are Catholics sprinkled in with a few Lutherans; almost all of us are Germans, though. Why do you ask, Chris?"

"I might want to try my hand at farming someday. Papa always had a large garden behind the shop, and as a kid, I'd often work for one of my uncles who had a farm just outside of Trockau. I like getting my hands dirty."

Johannes smiled. "Why don't you come visit us in the spring? I'd love to show you around. Maybe you'd like it there, and we could always use a carpenter in town."

Chris nodded. "Thanks, I'd like that very much."

Soon, it was time for him to go home. The Bauer's lived on Spruce Street; only six blocks away from the Zeilmann home. On his way out, he thanked his hosts and told Margaret again how much he enjoyed her recital. She blushed and said to Chris that she'd love to sing for him sometime. Little did he know then that one day she would be his bride.

In late February, the brothers received a letter from Trockau; it was from their brother, Johann.

> *January 20, 1844*
>
> *It is my sad duty to inform you that Papa died peacefully on January 17. In his last days, he mentioned each of you on several occasions with great love and affection.*
>
> *We began noticing a slight difference in Papa starting in September when he tired quicker, and he seemed to have some difficulty with his memory. He had been working on a standup chest for Duke Gottingen - it may be Papa's finest work. Shortly after he finished the piece around St. Barbara's Day, he suffered what we assumed to be a slight stroke. After a short while, however, he seemed to be getting better. That's why he didn't mention it in the Christmas letter.*
>
> *But for the first time in nearly thirty years, Papa decided not to sing at Midnight Mass, and in early January, he experienced a series of more severe strokes; the latter one proved to be fatal. He died three days ago in his bed with the family around him.*

Yesterday, Father Gerhard said a Requiem Mass for Papa at St. Boniface's, and the entire town attended it. Duke Gottingen spoke for a few minutes, and His Honor said some pleasant things about Papa. Later on that evening, we buried him next to Mother, Anna, and the rest of our family. May he rest in perpetual peace and may eternal light shine upon him.

In his Will, Papa left the shop and house to me. Chris, I fully realize that, as the oldest son, this should have been your legacy. If you ever return to Trockau, I am confident we can arrive at a suitable agreement. For now, Georg, Anna Maria, and her family will remain in the family home, and they'll participate in the business. Once I marry - which still may be a long time off - we will have to reconsider this arrangement.

Papa did leave both of you some keepsakes, and I will mail you the smaller ones over the next couple of weeks. Unfortunately, the grandfather clock - that you've so admired - will have to remain in Trockau at least now until we can figure out how to transport it to St. Louis without damage.

We are all heartsick at Papa's death, and I know you are deeply saddened, too. But he has been reunited with Mother and Anna, and they wait for us to join them in our heavenly home one day.

You will remain in our thoughts and prayers, and I know this will be a hard time for you, too. May the Good Lord watch over and keep you safe.

Georg, Anna Maria, and her family send their love. We pray we will see you again. Johann.

Almost immediately, Uncle Christopher saw the pain in Chris' face and realized that something terrible had happened in Bavaria. After he and Charles read the letter, the three of them closed up the mercantile and walked over to the Old Cathedral for prayer and reflection. It was a day which they'd not forget for a long time.

In late June, Chris finally accepted an invitation to spend a week with the Zeilmanns in Rich Fountain. On the morning of July 2, Chris left home, walked the twelve blocks to the depot, and bought a ticket. He had never ridden on a train before, and he was excited about the prospect. Ever since he saw the Alder steam engine pull into Mannheim four years earlier, he had wondered what it would be like to ride the rails.

The daily run of *The Central Missouri Railroad* left St. Louis right on time at 8 AM, bound west for Jefferson City, the capital of Missouri. He found a seat by a window and watched as the six-car long train left the city. In 1844, most passenger cars were constructed of wood, and while the trains could not travel very fast, these locomotives were able to haul many more passengers for a greater distance than any wagons pulled by horses.

The Central Missouri Railroad had been operating for almost two years then, and the one-hundred mile trip from St. Louis to Rich Fountain — which used to take two to three days by wagon — had been reduced to a mere two to three hours by rail.

The first passenger cars in the United States resembled stagecoaches. They were short, often less than 10 feet long, and had two axles. Leaving St. Louis that morning, the train consisted of an engine, a coal car, one passenger car, and three freight cars plus a caboose — was powered by a Stourbridge Lion steam engine. Imported from England, the smokestack threw ash and cinders as it moved along at an almost unheard of speed of 45 miles per hour.

Chris watched as the city of St. Louis passed by quickly before him as the train moved west into the rolling hills of Eastern Missouri. From his seat in the passenger car, he could occasionally see a small town sitting far away in the distance — but the vast majority of the scenery consisted of cornfields and pasturelands. It was hard for him to reconcile that only twenty years ago, hostile Indian tribes patrolled this now plowed and fenced prairie and the almost endless herds of buffalo and elk once roamed these now tranquil landscapes.

At approximately 11 AM, the train stopped at Bonnots Mill – the train-stop closest to Rich Fountain – where Johannes Zeilmann and his son, John, were waiting for Chris in a buckboard wagon. He waved at them as he stepped off the train.

"How was your trip, Chris?"

"It was great; it's my first ride on a train, but I know it won't be my last."

After shaking hands, John placed Chris' bag in the back of the wagon, and they began their short ride to Rich Fountain. It was a hot July day, but the winding country road to the Zeilmann farm was shaded with maples, oaks, and sycamores, making the trip quite enjoyable. Within thirty minutes, the three men were at the gate entering the farm.

As they drove through the opening in the split rail fence, Chris saw a wheat field laying off to his left and a small enclosure holding rooting pigs off to his right. About one hundred yards up a bumpy dirt road stood a two-story log farmhouse. It had ten rows of stacked hewed logs on each side of the building with perhaps four to six inches of mud to fill and seal the spaces between the logs.

Chris noticed one window in the middle of the wall of the southern side of the house, and two windows and a door on the front and on the back of the structure. A chimney stood in the middle of the northern-side wall. The house appeared to be about twenty years old.

As the wagon pulled up to the farmhouse, Frau Zeilmann and the other children came out of the front door and quickly walked up to the cart.

She said, "Welcome, Chris. I presume you remember our children."

"Indeed I do, Frau Zeilmann. Thank you so much for the kind invitation. I hope I'm not an imposition, Madam."

"No, of course not; you're almost family. Come in, let me show you around."

The interior of the home consisted of an entrance hall and three large rooms on the first floor. In the room to his right, Chris saw a fireplace, kitchen, a spinning wheel, and a small piano, and there was still plenty of space in the room for a couch, a large easy-chair, and an eight-person table and chairs. To enhance the beauty of the area, Frau Zeilmann had hung several family portraits on the walls and placed white lace curtains around the windows.

To the left, Chris saw two bedrooms. The bedroom on the front of the house was for Herr and Frau Zeilmann, and the bedroom in the back of the house was reserved for the three girls, Margaret, Ann, and Barbara. Also, the entrance hall contained a staircase on the left side and a lane that went directly to the back door.

The stairs climbed to a large upstairs room where the boys slept. The upstairs bedroom had one window each on the north and south sides of the room with a slanted ceiling which also comprised the roof. Chris would be staying there, too.

Frau Zeilmann asked, "Are you hungry, Chris? We're about ready to sit down for dinner."

"Yes, ma'am. Something smells good."

After dinner, Johannes took Chris for a tour around the farm.

"We bought the house and forty acres in 1839 from a widow who had lived here for over twenty years. She raised twelve children, and when her husband died and her children scattered, she could no longer handle the farm by herself. In the end, we received a pretty good deal, and we hope to replace the house with a modern wood-frame structure as soon as we can afford it. Perhaps you can help me construct it, Chris."

"It would be my honor to help, Johannes."

"We now have eighty acres, and we cultivate between twenty-five to forty acres per season, depending on the crop. The land agent told us that crop-rotation plus a fallow season or two would ensure a healthy use of the land."

Johannes bent down and picked up a handful of soil and moved it around in his hand. It looked quite moist and dark in color – good fertile soil. "We hope to transform our property from barely getting by to a profit-making enterprise, and I think we're making good progress. As you can see, the soil is rich, and it's good for corn, potatoes, and wheat."

He handed Chris the handful of soil. "We grow corn to feed the hogs which we usually sell in the fall. We sometimes get three wheat cuttings, and the potatoes we harvest are mostly for our use. Chris, we have potatoes for almost every meal. Thankfully, Dorothea has a great imagination for them."

Chris smiled. "The potato salad was wonderful; it reminded me of my mother's recipe."

"I'm glad to like it. Dorothea is a marvelous cook, Chris. Now let me show you the barn."

Once again, it was a log structure, and it consisted of a six-foot square building constructed on a dirt floor and with a slanted roof. On the southern side of the barn, Johannes had built a lower leaning roof, about four feet long, where he stored the buckboard wagon. Inside the barn, Chris saw all sorts of tools and implements, along with a long wooden table on the northern wall which Johannes used as a workbench.

After they left the barn, they began walking toward a smaller wooden building. "Now, here's the chicken coop. We have about forty laying hens and one rooster who keeps them happy, I guess. We rely on poultry for three major purposes: meat, eggs, and of course, money. John often collects forty eggs a day – sometimes more – and what we don't consume, we sell both in town and in Jefferson City."

"I like your farm, Johannes."

Then they walked further toward a fenced-in area. "Here, we keep ten Shorthorn cattle. We like them because they are good milk producers, good beef producers, and they make good oxen. We'll get two or three calves a year, and they bring a pretty good price at market. Let's walk back to the front now."

Retracing their steps, Chris looked beyond the fence lines and saw other farms. "Do you have good neighbors?"

"Yes, they're the best. We all help each other. I think John has his eye on one of their daughters. He's growing to be a man, and one day, he'll marry, and then, being our oldest son, he'll probably inherit the farm. Maybe Margaret will marry one of our neighbor's sons, but she's pretty picky. By the way, there's something I want to ask you about her – perhaps a little later."

The two men walked to the front of the house. Johannes pointed down the road. "Over there, we have our pigsty and pens. We'll keep about fifteen hogs over the winter, fatten them up all summer, butcher one or two in the fall, and sell the excess pigs to raise money. And over here, we have twenty acres of wheat and twenty acres of corn."

"Yeah, I see it."

"Finally, over there, we have an orchard with apples, apricots, pears, and plums plus a small truck patch for lettuce, radishes, cucumbers, tomatoes, beans, and other small crops. These crops are usually just for our use, but if we have some abundance, we sell some in town to raise some money."

"Sounds impressive, Johannes. By the way, do the kids go to school?"

"I think John and Margaret are finished with their schooling – we need them around the farm now – but Eli and Ann will go on for another couple of years, and Barbara will begin school in another year or so."

After supper, Margaret needed to practice for her upcoming performance at the 4th of July Picnic in Rich Fountain. The event would be held on the grounds of the Sacred Heart Catholic Church, and a lot of folks from the surrounding area would be attending the festivities.

Once the dishes were done, the family gathered around the piano, and Frau Zeilmann began playing the three selections Margaret would sing at the picnic. First, she sang "The Liberty Song" which was a pre-American Revolutionary War song with lyrics written in about 1768[i] by one the founding fathers, John Dickinson.

Then, she performed "My Country, 'Tis of Thee," whose words were written by Samuel Francis Smith in 1831. And lastly, she sang "Across the Wide Missouri," the tune Margaret sang the previous February at the Old Cathedral in St. Louis.

After each rendition, the family members gave the young girl thunderous applause. She bowed and offered her thanks.

When she finished singing the last song, she asked, "Herr Bogner, is there a song you'd like me to sing? Perhaps I know it."

"Do you happen to know 'The Leaving of Liverpool'?"

She frowned ever so slightly and replied, "No, sorry; I've never heard of it. How does it go?"

Chris chuckled, "Well, I haven't sung a song in public since my days in the school choir. But let me tell you a little bit about the song. I heard it first when I was sitting in a tavern in Liverpool – just before our ship sailed to Philadelphia."

"In Liverpool?" Margaret asked.

"Yes. It's an old Irish folk song, and it seems to be a story about sailors who are leaving for America and hope to return to Ireland someday. Then I heard it a couple of times while aboard *The Ballantine* – the ship which carried my brother and me to America. I'll give it a try, but I don't think I can give it justice."

Frau Zeilmann said, "Chris, just try singing a couple of verses, and I'll try to find the tune on the piano."

"Okay, here's how it goes."

As Chris started singing the song, Frau Zeilmann began finding the notes on the piano.

She said, "I believe you are singing it in B flat. Let me try to put the song in the key of either C or G."

Soon she determined that the best key was C, and she began following the words of the song with chords as Chris sang it.

As he finished singing, Margaret applauded and said, "Good job, Herr Bogner. If you write down the words, I'll sing it for you. Mother seems to have captured the chords and notes."

Ten minutes later, Margaret had learned the song, and it would become the fourth selection for her recital at the 4th of July Picnic.

As the clock struck nine o'clock, it was time for the kids to go to bed. After tucking them in for the evening, Chris and Johannes retired to the front porch for cigars and a glass of brandy. After a long hot day, it felt good to be sitting on the rocking chairs and looking out into the calm, clear July night.

Chris asked, "So, what chores to the kids do around the farm? I remember that as a child in Trockau, I always had a list of things to do. What do they do?"

"Well, the chores change from season to season, as you well know. Now, Barbie is four years old, and her major chores involve gathering eggs, working in the garden, feeding the chickens, and tidying up the yard. Ann, who will be seven this fall, has to milk the cows and feed and water the pigs each morning. And she needs to keep the girl's bedroom clean and do the family's laundry from start to finish."

"She's a busy little girl."

"Yeah, she is. Now, Eli has to milk the cows each morning, feed and water the chickens, fix any problems with the animals' pens, look for signs of chicken predators, and keep the upstairs room clean."

"How about John?"

"John will be fifteen in November, and he's my big helper. He does almost everything I do including plowing the fields and harvesting the crops. Also, he takes care of the tools and implements, scrubs and cleans the animal feeders and pens, trims the hooves of our large animals, and takes care of the garden; things like that. You know, he's a hard worker and seems to like the life of a farmer."

"I did a lot of those things as a boy; and Margaret, what does she do?"

"She'll be fourteen in October, and Dorothea is teaching her all the things she'll need to know when she becomes a wife and mother; such as, housekeeping, laundry, cooking, food preservation, gardening, raising poultry, knitting, sewing, carding wool, spinning, and of course, child-rearing. I'm certain there are many other things, too. She's Mama's big helper, I guess."

The two men sat quietly and smoked their cigars for a few moments. Chris asked, "You had mentioned you wanted to discuss something with me about Margaret."

"Oh, yes, Margaret would like to find a job in St. Louis this fall. She can live with Heinrich's family, and perhaps, Heinrich could find something for her to do. But I'm wondering, do you think you can put in a good word with your uncle about her? She's quite good with numbers and has fine handwriting. Maybe he has something in his business that she could do or knows someday who might use her skills."

Chris nodded, "I'll be happy to put in a good word for her. Maybe Uncle Christopher can find a position for her in the front office."

The two men sipped their brandy and puffed on their cigars as the evening was growing late. Johannes asked, "Well, how do you like it here?"

"I do like your farm, and I love the stillness of the evening."

Chris looked up at the cloudless night sky and said, "Except for those nights when we were far out to sea on *The Ballantine*, I've never seen so many stars; even in Trockau. It's so peaceful here; you know, I believe I can sit here all night and listen to the wind. You have a lovely life, Johannes."

"Yeah, we like it here. Maybe you'd consider moving here. We can use your talents in Rich Fountain."

"Perhaps someday; who knows?"

After finishing their chores on the morning of the 4th of July, Chris and the Zeilmann family climbed onto the buckboard wagon and drove the short distance from the farm to town. The parish church, Sacred Heart, was the site of the fifth annual Independence Day picnic, and people would be coming there from far and wide.

In 1844, the parish was about six years old. Father Ferdinand Benoit Marie Guslian Helias d'Huddeghem, the pastor, had celebrated the first Mass in Rich Fountain on May 16, 1838. Within two years, the twenty or more Catholic families in the vicinity built a small log church on the four acres of land donated by John Strumpf. Of course, they had grand plans for a much larger church to be built on that site one day soon, but for now, the log structure would have to do.

As the buckboard rambled up to the church building, Johannes saw Fr. Helias, as he was coming out of the church, and Johannes waved to him. After Johannes parked the wagon and settled the horse, the family walked over to Fr. Helias.

"Chris, allow me to introduce you to Father Ferdinand Helias."

And turning to the priest, Johannes said, "Father, permit me to introduce you to Christopher Bogner. Father is from Belgium, and Chris hails from a little village not too far from our village in Bavaria."

As he held out his hand to the priest, Chris said, "*Je suis heureux de vous rencontrer, Père.*"

Fr Helias looked surprised and replied, "*Parlez-vous français,* Herr Bogner?"

Chris smiled and said, "*Juste un peu. J'ai vécu à la Nouvelle Orléans pendant deux ans et ma copine était française, père.*"

"*Êtes-vous deux ensemble plus?*"

Chris shook his head and sadly replied, "*Père, elle est morte de fièvre jaune mais je l'aimais beaucoup.*"

"*Qu'elle repose en paix,* Herr Bogner."

"*Merci beaucoup, Père.*"

Johannes interrupted, "Will you both please speak English. We live in America, you know."

They laughed, and soon they began the process of getting the church lawn ready for the 4th of July picnic. As several other people set up tables and chairs, Chris and Johannes rolled the piano out of the church and on to the landing just outside the front door, and all around, folks were getting ready for the picnic to begin.

About 1 PM, Conrad Rottener, the unofficial 'mayor' of the town, walked up the stairs to the landing, turned around, and addressed the people below.

"Welcome, one and all. Isn't this a marvelous day? Not too hot and, thankfully, no rain like last year. Well, we have a wonderful day planned for you.

In just a minute, Fr. Helias will say a few words and the lovely Margaret Zeilmann will sing three or four patriotic songs. And then, it's time for dinner."

As the people cheered, Herr Rottener stopped an instant and looked down at the faces of the approving crowd. "Oh boy, do we have a good dinner today. John Strumpf has been cooking a hog on a spit for well over twelve hours now. I know you can smell it. And Willy Brenner and his sons spent all night fishing on the Missouri River, and they have brought us two dozen catfish and a few strippers for us to enjoy."

The 'mayor' stopped again, "And of course, the ladies have brought all of the trimmings, including potato salad, green beans, corn-on-the-cob, and freshly baked bread; and of course, Mrs. Wagner has brought her pies. We'll eat like kings and queens today."

Once more he stopped, "After dinner, we have a wonderful treat: Gunther Meissner and his sons brought their fiddles and banjos, and they will perform a little bit later. And yes, we'll have a square dance; Jules Jorgensen will call it again just like last year. It'll be a day you'll not forget for years to come. So, are we ready?"

The crowd cheered again.

"Then let's get started. Father, will you say a few words please?"

Father Helias rose out of his chair and looked at the crowd below.

"Good afternoon, friends and neighbors. I hope my English has improved somewhat since last year; in fact, I know it has! Well, I've been here in our lovely community – now, for over six years; and yes, I'm a long way from Brussels. Thank you for welcoming me so warmly into your community."

Father Helias stopped as the audience applauded. "You know, my former King and sovereign, King Leopold, decided he would not tolerate any dissent in his realm; he believed it's just too bad that the good people of Belgium were born poor and ignorant. He called their misery 'God's plan.' And perhaps, I am just a Jesuit troublemaker, and I opposed him. King Leopold didn't like my opposition, and to escape his persecution of freedom and light, I came here to America to seek both."

Father Helias stopped again, as the crowd cheered. "I guess it's a good way to celebrate the Fourth of July is by reading the Declaration of Independence which Thomas Jefferson wrote sixty-eight years ago. Thus, I reread it this morning, and once again I find it's an amazing political and social document. Jefferson wrote in the manuscript that the thirteen British Colonies in the New World are now independent, and he provided a compelling case for its conclusions. As many of you well know, he wrote that governments gain legitimacy from the consent of the governed and all people have certain unalienable rights of life, liberty and the pursuit of happiness. This philosophy constitutes the political essence of what we practice today on our great land."

Once again, the crowd showed its approval. "Yesterday, I began thinking about my talk today; so I rode my horse down to the Missouri River and sat on the bank just looking at the opposite shore. I was alone on the riverbank, and I thought about how precious freedom is; how I didn't have to bend my knee or answer to a Lord or a Prince; and how people who share my same dreams of opportunity and peace can come to this land and find it here. Our American forefathers fought and died so we could have this grand picnic today."

Fr. Helias stopped again and waited for the cheers to subside. "I love the Fourth of July; our gathering, our fellowship, our food, the dancing, and the patriotic music; all of it. To help us celebrate, Margaret Zeilmann will sing three or four patriotic songs in just a few minutes which define and testify to my dreams of this land of ours."

The crowd showed its approval again.

The priest continued, "But to most Americans, patriotism must not be so much about the land as it is about the ideas that created and sustain our country. The underlying idea is that people can come here from all over the world – bringing with them different beliefs, traditions, languages, and cultures – and still feel welcome here."

He stopped one more final time to build to a crescendo. "Consider this for a moment; that from the beginning of time when the first human settlements arose in ancient Egypt, Babylonia, and Palestine until now, men were controlled by their leaders. Now our precious documents remind us that all men are created equal, and governments derive their power from the consent of the governed. This philosophy goes against the basic acts and proclamations of all regimes and political institutions which had ruled the world long before we began our shared experience in democracy."

He shook his head and looked out well beyond the people in the audience before him; out to the foothills and valleys of the land that he loved so much.

Then he said, "Equality, consent of the governed – these were radical, new, fragile, powerful ideas that the ancient Greeks and Roman wrote about, and perhaps for a little while, these ancient people practiced on a much smaller scale than we do today. These grand ideas that Jefferson formulated are worth living for and dying for; concepts that human beings have worth and dignity, and that no lord, no government, no religion, no master, and no army has the right to disturb or compel. These ideas, my friends and neighbors, consist of the social and political fabric which people all over the world yearn for and dream of every day. Cherish them and practice them in your daily lives and your actions, and he proud to call yourself an American. God bless you and God bless the United States of America."

After thanking the audience, Father Helias asked Margaret and Frau Zeilmann to come up to the landing. To her mother's accompaniment, Margaret sang the four songs she had practiced at the farm – 'The Liberty Song,' 'My Country, 'Tis of Thee,' 'Across the Wide Missouri,' and 'The Leaving of Liverpool' – to the delight of the audience.

Then it was time for dinner, and for the next hour or so, the people sat down at the tables or on blankets in the shade, and enjoyed a community meal. Once in a while, several of the men would excuse themselves from their families, and partake of a sip or two of Kentucky bourbon behind the parsonage.

When dinner was over, Mayor Rottener walked up to the landing and announced that the music would commence at 2 PM, and as Gunther Kemmerer and his sons began tuning their instruments, the people started walking over to the dancing area.

Margaret asked, "Herr Bogner, will you dance with me?"

"Me? Margaret, I don't know how to dance."

"It's simple; anyone can square dance. There are just a few basic steps, and I can show them to you. You'll have a great time."

Chris was hesitant; but Johannes said, "Don't be bashful, Chris. Dance with Margaret; you know, you owe her; she sang the song about Liverpool for you. Please, dance with my lovely daughter."

"Well, I guess I could try but first, Margaret, tell me about it; what is square-dancing anyhow?"

Margaret smiled and took Chris' hand. "Come on, let's walk over there and watch them dance for a while. I'll explain it all to you."

When they arrived at the dancing area, the first couples had already begun their steps.

Margaret said, "As you can see, a square dance is meant for four couples – eight dancers. They are arranged in a square, with one couple on each side facing the middle of the square. The man over there is referred to as a 'caller,' and he mostly tells the dancers which steps to take."

The music started, and the dancers turned to face their partners, bowed, and circling an arm around their partner's back while standing side-to-side, they began to move around the dance floor in unison. The caller yelled the 'allemande left,' and the dancers grasped the left hands with their partner, and pulling away from each other slightly, they walked halfway around a central axis and began stepping through.

As the dancers maneuvered around the floor, Margret explained the dance steps to him. Then she described the steps in the 'promenade,' and the indispensable 'do-si-do' (which is a corruption of the phrase 'dos-à-dos'), and in French means 'back-to-back.'

Soon the music stopped, and the eight original dancers left the dancefloor as eight new dancers took their places. Soon the band began playing another tune.

"Herr Bogner, are you ready to try?"

"Margaret, please call me Chris. Herr Bogner sounds so old and stuffy."

"Okay. Chris, are you ready to dance with me?"

The music stopped for a second time, and when eight new dancers walked onto the floor, Margaret and Chris were among them. At first, he was a bit clumsy and hesitant, but soon he developed a feel for it.

By evening's end, he had learned the circle left, the circle right, the halfway around, the full way around, the courtesy turn, the forward and back chasse, the pass thru, the right and left grand spins, the stars (both left-handed and right-handed), and the weave the ring.

All in all, Chris had a wonderful time, and he left the dance sweaty and exhausted. For her part, Margaret began planning for the day when she'd see him again.

A few days later, Chris was back on the train for his return trip to St. Louis. Waving farewell to Johannes and John as the train pulled out of Bonnots Mill, Chris reflected on his wonderful week in Rich Fountain. Yes, he'd come back again, and perhaps he'd even settle there one day. He liked the area that much.

As the train made its way east, Chris picked up a copy of *The Jefferson City Inquirer* and looked at the stories which were headlining the local paper. He read:

- An organization called *The Young Men's Christian Association* had formed in London;

- The Texan envoys signed *The Treaty of Annexation* with the United States; Texas would soon be admitted to the Union as a slave state;

- An electrical telegram was sent by a man named Samuel F. B. Morse from the U.S. Capitol in Washington, D.C. to *The B&O's* outer depot in Baltimore, Maryland, saying "What hath God wrought." Later the same day, the first telegraphed news dispatch was published in *The Baltimore Patriot*;

- Joseph Smith, founder of *The Latter Day Saints* movement, and his brother Hyrum were killed in Carthage, Illinois by an armed mob;

- The U.S. signed *The Treaty of Wanghia* with the Qing Dynasty of China, the first diplomatic agreement between the two nations in history;
- *The Exclusion Law* was passed in Oregon prohibiting negroes (including slaves) from entering or remaining in the territory; and
- *The Whig Convention* nominated Senator Henry Clay of Kentucky as its presidential candidate.

Chris marveled at all of the things which were going on in the world, and he wondered what the future might bring.

Soon, life returned to normal for Chris. In September, Margaret was offered a job at Bauer Mercantile as an office clerk, and she moved into the Heinrich Zeilmann family home a few weeks later. She also joined the choir at the Old Cathedral and soon began being called upon as a soloist on many Sundays and Holy Days.

Margaret proved to be an excellent worker and a delightful young woman to have around the store. Chris initially treated her as his little sister, and although he felt an emotional attachment to her, Chris realized she had not yet reached her fourteenth birthday, whereas he was over twice her age at twenty-nine.

He was frequently a guest at the Heinrich Zeilmann home for supper, and Chris would often escort Margaret home from church – and then, perhaps, linger a little bit longer than he should have at the Zeilmann home.

On October 26, 1844, Margaret turned fourteen years old, and Chris escorted her to dinner at a local restaurant to help celebrate her special day. As Christmas approached, Chris could sense that Margaret was feeling adult thoughts about him, and he began thinking of her as being more than just a little sister.

As winter turned to spring, Chris and Margaret often rode the train back to Rich Fountain for short visits. He would spend most of his time there working with Johannes on the plans for the new Zeilmann farmhouse, and Chris would also work with Father Helias on the design of the new sanctuary. The more time he spent in Rich Fountain, the more he liked the area, and the more comfortable he felt with the Zeilmann family.

Also, Chris noticed Margaret devoted a considerable amount of time while in Rich Fountain whispering to her mother, and once in a while, the two of them would look over at him and smile.

In late December 1845, Chris and Margaret rode the train again to Rich Fountain to celebrate Christmas. As the snow was falling, Johannes picked up the two of them at the station. The pines were already covered in thick wet snow, and the air was full of wood-smoke from the firesides of the stores and family farms they passed on their way to the Zeilmann home.

Margaret sat in the middle, and she wrapped her left hand around Johannes' arm and placed her right hand under a blanket where she held Chris' hand tightly. She had an enormous smile on her face.

The Zeilmann home was beautifully decorated for Christmas, with candles in each of the front windows, a big pine wreath hanging on the front door, and of course, a large (undecorated) evergreen tree standing in one corner of the living room. A warm fire was burning in the fireplace.

That evening, December 23rd, the family members began decorating the tree with paper ornaments, gilded nuts, kuchen (homemade cookies chiefly made of confectionery), and red and green ribbons. On the top of the pine tree, Johannes set the same Christmas star which he brought with them from their prior home in Bavaria.

As the family finished decorating the tree, Frau Zeilmann played the piano, and the others sang:

O Tannenbaum, O Tannenbaum,
wie treu sind deine Blätter
Du grünst nicht nur
zur Sommerzei
Nein auch im winter, wenn es schneit
O Tannenbaum, o Tannenbaum,
wie treu sind deine Blätter.

After supper, Chris asked Johannes if the two of them could go for a walk. The snow had stopped falling, and the sky had cleared so that Chris could see a 'million' stars. As they left through the front door, Margaret gave Chris a sweet smile, and whispered, "Don't be too long now."

Walking along the road leading to the farmhouse, Chris felt the snow crunch under his boots. A cool breeze pushed through his beard and pushed his hat a little higher on his head. As they approached the front gate, he said,

"Johannes, I have two things I'd like to speak to you about. Each question is dependent on the other question."

Chris took a deep breath, as the two men stopped near the front gate and looked directly at each other.

Johannes said, "Okay, I'm listening."

"Well, I want to buy a farm in Rich Fountain. I've saved several thousand dollars, and I'm ready to start anew here. Can you help me find a farm?"

Johannes smiled – almost relieved. "Yes, I'll be happy to help. I know Widow Nelson has been talking about selling her farm since her husband died last spring; she says that it's too much for her. It's a forty-acre freehold of rich bottom land with an older farmhouse, but I think she may sell it for a good price to the right buyer."

"Great, maybe you could approach her while I'm still here."

"I will. Now, you said that there were two things you wanted to talk to me about?"

"Yes, and I'm not certain you'll want to hear this one, my friend. But, here it goes; I'm in love with your daughter, and I want to marry her. However, I realize she's half my age, and if it's a problem, I can wait for a couple more years or I can go away and never bother you again."

For an instant, there was silence; just two men looking carefully at each other.

Finally, Chris said, "So, what do you think? I will not marry her without your consent."

Suddenly, Johannes replied, "Have you asked Margaret yet?"

"Yes, and she agreed to marry me, but I reaffirm to you that I will not marry her without your consent – and I told her that."

Johannes smiled, "Her mother and I have waited several months to hear this wonderful news. Yes, Chris; you have our permission but with one condition: that you won't call me 'Father'; 'Johannes' is still okay for me."

Chris smiled and nodded his head. "Then it will stay 'Johannes.' But aren't you concerned about our age difference? I'm thirty, and she's only fifteen."

"As a parent, of course, we are concerned about whom our daughter marries. But Chris, she's been a woman now for almost a year, and it's time for her to begin to have children. Her mother and I want her to have a good life. Yes, you're a bit older than her; but you'll make a fine husband for our daughter, and she'll bring you so much love and joy that you cannot begin to imagine."

And with that being said, Johannes hugged Chris and kissed him on his cheek. "No Chris, I am very pleased. Now, be faithful to her in return, and she'll make you a very happy man."

As they walked in through the front door, Margaret saw the broad smile on Chris' face, and trying to hold back the tears, she ran and almost leaped into is outstretched arms, kissing him deeply on his mouth.

Then Frau Zeilmann hugged Johannes, and then Margaret, and finally embraced Chris, saying, "Christopher Bogner, welcome to the family, and please call me 'Mama.'"

A few moments later, Johannes opened the cupboard and brought out four glasses and a bottle of white wine – a Moselle wine from a small German town near Koblenz.

"Here's to your union, and may the two of you be happy together for a long, long time – and give us plenty of grandchildren, too."

Then Johannes picked up his glass and saluted the couple, saying in German,

"Ichmöchte einen toast, auf Margaret und Chris ausbringen! Prost!"

And Chris and Margaret replied, "Prost!"

Frau Zeilmann was crying too hard to partake in the toast.

On Christmas Day, Father Helias announced the engagement, and for the next four weeks, he published the bans of marriage in the local church bulletin. The couple set the day of their wedding on Tuesday, May 5, 1846.

For the months preceding their marriage, Chris and Margaret returned to St. Louis to sever their ties with the city. Chris transferred his ownership of the cabinetmaking business to Charles, and the couple attending Pre-Cana classes at the Old Cathedral. In late April, farewell parties were held for the couple in the church hall and at the residences of both Heinrich Zeilmann and Christopher Bauer.

On Saturday, April 26, the couple gathered up their belongings and boarded the train to Rich Fountain. Before leaving the Bauer residence that morning, Chris went to the garden and cut off several twigs from the same grapevine he had carried to America from his boyhood home in Trockau. A few hours later, the couple arrived in Rich Fountain.

The following Monday, Chris purchased the family farm from Widow Nelson, and he spent the next week readying the home for his new bride. He reconstructed the sagging front porch, replaced windows and curtains, and made significant and long-overdue repairs to the interior.

Furthermore, Chris repainted the entire structure – both inside and out. Finally, he bought a brand new featherbed, and on the Sunday before the wedding, Father Helias blessed the house with prayers and holy water.

The home was ready for his new bride.

May 5th turned out to be a beautiful springtime day. The sun rose up into a cloudless blue sky, and the temperature would eventually rise into the mid-70's. Father Helias held a Nuptial High Mass in the church building but permitted the couple to exchange their vows on the church lawn after the

Mass concluded.

He mentioned he was uncertain whether the Bishop would approve of the bifurcation of the ceremonies but added, "It's easier to apologize than ask for permission."

Chris and Johannes built a trellis on the church lawn, and Margaret and her mother decorated its top and sides with daisies, roses, day-lilies, amanita, bluestem pricklypoppy, aster, beebalm, bugleweed, iris, and other local spring flowers. In a simple ceremony, Charles acted as the best-man and Margaret's best friend in St Louis, Clara Bankhead, was the maiden of honor.

Margaret wore her finest dress – a red print floor-length design – and a white veil. Chris wore the suit he had purchased in Bayreuth before the opera in 1839, and it was the one he had worn to Chéri's funeral in 1842.

Frau Zeilmann played "Jesu, Joy of Man's Desire" by Johann Sebastian Bach and "Canon In D" by Johann Pachelbel, and Father Helias blessed the couple after they exchanged their vows. The reception was held at the Zeilmann home with most of the townsfolks attending.

That evening, Chris and Margaret Bogner climbed into their buckboard and rode the short distance to their new home. After hitching the team, Chris lifted his bride out of the wagon and carried her through the front door and into their living room.

Time swiftly passed for the new couple, as Chris began learning the trade of a Missouri farmer. He raised oxen and planted a large fruit orchard. Furthermore, he became a beekeeper and winemaker, and he opened a small cabinetmaking business in 'downtown' Rich Fountain to supplement his income.

On July 1, 1848, Chris bought an additional forty acres of land adjoining his property, and he grew corn and soybeans on the new acreage to help feed his livestock. These were bountiful years for Chris and Margaret.

Their first child, George, was born on January 19, 1847. George was followed by John (March 22, 1848), Joe (September 27, 1849), Mike (January 4, 1851), Frank (April 12, 1853), Alois (January 30, 1855), Anna Lena

(November 2, 1856) and Barbara Maria (October 30, 1858). Thus, by Christmas Day of 1858, Chris and Margaret had seven healthy children and a prospering farm.

Everything seemed to be going well for the Bogner family. Although there was tension on the national scene involving the matters of slavery, states' rights, and tariffs, prominent politicians such as Senators John C. Calhoun of South Carolina, Daniel Webster of Massachusetts, and Henry Clay of Kentucky always seemed to forge compromises despite continued partisan bickering. So far, so good.

Chris' brother, Charles, married Annette Virginia Barnhart in 1848, and the couple moved to her hometown, Corning, Arkansas, where Charles began a cabinetmaking business with the help of her family. He would thrive financially through the decade of the 1850s as would the Bauer Mercantile in St. Louis.

But underlying the relative calm and serenity of those years, dark clouds loomed over the horizon. A boat can be tossed from side-to-side only so many times before it is swamped. The Bogner family and the Nation would soon experience hard times and difficult choices as the calendar moved toward the spring of 1859.

CHAPTER TWELVE

O ne of the highlights of the summers I spent in Nebraska was the annual *Knox County Fair.* Usually occurring over the third long-weekend
of August, people from all over Nebraska and South Dakota would drive
for hours to attend the four-day event at the fairgrounds in the town of
Bloomfield.

In 1964, *The Know County Fair* was celebrating its eighty-first season, and
the festivities featured a large mid-way, carnival rides, a tractor-pull, a beer
garden, and food and dessert competitions of all sorts. The Fairgrounds also
contained a large livestock facility and a grandstand where spectators could
enjoy a different a live musical act on each evening of the Fair.

Furthermore, *The Future Farmers of America* and *The 4-H Clubs* provided classes and exhibits which ran throughout the four-day fair.

The Thursday edition of *The Yankton Daily Press* reported:

> As of the last available count, the 4-H entries included 147 buck-
> et calves, 113 pigs, 45 lambs, and 33 goats. Those figures don't
> include FFA members who have enough stock to have their own
> shows on Saturday for all species.

The newspaper also noted that Bobby Vee – one of the teen idol rock stars
of the early 1960s – would be performing in concert on Saturday evening.
Like many of the teenage heart-throbs of the time – such as Frankie Avalon,
Ricky Nelson, and Fabian – Bobby Vee's star had been eclipsed by the arrival
of the Beatles and the British Invasion. Nevertheless, Sarah picked Saturday
night to attend the Fair.

After the conclusion of my ballgame on Saturday afternoon, we hopped into
the Hudson and drove the twenty-mile distance from Crofton to Bloomfield.
We arrived at the fairgrounds just after six o'clock.

After eating a couple of hotdogs and taking rides on the Tilt-A-Whirl, the Cuddle-Up, and the bumper cars, we sat on two seats situated about twenty rows down from the stage to await the arrival of Bobby Vee.

Shortly after 9 PM, the emcee took the stage to introduce the evening's headliner. Born Robert Thomas Velline on April 30, 1943, in Fargo, North Dakota, Bobby had produced thirty-eight Hot 100 chart hits, ten of which reached the Top 20.

It was an overflow crowd that night.

Sarah (and almost all of the other teenage girls in the audience) leaped to her feet and began screaming as Bobby Vee walked on stage singing one of his best-known hits, "Devil or Angel," and she kept screaming throughout the entire ninety-minute concert.

Dressed entirely in black (except for his trademark white high-school letter sweater), he wore his hair in the famous 'Duck Ass' motif – with a front curl standing high on his forehead. He also sported a series of scarfs around his neck which he removed from time-to-time to present to several of the young women seated in the front rows – *a la* Elvis Presley.

During the evening, Bobby Vee performed about twenty songs including several of his biggest hits, such as: "Rubber Ball," "Run to Him," "The Night Has a Thousand Eyes," and "Please Don't Ask About Barbara." Sarah knew the words to almost all of his songs, and I'd never seen such joy on her face.

For his encore, Bobby Vee sang his signature song, "Take Good Care of My Baby." As he ran through the final verses of the song, I hugged Sarah and whispered, "Yes, dear Lord; please take good care of my baby."

She kissed me and kept singing along to the words of the former number 1 song. As the concert concluded, we both knew I'd be leaving Nebraska in less than two weeks, and our beautiful summer together would soon be over.

After the concert, we strolled through the midway, eating cotton candy, and later stopping for a root-beer float. Along the way, we ran into many of our friends from Crofton, and we rode the Ferris wheel and the Whip.

Later, I tried my luck at the 'Milk Bottle' game. The objective of the game is to toss a wooden loop onto rows of milk bottles. If the loop wraps around the top of a milk bottle, the player wins the prize of his/her choice. She had her eye on the large pink stuffed puppy, but no matter how many times I tried, the wooden loop merely bounced off the milk bottles and fell into the case below.

Sensing my frustration, Sarah said, "Let me try," and she won the puppy dog on just her second throw, causing me endless embarrassment.

Before leaving the midway, I tried my hand on the 'basketball toss" which required the player to shoot a ball into a twelve-foot high basketball hoop that was slightly smaller than a regulation hoop. After three shots, I finally won my consolation prize – a red-stemmed goblet that I still have today.

Just before leaving the Fair, we stopped at the 'Kissing Booth,' paid the attendant the sum of fifty cents, and took two photos of us – one with us smiling and one while kissing. Sarah kept both images.

As 10 PM approached, it was time for us to begin our drive back to Crofton. After finding the car, I grabbed a couple ice-cold Hamm's out of the trunk and started rolling out of Bloomfield. Sarah turned on the radio, and we were able to pick up radio station KOMA from Oklahoma City.

Along the way home, the Beatles sang 'I Should Have Known Better,' the Beach Boys performed 'All Summer Long,' and The Four Seasons crooned 'Dawn, Go Away' – along with many other songs that were at the top of the American pop charts.

After a song ended, the disc jockey often howled:

". . . and the hits just keep on coming."

They did – and we sang together the entire way back to Crofton.

CHAPTER THIRTEEN

Rich Fountain, Missouri, February 1859

Following the formal requirements of the U. S. Constitution, the Missouri territorial legislature submitted a request to Congress in December 1818 for admission to the Union as a slave state. In what would otherwise have been a routine admission suddenly became contentious due to the delicate balance between the slave and free states.

After considerable negotiations conducted by Senators Clay, Calhoun, and Webster, Congress agreed to *The Missouri Compromise*, clearing the way for Missouri's entry into the Union as a slave state. To preserve the delicate balance, Maine was admitted as a free state. The Missouri Compromise also provided that the remaining part of the Louisiana Territory above the 36°30′ line was to be free from slavery.

The following year, Missouri was admitted into the Union as the 24th state, with Jefferson City designated as its state capital. Thus, Missouri was the first state entirely west of the Mississippi River to enter into the Union.

As with many other Southern states, Missouri laws treated slaves as property which could be bought and sold. Because of the legal status, incidents of brandings, beatings, rape, and family separation were not infrequent.

Moreover, slaves were prohibited from serving as witnesses against white people, and they were forbidden from holding assemblies, including church services, without a white person in attendance. Finally, a slave could not buy, keep, or sell property without the permission from an owner, and slave marriages were not legally acknowledged.

Therefater, Congress enacted *The Fugitive Slave Act of 1850* which declared all fugitive slaves must be returned to their masters – even if the slaves were captured in a free state. Upon return to bondage, many escaped slaves faced harsh punishments, such as the amputation of limbs, whippings, brandings, and many other inhumane acts.

Individuals who aided the escape of fugitive slaves can be charged with a felony and severely punished under this Act.

Following a cold January, the month of February brought with it the promise of spring to Rich Fountain. One late morning, Chris and his three oldest sons, George, John, and Joe, had begun the cutting of the winterkill and the preparing of the fields for spring planting. After several tough years, the Bogner farm was finally producing bumper crops.

Chris was talking to Margaret on the front porch when he noticed George, age 12, came running out of the barn toward the house.

"Papa, Papa," George yelled, "There's a black man in the barn. I think he may be hurt."

"What are you talking about?"

"A man is hiding in the barn – he may be a runaway slave, Papa."

Chris looked at Margaret; she appeared to be startled. He said, "I'm going to get my rifle. George, go and find Joe and John and bring them into the house. Stay here – all of you – until I come back. I'll be back as soon as I can."

With his rifle tightly in his hands, Chris walked slowly to the barn, opened the door, and stepped inside. He didn't see anyone there.

"Okay, I've got a gun, but I'm not going to hurt you. I need to see you come out with your arms above your head."

At first, there was only silence. Then Chris saw a stirring in the rear of the barn near the milk cow's stall. He aimed his rifle at the movement.

"I see you. Now come forward into the light. Don't be afraid. Come now."

A few moments later, a young black man hobbled out of the shadows with his arms raised. "Please don't shoot me, sir. I ain't armed."

"Who are you, and what are you doing here?"

The man looked to be in his early twenties, and he was dressed in white homespun linsey pantaloons and roundabouts. He seemed to be very frightened.

"Sir, my name is Amos, and I need help. I'm hungry, and I hurts my ankle, Sir. Please help me. I won't hurt nobody. Please, sir."

Chris exhaled and lowered his gun.

"Are you a runaway, Amos?"

Amos lowered his head, "Yes, Sir."

"Where are you from?"

"The Ridgely Plantation, near Hancock, sir."

"How long have you been on the run?"

"Almost two weeks, sir."

"Are you hungry, Amos?"

"Yes, sir – I'm mighty hungry."

"Well, stay here. I'll bring you some food and water. I see you hurt your foot; maybe I can look at it, too."

Chris paused briefly and then said, "Don't go nowhere, Amos. I don't plan to turn you in. We'll talk some more after I get back."

"Thank you, sir. I'm much obliged."

Chris nodded his head and returned to the house. He didn't know what he wanted to do.

As he walked into the living room, Margaret asked, "What's going on? Who is the boy?"

Chris placed the gun back on the rack that hung over the fireplace, and then he told Margaret and the children about what we knew so far.

Margaret replied, "He can't stay here; they're probably looking for him right now. We can't hide a runaway slave; we could lose our farm. You're not going to help him; are you?"

Chris shook his head and replied, "Honey, I can't turn him over to the authorities; they'll return him to his plantation where he'll probably be whipped and beaten. But you're right; he can't stay here, either."

"So, what do you plan to do?"

"I'm not entirely sure; but first, we need to feed him and tend to his ankle. Then I'm going to talk to Father Helias. Maybe he'll know what to do. Until then, everyone needs to stay out of the barn. The boy is hurt; so he can't walk too far. But stay here and watch the barn from the windows. If necessary, George knows how to handle the rifle; don't you, son?"

Father Helias was working in his garden when Chris arrived at Sacred Heart Church.

"Hey Chris, your Papa's grapevines seemed to have made it through the winter; and they're beginning to bud already. They're a hearty breed."

When Father saw the look on Chris' face, he asked, "Is this a social call or do you have something you'd like to talk about? Gosh, I hope the family is fine."

"Yeah, Father, everyone's fine. Can we talk privately in your office?"

After closing the door in the rectory, Chris explained to Father Helias all of the circumstances relating to his visit.

"So, what do you want to do?"

"Father, I can't give him back to the slavers, and if I give him to the police, that will be the same result. Is there any way we can help him reach safety across the river into Illinois?"

"Are you sure you want to help him? You'd be breaking the law – in fact, you are breaking the law right now – and it could cause severe consequences for you and your family."

Chris nodded and said, "Yes, I am, Father. I'm sure."

"You know, Chris, I'm not confident that even getting Amos to Illinois will resolve his dilemma. You are aware of *The Fugitive Slave Act*, aren't you? Bounty hunters can go anywhere in the North – and even into Canada – and find a runaway there and bring him back to his masters. And believe me, they'll find ways to make him talk. You might remain in jeopardy for a long time, my friend."

Chris tugged at his beard. "I need to help this man."

"Are you quite certain?"

"Yes, Father, I am."

Father Helias looked into Chris' face for a long time. Then the priest stood up and walked around his office for a few minutes before sitting down again.

Finally, he said, "Well, I think I may be able to help you – but I don't want to go into any detail right now. So, go home, and I'll look into the matter. I'll ride over to your farm in a day or two. Until then, be careful. Make certain nobody else knows anything about this matter. Be sure your kids stay away from other children and hide Amos well."

Two days later, Father Helias rode out to the Bogner farm and provided Chris with the particulars and the directions to a safe house. But there was a catch; he would have to carry Amos in the wagon and drive to a farm just outside of Clover Bottom – a little village situated almost fifty miles away from Rich Fountain.

There was no telling whom or what Chris might encounter on the way to Clover Bottom. Of course, Margaret was firmly against the plan, but Chris decided to leave the following morning with Amos, and hopefully, make it to Clover Bottom safely in one day.

Before leaving the farm, Father Helias spent an hour or more talking with Amos alone. Then Father went back to the house, blessed the Bogner family, and wished Chris good luck.

The following morning, Chris prepared a dry, warm spot in the wagon bed where Amos could hide, and shortly after 7 AM, the two of them began the long journey to Clover Bottom. As luck would have it, it was a cold, nasty, rainy day. In an attempt to stay dry, Chris wore the yellow slicker he'd utilized on his voyage aboard *The Ballantine*, and thankfully, there were few fellow travelers during their journey that morning.

Unfortunately, the roads were often muddy, and in some places slightly slick, as the temperatures remained in the low forties all day long. Every once in a while, Chris saw scattered flurries, and he hoped that snow would not be a factor he'd have to deal with later on in the day.

Every two hours or so, Chris stopped the wagon in a secluded spot so Amos could get out of the buckboard and stretch his legs for a short time. Probably because of the cold temperature, the men were not stopped by the authorities.

Even when driving through the little villages of Rosebud and Beaufort, he noticed only a handful of people were out and about. But every time he passed someone on the road or saw someone while driving through the small towns and villages along the way, Chris prayed his luck would last – and it did.

Carefully following the directions provided to him by Father Helias, Chris eventually found the rutted lane to the safe house – a small farm located about two miles south of Clover Bottom. As his wagon approached the house, he was determined to follow the prearranged protocol carefully.

When he drew the wagon to a halt, two men walked out the door of the cabin, each one holding a rifle pointed at the cart. Exactly as he had rehearsed, Chris looked up at them and asked: "Do you have any molasses for sale today?"

The shorter man replied, "Yes, how many pints do you need?"

"Just one."

One of the men nodded, and Chris exhaled with a heavy breath; the connection had been made.

After looking around to make sure the wagon hadn't been followed, the men helped Amos out of the wagon-bed and safely into the farmhouse. They directed Chris to hide the buckboard in the barn. There, he unhitched the team from the buckboard.

Because of the long ride, he needed to tend to his horses before going back to the house. One-at-a-time, Chris walked them around the inside of the barn for several minutes, letting their muscles relax and allowing their body temperatures to cool off. Even though it had been a chilly day, the horses were sweating heavily, and he dried them with a blanket.

Once the horses were calm and dry, he gave them warm water to drink (to prevent colic), and after the horses drank their fill, he gave them food, cleaned their hooves, and thoroughly brushed them. After leading them into a vacant stall, he made sure the horses had plenty of hay to eat throughout the evening and night. Confident that his horses were well taken care of, he went to the house.

The Jasper family, members of *The Religious Society of Friends* (also known as Quakers), offered Chris and Amos dry clothes and a warm meal. It was understood Chris would remain in the safe-house for the night – the six-hour ride had been hard on his horses, and they would need time to recover from their long journey.

Over a warm dinner of salted pork, brown beans, and cornbread, Chris began to tell Hiram Jasper and his family all about the journey from Rich Fountain when Hiram's oldest son, Virgil, stopped Chris in mid-sentence.

"Friend, we wish to know very little about you – and you about us. If one of us is arrested, the posse will use all measures of torture to learn the identities of the co-conspirators. The less we know about each other, the less we can tell them."

Chris nodded his head, "Yes, I understand."

Virgil continued, "But with that said, let me give you some advice. Tell no one anything about Amos' escape, and when you get back home, be sure to wash and clean anything Amos may have touched; such as the wagon, the blankets, and the area around wherever he spent his nights while in your care. Burn anything which might later give Amos away."

"Why?"

"Should the posse find its way to your home, they'll undoubtedly bring bloodhounds with them. These dogs have an acute sense of smell, and the dogs will be able to locate any lingering scent Amos may have left behind – even after weeks. Friend, while I know it's difficult to wash everything, remember that Amos' scent will probably remain in your barn for many weeks to come."

"So, if they should come, what shall I do?"

Hiram replied, "Admit to them that the runaway slave – but don't give him a name – had spent a night in your barn. Tell them you scared him away. If you say you've not seen the runaway, the dogs will prove you wrong."

For the next several hours, they talked about several additional measured to undertake to safeguard Chris' family. After a couple of pipes of tobacco, they prayed together for good fortune before retiring to their beds.

Being mid-February, dawn came late the following morning; but it was a bright, crisp day this time. After breakfast, Chris went out to the barn to ready his team of horses for the long trip back to Rich Fountain.

As he was hitching the team to the wagon, Amos walked into the barn, stopped directly in front of Chris, got down on one knee, and bowed his head. "Sir, I wish to thank you for all you've done for me. I'll be forever in your debt, Sir."

Chris took Amos by the hand and raised him to his feet. "Amos, you will always remain in my prayers, and I hope you'll find a way to keep your freedom."

Amos had tears in his eyes. "Thank you, Sir. God bless you, Sir."

"I do have one question. What did you and Father Helias talk about in the barn?"

Amos smiled. "Sir, the priest told me that Jesus loves me, and then the priest told me stories about his life and his struggles with his faith and freedom. Sir, I felt he cared for me – it was the first time a white preacher has ever shown me any compassion. Then he blessed me."

Upon saying his goodbyes to the Jaspers and Amos, Chris began his relatively uneventful but long journey back to Rich Fountain. The day was much warmer; the sun felt warm on his face, and the sky was a deep blue. The six-hour journey seemed to pass much quicker this time, and as he pulled the wagon up to the farmhouse, the entire family ran out the front door and embraced him.

Later, with the help of George and Joe, he thoroughly washed the wagon and attempted to remove all traces of Amos from the barn. They fed the hay (where Amos had slept) to the cattle, and Margaret carefully washed all of the blankets and towels. Finally, with prayers of thanksgiving and deliverance, they burned Amos' slave clothes.

That evening after the kids had gone to bed, Margaret placed her arms around Chris' waist and said, "Honey, I'm so proud of you; but I was so scared of being caught by the posse. I've heard some terrible stories of what happens to people who help the slaves escape. I was so worried you'd be caught, but it looks like everything will work out okay."

Relieved, Chris held his wife in his arms as she cried happy tears, and he thanked God for his many blessings.

But often during the next several weeks, Chris would lay awake in bed at night and wonder whether a posse or the sheriff would soon find their way to the Bogner farm; he pondered whether Amos or a member of the Jasper family might be caught and later tortured to reveal the identities of the other participants. And in his dreams, armed men with ferocious bloodhounds would descend on the farm and demand information on Amos and the Jaspers. But as the weeks went by without an arrest or provocation, Chris began to sleep a bit more soundly. The danger had passed.

Chris and Margaret's oldest daughter, Anna Lena, had been born on November 2, 1856. From the outset of her birth, she was a sickly child, and although Margaret loved all of her children, she had a special area in her heart for little Anna Lena.

In early June 1860, the child came down with a bad cold. Despite all the remedies that Margaret and Chris tried in an attempt to cure their daughter, Anna Lena died on July 1 as fluids filled her lungs and eventually suffocated her.

Just before she died, she looked up at her father and said, "Papa, I'm so cold."

As she drew her last breath, Chris wept bitterly; he had not cried so hard since Chéri's death in 1842.

On the 4th of July, Father Helias celebrated a Requiem Mass for the little girl. Anna Lena was the first Bogner to be buried in Sacred Heart Cemetery but unfortunately, not the last one.

Margaret took Anna Lena's death very hard, and she never fully recovered from the pain of losing her daughter. As a result, Margaret stopped singing in Church on Sundays and began suffering from bouts of severe depression.

A son, Ignatius (whom they called Ignatz), was born on December 2, 1860, and he was soon diagnosed as being a deaf-mute. Two subsequent children, Elias (born on March 16, 1862) and Anna Dorothy (born on December 11, 1863) were also later determined to be deaf-mutes.

Despite regular counseling from Father Helias and the loving support of her family, Margaret couldn't understand how the Lord God would allow these infirmities to fall upon her children. Eventually, she blamed herself for all of these misfortunes as she slowly but surely removed herself from the prior joys of her daily life.

On November 6, 1860, Abraham Lincoln was elected as the sixteenth President of the United States. In a highly contested four-way race, Lincoln eventually secured only 39.8% of the voting electorate; but it was enough to win the presidency.

As such, he carried all of the Northern and Western States but lost the entire South plus the States of Delaware and Maryland to the second-place finisher, U. S. Attorney General John C. Breckinridge. The border States of Virginia, Kentucky, and Tennessee chose Senator John Bell, and Missouri was the only State to select Congressman Stephen A. Douglas.

Shortly after Lincoln's victory, South Carolina announced that it would secede from the Union, and by February 1, 1861, six other states had followed South Carolina's lead. The former U.S. Secretary of War, Jefferson Davis, was inaugurated on February 18, 1861, as the President of the Confederate States of America in Montgomery, Alabama – the Confederacy's first capital.

Shortly after that, the newly-formed Confederate government began seizing

Federal forts, arsenals, and other Federal property located within its jurisdiction. By the time Lincoln was inaugurated on March 4, 1861, only Fort Sumter (situated in the harbor just outside of Charleston, South Carolina), Fort Pickens (positioned on the Gulf Coast near Pensacola, Florida), and one or two other outposts in the South remained firmly in Federal hands.

Once the Confederacy was formed, Missouri, along with the States of Virginia, Tennessee, North Carolina, Kentucky, Delaware, and Maryland decided to place the issue of secession to a vote of their citizens.

In March 1861, representatives from all over the State of Missouri met at Jefferson City to discuss the secession initiative. Lieutenant Governor Thomas Caute Reynolds represented the Secessionist movement, and Oliver D. Filley, the Mayor of St. Louis, spoke for the Unionists. Deeply concerned with the outcome of the matter, Chris rode the train to Jefferson City to listen to the discussions.

On the final day of the convention, Lt. Gov. Reynolds and Mayor Filley debated the issues for several contentious hours in the legislative chamber. Chris was lucky to find a seat near the back of the balcony as the two men traded arguments.

The secessionists' spokesman, Lt. Gov. Reynolds, maintained: "Yes, Mayor Filley is correct in saying that the Constitution does not directly mention the matter of secession. However, that omission, by itself, doesn't mean a state may not secede. If anything, the Constitution's silence on this notion must be interpreted as 'implied consent.' I also note that the Tenth Amendment to the Constitution says explicitly, and I quote:

> The powers not delegated to the United States by the Constitution, nor prohibited by it to the States, are reserved to the States respectively, or to the people.

Because of the Tenth Amendment's specific language leaving this option to the States and its citizens, I argue Missouri has retained the inherent right to secede."

Mayor Filley stood up, slowly walked to the podium, and replied. "Not so.

I can find no legal basis in any of our national documents which provide, or even implies, that a State can unilaterally secede from the Union. Our Republic is a unified nation where the individual states have permanently merged their sovereign rights."

Mayor Filley stood for an instant and looked around the hall. Then he said, "I ask you to recall the words contained in the Articles of Confederation – the document which governed our Nation from 1782 until 1789 and was repealed and replaced by the Constitution. The Articles explicitly provide the Union is 'perpetual.' I note further the Preamble of our Constitution reads that this document is designed to make an even 'more perfect union.' No, I hold that a State once joined to the Union may not sever the bonds."

Reynolds quickly retorted, "I see where you mentioned the Constitution, but let me refer you back to the Declaration of Independence where Jefferson wrote the following words, and again I quote:

> Governments are instituted among men, deriving their just powers from the consent of the governed, that whenever any form of government becomes destructive of these ends, it is the Right of the People to alter or to abolish it, and to institute a new government, laying its foundation on such principles and organizing its powers in such form, as to them shall seem most likely to affect their safety and happiness.

This power to sever the bonds of our union is explicitly provided in our primary document."

Reynolds stopped for a moment to let his point settle in. Then he continued:

"I also note that President Jefferson later wrote, and again, I quote:

> I am not an advocate for frequent changes in laws and constitutions, but laws and institutions must go hand in hand with the progress of the human mind. As that becomes more developed, more enlightened, as discoveries are made, new truths discovered and manners and opinions change, with the change of circumstances, institutions must also advance to keep pace with the times. We might as well require a man to wear still the coat which fitted him when a boy as civilized society to remain ever under the regimen of their barbarous ancestors.

Now, I ask you, was Jefferson wrong?"

Many people sitting in the chamber rose to their feet with thunderous applause.

Reynolds continued, "The government's power is derived from the consent of the governed – and that the people retain the right to alter or abolish it. These are Jefferson's exact words, Mayor Filley. Jefferson believed we have the right to change the ways we are governed, and I fully agree with Mr. Jefferson."

Following each retort from the opposing side of the issues, many people in the chamber would rise and cheer their particular side of the argument they espoused, and the hotly debated discussions went on until almost nightfall.

Ultimately, the convention rejected Lt. Gov. Reynold's Motion calling for Missouri to secede from the Union and join the Confederacy. Instead, the assembly voted to instruct the U.S. Congress to preserve the institution of slavery in the Southern States, and the convention recommended that the federal government remove its armed forces from seceded states to avoid the possibility of a military conflict.

Although Chris vehemently disagreed with the compromise, he fully concurred with the convention's vote to remain in the Union.

As springtime arrived once again in Rich Fountain, Chris and his older boys began plowing the fields and planting tobacco, corn, and hay for the upcoming season. There was always something to do on the farm. In recent years, he had set aside half of his eighty-acre farm for the raising of mules and horses.

Furthermore, his vineyard was producing bountiful grapes, and he still spent many hours a week in his carpentry and cabinetmaking business. All in all, things were going well for the Bogner family in the spring of 1861.

On April 12, the War Between the States began in earnest as the South Carolina government and its military forces under the command of Confederate Brigadier General Pierre Beauregard started a bombardment of Ft. Sumter; a fortification built in Charleston harbor shortly after the War of 1812. At 4:30 a.m., the Confederate batteries opened fire and shelled the fort for thirty-six straight hours. On the evening of Saturday, April 13, the fort surrendered and was evacuated.

Over the next several months, four additional States in the middle and upper South (which had repeatedly rejected Confederate overtures), Virginia, Tennessee, Arkansas, and North Carolina, voted to join the Confederacy. To reward Virginia, the Confederate capital was moved to Richmond.

Relying on the promise that they can keep their slaves, the Border States of Missouri, Kentucky, Maryland, and Delaware elected to remain in the Union despite large contingents of Southern sympathizers among their populations.

As the war ensued, both sides began to mobilize and build armies. At the beginning of the hostilities, the entire U.S. Army numbered only 16,000 troops, and of course, the Confederate army had to start constructing its forces from scratch. During the first year of the War, both sides had far more volunteers than they could adequately train and equip. But after the initial enthusiasm faded, the drafting of soldiers began.

In the summer of 1861, Chris was 46 years old and was considered to be too old to serve in the army. His sons, George (age 14), John (age 13), and Joe (age 12) were still too young to be conscripted. Every night, however, the Bogner family prayed for a quick end to the war so that the boys could remain safely at home.

In September, Chris received a letter from Charles.

September 20, 1861

Dear brother,

I hope you and your family have escaped the War so far. Unfortunately, I have been drafted, and because of the recent hostilities, mail service has been disrupted between Missouri and Arkansas. Please reply to me by way of Annette's sister, Clara Johnson, in Kenneth, Missouri, at the address found on the bottom. She'll make sure Annette eventually receives it.

Currently, I am a private in the 7th Brigade of the First Corps of the Army of Arkansas, and I serve under the command of Maj. Gen. Leonidas Polk. Just last week, our Corps has been placed under the authority of Gen. Albert Sidney Johnston, the commanding General of the Army of Mississippi.

Annette has always fully supported the War effort and had initially encouraged me to volunteer to enlist, but I've resisted. Not having any children, however, has made me a prime target for the draft, and two weeks ago, I was conscripted.

I have mixed feelings about the War. As you well know, I oppose slavery, but I also agree with Annette that the federal government has instituted policies going against the best interests of Arkansas; such as enacting the oppressive tariffs which have paralyzed the South.

Furthermore, Annette and many of my fellow Southerners believe that if the federal government were to attempt to abolish slavery, the prohibition would be an intolerable infringement on our States' rights.

Often at night, I dream about those days when we spent sailing the Atlantic on The Ballantine. It was so peaceful there on the ocean, especially when we sailed into St. Augustine and along the Gulf of Mexico. Do you remember how I fell in love with Colleen McConnell? Sometimes I wonder what became of her.

Brother, how I long to be back at sea today rather than in this dreadful army camp.

Through Annette, I'll try to keep you informed regarding my whereabouts, and I ask you to pray that the Lord will keep my fellow soldiers and me out of harm's way.

Have you heard anything from Trockau? Please pass along all of the latest news to me through Clara. She'll ensure your letters eventually will get to me.

Please give my love to Margaret and your children. How I wish to see you again.

Affectionately, Charles

As often as he could, Chris took the buckboard to Rich Fountain to read the daily edition of *The Jefferson City Inquirer* to learn what he could about the progress of the War. He was especially interested in the movements The Army of Mississippi.

In late March 1862, Chris read that a Union force, known as The Army of Tennessee under the command of Major General Ulysses S. Grant, had moved into Southern Tennessee to await the arrival of The Army of Mississippi.

Beginning on April 6, the two armies engaged in a bloody battle producing over 13,000 Union casualities and the loss of nearly 12,000 Confederate troops. Known as the Battle of Shiloh, the mêlée became the costliest engagement in American history up to that time and resulted in the defeat of the Confederate army. Its commander, General Johnston, was shot in the leg and bled to death while personally leading an attack on the Union lines.

Chris was shocked to read about the carnage which caused more than four times as many casualties as the Battle of Bull Run (which had horrified the nation nearly ten months earlier), and he prayed Charles had escaped the battle unharmed.

His fear, however, soon proved to be telling. In early June, Chris received a letter from Annette. It read,

May 20, 1862

Dear Christopher,

I deeply regret to inform you that Charles died bravely at the Battle of Shiloh while attacking Union lines. His commander, Lieutenant Peter Singleton, wrote to tell me that Charles died instantly from a head wound on April 6 and he was buried in a mass grave on the battlefield the following day.

Lt. Singleton noted that while the Yankee shell had

obliterated Charles' face, the lieutenant recognized the R tattoo branded on his right hand.

Lt. Singleton also reported that because of a large number of casualties and the oppressive heat there was no way to ship Charles' body home for a proper Christian burial. I will, however, have a requiem Mass said in his honor here.

I know this news troubles you terribly, but please take comfort in the thought that Charles' death was merciful, as so many other soldiers died in more horrific ways that day.

My husband always spoke dearly of you and your family. My most profound regret is not visiting with you more often over the years.

Charles deeply loved you. He often said you were his best friend in the entire world, and he delighted in telling stories to us about your many adventures together. We had hoped to have a son one day and name him Christopher.

I have grown to hate this damn War, and I genuinely regret encouraging Charles to enlist. I miss him more than anyone can ever know.

Please keep me in your prayers. I simply don't know how I will ever fully absorb Charles' death. He meant the world to me.

Affectionately, Annette

In a state of almost disbelief, Chris dropped the letter to the ground and stood for several minutes in the post office just clenching his hands tightly. He felt intense anger, which was closely followed by overwhelming sorrow. Then, after he slowly walked out of the building, Chris sat down on a bench and began to weep.

During the first years of War, the economy around Rich Fountain boomed. The Union Army needed horses and mules, and the supply officers obtained, at fair prices, every animal that Chris had to offer. The Zeilmanns also prospered, selling the Army bushel upon bushel of corn, wheat, and hay at market value.

But there were dangers, however; any farmer caught selling its crops or animals could be targeted by a renegade Rebel group called 'the bushwhackers' – a group of Confederate guerillas who roamed the countryside instilling fear into the hearts of so-called 'Yankee collaborators.'

The work on the farm was hard, and often the only days the Bogners left their fields was to attend church. In ease their burdens, Father Helias often planned social events for his parishioners after each Sunday Mass when neighbors had the time to meet and to share their news.

In the 1850s and early 1860s, the Zeilmann family continued to grow. The oldest boy, John (then age 33), married Margaret Bock on April 22, 1850, and by the spring of 1862, was living with their five children on a farm in nearby Westphalia.

Elias, then age 30, was engaged to Elizabeth Eichel. Johannes' oldest daughter, Ann (age 25), married John Adelhardt on May 10, 1859, and had given birth to three children – one of whom, named Christopher, died when he was less than one year old. Finally, Barbara (age 22) was engaged to a local boy, Eberhard Eikel. She also sang in the church choir.

On September 22, 1862, President Lincoln issued a preliminary warning stating he intended to order the emancipation of all slaves in any State which did not end its rebellion by January 1, 1863. Because none of the Confederate States restored themselves to the Union, and the President's Executive Order became effective on that date.

The Proclamation, however, applied only to those slaves who were held in Confederate-held areas; the Order did not apply to the States of Kentucky, Maryland, Delaware, and Missouri. Furthermore, the Order did not apply to territories that were then in Union hands, such as Tennessee, lower Louisiana (including the city of New Orleans), and much of Virginia.

The Proclamation was immediately denounced by the Democrats who opposed the War and who advocated for a restoration of the Union by allowing slavery. The Confederate response was one of outrage, as they viewed the Proclamation as a justification for the rebellion. It provided further proof;

they maintained that President Lincoln would have abolished slavery even if the states had remained in the Union.

The Jefferson City Inquirer ran an editorial which read in part:

> In the name of freedom of negroes, the Proclamation imperils the liberty of white men; to test a utopian theory of equality of races which nature, history and experience alike condemn as monstrous, it overturns the Constitution and civil laws and sets up Military usurpation in their stead.

It seemed like much of the Union population, including several of the Army Generals (who had to house and feed the ex-slaves), were also displeased with the Proclamation. Nevertheless, while the national emancipation of the slaves had begun in earnest, it was not until December 18, 1865, when the passage of the Thirteenth Amendment freed the last slaves.

Chris was angry at the limited scope of the Proclamation because the Order did not free the thousands of slaves who resided in the Union or Union-controlled Southern land. Moreover, he viewed the Order has a strategic military move aimed at causing upheaval in the Southern-held territory, and that it was not a humanitarian effort to abolish the heinous practice of involuntary servitude.

The fact slavery was still legal in Missouri greatly disappointed Chris.

In what was first hoped to be a short war, dragged on unmercifully; but by July 4, 1863, the tide had turned sharply in the Union's favor following the battles of Gettysburg and Vicksburg. Then in the autumn of 1863, Lincoln appointed General Grant as the commander of all Union armies, and shortly after that, Grant placed Maj. Gen. William Tecumseh Sherman in command of most of the western troops.

Soon Grant aimed The Army of The Potomac at the city of Richmond, and Sherman set his eyes squarely on Atlanta. Ever vigilant regarding the progress of the War, Chris prayed that the insurgency would be over long before his sons were of fighting age.

On one afternoon in late November of 1863, Chris had just finished selling the remainder of his non-breeding stock to Union Army buyers when he saw a band of six 'irregulars' galloping up the lane to the farmhouse. Instantly, he could tell they were Confederate Bushwhackers.

Chris yelled, "George, John, Joe – run out the back door and hide in the barn; go now; be quick!"

The three brothers immediately put down their dinner forks and ran out of the house. Chris grabbed his rifle and stepped onto the front porch, just as the guerrillas approached the house.

Aiming his weapon directly at the lead soldier, Chris said, "Good afternoon, boys. How can I help you today?"

The troops stopped in front of the house. The lead officer replied, "Well now, you don't look too friendly, old man. I hope you don't get yourself hurt with that musket."

"I'm just protecting what's mine, friend. Now, what do you want?"

"We heard you've been selling mules to the Yankees. Have you now?"

Still aiming his rifle at the lead man, Chris replied, "Last time I checked, it's still a free country."

"Sounds to me that you're on the wrong side of this fight, old man. I saw a couple of mules over in the pasture that President Davis would like me to requisition. How much you want for them?"

"They're not for sale; they're my breeding stock. I need them to replenish my herd."

"Well, that's not very friendly, old man. Now, we'll have to take them off your hands."

Chris wondered for a moment; should he stand his ground. He replied, "If you leave right now, you can have six of them, and I won't have to put a bullet through your head."

"Much obliged, old man. But we also heard you have three sons of fighting age. We want them too. I think I saw them running into the barn."

"I warn you; stay away from my boys."

At that, the leader turned to his men and said, "Virgil, take two men and go find those boys."

"Yes, Captain."

Chris knew he was outnumbered but kept the rifle pointed directly at the captain's head.

Three of the bushwhackers turned their horses and rode off at a gallop toward the barn – where they dismounted, drew their pistols, and slowly entered it.

One of them yelled, "Come on out, boys. It's time for you to be heroes for 'the cause.'"

The guerrillas opened the door, and at first view, it appeared that the building was empty. After looking around, one of the bushwhackers noticed the brothers were hiding in the loft.

"They're up there; let's get 'em."

As two of the guerrillas began climbing up the ladder to the loft, Joe and George grabbed bales of tobacco and threw them down at the bushwhackers, causing the men to fall and stumble down the ladder. Then the three boys opened an outside door, jumped out of the back of the barn, and ran as fast as they could toward the woods.

The bushwhackers, seeing the boys scrambling away, rushed out the front door, sprinted around to the rear of the building, and began firing their pistols at the fleeing brothers. Although one bullet grazed George's left arm, the boys reached the safety of the woods mostly unscarred.

After emptying their pistols, the guerrillas mounted their horses and rode back to the captain who asked:

"I heard gunshots. Where're the boys?"

"Sir, they got away; but I think we may have hit one of them. Do you want us to try to find them?"

"No, dammit, the Yankees may have heard the shots; now we need to get out of here quick. Grab six of the best mules and meet us down by the fence.

Go now, sergeant."

"Yes, sir."

The captain turned back to look at Chris and said, "We'll be back for your boys, old man, and if you ever sell another damn thing to the Yankees, I swear that we'll come back in the middle of the night and burn your goddamn farmhouse to the ground. Then we'll hang you and your wife from the highest tree. Do you hear me, old man?"

Chris still had his rifle pointed directly at the leader's head. "I hear you; now go."

The captain stared for a second at Chris, and after saluting, he rode back down the lane at a trot.

After the bushwhackers left, the door flew open, and Margaret and the other children came out. Margaret asked, "Are they gone? Husband, I was so scared; I heard gunshots."

He placed his arms around her. "Yes, they're gone, my dear, and they stole five or six of our mules; but not any of the horses."

The remaining children were crying. He hugged them, too, and told them everything was alright. Chris said, "Mike, Frank, run out to the woods and find your brothers. Bring them home."

"Yes, Papa."

After treating George for a minor gunshot wound, Chris helped the boys hide in the woods for the next few days. The bushwhackers, however, never returned to the Bogner farm.

The next twelve months turned out to be a time of both great joy and sorrow. Margaret gave birth to her last child, Anna Dorothy, on December 11, 1863. Just like her previous two children, Ignatz and Elias, Anna was later determined to be both deaf and mute. After that, it seemed that Margaret's depression deepened with every passing day; she often spent days upon days in bed.

As Christmas arrived, Margaret grew even more despondent; even more locked up within herself. Her face wore a lethargic expression that had become almost routine for her during those days; a state of profound melancholy which lay upon her that winter as if her whole presence seemed to reflect an endless struggle with either guilt or bitterness.

Her spirits were lifted briefly in January when two of her siblings married. On January 14, her youngest sister, Barbara, married Eberhard Eikel, and about two weeks later, her brother, John, married Margaretha Elisabeth Eickel. On both occasions, Margaret sang 'Ave Maria' during a Nuptial High Mass performed by Father Helias. These would be, however, the last times that Margaret sang in church.

A joint reception for both couples was held in the Zeilmann home on January 26, 1864, and the entire town was invited. Once again, Gunther Kemmerer and his sons played music in the parlor, and Father Helias provided the blessings.

After most of the people had left that afternoon, Johannes and Chris went out on the front porch, lit their pipes, and sipped a glass of Tennessee whiskey. Soon, Johannes set down his glass and said, "Well, they're all married now, and I can't believe I already have sixteen grandchildren. Where has the time gone?"

Chris just shook his head, "Margaret and I have nine children, and two of the boys are courting local girls. Soon, all of them will marry. I guess it's a perpetual cycle. All of my brothers and sisters in Trockau are married, but unfortunately, I've never met any of their spouses nor seen any of their children. I suppose I never will. And of course, Charles lies in a Rebel grave. How I miss him."

They both sat quietly for a few moments. Johannes said, "So many families have suffered during this damn war. I wonder how things will be after it ends."

After a long silence, Chris said, "You know, I'm so worried about Margaret, and I don't know what to do. She blames herself for so many things; I don't know whether to listen to her or to tell her to get on with her life. I don't think God is punishing her, do you?

"I guess the Lord moves in mysterious ways, but I can't believe He'd punish such a virtuous woman – but then I remember Job and what happened to him."

Once again they sat in silence. Then Chris said, "Dorothea looks better today. I was almost thinking that she'd be dancing tonight."

"Yes, she has her good and bad days now. You know that she's just turned 65, and I've heard the Bible says God will only give us three score and ten years. I wonder, too, how much longer I'll live. Later this year, I'll also turn 65."

"I believe we all have a long time to go on this earth. Let's have another taste of the whiskey. Then I'll have to go home. Tomorrow's another day, you know."

Dorothea Redel Zeilmann died peacefully in her sleep on May 16, 1864. Less than a month later, Margaret contracted erysipelas and died on June 3, 1864, at age thirty-four.

Erysipelas is a skin rash which usually begins to form on the arms and legs. In late May, she began to develop a high fever that was followed by chills, shaking, diarrhea, and vomiting. She became severely dehydrated, and toward the end of her illness, she began hallucinating.

In one of her last lucid times, she cried out, "Why is God punishing me? What have I done to offend Him so much? Whatever it was, Dear Lord, I am heartily sorry for having offended you. I beg you; please forgive me; I don't want to die. Please, Lord, please."

Father Helias was called to the house on June 2, and Margaret passed away on the following morning. Chris was kneeling there by her side, holding her hand, and the older children were also by her bedside, praying and weeping – and saying the rosary.

Two days later, Father Helias consecrated a Requiem Mass at *Sacred Heart*, and after reciting the gospel, with tears in his eyes, he stood at the pulpit to give the eulogy:

"My dear brothers and sister in Christ, the Holy Bible says,

To everything, there is a season and a time for every purpose under heaven. There is a time to be born and a time to die.

Tuesday was Margaret's day to go home to the Lord.

Margaret was a lovely woman. She embodied all of the attributes of a perfect wife and mother. Margaret was caring, thoughtful, hardworking, compassionate, loving, and so much more. And she had the voice of an angel – I've never heard anyone with a more-perfect pitch, such a precise tonal quality, and an extensive range as Margaret. For a while, I believed she was an angel. For almost twenty years, she sang soprano in our church, often with just her mother, Dorothea, accompanying her on the piano. Now, she sings for God.

I remember one Christmas morning about ten years ago when she surprised me when she sang 'O Holy Night' in French here in this church. I'd never heard the song before, and with Dorothea playing the piano, Margaret sang:

> Minuit, chrétiens, c'est l'heure solennelle,
>
> Où l'Homme-Dieu descendit jusqu'à nous
>
> Pour effacer la tache originelle.

I still recall weeping upon hearing the carol which contained such beauty, and I remember feeling so much love which she brought to you and me on that Christmas Day. I know each of you recalls that's she sang in this church for the last times less than six months ago at the weddings of her brother and her sister. I dread to think I'll never hear her angelic voice again on this earth. Now I'll have to wait until I listen to her in heaven.

Margaret grew up in a large family. She was the second oldest of five children, which is how she later became such a wonderful mother. Margaret spent much of her childhood helping Dorothea raise her kids. Margaret worked as hard as any woman I've ever known, and despite all of her hardships in raising her eleven children and work-ing hand-in-hand with Christopher in the fields, she often found time to help me here at Sacred Heart. It was the Bogners, along with the Zeilmanns and so many other families, who raised this building from the ground to the sanctuary it is today."

Father Helias talked for another thirty minutes or so, and he was followed by three of Margaret's sons: John, Joe, and Mike. Then Chris rose to speak; but with less than ten words into his eulogy, he broke down and had to be helped back to his pew.

When she was interred in Sacred Heart Cemetery later that afternoon, Chris spoke for a few moments. He ended up by saying:

"Rest in peace, my love. Now, little Anna Lena will have her mother with her for eternity."

Margaret's passing was a terrible blow to Chris, and it resurrected all of the pain he'd felt resulting from Chéri's death and the loss of his beloved, Sonia. He was now a widower who had four children under six years of age, and three of them were disabled. After talking to Father Helias, the priest suggested that Chris consider hiring a widow to come into the Bogner home and raise his children.

A few days later, Chris welcomed Martha Gruden, a widow who had lost her only child in the War, into the household. Martha would remain with the Bogner family for almost the next ten years.

In November 1864, President Lincoln won a second term, and by April 1865 the War was nearly over. Shortly after General Robert E. Lee's rebel army had reached Appomattox Court House in Central Virginia, Lee decided the fight was now hopeless. On April 9, 1865, he surrendered the Army of Northern Virginia to General Grant.

Then on April 26, 1865, General Joseph E. Johnston surrendered nearly 90,000 men of the Army of Tennessee to General Sherman at the Bennett Place, North Carolina. It proved to be the largest surrender of Confederate forces, effectively bringing the War to an end.

In the interim, however, President Lincoln had been shot by John Wilkes Booth, a Southern sympathizer, on April 14, 1865. Lincoln died on the next morning, and his vice president, Andrew Johnson, became the new president.

After that, President Johnson officially declared the end of the Southern rebellion on May 9, 1865, and Confederate President Jefferson Davis was captured the following day. The War resulted in the deaths of approximately 620,000 soldiers and 50,000 civilians.

On May 4, 1865, Chris celebrated his fiftieth birthday at a dinner held at the Zeilmann home. Johannes had invited the entire family, and Chris and the other well-wishers enjoyed a delicious pork dinner with all of the trimmings. After two or three toasts to his health and long life, Chris was asked to speak. He took a swallow of cider and arose from his chair at the head of the table.

"Johannes, I am honored by your hospitality, and I thank every one of you for making me feel so happy today. It has certainly been a tough five years for all of us. First, my baby, Anna Lena, died in June of 1861, and then my brother Charles was killed in the Battle of Shiloh in October 1862. Our beloved wife, mother, and grandmother, Dorothea, died on May 16, 1864, and finally, my dear wife, Margaret, followed her mother to heaven on June 3. How I miss each one of them."

Chris stopped for an instant and wiped his eyes. "But, wow, fifty years of life – where did it all go? I still remember waking up in my brother's bed in Trockau and going off to school each morning. I was probably about six years old then, and it feels like it happened just yesterday or maybe last week. Those memories are still so vivid for me. Though my father has been gone nearly twenty years and my mother dead for almost forty, I still see them in my dreams, and I miss them so much."

He took another sip of cider. "I remember our last day in Trockau – the day after Christmas, 1839 – when Charles and I began our long trip to America. After shedding tears and hugs, we rode on boats down the Danube to Ulm, and later up the Neckar and the Rhine to Rotterdam. And then we sailed on *The Ballantine* across the Atlantic to Philadelphia, and finally south to New Orleans. Those were heady days for us."

He laughed to himself as a memory filled his mind, and then continued,

"Charles and I lived for a year and a half in New Orleans, and after that, we rode on *The Mississippi Queen* to St. Louis where we lived with my cousin, Christopher Bauer, and worked in his business. Johannes, I still recall the day you walked into Bauer Mercantile and invited me to the cathedral to hear your daughter sing. I fell deeply in love with her from the first instant I heard her voice and saw her lovely face. She is the best thing that has ever happened to me."

Chris talked about later on getting to know the Zeilmann family, his marriage to Margaret in 1846, and their first ten years together where the Bogner family struggled to make the homestead both profitable and joyous. He also talked about the prelude to the War, and about the War itself; how so many soldiers died; and how so much damage resulted from the battling armies.

"Now that the War is over, we all need to, as Abraham Lincoln said, bind up the nation's wounds and move forward. I have six sons between ages ten and eighteen; and four little children, between ages one and six. Even after all of this sorrow, I am a blessed and happy man."

He smiled and looked at the younger people around the table. "These next decades will be theirs and yours, and I can't wait for the next fifty years to pass by to see how well you all did. Johannes, thanks for your love and kindness."

Almost as if a veil had been lifted, Chris was once again a happy man.

One Sunday afternoon in October 1866, Alois was looking out of the front window when he saw a man walking up the lane to their house. "Papa, a black man is walking up the road."

Chris got out of his chair, grabbed his rifle, and went out to the porch. After the War, many former slaves and soldiers were looking for work or for opportunities to steal.

The man, however, seeing Chris, began waving. "Mister Chris; Mister Chris."

Chris looked hard at the man and replied, "Amos, is that you?"

"Yes, sir, it's me."

Chris put down his musket, and began walking swiftly toward Amos, "Well, I'll be; Amos, it's so great to see you."

Amos reached out his hand, but Chris said, "Come on, Amos; give me a hug."

The two men hugged for a long time until Chris said, "We're about ready to sit down to Sunday dinner. Would you like to join us?"

"In the house, sir?"

"Yes, in our house; you're a free man now; you can go anywhere you like."

"Thank you, Sir, I am mighty hungry."

The family sat down at the table and soon began passing the dishes to each other. After grace, Amos started telling the family all about what happened to him after Chris had left the Jasper family home.

"Two days later, Misters Hiram and Jasper hid me in their wagon and drove to a spot on the Missouri River. Later that night, a man named Kent rowed me over to the Illinois side, and I stayed with another Quaker family until I was able to walk okay."

"We were praying for you; you know that, right?"

"Thank you, sir. I eventually found my way to a Union camp and joined the Army. I was in North Carolina in Sherman's Corps when Joe Johnson finally surrendered. I was lucky; I never really saw any action; we just marched and marched from Atlanta to Savanah, and then up to Carolina."

Amos also told the family that when the War was over, he was given his pay and a train ticket to St. Louis. The money didn't last long, and then he set out to find his family who lived at the Ridgely Plantation, near Hancock, Missouri.

"When I got there, everyone was gone. I was told that my people had burned the house down in 1864 and later on, several of them were hung. I spent a couple of days there asking about my family, but nobody would help me. I was afraid they'd hang me, too; and if I hadn't served in the Army, I think they would have, Sir."

Chris asked, "So, what are you going to do now?"

"I want to find Father Helias and be baptized as a Catholic."

"After dinner, I'll ride you over there."

Father Helias couldn't believe his eyes, and he immediately offered Amos a place to live in the parsonage. After receiving instructions in the faith, Father Helias baptized Amos on Christmas Day, and he spent the next several years helping out in the rectory.

On August 3, 1867, Father Helias celebrated his 70th birthday, and at the reception in the church hall following Mass that Sunday, he announced he would be leaving Sacred Heart and retiring on a farm near his brother in Taos, Missouri – a town about twenty-five miles from Rich Fountain. Father Helias would help out in the local church, St. Francis Xavier, up until his death on the morning of August 11, 1874.

In reporting his death, *The Jefferson City Inquirer* wrote:

> In 1867, Father Helias transferred his residence from Rich Fountain to Taos, and from then until his death, he lived amongst the people he loved, and whom he served so faithfully for so many years. On the morning of August 11, the 'Apostle of Central Missouri' was found lying in the yard near the church – a stroke had ended his life. He was buried in the church cemetery in Taos.

During the one occasion when Chris was able to visit Taos, he laid a bright bouquet of summer flowers on Father Helias' grave.

Chris left the cemetery with a heavy heart.

CHAPTER FOURTEEN

Oleyen, Nebraska, July 1874

In the middle of the Civil War, Congress passed *The Homestead Act of 1862*. The act provided that the lands west of the Mississippi River, acquired as a result of the Louisiana Purchase, would be given away in one-hundred-and-sixty-acre parcels to men who were intent on living on the property and cultivating it for at least five years. Thus, any citizen who had never taken up arms against the Federal Government, and was at least twenty-one years old, could apply for a federal land grant.

The Act required a three-step procedure: apply, improve the land, and register for a deed of title. Proof of a man's intention was relatively simple: a man was required to build a home on this land; live on it for at least nine months each year; and farm at least forty acres of his grant for five years. At the end of this time, he'd receive the title, and the land was his in perpetuity. The property which was not claimed by the homesteaders (much of it was not suitable for farming) remained the property of the government.

By 1900, over six-hundred-thousand claims had been filed for approximately eighty million acres of public land.

For the area around Rich Fountain, it was a prosperous time for most farmers following the end of hostilities. There had been minimal fighting in Central Missouri during the War, and the Federal Government had been buying almost everything the farmers could grow.

In the South, however, the economy was in shambles. Farms were in disrepair, and the pre-war stock of horses, mules, and cattle was severely depleted. Most of the railroads had been destroyed, and the Confederate dollar was worthless. Moreover, over a quarter of Southern white men of military age died during the War, leaving countless families destitute.

As for the Christopher Bogner family, their prosperity abruptly ended when the Union army stopped purchasing the family's mules and horses. Although the Bogners were by no means poor, the steady income resulting from the federal purchasing agents had diminished considerably.

In 1872, five of Christopher's sons were 19 years old or older, and they were ready to strike out on their own with farms and families. Due to the relative prosperity in Central Missouri, the price of land had skyrocketed, and Chris had little extra money to help the boys purchase farms of their own.

George, the oldest son, began courting Mary Stuckenschneider in 1871, and the two of them were talking seriously about marriage. Before a wedding could occur, however, the couple agreed that George would need to buy a farm of his own. The lack of farmland at a reasonable price was quite frustrating to George and Mary.

One day, Chris was reading *The Jefferson City Inquirer* when he noticed an advertisement on the bottom of page three. It read:

HOMESTEAD LAND OFFICE IN OMAHA, NEBRASKA

Under the provisions of The Homestead Act of 1862, Congress will be releasing additional tracts, consisting of 160 acres each, to secure homesteads for actual settlers in the following counties, beginning on July 1, 1872:

Butler, Colfax, Polk, and Stanton.

Interested applicants must satisfy all of the Act's requirements, and may inquire for further information at the Homestead Land Office in Omaha, Nebraska.

Cornelius M. Atkinson, Federal Land Agent
234 Dodge Street
Omaha, Nebraska

Chris showed the advertisement to his sons, and immediately, George sent a letter to the land office agent in Omaha. Two weeks later, he received an envelope with the information he needed to make his decision.

In early June 1872, George and his brother, Joe, hitched a team of horses to the buckboard and began the roughly five-hundred-mile trek to Omaha. The understanding between Chris and his two sons was that should they find good available land, each brother would file a claim and remain on the property until spring. Mary Stuckenschneider was in full agreement.

With George and Joe gone, the management of the Bogner farm fell squarely on the four remaining boys: John (age 24); Mike (age 21), Frank (age 19), and Alois (age 17). Martha Gruden and Barbara (age 14) ran the Bogner household. Every couple of months, Chris would send George and Joe some money to help finance their homesteads in Nebraska.

The acquisition of the land, however, was no immediate remedy the George and Joe. Very few homesteaders could afford the costs related to building a farmhouse or acquiring the necessary food, tools, livestock, and seed to make the farm successful. Additional money was required for the lumber needed for the construction of houses, barns, sheds, and fences. Each of the brothers would need significant help to survive long enough to make the farms profitable.

In September 1872, Chris received a letter from George and Joe. It read:

August 21, 1872

Papa,

We know you've been worrying about us, but we decided to wait to write until we could give you some news. It took us nearly four weeks to drive the wagon to Omaha, but we made the trip without any serious setbacks. For the next several weeks, we rode around the four counties until finding good available land near the town of Oleyen in Colfax County.

On July 12, we filed claims for adjacent farms with the land office in Grand Island, and now we are beginning the process of staking the land and building a sod house on George's homestead. Next year, we'll construct a sod house for Joe.

The land is beautiful; it's mostly flat but has an occasional rise. A stream named Maple Creek flows directly through our properties. Perhaps the most remarkable features are that the land is covered with high grasses and it has absolutely no trees on our homesteads. The view in all directions goes on seemingly forever.

The town of Oleyen is tiny - only three businesses - but it has a post office. Please send mail to us at Box 34, Oleyen, Nebraska. We are almost out of money; please send us as much as you can spare as the costs are much steeper than we had anticipated.

We miss all of you so much. Please let Mary read the letter, and please tell her that I am working as hard as I can to keep the dreams we've made together.

Finally, I am enclosing the Homestead Grant. Please keep it safe as the conditions here are not dependable.

There are several other homesteads available adjacent to ours, and please tell John, Mike, and Frank that if they wish to join us next spring, the land agent assured Joe and me that he'd hold them for one year.

Please pray for us. We have heard stories on how rough the winters can be here on the prairie.

Love, George and Joe

Chris put down the letter and just shook his head. Then he prayed the boys would be strong enough to endure the hardships that he knew stood before them.

He opened the folded land grant and read it.

Duplicate Receiver's Receipt, No. _3026_   Application No. _3093_

HOMESTEAD

Receiver's Office, _Jesse Turner_
Grand Island, Neb. _July 12th, 1872_

Received from _George Bogner_ the sum of _Fourteen dollars_ and _no_ cents; being the amount of fee and compensation of Register and Receiver for the entry of the _____ _North ½ of the NW ¼_ _____ of Section __22__ in Township _____ _20 North_ _____ of Range _____ _4 East_ _____ under The Acts of Congress approved May 20, 1862, and March 31, 1864, entitled: "An act to secure homesteads to actual settlers on the public domain."

Jesse Turner
Receiver

Chris immediately placed the document in his safe.

Mike and Frank joined their brothers in Colfax County the following year, and they applied for federal homestead grants on the two adjacent properties which the land agent had held for them. Soon the brothers were asking Chris to sell the farm and join them in Nebraska.

By the autumn of 1873, Chris was 58 years old and beginning to feel the effects of aging. He was becoming hard of hearing and was experiencing arthritis in his hands, feet, and back. John, the oldest remaining son, was 25 and betrothed to Theresia Luebbert. They were planning an April wedding and busy looking for a farm to purchase. Alois would soon be 19, and Chris still had four children under the age of 16.

The Nebraska brothers came home to Rich Fountain from time-to-time on the train. Although it can take as long as two months for a traveler to ride a buckboard the distance of almost five hundred miles from Rich Fountain to Oleyen, the railroad service was much faster – often only two days. The boys could ride the train from Omaha to Kansas City, and then board another one which would stop at Bonnots Mill – the depot closest to Rich Fountain. During their visits home, the brothers talked endlessly about the beauty and opportunities in Colfax County, and Chris was sorely tempted.

In March 1874, Chris rode the train to Omaha, and Mike and Frank picked him up at the depot. After a four-hour ride in the wagon, the brothers arrived at George's home. Because of the shortage of lumber in Nebraska, George was still living in a sod house.

The plan of the house was 'L-shaped' in design with rooms projecting to the east and the south. A small bedroom occupied the northwest corner - at the angle of the 'L.' The eastward portion of the house contained a large kitchen and hall, and the southward projection included a somewhat smaller parlor and dining room.

After dinner, Chris inquired about the construction of the house. "How long did it take you boys to build the house?"

George replied, "Once we got the hang of it, Joe and I finished it in about two weeks. We cut patches of sod in rectangles – maybe two feet by one foot by six inches – and began piling them up to set the walls. We used what little lumber we had for the doors and window frames."

Chris asked, "How about the roof?"

"Well, the roof is also made of sod but we used 2x6's for the ridge posts and some of the rafters, and we covered it all with tarpaper. The whole cost of the house was only about five bucks."

"Wow, that's amazing. How did it do in the winter? I'll bet it was quite cold here."

George smiled, "Yes, the winter was brutal, Papa – much colder than anything I've ever felt in Rich Fountain. But we were pretty warm inside. Joe stayed here with me in the house during the first winter, and all four of us lived here together last winter.'

"That's good."

"The thick sod walls provided pretty good insulation against the cold, and often, we'd burn corncobs, slough grass, or dried buffalo dung for us to stay warm. Once in a while, we purchased some coal in Oleyen. We got by – but it's still no place for a woman and kids."

Chris just looked around the inside of the home. Canvas lined the interior walls, and it was dark, damp, and musty.

"Papa, we need you to join us here. You can help us build proper homes and the furniture which we need. I want to bring Mary here next year and begin our family. She's waited almost four years for me, and I don't want to lose her."

Then the brothers talked about their life in Nebraska; the occasional bands of Indians and herds of buffalo. They also mentioned instances about meeting their neighbors and the townsfolk, and about the strange insects, the number of tornadoes, the drenching thunderstorms, and the all-consuming fear of prairie fires. But what seemed to have what bothered them most was the intense loneliness of living in such an isolated space.

Mike said, "Papa, I thought that the winter would never end. The wind never stops blowing, and it's so dark here at night. And there are no trees and no birds; but still, this place calls to me."

"How so?"

"Because in four years, it will be mine. There's so much potential here. We see settlers coming in just about every week – some were passing through in long wagon trains on their way to Oregon and California; some were bound for the Colorado and Wyoming Territories. But more and more folks are coming to Colfax County and building shops in Oleyen. There's talk of schools, churches, and local government; things are changing so fast, Papa."

Chris asked, "How good is the land?"

Joe answered, "Papa, much of the soil here has never been turned over, and it was as hard as a rock the first time we planted. But the soil is rich, and during the second year, the soil turned-over easily. It's good for corn and wheat, and probably excellent for orchards and vineyards. Anything that can withstand a hard winter will thrive here."

Over the next two weeks, the boys took Chris to see their farms, and later over to Oleyen. Then they rode south to the Elkhorn River to show Chris the area where some trees grew along the riverbanks. He liked everything he saw. Before he left for Missouri, he looked at a farm that was going up for sale and adjacent to Frank's homestead. The farmer said he wanted the sum of $4 per acre, and that he would be willing to sell the property after September 1 when the harvest was over.

Chris gave the farmer the sum of $10 to hold the farm for a couple of weeks, and just as soon as Chris had arrived home in Rich Fountain, he accepted the farmer's offer to purchase the property. While Chris believed the price was a little high (he presumed the sum of $2.50 to $3 per acre would be more reasonable), the homestead already had a two story house, two large barns, and a couple of sheds. Furthermore, most of the land was already under cultivation.

Come summer, Chris and the remainder of his family were going to join his sons in Nebraska.

On April 21, 1874, Chris' second oldest son, John, married Theresia Luebbert in Westphalia, a little town situated roughly ten miles northwest of Rich Fountain. As a wedding gift, Chris promised the couple twenty percent of the proceeds from the sale of the Bogner farm. Two of John's brothers, George and Joe, rode the train from Omaha to attend their brother's wedding. It was a joyous event, and Chris began thinking that soon he'd be a grandfather.

The union of John and Theresia eventually produced nine children and forty-seven grandchildren. Their marriage would last for over forty-eight years, and John would live to be seventy-four, and Theresia would die at age ninety-one.

After only a two month search, Chris found a buyer for the Bogner farm, and in early August 1874, he and his remaining five children began preparing for their long journey to Nebraska. To lighten their load, they sold as much of their belongings as they could sell – most of which went to the new buyer. Chris gave away much of the rest of his household belongings to John and Theresia, so they had items to furnish their new home.

In the end, Chris decided to bring along twenty-seven horses and mules (which he shipped to Lincoln, Nebraska in a cattle car), several cuttings from his vineyard and orchard, their clothes and personal items, a few mementos, and a couple bags of acorns Chris would plant on the barren prairie once they reached Oleyen. He also brought along the brown leather chest he and Charles had carried with them all the way from Trockau.

On the afternoon before the family began their journey north, Chris rode in the buckboard to Sacred Heart Cemetery to make one final visit to Margaret's grave. It was a hot August day, and he could feel the heat and humidity soaking through his broad-brimmed hat and black jacket. Sitting down by her tombstone, he removed his cap, and like so many other times before; he began talking to her.

"Darling, we'll begin our trip to Oleyen tomorrow morning, and I've come to say goodbye. I can't believe you've been laying here for over ten years now. I still can't fully accept you're gone, even after all of this time."

He stopped for an instant and wiped a tear from his eye. "You still fill up my dreams almost every night, and I can't count the number of times when I've said to myself, 'I have to tell this to Margaret.' Oh my darling, I still miss you so very much. Why did you have to die?"

He stopped once again. "You and I have eight wonderful sons, and except for the two youngest boys, they still remember you and cherish the time they spent with you. Little Barbara still remembers some things, and I've let the three youngest ones know how wonderful you were. The three – Elias, Ignatz, and Anna – have learned sign-language, and they talk to each other all of the time. Martha has learned it, too, and we're so sad that she's has decided to remain in Rich Fountain. I understand her reasons for staying here, but the four little ones think of her as a dear, dear aunt. They will miss her so much. You would have liked her, too."

Chris looked around and noticed an older woman was walking into the cemetery – probably to visit her late husband. "Darling, John's wife is a wonderful woman; she's made him so happy. And George plans to wed Mary next spring here in Rich Fountain. So, I'll be back to see you in April."

He couldn't continue; tears were flowing down his cheeks. He bent over and kissed her gravestone, and tried to say something more but the words wouldn't come. He stood up and mouthed the words 'goodbye, my darling' and slowly walked out of the cemetery.

On August 12, 1874, Chris and his family boarded *The Central Missouri Railroad* and rode the train as far west as Kansas City. There, they boarded *The Chicago, Burlington and Quincy Railroad,* and rode on that train north to Lincoln, Nebraska, where the twenty-seven horses and mules had been offloaded on the previous day and positioned into a holding corral.

As the Bogner family got off of the train in Lincoln, George and Mike were already waiting there for them. After some hugs and tears, the family loaded themselves and their possessions onto two wagons, rounded up the horses and mules, and set off on the final leg of their journey to Oleyen.

On March 1, 1867, Nebraska became the 37th state, and shortly after that, the legislature moved the state capital from Omaha to Lancaster (which was later renamed 'Lincoln' after the late President). During the 1870s, Nebraska experienced substantial growth in population primarily because its vast prairie land was perfect for agriculture. The recent inventions of barbed wire, windmills, and the steel plow, combined with the favorable weather, enabled settlers to utilize Nebraska as prime farming land.

The distance from Lincoln to Oleyen (later changed to Olean) is approximately eighty miles, and the trip would take the family four days. By the evening of the third day, each member of the family had his or her tasks to perform and was well used to them.

Mike would remove the wood from under the lead wagon (consisting of dry branches and small logs they had gathered from the last thicket they passed) and set them down near the fire-pit. George took two iron rods, drove them into the ground around the perimeter of the fire-pit and placed another rod parallel to the other two so that a cooking pot could be hung from it. Then he prepared the fire.

As Alois unhitched the teams, Chris attended to the horses and mules and later turned them all loose to graze on the prairie grasses. While Barbara waited for the pot to boil, she and Anna spread a blanket on the ground and put utensils around the edges. Once the meal was ready, the family sat down, said a blessing, and began eating.

Mike asked, "Papa, tomorrow he'll be home; how are the horses and mules doing?"

"Several of them were a bit roughed up as the result of their time riding in the cattle car, but they seem to be healing fine. Some have scratches and sores from the ride, but there's only one I'm anxious about – Drake – he's come up lame."

"What are you going to do?"

"Well, I won't shoot him, and I can't leave him. Drake is one of my prime suds; he's sired maybe twenty foals; perhaps more. He's getting a bit old, but he's my best one. Hopefully, he'll be better by morning."

They passed bowls of food around the blanket and talked about the day's drive.

George said, "Tomorrow, we'll cross the Platte River. It's a bit hilly around the ford, but I believe the wagons will make it okay. We'll all probably get wet, though. It's running a little high after our wet summer."

Alois said, "You know, I'll be glad to see the farms. I still can't believe all of this seemingly endless grasslands; it's truly quite amazing."

Around eight o'clock, it suddenly turned dark – as if a curtain had fallen across the land. Then, the western horizon swelled with a mystical light – a glow of pale yellow mingled with touches of gold, purple, and red. The colors enveloped the entire western sky, and with every passing moment, the sunset grew even more spectacular.

Chris looked easterly and said, "Look, here comes that ol' moon-rising; I think it's gonna be full tonight."

In the minutes that followed, a massive golden moon rose just above the plains. The family had watched it rise over the past two nights – in fact, Chris had watched it from the train as *The Central Missouri Railroad* had sped through western Missouri. But each evening that the family saw the moon, it seemed grander than the night before.

As a hush fell upon them, they looked east and then west and finally, west again. Each side of the sky seemed to mesmerize them as they 'oohed' and 'ahed.' As the sunset began to diminish, the silvery moonbeams grew even brighter, and for many minutes, there was silence in their little camp on the prairie.

A few moments later, Chris removed his pipe from his coat-pocket, knocked out the ashes from the previous evening, and after filling it with tobacco, lit his pipe again. George opened the bottle of Tennessee whiskey and passed it around making toasts for family and good fortune.

As Chris was exhaling a flow of tobacco smoke, he couldn't quite believe the beauty of the evening prairie, and he wished quietly to himself that Margaret could have seen it with them that night.

As a chill finally engulfed them, the family spread out their bedrolls and lay under their quilts still gazing at the moon.

Mike asked, "So, Papa, do you think Drake will be okay?"

Chris answered, "Yeah, I believe so. He's a hardy one."

He yawned once or twice – long and slowly – and then rolled over onto his side.

At about ten o'clock on the following morning, the family arrived at the southern bank of the Platte River. Formed from snowmelt in the eastern Rockies, the Platte is the principal river in the State of Nebraska, and it meanders for over one thousand miles until it empties into the Missouri River just south of Omaha. For over most of its length, the Platte is a murky, broad, shallow, snaking stream with a muddy bottom and many islands.

As the Bogner family approached the steep riverbank, they halted and searched for the best place to make a crossing. After finding one, George and Mike were the first to enter the water, taking the stray horses and mules to the other side.

With Mike remaining on the northern bank tending to the horses and mules, and the children sitting safely aboard the wagons, Chris, George, and Alois began pushing the buckboards from behind. As Ignatz and Elias held onto the reins, the two teams of horses were lured into the river.

Slowly the buckboards sank until the water was even with the top of the wheels which allowed the horses to pull the cargo slowly toward the northern bank. When the horses felt the rushing current, however, they began to panic; but with the men riding alongside, the animals started walking with confidence.

With much clambering, scrambling, snorting, and grunting, the horses finally regained their footing and eventually made it safely across the Platte and up the northern slope of the riverbank.

Four hours later, the wagons, horses, and mules reached George Bogner's homestead. Looking back, Chris could see Alois slowly leading Drake toward the farm, walking about a hundred yards behind the others. The horse was limping badly, but his leg would eventually heal. Drake would live for another twenty years or so, and acting as a stud, the prized sire would produce dozens of foals.

The Bogners were finally home and safe in Oleyen, Nebraska.

With the harvest done, Chris and his family gained possession of their farm in mid-September. During the first days, there was so much to do that they hardly had time to eat. They unloaded their wagons, set up the kitchen, and began rearranging the furniture which the prior owner had left behind for them. Until more beds could be acquired, most of the family members slept on the floors in their bedrolls. Initially, the younger ones thought this was great fun but soon tired of the hard floors.

About a week after moving in, all of the brothers gathered at Chris' home and sat out on the front porch as the first sunset colors of evening began to spread westward over the plains. Soon the talk turned to a serious nature; how to establish their priorities as winter was coming on.

As the evening grew late, a strange silence descended upon them; the very vastness of the prairie and isolation from the comforts of civilization seemed to stymy their conversation. They wondered, would they survive another Nebraska winter? And where would the boys get money for their necessities now that Chris had sold the farm in Rich fountain and invested all the remaining money he had left in this world into his new farm in Nebraska?

But the Bogners were hardy souls; Chris seemed to have had lived many lives and was always straying farther away from his boyhood home in Trockau. He crossed an ocean and then built a good life in Missouri, and his four older sons had already survived one or two winters in the bleakness of these grasslands. All of them had been tested.

Even in the evening's shadows, Chris could see lines of strength and determination engraved on the faces of his older sons, and he knew that the Bogner family would eventually thrive in this wild and desolate land.

Once more, his soul filled with a profound sense of peace and contentment. The family members would seize this opportunity and farm this big stretch of excellent grassland; each year, it would be easier, and each year, the family would grow and claim this land as their just inheritance.

In October – before the first snows fell – Chris, Mike, and Frank rode out in a wagon on the forty-mile journey to Fremont to fulfill the filing requirements on their homesteads. Mike and Frank had initially received only temporary deeds to their properties, and Chris had to file his documents with the appropriate land office. They would also need to bring back supplies to help them make it through the long cold winter. Once the snows set in, the journey would be almost impossible.

In those days, a trip to Fremont was always a serious affair, and it had to be carefully planned from the beginning to end. It was a forty-mile journey over an open range, and the roundtrip in a buckboard could take three or four days. All sorts of supplies would be needed to make it through the winter and to prepare for the spring planting season.

Of course, there was always the matter of food – once the wild animals hibernated for the winter, fresh edible game would be nearly unobtainable. Then, they'd need to purchase lumber to build furniture, repair the homesteads, barns, and sheds, and construct new ones. The livestock would need to hay and corn once the prairie grasses were dry or snow-covered. Farming implements and tools were required to plant and plow in late March, and of course, clothes were needed for his growing children.

And then there were the Indians – an ever-present unknown. Tales of uprisings and massacres still circulated among the townsfolk, and even though most of the tribes had been moved on to government reservations, wandering bands of renegades would often leave these outposts when times became tough. Starving Native women and children needed to be fed, and the government's supply of necessities was always too little and too late.

The settlers, however, never spoke of Indians when the women and children were around.

Four days later, the three men returned home to Oleyen with a wagon full of the treasures. There were bags of food; yards of cloth to make clothes, bedding, and curtains; rakes, shovels, and plows; and a big stack of lumber that Chris would utilize all winter long to build furniture for his home and those of his four boys.

While the goods and materials genuinely interested the members of the family, everyone wanted to know every detail of their adventures and the problems they encountered along the way. Did they see any Indians? What were the people like in Fremont? Did they meet many other settlers moving west? What was the news?

For the next several hours, the three men talked and talked about their escapades – answering questions and telling tall-tales to amuse the children. As Chris knelt in his bedroom to say his prayers at night, he almost cried at recounting the blessings the Good Lord had bestowed on him and his family. He knew that now they could survive the long cold, winter and begin planting new crops in the spring.

Toward the end of October, the first white, large snowflakes began falling – hovering in the air and floating all about in great oscillating circles. Even on those days when the sun shined, it was without any power, and the angle of the light made the sky looked so much different from the summer brightness. Sundown came to the prairie much earlier, and the sun rose later as it traveled northerly in the heavens.

In early November, the first measurable snow arrived on the plains. It came in the form of darkish blue skies from the Rockies, and the snowfall was accompanied by a wind that never seemed to cease. It snowed all night on November 11th and on into the next morning. By noon of the second day, there was almost a foot of snow laying on the ground. For the next six months, there was hardly a day when snow did not cover some portion of Chris' farmland.

Because he resided in the only wooden home (the four brothers lived in sod houses or dug-outs at that time), the family often gathered at Chris' farmhouse when the conditions allowed for travel. All of their homesteads were situated near the Maple Creek bottom, adjacent to each other, and lying within a radius of six miles.

Three of the farms were located south and southeast of Oleyen and located approximately one to three miles from town. The other two farms were due east of Oleyen. Over the next three years, he built houses for each of the four boys.

As December arrived, the winter was ever tightening its grip. The snow drifted high – often above four feet – and it gathered in every corner of a building or shed. It seemed the entire universe was a swirling mass of white.

Whenever the snow stopped, the wind would continue to blow in a maddening furry, and the temperature outside was so cold that should someone touch a piece of iron, a bit of skin would be torn away. Chris' breath hung in the air, and the horses and mules – used to the warmer Missouri weather – suffered considerably during their first winter in Nebraska.

When the sun shone brightly, the whole vastness gleamed as the sunlight danced and sparkled on the snow – producing illusions of diamonds and crystals. Often the glare was so intense that Chris' eyes would blur or tear up. But whenever the outside world became a bitter cold and dangerous place to venture for too long, the fireplace produced a steady heat and a warm environment for the family.

Although the days and months seemed endless and unchanging, Chris spent much of this time the first winter repairing the old buildings situated on his farm and making furniture for his boys. After spending twenty years in Rich Fountain, Chris had not anticipated the bleakness of the Nebraska winter. To him, the prairie seemed to be a white wasteland; silent, except for the wind and a perpetual coldness.

In January and February, there seemed to be one blizzard on top of the last one. There was drifting snow, intense cold, cloudy skies, and smothering blizzards that would last for days on end.

Perhaps no one suffered more than the younger children. There was no formal schoolwork to attend, no church for them to join, and no interactions with other children; just busy work and school lessons when Barbara had the time. On the few occasions the children could go outside and play, they had to be watched carefully; if one of the three youngest got lost, there'd be no way to find them.

Barbara, and to a much lesser extent, Anna, spent their days cooking, cleaning, washing, mending and taking care of the Bogner men – including the five older brothers – who would often be found at the house for dinner.

In late February, the region warmed up enough so that Chris and the older boys believed they could soon hitch the wagons and travel to the Elkhorn River to cut and gather wood. The men delayed their trip for several days, and then one morning, the sun rose a little higher in the sky, and a warmer breeze came in blowing from the south. It was the first breath of spring, and it was time to give it a try.

The two wagons left Oleyen in bright sunshine early one morning. Three hours later, they made it safely to the Elkhorn River and began cutting the trees and stacking the wood in the buckboards. However, about 3 PM, the skies darkened, and the wind switched from coming in from a southerly direction into a crisp west wind.

Almost all of the work stopped at once, and the men gathered together; they knew what was coming. They had two choices; either hunker down in place or try to get back home before the blizzard hit. They decided to make a run for home.

Soon the snow was falling so fast that they could barely see the horses pulling in their harnesses directly in front of them. The wind began howling, and as the blizzard broke with all of its ferocity, it blew against them in angry blasts.

It was the worst part of the storm, and as the whiteness enveloped them as if they were in a raging cloud, they still had at least one hour to go before reaching the safety of their home. The men needed to stay together; they'd all make it home or none of them would.

The horses neighed and cried; stumbling along at a plodding but deliberate pace. Soon one of the lead horses became distressed and began panicking. The horse reared up, but Chris' steady hand calmed the animal to a degree and, after a few seconds, the wagon continued moving forward.

As the snow became deeper, the wind became unrelenting, and the horses picked a cautious route between the drifts to find their way safely down the steeper slopes. Had the men waited another hour before departing the Elkhorn River site, the route home would've been nearly impossible.

Leading the first wagon, Chris rode in silence; carefully listening to the horses' hooves crunching in the ever-deepening snow. Finally, the troupe crested the last hill, saw the rooftops of the Bogner farm, and smelled the wood-smoke rising from the chimney. Realizing they were home, the men and the horses rejoiced – they'd barely outlasted the teeth of that crushing blizzard.

Right after they drove the buckboards into the barn, the night suddenly pressed down upon them, and the evening suddenly became nearly pitch black. Although the snow was not falling as intensely as it did during the afternoon, the temperature had dropped considerably.

After taking care of the horses, the men walked into the farmhouse and shook off the snow which had encased them for the last four hours. Together, they sat in silence by the hearth – rubbing their hands together and picking the snow out of their beards.

For the next three days, the storm raged on around them, and the men lamented upon 'what could have been.' But Chris had learned a hard lesson; the weather can change so hurriedly in these vast grasslands that one should not venture too far away from home until the springtime thaw.

As March arrived, the sun returned in earnest, and the evenings grew longer. Soon the snow melted, and grasses started growing again – the bluestem, the bluegrama, the fleabane, and the buffalo grass. As May arrived, the land bloomed with milkweed, purple coneflower, and stinging nettle, and the wild animals returned from hibernation — elk, deer, rabbits, coyotes, prairie dogs, and an occasional badger, bobcat, and fox. A once seemingly dead world had suddenly sprung back to life.

Aside from spring plowing, one of the first tasks for Chris and his boys was for them to build a wooden farmhouse for George and Mary, his bride-to-be. Together, the brothers had decided earlier to construct George's home first, and after that, in succession, build wooden dwellings for Joe, Mike, and Frank.

The brothers also understood Alois would operate Chris' farm, and then Alois would eventually inherit it. Chris and his sons jointly decided that once Alois married, he would receive title to the property as long as he and his wife agreed that Chris, along with the four other younger children, could remain on the farm as long as they wished.

With the house nearly completed, George and Chris boarded the train in Fremont on April 1, 1875, and arrived safely in Bonnot's Mill the following day. Then on April 6, 1875, George married Mary Stuckenschneider in Westphalia, Missouri.

The church, St. Joseph's, had been founded in 1835 by Father Helias a few years before he moved to Rich Fountain, and it was the same church where Chris' son, John, and his bride, Theresia, had married the previous year. It was a special occasion for the Bogner family. He only wished Margaret and Father Helias (who had baptized George) were alive to witness the marriage.

George and Mary had been betrothed for nearly four years, and tears of joy rolled Chris' face as the couple exchanged their vows. The following morning, George and Mary Bogner boarded the train and left for Oleyen. They didn't want to wait any longer to begin their lives together. Their union lasted thirty-four years and produced eight children. George died on July 16, 1909, at age 62, and Mary passed away on November 19, 1940, at age 86.

On April 4, 1875, Chris celebrated his 60ᵗʰ birthday at the Zeilmann home surrounded by family and friends. His father-in-law, Johannes, had turned 75 on March 21ˢᵗ and the family had waited for Chris' arrival so they could have a joint birthday celebration. After most of the people went home in the evening, Johannes and Chris sat on the front porch smoking their pipes and sipping Kentucky bourbon.

Chris said, "I remember the first time I came here. It was nearly thirty-five years ago, and after Margaret sang 'The Leaving of Liverpool,' you and I sat out here and smoked cigars. You know, the view looks almost the same as it did back then; maybe the trees are a little taller."

"Yeah, things don't change much around here – but where has the time gone? You were 30, and I was 45. I don't feel much older, but I am, dammit."

"Yeah, where has the time gone? The day you walked into our shop in St. Louis changed my whole life. Had I not met you, I probably wouldn't have met Margaret, and I would have missed out on all that happened after we married. It was my lucky day."

They sat in silence for a while. Then Chris said, "Well, Margaret died ten years ago, and now I live in Nebraska. Can you believe it's been ten years since we lost Margaret and Dorothea?"

Again they say in silence sipping their bourbon and smoking their pipes. A quarter-moon rose over the countryside, and a soft breeze was blowing through the trees.

Johannes said, "Tell me about the land; what's it like living on the prairie in Nebraska?"

"Well, the terrain is nearly flat and virtually treeless. The summers are hot, and the winters are long, windy, and cold. A man needs to keep himself busy in winter, or he'll surely go crazy."

"Why are there no trees there?"

"I've been told that every couple of years, prairie fires scorch the grasslands and kill most of the vegetation – including any saplings which had taken hold. These fires usually occur in the fall when the grasses are dryest."

"Did you say prairie fires?"

"Yes. If a fire comes, we need to get into our storm cellars rapidly. But the grasses' roots are deep, however, and it comes back each year – even in the cultivated areas. These weeds can be a nuisance come summer, but in the spring, the grasslands are a sea of flowers. It's quite a sight."

Johannes asked. "You said you had a harsh winter in Oleyen; did the livestock make it through okay?'

"Yes, we arrived there with twenty-seven animals, and we had ten live births over the autumn and winter; all but one foal made it through the winter okay. But it was tough. I learned that Nebraska is no place to raise horses and mules."

"So are you going to make some changes?"

"Yes, we decided to sell off most of our livestock – we'll keep only a few for breeding – but we're using the money that we receive from the sales to purchase lumber. You know the four boys have been living in sod houses or dugouts for a couple of years now. We've pretty much finished with George's house, but the other boys are ready to marry, and they all will need decent homes soon."

"What about Alois?"

"He wants to be a corn farmer, and as I told you, one day he'll inherit my farm; so we're trying to get the homestead to the point where he can take it over pretty soon. The previous owner of our farm planted corn, and apparently, he did well financially. All of our fields are designed for growing corn, and the weather seems to be ideal. So, I think we're moving in that direction."

Then they talked about Frank, Mike, and Joe, all of whom were also planting corn. Chris mentioned that Joe had developed an interest in bees and he had twenty working hives.

Then Chris said, "All of the boys have planted orchards, and many of the cuttings I carried from my old homestead – including the grapevines I brought here from Trockau – have flourished in Nebraska. I'm quite optimistic about our orchards and vineyards."

"How are the three youngest kids doing?"

"Well, with them being deaf, it's tough on all of us – but they're making good strides. You know, I heard about a government school for the deaf in Lincoln, and after the harvest, I plan to send the three of them there for the winter. I think it'll be good for them to be with other deaf children. Of course, they'll come home next spring."

Soon, it was growing late, and on the following day, Chris would begin his long journey back to Nebraska.

"Johannes, you need to come visit us someday. With the railroad, it's rather easy. You need only to change trains twice – once in Kansas City and again in Omaha. Then we can pick you up in Fremont. It's only forty miles from there to Oleyen, and we hear that one day soon, the railroad will make it there, too. It's a marvelous age to live in, you know."

The following morning, Chris and Johannes hopped on the buckboard to make the final trip to Bonnot's Mill. First, though, they stopped at the cemetery to visit the graves of Dorothea, Anna Lena, and Margaret. Once again, tears came to Chris' eyes, and after saying their farewells, the two old friends drove to the train station.

The Central Missouri Railroad arrived right on time at the depot, and just before stepping on to the train, the two men hugged. Somehow, both men knew in their hearts that they'd never see each other again. Although they wrote to each other several times a year, Chris never returned to Rich Fountain, and Johannes never rode the train to Oleyen.

As the train left the station, the two men waved goodbye to each other, and Chris watched as a significant part of his life disappeared from view in the tall forests of Missouri.

When the Bogners first arrived, there was no Catholic church in Oleyen. To fulfill their obligation, the family attended St. Charles' Catholic Church near West Point, Nebraska – located some twenty miles away from their farms.

Because of the distance and the poor roads, however, it would often take them all day to get to church and back to their farms. In the winter, the trip was nearly impossible.

As the area surrounding Oleyen began to grow, a small wooden chapel was erected in there in 1874. Father Uhing, the pastor at St. Charles, said Mass at the mission church on alternating Sundays.

On July 4, 1876, America celebrated its 100th birthday, and Father Uhing officiated at a Centennial Mass. In a clear break from the Catholic tradition, the choir sang *The Battle Hymn of the Republic* as its recessional song, and the mission church held a picnic on the grounds on that day to celebrate America's Centennial.

As a result, neighbors got to know neighbors better, and young people spent time with other young people. Soon, the gathering on the 4th of July became a tradition which would endure in Oleyen for many years to come.

On August 30, 1877, the Bishop of Omaha officially established Oleyen as a parish, and Father John Blaschke was appointed as its first resident pastor. The Bogners, among many other local families such as the Peitzmeiers, the Kassmeiers, and the Kampschneiders, were instrumental in building the sanctuary which was eventually christened as 'Sacred Heart' – the same name as the church the Bogners had attended in Rich Fountain.

In 1882, Father Turek succeeded Father Blaschke as the pastor of Sacred Heart. When the original church building became too small for the growing Catholic community, a second sanctuary was erected in 1883, and the old church was turned into a school. Even to this day, the Bogners attend Mass there.

Now well-established in Oleyen, the Bogner family began growing. In the course of one year, four of Chris' children married. Frank wed Josephine Kovar on February 21, 1878, and then Joe married Katherina Becker on February 26, 1878.

After that, Mike and Mary Laur went to the altar on July 16, 1878, and finally, Barbara married Nikolaus Becker (Joe's wife's brother) on January 14,

1879. The remaining oldest son, Alois was 28 years old, and Anna Dorothy, the baby, had just turned 16 and was the mistress of the household.

With a shortage of eligible women in the Oleyen area, Chris sent Alois to St. Louis in September 1881 to find a wife. While there, Alois lived with Christopher Bauer – whom Chris and Charles had worked for over forty years before. Almost immediately after arriving there, Alois met Sibilla Sepbolla Pickel who had immigrated from Koblenz, Germany in 1869.

Born on August 8, 1858, Sibilla – the youngest of five children - and her family arrived in Baltimore, Maryland on June 4, 1869. Shortly after she met Alois, they married on February 1, 1882, and on the following day, the newlyweds took the train to Fremont.

Although she was initially hesitant to leave the comforts of St. Louis and move to Nebraska, Alois promised her that she would never have to work in the fields and she could make their home as elegant as she wished.

Almost immediately upon arriving in Oleyen, the new bride hung lace curtains on the windows and placed rugs on the floors. Sibilla insisted that screens be set tightly on the windows and doors, and she later became known as an excellent cook and baker.

On November 20, 1883, their first child, Otto, was born, and his birth was followed by seven other boys and one girl, Martha, who was named after the woman who helped raise Alois in Rich Fountain after his mother died in 1864.

As the years passed, the Bogner farms began to expand and thrive. After a couple of initial lean years, the boys adapted to their new environment and made many changes to their farming methods which substantially increased their harvests. Furthermore, each brother planted an orchard containing many different varieties of fruit trees, and as the trees matured, they picked the fruit and made jellies, jams, and preserves.

Each brother also had milk-cows, chicken, pigs, and squabs, and Joe raised bees – eventually having over twenty hives. The families also kept extensive vegetable gardens and sold off their excess produce in town to raise additional money for their families. By 1880, Chris had sold most of his breeding stock but kept his best stud, Drake, and several mares, and each year Chris had four or five foals to sell.

In the spring of 1883, John and Theresia Bogner moved from Rich Fountain to Oleyen and bought a farm which was adjacent to those of Chris and the other brothers. So, for the first time in nearly a dozen years, the whole family was living together in one place.

By Christmas of 1883, Chris had twenty-one grandchildren to go along with his ten living children. The Lord had been kind to Chris, indeed.

In the summer of 1869, *The Fremont, Elkhorn and Missouri Valley Railroad* laid its first ten miles of track from Fremont to Blair, Nebraska. Ten years later, the rail-line stretched all the way to Wisner, and in 1881, the rail company pushed even further westward to Long Pine, Nebraska.

In 1884, the railway decided to build a 'branch line' stretching from Fremont northwest to Creighton, Nebraska. In July, the railway served notice on the Bogners of its intent to seek easements through their farms.

"The damn railroad can't just force its tracks onto our property; can it? We own this land!"

Chris, Mike, and Frank were sitting in the law office of Eli Schuster in Fremont. Chris was holding a letter from *The Fremont, Elkhorn and Missouri Valley Railroad* advising the Bogners of their intentions. Mr. Schuster was reading the letter carefully. He wasn't smiling.

After he finished reading it, the attorney said, "Well, Mr. Bogner, unfortunately, they can – and probably will. Permit me to tell you a little about the law. *The Railroad Act of 1862* allows railway companies to condemn private property from landowners whose property lies along a proposed route or an existing route that the railroad's plans to expand. If the property owners could legally prevent the railroad from acquiring parts of their land, none of the railroads would get built except on public land."

Chris frowned, "Sir, it will destroy our farms. We've worked hard to make our land productive. I won't let them steal it from us; dammit. I won't."

Mr. Schuster frowned, "Let me briefly tell you how the process works. Perhaps you'll feel a little better once I explain it. Section 26 (a) of the Act provides that 'No land can be taken without consent except within two years of approval of the location of the route.' The State of Nebraska approved the route last month, so we are now within the two-year window."

"Okay."

"Next, the railway must enter negotiations with you – they cannot take it – and then hopefully, you and your sons can arrive at an agreement with the railroad's agents regarding the value of the land to be taken. If you can't agree, you can go to court."

"Court? Are you talking about a trial?"

"Technically, it's called a 'hearing' – not a formal trial; but yes. The Act also requires in Section 26 (b) that 'Before a court may approve the layout of a railroad or the taking of any land for it or any change or alteration, it must give reasonable notice to all people who may have an interest in the land to attend and to be heard.' Mr. Bogner, there and then, you can present your facts and arguments to the judge."

"I see. What if we still oppose the taking of our land; what happens next?"

Mr. Schuster swiveled in his chair, and after taking another sip of coffee, he continued. "That's when the railway can make use of a legal procedure called 'eminent domain.'"

"What's that?"

"It's a condemnation process whereby the rail-line can purchase the land from you at fair market value."

"Is this all legal?"

"Yes, I'm afraid so. The statutory basis of the remedy known as 'eminent domain' comes from the 5th Amendment to the Constitution which provides that the government can't seize private property unless 'just compensation' is given to the owner. Traditionally, this is interpreted as the providing the owner with the fair-market value of the land."

Mike asked, "Do the courts always side with the railroad?"

"Well, the courts try to determine whether the taking of the land is 'necessary for the public good.' It's often a difficult process, Mr. Bogner, but the railroad companies usually prevail. Their attorneys have gotten rather good at it lately. For some lawyers, that's all they do."

Frank asked, "How does the court establish the 'fair market value' of our land?"

"The railroad's agents would first send an appraiser to look at your land. Then he compares your farm's characteristics to your neighbors' land to establish the local market price. Because they're taking only a part of your land, the agent must also determine how the taking of the portion would either harm or benefit your farm. In some cases, the right-of-way makes the remaining property more valuable; but probably not in your case, Mr. Bogner."

Chris asked "Are we bound by what the agent's finds? Can we appeal that, Mr. Schuster?"

"Should you disagree, the court would tell the agent to consider the property owner's arguments and provide the court with a 'second look' at the property?"

"If there is still no agreement, what happens?"

Mr. Schuster leaned forward and said, "If the railroad company demonstrates to the court that they've gone through a fair and reasonable appraisal process and the parties still can't reach an agreement, the court determines the fair market value. Then the property is deeded to the railway company. Hopefully, though, with my help, we can reach a satisfactory agreement."

After rejecting the first offer made by the railroad, Chris and his sons accepted the second proposal. The tracks would eventually run through parts of three of the six Bogner farms, and by the autumn of 1885, the work on the rail line was completed. Although none of the family members was happy with the intrusion, George and Mike assumed that perhaps one day the value of their land would increase significantly because of its proximity to the tracks.

One the benefits of the rail-line came into play in late 1885 when the railroad purchased two-hundred acres from a local woman, Antonia Busch, for the sum of $4000. After that, the railroad platted a town on the acquired acreage, and named the village 'Howell,' in honor of James Howell, the railway's chief surveyor.

The incorporation of the village of Howell (later changed to 'Howells') proved to be the deathblow to Oleyen as many of its businesses were merely placed on wheels and moved to the new town.

By July 4, 1887, Howell had reached a population of over two-hundred residents, and new town mayor, John Kloke, announced at the Independence Day celebration held at Sacred Heart that a post office and a railroad station (complete with a working telegraph office) would soon open in the bustling new metropolis.

The location for Howell was advantageous to the Bogners; the town was situated only a short walk from Chris' farm Because the tracks were straight and level, the new route was a better alternative than walking the long and winding dirt road from his farm to the new village. Shopping, banking, and communications with the outside world suddenly became much easier and more convenient.

The tracks would also, however, proved to be Chris' eventual downfall.

The eighteen month period between January 19, 1888, and June 25, 1889, was a period of extreme sorrow for Chris and his family. While walking home on the tracks in a snowstorm from his brother's farm, Elias (who was deaf) was hit by a train and killed on January 19, 1888.

Three months later, Frank's son, Bernard, unexpectedly died at age six months, and on September 10, 1888, Joe's daughter Katharina died at the age of nine years. After that, George's son Peter was born prematurely on

December 8 and died two weeks later on December 22, 1888. Finally on June 25, 1889, Frank's wife, Josephine died at age twenty-five.

Unfortunately, these five deaths would not be the only ones the Bogner family would experience during the decade.

On May 4, 1890, Chris celebrated his 75th birthday, and Alois and Sibilla invited the entire family over to join him in the celebration. All eight of his surviving children, their spouses, and Chris' forty-one grandchildren assembled at the farmhouse for dinner and dessert. The occasion would mark one of the happiest times of his long life.

Sibilla prepared his favorite dinner – pig-hocks, sauerkraut, and dumplings – and every family brought along cakes, cookies, and pies. As expected, Chris stood up after dessert and talked about his life and good fortune, and he even vowed the family would to do it all over again on his 100th birthday.

After dinner was over, Chris and his grandchildren gathered in the backyard – under several of the trees he had planted just after arriving in Nebraska – for dessert and to hear stories.

After the grandchildren were served and seated, Chris asked, "Okay, who wants to hear one of Grandpa's stories? Raise your hands!"

Almost every grandchild above three years of age raised a hand, and Chris said, "Okay Annie, what story would you like to hear?"

Annie, George and Mary's ten-year-old daughter, said, "Grandpa, please tell us about Dieter and the sailing ship."

He smiled, "Oh, that one. It so happened that my brother, George, and I had just arrived in Liverpool – that's in England, by the way – and we were waiting to cross the mighty Atlantic Ocean on a wooden ship called *The Ballantine*. The ship had three huge masts with sails stretching over thirty yards in length. It was a good ship, but its master was a demon named Dieter who had only one eye and one leg. He . . ."

And Chris went on and one telling his grandchildren a tall-tale about his voyage to America. They laughed and squealed all along the way from beginning to end. After he finished his story, several of his grandchildren asked him questions about his voyage, and the 'tall-tale' grew even more absurd to the adults standing around them.

After he finished his first story, Chris asked, "So, do you want to hear another story? Yes, how about you, Cecelia; what story would you like to hear Grandpa tell?"

Cecelia was Mike and Mary's seven-year-old daughter. "Tell us about Amos and how you saved him from the police."

He smiled again, "Well, Cecelia, they weren't police; they were slave-catchers – and a nasty group was they. So, one day while we were living in Missouri, your Uncle George told me a young black man was hiding in the barn . . ."

As Chris told the story, he exaggerated the tale to the point where even he started laughing at his version of the story; but his grandchildren loved it.

Finally, Chris said, "Okay, we only have time for one more story. Dorothea, which one would you like to hear?"

She was five years old and Frank's daughter. Her mother, Josephine, had died the previous year.

"Grandpa, tell us about swimming in the ocean; and did you really take off all of your clothes?"

She put her hand to her mouth and tried to stifle a giggle.

"In fact, yes, I did – but I was so much younger then. I certainly wouldn't do that now."

And all of them laughed again.

After the guests went home and the rest of the family had gone to bed, Chris went out to sit in a rocking chair on the front porch. It was an unusually warm evening for early April, and for the first time since October, he could hear the tree-frogs and crickets peeping in the trees and bushes. It was a lovely evening, and as he sat down, he could see a waning moon rising in the east.

He pulled his pipe out of his jacket, struck a match, and began inhaling the warm, smoky tobacco. Alone with his thoughts, he started thinking of the members of his family who were not present at his birthday celebration: Margaret, little Anna Lena, and Elias (who had died two years earlier after being hit by a train).

And then Chris thought about Charles – whose body was lying in a mass grave in Tennessee, and his father – who had died almost fifty years before. Whether it was the stillness of the evening, the three glasses of tawny port wine after dinner, or the incredible weight of loneliness, he began crying.

A few moments later, he heard the door open and a voice saying, "Grandpa, are you crying?"

Looking around, he saw his grandson, Otto, who was seven years old.

"Yes, Otto; I was thinking of your Uncle Elias and your grandmother who couldn't be here tonight. But I'm okay; old people cry sometimes."

"Are you worrying about dying?"

"No, I'm not afraid of dying; when I die, Otto, I'll go to heaven and see so many people who have gone there before me."

Otto just looked at him; somewhat bewildered.

Chris said, "Come and sit on grandpa's lap for a minute. Are you cold, son?"

"A little."

"Well, come and sit on my lap. I'll make you warm."

Otto crawled up onto Chris' lap, and he held the little boy close for a long time. The two of them had always had a special bond.

Otto asked, "What was Grandma like?"

"You know, she was beautiful and could sing as well as any person I've ever heard. She loved her children very much, and your grandma was such a wonderful cook. She would have loved you, too, Otto. She died just after your Aunt Anna was born, and Grandma is buried in Rich Fountain."

"Is that in Missouri?"

"Yes, it is, and I hope to take you there one day to meet the rest of our family. We can ride on the train; would you like that?'

Otto nodded affirmatively.

"You know, your great-grandfather and lots of your uncles, aunts, and cousins still live there. You need to meet them; Otto, there's nothing better in this whole world than family. You know that, right?"

Otto smiled.

The two best-friends sat and talked on the front porch for another thirty minutes or so until Otto began tiring and eventually fell asleep on Chris' lap. Gathering him up in his arms, Chris carried Otto to his bedroom and laid the sleeping little boy on the bed next to his brothers Martin, Alphonse, and Anton.

Closing the door behind him, Chris quietly climbed the stairs to his bedroom, knelt and said his prayers, and the next thing he knew, it was morning.

When the weather was favorable, Chris would often get on the railroad tracks and walk to Howell — usually a thirty-minute journey. After Elias' death, Chris was careful to be on the watch for trains as there were several long curves on the line which could hide the approach of a locomotive until it was almost too late.

On the morning of June 16, 1890, he hiked to town. It was a beautiful late-spring day, and walking up Main Street from the depot, Chris stopped at the general store and the livery to talk to friends about politics and farm prices. Everyone agreed that 1890 would be a good year for farmers. Before leaving town, he stopped by the post office.

He said, "Hey Bill – any mail for me today?"

Bill Hastings, the town's postmaster, replied, "No mail, Mr. Bogner, but you have a telegram."

"A telegram? I don't believe I've ever received one before."

Bill hand Chris a sealed envelope. He looked at it and then sat down on a chair to read it. The telegram read:

```
Johannes Zeilmann died peacefully last night at
age 90. More to follow by letter.
```

He reread the telegram several times. Taking a deep breath, he whispered, "Oh, no."

Although Johannes was Chris' father-in-law, he was also much more like a big brother.

Chris sat there for about five minutes until Bill asked, "Bad news, Mr. Bogner?"

Chris looked up at him and replied, "Yes, I lost my best friend."

He walked home slowly that day.

By the summer of 1890, Alois had taken over the day-to-day operation of the farm, and Chris concentrated more on making furniture for his children and their families. He stayed busy but always looked forward to his walks into town.

By 1890, Howell had grown from a platted map to a village with well over six-hundred residents. In just five years, three churches and a school were constructed within the town's limits. *The Congregational Church* was organized in 1887, and *The Sisters of St. Francis* built a parochial school in 1888 (although the parish center, *Sacred Heart*, remained in Oleyen). Also, the Czech population erected *St. John of Nepomuk*, and *Trinity Lutheran Church* had just begun construction during the spring.

It seemed that the builders of the town were busy from night to day.

During the afternoon of July 15, Chris walked into town, and after a couple of social calls, he stopped by the post office to pick up the mail. Aside from a few other items, he received a letter from his brother, Johann. Being a beautiful day, Chris decided to look at it on his way home.

While walking slowly on the tracks, he opened the letter and began to read it:

June 20, 1890

Dear brother,

I enjoyed reading your last letter. It's difficult for me to accept that you are now 75 and I am nearly 68. I remember so well when we were mere boys in Trockau.

After my patron, Richard Wagner, died a few years ago, our business has been much slower. He referred me to several of his friends, but after his death, the work we used to get from Bayreuth has wholly disappeared. My boys, Charles and Georg, are taking a leading role in the family business now, leaving me time to travel. Tomorrow, I'm taking the train to Rome, and I hope to see the Pope.

I do have some sad news for you. Duchess Sonia Therese Von Furstenberg D'Ousterling died last week. I understand she was a childhood friend of yours. Although she was buried in Vienna, her family held a Requiem Mass for her in Trockau.

Of course, her brother, Duke Gottingen, and his family attended the service. After Mass, we talked for a little while, and he asked me to tell you about the Duchess. He seems to think that you two were lovers once. Is it true, brother?

The Duke also said that she often asked about you and she named one of her children after you. It's funny how we learn little secrets in the most unusual ways, isn't it?

All is fine in Trockau. In tiny towns like ours, very little changes; it's not like in America. But our Bogner family has grown, though.

Like you, I am a grandfather many times over. I only wish I could see you again. Perhaps you can come home one day. I still can't believe that you've been gone for almost fifty years now.

As always, you will remain in our thoughts and prayers. May the Good Lord watch over and keep you and your family safe.

Anna Maria and her family send their love. Write us when you can; we so like hearing about Nebraska and your growing family.

Johann

Johann's letter included a newspaper article about the life of Sonia Therese and a recent photo. In Chris' mind's eye, she was still in her mid-twenties, but the newspaper photo showed her as a seventy-three-year-old woman.

He read the newspaper article over and over again – telling the readers about her life and her children and grandchildren – and then he just stared at the photo of the old woman. He kept asking himself, 'what happened to the girl whom I first fell in love with?'

Chris looked at the photo for a long time – trying to reconcile it with his last memory of her while in prison in Bayreuth. Yes, it was her; he recognized her eyes.

Chris shook his head and whispered to himself, "Oh, Sonia, we had such hopes and dreams. Did yours come true, my darling?"

Absentmindedly, he dropped the envelope on to the tracks, and while reaching down to pick it up, he felt the sharp vibration of an approaching train. Just as he turned around to look at the locomotive coming quickly down the tracks, the engine struck him on the left shoulder and propelled him high into a grouping of sycamore trees and then down into the ditch.

Seeing what had happened, the engineer immediately sounded the whistle and began the task of stopping the train. The locomotive eventually arrived at a complete stop about two miles down the tracks, and the engineer immediately told the farmers who had gathered outside his window about the horrible accident. By the time Frank and his sons, John and Mike, located Chris, he was dead – but still clutching in his right hand the letter he had received from Johann.

The men carried Chris back to his farmhouse, and according to his instructions, Alois and Sibilla dressed Chris in his dark suit. It was the one he wore at the opera house in Bayreuth; the one he wore at Chéri's funeral; and the same one that he wore on the day he married Margaret. Because Sibilla presumed the newspaper article was significant to Chris, she carefully folded it and inserted the item into his breast-pocket.

Chris laid in an open coffin in the parlor of his residence for three days as family and friends visited him to pay their respects. After that, the family placed the coffin in the buckboard and carried it to Sacred Heart Church for the funeral.

On July 18, Father Turek celebrated a Requiem Mass for the Bogner family, and Chris' oldest son, George, and Chris' oldest living daughter, Barbara, each provided a eulogy. During the interludes and under his specific instructions, the pianist played mournful versions of 'Across the Wide Missouri' and 'The Leaving of Liverpool.'

Before the Mass, the pallbearers had wheeled the bier holding the coffin into the sanctuary with Chris' feet positioned toward the altar, and as the Mass concluded, Father Turek walked down to the coffin and began sprinkling holy water on Chris' remains. Then the altar boy brought forth a canister of incense which the priest lit. As the priest started reciting the absolution of the dead, he began walking around the coffin and slowly shaking the fragrance over the casket.

This form of absolution is not intended as a means to forgive sins or a substitute for the Sacrament of Penance. Instead, the ceremony consists of a series of prayers to God that the person's soul will not have to suffer the temporal punishment in Purgatory due to the sins which had been forgiven during the person's life.

During the absolution, Father Turek sang the *Libera Me Domine,* and upon blessing the body, he ended the ceremony by saying in Latin, "*Requiem eternam dona eis, Domine; et lux perpetua luceat eis.*"

After the Mass concluded, the pallbearers wheeled the bier out of the church and slowly rolled it a few yards to the cemetery. As the family gathered around the gravesite, Father Turek provided one final blessing, saying:

"May Christopher Bogner's soul and the souls of all the faithful departed through the mercy of God rest in peace."

The mourners whispered, "Amen."

Then the priest sprinkled the coffin with holy water, and the pallbearers lowered the casket into the grave. As the graveside portion ended, many of the family members picked up a handful of dirt and tossed it onto the lowered coffin.

A few months later, the family erected a burial stone at the head of Chris' grave. The inscription provided the dates of his birth and death, and on the bottom, the carvers engraved the following words in Latin:

Curru viae ferrae necatus, vir bonus et pius.

The English translation is as follows:

Killed by a train, he was a good and devout man.

CHAPTER FIFTEEN

"Do you remember much about his funeral, Grandpa?"

He leaned back in his chair and responded: "Well, because I was only seven years old, my parents didn't let me and my brothers attend it. But I do have several memories from that time."

"You do?"

"My brother, Martin, was five years old at the time, and I distinctly recall him tugging on Grandpa's jacket and saying, 'Get up, Grandpa; get up.' Also, I remember that on the third day, there was a noticeable smell in the room."

"A smell?"

"Yes, I guess his body had already begun to deteriorate."

"I wish I could've known him. What was he like?"

Grandpa thought for a second and said, "My grandfather was an optimist. He always told me it's easier to be a pessimist because a pessimist is rarely disappointed. But being an optimist is much more rewarding in the long run. Also, my grandfather always looked forward to the next day. He told me that he could always see a promise in the morning sky."

"He did?"

"Yes, I remember he used to get up early and watch the sunrise, and when I'd join him on the front porch of our house, he'd say,

'Otto, today is another opportunity to excel. Try to make this day as best as you can make it. You'll have only one chance; make it a good one.'

But he also reminded me that not every day can be shining bright; some days are meant for rain."

I asked, "What did he mean by 'some days are meant for rain?'"

"Well, I guess he was saying that we must expect problems in our lives; but we can benefit, too, from our throwbacks. He'd tell me that even a rainy day can be good for our crops and our peace of mind. Do you understand what I'm saying?"

"Yes, I believe so. What else did he tell you, Grandpa?"

"He suggested I keep a journal and write done my thoughts, accomplishments, and errors in judgment. He said that it would be helpful to me in the future to determine how far I've come and how much further I still needed to go. He told me not to procrastinate. He'd say 'Do it now, Otto.' Yes, he would."

"But isn't that your motto, Grandpa?"

"Yes, it is – I took the saying from him. He'd also tell me that, as much as I possibly can, to be on good terms with all people, and don't hold grudges, especially with the ones whom we love. And to always forgive my friends and family members, and ask for forgiveness from them, too; and to remember that God and family are the two most important things in this life."

I smiled and said, "I know you loved him very much."

"Yes, he and my father were my first heroes; and I guess, they still are my role models."

I heard a noise outside and looked out the window. A car was going into the driveway at Max Sprakel's house across the street.

I asked, "Grandpa, do you think your grandfather had any regrets?"

He smiled and leaned back in his chair. "You know, Bobby, when people get to be my age, we always look back at missed opportunities – of the roads not taken. I suspect that my father had some regrets, too. You know in the Catholic Church, our priests talk about sins of omission and sins of commission. Do you know what those terms mean?"

"No, not really."

"Well, sins of commission are things that we've done, and sins of omission are things we failed to do. You know we say to those words in the Mass."

"Yeah, right in the beginning when we say 'I confess . . .'"

"You're right. I assume my grandfather had regrets, but we all have them – it's quite natural. But although Grandpa could have taken different paths in his life, I think in the end, he made some very wise choices. You know, neither you nor I would be here today had he remained in either Trockau or New Orleans."

"Yes, I'm glad he did what he did."

We both sat in silence for a few seconds, then I asked, "When did you leave Howells and move to Crofton?"

"I first left Howells in 1907 and tried to homestead on a small farm near Ft. Pierce, South Dakota; but I didn't like it – it was so isolated and desolate. So I came home, but the experience certainly gave me an idea about what my Uncle George and Uncle Mike went through during those first years in Olean."

He stopped for a moment, and noticing that his pipe had gone out again, he relit it and continued talking. "I married Grandma in 1909, and shortly after that, we settled here and began our family. Just like the time so many years ago when all of Grandpa's children eventually left Rich Fountain and settled in Olean, four of my brothers later settled in Crofton, married lo-cal women, and raised large families. In turn, their children have grown up, married, and have large families of their own. There are a lot of Bogners here now, Bobby."

"Whatever happened to your father and mother?"

"Dad sold the farm in 1913 – he was 58 years old and was suffering from arthritis – and they moved into Howells. When my youngest brother, Lawrence, graduated from high school in 1921, Dad and Mama moved to Crofton. We built the house next door for them - the one where Uncle Albert lives right now – and they resided there together until 1931 when Dad died suddenly on January 29th. It was the day before his 76th birthday, and it was only two days before their 50th wedding anniversary."

"Wow; that was unfortunate."

"Yes, it was. So, instead of it becoming a happy occasion, we buried Dad.

Mama lived in the house with Lawrence and Albert until she died on January 9, 1947; she was 88 years old."

Once again we sat in silence. After a few moments, I asked, "Is it hard growing old?"

"You know, Bobby, time moves both quickly and slowly. While a person is aging, he doesn't notice time slowly passing by. But time has a way of moving pretty rapidly, too. It seems that just yesterday, I was a young man – and now, I'm old. I knew that I would age but I thought growing old would take longer."

I sat and thought about what he was saying.

Then he continued, "I remember years ago seeing old people and thinking that I still had so much life waiting ahead of me. Now, most of my friends have either died or retired – and those folks who are still alive move slower and have more health problems. Of course, some are in better shape, but I see a major change in all of them. Take my brothers – I remember them as being young and vibrant – but like me, their age is betraying them."

"I know, I see a lot of old people around Crofton."

"Yes, there are lots of them here. But it seems like people live a long time in our family; in fact, I read in the paper last week that folks live longer in Nebraska than in any other state in the nation."

"Is that true?"

He smiled, "Well, I'm not sure we live any longer; it just feels that way."

And we both laughed at his joke.

Then he said, "Let me give you some advice. Don't put things off for too long. Life goes by so quickly. So, whatever you'd like to accomplish during your life, try to do it as rapidly as you can. Also, be willing to work hard and don't be afraid of failure. Remember, life is a gift from God – make it worth all the joy and pain that you'll encounter along the way."

"That's good advice."

"It's what my grandfather told me so many years ago."

He stopped speaking for a moment. Then he placed his hand on my shoulder, looked me in the eyes, and said, "In the end, try to be a part of something good and leave something worthwhile behind which you'd want your loved ones to remember you by."

"I will, Grandpa, I will."

Finally, he said, "Look, Bobby, it's almost time for the 10 o'clock news. If you come back to Crofton next year, I'll tell you some more about Papa and Mama – and maybe I'll even remember a few more stories about my grand-father, too. But let's watch the news now."

After the news ended, I asked Grandpa if I could take a beer from the refrig-erator and sit for a short time on the front porch.

"Yes, but don't stay up too late. Your parents will be here tomorrow afternoon."

I sat down on one of the rocking chairs and looked at a full moon which was rising slowly in the east. Sipping a cold can of Pabst Blue Ribbon, I watched as cars occasionally passed down Iowa Street – honking their horns at me and waving hello.

Down the street, I could hear the occasional pop of firecrackers and the lonesome sounds of a barking dog; but otherwise, the evening was calm and still. Shivering slightly, I could detect a definite hint of the autumn in the Nebraska air.

Yes, the nights were getting a little longer and cooler, and a gentle breeze was pushing through the still-green leaves of the maple trees standing guard out in Grandpa's front yard.

Alone with my thoughts, I began thinking about Christopher Bogner and all the adventures he experienced during his seventy-five years on this earth: the riots and imprisonment in Bayreuth; sailing the Atlantic Ocean and the Gulf of Mexico on *The Ballantine*; spending several terrible winters on the flat grass-covered prairies; and losing the companionship of the three wom-en whom he loved so much in such different ways.

Suddenly, I wondered about Sarah; would she be one of the women whom

I'd remember for the rest of my life?

After finishing my beer, I went inside and climbed the stairs to my bed-room. Dick was still working in the steakhouse and would not be home for several more hours. That night I dreamed of tall-ships, grand palaces, and long empty grasslands, and my ears were filled with music from churches, operas, taverns, and symphonies.

Sometime toward morning, I got out of bed, went downstairs, and sat down once again on the front porch. There, I saw a full moon laying on the western horizon – smiling back at me like a lover.

As the time passed, I began to hear the familiar sounds of the morning: the birds chirping, the roosters crowing, and the cows mooing in the barns nearby in anticipation of a meal or milking. Things were coming back to life in this small town.

In the east, I could see the beginnings of a glorious sunrise; the purples, reds, oranges, and yellows – all gathering together in a kaleidoscope of hues and colors.

In some unexplainable way, I felt the presence of Christopher Bogner – standing beside me with his hand resting on my shoulder.

Whispering a silent prayer, I thanked God for allowing me to be a part of this family, and then waiting patiently for the sunrise, together we shared the promise in the morning sky.

CPSIA information can be obtained
at www.ICGtesting.com
Printed in the USA
FFHW020200180219
50586809-55922FF